W9-BNT-196

Shortly after midnight, when they were sitting on the floor, stapling their material and labeling file folders, the phone rang. The answering machine was on, but immediately after the recorded message, screaming filled the room, a woman's scream, high and shrill, panicked. "WHAT'RE YOU DOING? WHY'RE YOU DOING THIS? HE'S JUST A CHILD, HE HASN'T HURT YOU, OH, GOD, PLEASE . . . NO, PLEASE . . . DON'T HURT HIM. . . ."

The hairs on the back of Aline's neck stood on end; the voice belonged to Jenny Michael. "My God, what . . ."

A child's shrieks and wails shredded the air, then stopped quickly, suddenly. The two or three seconds of subsequent silence pulsed against the walls in Aline's den. She waited. She heard Kincaid swallow. She closed her eyes, knowing it wasn't finished, that even when it was, it would remain with her, a hideous echo. . . .

Also by Alison Drake
Published by Ballantine Books:

TANGO KEY

FEVERED

Alison Drake

J

c.1

BALLANTINE BOOKS · NEW YORK

Copyright © 1988 by Alison Drake

All rights reserved under International and Pan-American Copyright
Conventions. Published in the United States of America by Ballantine
Books, a division of Random House, Inc., New York, and simultane-
ously in Canada by Random House of Canada Limited, Toronto.

Library of Congress Catalog Card Number: 88-91964

ISBN 0-345-34775-7

Manufactured in the United States of America

First Edition: September 1988

for Mom & Dad with love
& thanks

Barque of phosphor
    On the palmy beach,

Move outward into heaven
Into the alabasters
and night blues.

Foam and cloud are one.
Sultry moon-monsters
Are dissolving.

Fill your black hull
    with white moonlight.

There will never be an end
    To this droning of the surf.

—Wallace Stevens

PROLOGUE: THE JUDGE

1

Pain.

He was clawing his way through the pain, trying to surface, to lift above it, beyond it. But the pain burned through his legs, pulling him under again.

2

The screams awakened him.

They fluttered through the house like bats, rising and falling, slapping the cool air. He couldn't tell where they were coming from or who they belonged to—his wife? His sons? Himself? His hearing faded in and out, as though he were perched at the edge of a canyon, listening to an echo as it made its way toward him—and then away again.

Henry Michael tried to rise, but couldn't. His hands were bound, and his legs refused to work. He couldn't feel them from the knees down. *Get up, old man, get up.*

Up from where? Where was he? Why were his hands tied? Why was everything so fuzzy? His glasses, right, he wasn't wearing his glasses. No wonder he couldn't see worth a damn. He moved his back and felt the hard surface of the floor, its wood. . . . *Why am I on the floor?*

The screams were rising again, pounding the air around him, terrible screams, and once more he tried to lift up and failed. A sob wrenched from his throat as shoots of hot pain burned through his thighs, fanning out across his groin, his belly. *Please, oh God, please, make the screams stop. No more screams. Please.*

The pain blinked off, then on again, then off, and he squinted his eyes, attempting to focus on something, on anything, but it was useless. A gray fuzz sprouted like fur at the edge of his perception; the pain bit more deeply, and he fell back against the floor, his chest heaving from the exertion. *Be calm, old man. Be calm. You're imagining those screams. They're inside your head.*

Yes, all right. He would think backward from this moment to the moment when . . .

What? What was I doing before this?

Sleeping.

No, Christ no, he'd been . . . reading. He'd been reading through a case and

(But why are my hands tied?)

his youngest son had been sprawled in the beanbag chair, watching TV, and his wife, Jenny, had been

(Why do my legs hurt so much? Why . . .)

in the kitchen, cleaning up after supper. His oldest son had been in the kitchen with his mother, doing his homework. An ordinary evening,

(. . . my legs, the stink of blood, oh God, what . . .)

until the doorbell had rung, until a woman had arrived and . . .

no God no lemme be wrong please please

Henry Michael started to whimper. His teeth chattered. Terror and revulsion broke loose inside him as the screams spurted into the air once more and then died abruptly, like an artery that had been sucked dry. The fuzz, the webs, were clearing from his mind, and he knew the woman would come for him now, to finish what she began when she blew off his kneecaps and shot his youngest son in the chest.

He heard her footfalls, rapid and urgent, moving toward him from the kitchen, the dining room. He caught a whiff of her perfume. He heard her breathing; the sound of it echoed inside him as the screams had. He sensed her stopping just behind him, at his head, and felt her eyes boring into him. He pressed his elbows against the floor, pushed, pressed, and pushed again to propel himself away from her, but his legs felt like two-ton lead pipes. They wouldn't budge.

"How're the knees, Judge? I bet they smart, huh."

"Wh-why're you doing this?" He moved his head back, but the only thing he could see were her legs, blurred and gray, like distant tree stumps. "Wh-why?"

"You *really* don't know, Judge? I thought you were a bright man. That's what everyone says, you know. That you're a very bright man, the biggest supporter of capital punishment in the state of Florida. Yes siree, Judge Henry Michael, hotshot." She touched his forehead and he winced. Her skin was cold, clammy, like a corpse's. "Bet you don't feel like much of a hotshot now, do you." She patted his cheek. "Your wife wasn't very brave, Judge. I was really very disappointed in her."

"Please," he sobbed, trying to wiggle away from her but failing. "Wh-what do y-you want?"

"Don't squirm like that, Judge. It's very unbecoming. And besides, there's no place to go. You can shriek if you want, but that won't do much good, because all the windows are closed. I kept telling your wife that, but she didn't care. She just screamed and screamed, and I got fed up with it."

"Pl-please . . ."

"All you have to do is die, Judge." She was doing something to his legs now. Sitting on them? Tying his ankles together? He couldn't tell because he had no feeling in his legs and he couldn't see her clearly enough. "Nothing is simpler than dying. Even being born isn't as simple as dying, Judge. That's one of those cosmic thoughts you get sometimes when you're about to fall asleep. Like you, Judge, you're about to take a long nap." She laughed. "And if I were you, I'd sure be thinking about how easy it is to die."

"Please," he whispered.

"You can think of me as . . . let's see . . . what would be a good name for me. Oh." She snapped her fingers. "I know. The Avenger. I'm the Avenger, just like on the old TV show. Remember that show, Judge? With Emma Peel and that turkey sidekick of hers?"

Another laugh. Dear God, how that laugh terrified him, hurt him, pressed down against his gut with its horrible weight, its unbearable weight.

"I don't believe in getting back at someone, Judge. I just get even."

And she laughed some more, a weird, high cackle, and Henry Michael began to pray. *Bless me Father, for I have sinned. . . .* The prayer, what was the rest of the prayer? He couldn't remember because now she was touching something sharp and cold to the side of his neck. "You know what this is, Judge? It's an old-fashioned hat pin. It belonged to my grandmother. On Sundays, she would fix a couple of these pretty pins in her hat and off she would go to church. Can you see it, Judge?"

He knew she was holding something above him, but it was a long, gray blur. *Old and tired eyes, like your bones, Henry, like your bones.* "I . . . I . . . my eyes . . . aren't very good."

How normal his voice had sounded for that moment. *My eyes aren't very good,* as if he were talking to someone at the courthouse, an acquaintance. *My eyes are old. . . .*

"Oh, your glasses. Right. I forgot all about your glasses." She slipped them on over his nose. One lens was shattered and it fractured her features, created a mosaic of her face. But through the other lens he could see her soft skin, her bright, mad eyes, and there, the hat pin. It was long, slender, with a small red bulb on the end like a tiny impaled radish. "Isn't it pretty, Judge?"

"Pl-please," he stammered, "d-don't hurt Jenny. Don't hurt m-my sons, don't . . ."

She smiled. "Too late, hon. Jenny's taken the route of the big sleep. Remember? And your sons, too."

No no no

". . . You should've thought of that four years ago. He didn't deserve the chair, you know. Have you ever seen anyone fry in the chair, Judge? You know what burning skin smells like? You know what happens when all the juice zips through you? I . . . I was there. I saw him fry. I saw him twitch. I smelled him b-burning, you son of a bitch.''

"Who? *Who?*" he cried.

"God will have to tell you, Judge. Say your prayers, okay? It's only fair you should have a chance to say your prayers. Even a man going to the chair has that chance. I'll say them with you. 'Now I lay me down to sleep. . . .' C'mon, Judge, say it along with me. 'Now I lay me . . .' "

But when he opened his mouth, only his raw, ragged breath came out.

"Oh Christ," she snapped. "I give you a chance to say your prayers and you blow it." She removed his glasses. "I'm afraid you've exhausted my patience, Judge Michael. Now, this is going to smart a little. You'd better not move your head, either, because that'll just make it worse."

Pain exploded in his right eye as she slid the hat pin into the corner of it, down under the lid, deeply into the eyeball. It ruptured. It bled and oozed. He shrieked and bucked against the floor, and she straddled his chest and kept working the pin back into the eyeball, through the optic nerve, cooing, "Now, now, Judge, you're not very brave, either." She pressed something cold and sharp against his throat. For a blinding second he felt a warm rush of blood against his chest. He sucked at the air, but there wasn't any. There was no air, no light.

There was nothing.

PART ONE

1: BIRD'S EYE

1

They were third in line for takeoff. The Cessna's engine hummed, the blades of its propeller blurred, its red and white wings baked in the hot Tango Key sun. The dials and needles on the instrument panel said everything checked out fine, just fine. So how come she felt like she was suffering from sunstroke? Faintness, thirst, a dull thud in her temple, a certain queasiness in the pit of her belly.

Aline Scott's eyes slid over the instrument panel again, seeking irregularities: soaring oil pressure, a faulty altimeter setting, a red warning light. But everything looked okay. The only thing to worry about, then, was the unexpected: a meandering gull, a snapped rudder cable before she reached the front of the line, a blown tire during takeoff.

"You're fretting," Kincaid said over the din of the engine.

"I'm not. Really. Could you pass me my sunglasses?"

"Where are they?"

"In my purse. It's in the back seat."

"You should've thought of this before."

"I'll add it to my checklist. Just get them, okay?"

The Comanche at the head of the line was racing forward now, speeding into the sun, then lifting into the air. The Piper Cub in front of her inched forward. She let up on the brake, pushed the throttle in a little, and swung into second place.

Kincaid fitted her sunglasses onto her nose. "Relax, Allie, you're going to do just fine. It's not like you've never done this before."

But she'd never done it completely alone. Always before,

Kincaid's hands rested on the other wheel and his feet were on the other set of rudder pedals, ready to correct if she did something wrong. Always before, he'd taken her through the basic maneuvers so she could become accustomed to the plane. He contended that her fear of flying was simply a lack of familiarity with the mechanics of it all. She suspected the fear went deeper than that, could be traced, in fact, to a close call on an Eastern flight fourteen months ago. Close call: as in a go-around when the wheels hadn't come down and the plane was less than 200 feet from the runway. Close call: as in *Pillow in your lap, head down, remove eyeglasses and high heels and be prepared to evacuate the cabin . . .*

Her symptoms were worse now: serious nausea, dizziness, black dots in front of her eyes, blood draining from her face. She took several deep breaths, meditative breaths; it helped some. She looked over at Kincaid and that helped, too. He was the very picture of serenity: buckled into his seat, dark shades covering his lapis eyes, sunlight laced through his sandy, gray-speckled beard and spilling down the front of his shirt. He ran a hand over his sandy hair and folded the map in his lap into a neat rectangle.

"November Tango four niner niner, you're cleared for takeoff," said a voice in her earphones.

Her throat went as dry as tissue paper. She could barely spit out: "Roger, tower."

"You're on, Allie," Kincaid said, then repeated instructions she already knew by heart, but which she seized upon as if hearing them for the first time. "Taxi up to the front and push the throttle all the way in. As you head down the runway, keep to the yellow line that divides it. Around seventy-five, start your roll and lift."

"Right."

She moved into place. She pushed the throttle in, and the roar of the engine filled the cockpit. The plane leaped forward. It sailed straight down the yellow line, gathering speed, gobbling up the runway, the world to either side of her blurring. Her feet played the rudder pedals. The plane veered to the left.

"Keep her straight," Kincaid warned.

She coaxed the nose back so it was parallel to the yellow line. Her hands tightened on the control wheel. The sun blistered her forehead. Suppose the runway wasn't long enough?

Suppose the engine quit? *Suppose Kincaid has a heart attack while we're up here?*

"Get ready to pull back on the wheel. You're approaching liftoff speed, Al."

Panic. The needle quivered now at 68.

She was going to do it.

70 . . .

Nothing would go wrong.

73 . . .

A sense of exhilaration hissed into her as the needle struck 75 and she pulled back on the wheel and the Cessna's nose tilted upward. The plane rose effortlessly into the clear cerulean sky, out toward the sea. "I'm doing it!" she shrieked.

Kincaid laughed. "Great. You're doing great. But don't bring the nose up too steeply. There's no future in stalling out the plane."

Stall: a nasty word. She had visions of the Cessna's nose lifting higher and higher until it was pointed toward the sun. The engine would falter and die. The plane would shudder; the nose would plunge forward and begin a death spin toward earth. She lowered the nose.

"When you reach eight hundred feet," Kincaid said, "bank left to get out of the airport pattern, and keep climbing to a thousand feet. Then level out and head north along the shore, climbing gradually to fifteen hundred."

She followed his instructions to the letter, and when she leveled out at fifteen hundred feet she peered below at the island, delighted with the bird's-eye view. The strip of wheat-colored beach along the east shore of Tango Key was crowded with tourists, and they'd spilled over into the celery-green shoals. This high up, they looked like little dolls, bobbing in the waves, baking against the sand. Running parallel to the beach was the Old Post Road, which circumnavigated the island—a strip of black asphalt where cars looked no larger than toys. The ancient banyans and slender, graceful pines that proliferated along its edges seemed too green and dwarfed to be real. She raised her eyes, drinking in the sky and the island to the west.

Tango Key measured eleven miles at its longest point and seven at its widest. It was shaped roughly like a cat's head. The mouth fell around Tango, the main town to the south. The nose and whiskers were marked by the hills, where the airport was located. The cat's left ear was occupied by Pirate's Cove, the exclusive development on the island, with its $2 million marina. The right ear, which they were approaching, rose steeply from the shore, ending in a cliff that marked the beginning of a virtually uninhabited wilderness. It fanned south and west, creating an almost perfect square filled with banyan, pine, and ficus trees.

Off to her right, about twelve miles east and a little south, lay Key West. Connecting it and Tango Key was the bridge—an architectural marvel that arched high over the blue waters and which local bookies predicted would be devastated in the next five years by a hurricane or a tanker. It was thick with traffic, just as it always was during the tourist season.

"Well?" asked Kincaid.

"I love this. I absolutely love it. Why didn't you talk me into this sooner?"

"I tried." He laughed. "All right. Even though you've logged some hours, we'll keep things simple today. Head due west and then south. We're going to go around the island once, then slide into a landing pattern. We'll try a couple more takeoffs and landings, then go over everything when we're back on the ground."

Kincaid's voice was that of a man who was at home in the air, a regular Saint Exupéry. He'd bought the Cessna at an estate auction almost three years ago, even though he'd never flown an hour, and dubbed it Cat, short for Kathmandu, his favorite spot in the world. He claimed he was sick to death of battling traffic during the tourist season and now he could get to Key West in six minutes instead of thirty and to Miami in just under two hours. She'd expected the plane to sit on the airfield, a stepchild of Kincaid's whim, and thought the purchase was an enormous waste of money. But Kincaid had pursued his new hobby the way he did everything else, with a relentless diligence that had earned him four ratings so far—private, instrument, seaplane, and instructor's.

He presently had six students—counting her—enough to keep him busy, he said, when the private eye business got slow. She had yet to figure out when that was.

"Let me take over for a second, Allie." Kincaid placed his hands on the wheel on his side.

She surrendered control and followed his gaze to the terrain below. They were at the western side of the island now, near Suicide Cliff, where two dozen expensive homes dotted the hillsides. A cluster of cars sprouted like exotic white wildflowers from one of the crescent driveways. Even before Kincaid took the plane down to 800 feet, she knew the vehicles were police cruisers. It looked like most of the Tango Key police department was there.

"Want to go take a look?" Kincaid asked.

"Yeah, maybe I should."

He smiled, as if this was exactly the answer he'd expected.

2

The February air, as sweet-smelling as a kitten's breath, poured through the sunroof of Kincaid's white Saab. The car negotiated the hills toward the west end of the island with ease. He seemed to know exactly where they were going. But then, unlike her, he was one of those people who had a sense of direction as precise as a migrating bird's. A long time ago, she'd believed it was a talent he'd developed during all his years of traveling—a hundred-some-odd countries in thirty-eight years. But now she knew it was an innate talent, instinctive.

He was a tall man—six foot three in his bare feet—with curly hair a shade lighter than his beard, and wide-set lapis eyes. They'd been lovers for a little longer than he'd owned the plane, and although they'd talked about getting married, she was in no hurry to change what was so obviously a good thing.

"I think the house we saw belongs to Judge Michael," he said.

"We weren't really low enough to see the house."

"We were close enough to see where it is in relation to the rest, and it's the nearest place to Suicide Cliff. So is the judge's house."

She suddenly wished they'd stayed in the air. This was their first full day together in more than a month. They'd saved for it, planned for it, mapped it out—a flying lesson, a hike into the woods at the northeast tip of the island, and this evening, a flight into Miami for a jazz concert in Coconut Grove. Why risk blowing all that just to see what the ruckus was? This was her day off.

"I changed my mind. Let's go have breakfast or something."

"We already had breakfast."

"Then we can start our hike."

"Al, we're practically there."

"We drive in, then out, okay?"

"Absolutely."

But she didn't think he believed it any more than she did.

The house was a rambling two-story affair, made of cedar, and set back in a clearing surrounded by pines. The glass in its tall front windows had seized the chaos in the yard and frozen it: two ambulances and four paramedics, five cruisers, the chief's Chevy, and a ten-year-old Mercedes that belonged to the coroner, Bill Prentiss. It couldn't get much clearer than that.

Radios barked, two officers were roping off the area, and a handful of gawkers lined the edge of the driveway as the Saab pulled in. Claudia Bernelli was on the front porch, her thin bones zipped into a pair of skintight jeans, watching as one of the coroner's skeleton crew dusted an overturned bicycle for prints. Bernie glanced up as they ascended the stairs; her face was alarmingly pale, almost the same color as her very blond hair.

"What're you guys doing here?"

"We saw the cars from the air," Aline replied. "What happened?"

Her taffy eyes skewed against the light. "Unless you've got a strong stomach, don't go in there. The judge, his wife, their two kids . . ." She shook her head. "The bodies are gone, but it's bad. Real bad."

And that was when they should've walked away. But they didn't. They stepped into a foyer steeped in light and an eerie stillness. Everyone was upstairs, and the place seemed utterly devoid of life. Kincaid headed for the stairs, and Aline went left, toward the living room. She stopped abruptly in the doorway.

The living room looked like it had been turned upside down, shaken, and then someone had tossed a couple of buckets of blood into the ruin. Blood smeared the walls, had spattered the overturned furniture, and had caked in dry pud-

dles against the dove-gray rug. Two small, bloody handprints
marred the wall over the telephone stand. Directly in front of
the stand was the chalk outline of one of the children.

The cushions of the couch across the room stood on end
and had been torn open. Stuffing had leaked out and littered
the floor around it. A rocking chair nearby had been tipped
over; it reminded her of a Moslem bowing toward Mecca,
forehead touching the floor, legs bent at the knees, heels
sticking up. Next to it was the only undisturbed piece of
furniture in the room—a coffee table strewn with magazines.
Between it and the couch was the second chalked silhouette—
larger, either Judge Michael or his wife. Just beyond the head
lay a pair of glasses with a shattered lens.

Two men from forensics came into the room, but they
worked so quietly, Aline barely noticed them. She stepped
carefully around shards of glass where a display case had
been toppled. A lone figurine had escaped damage—an old
woman selling balloons. The entryway between this room
and the dining room was strewn with law books from a low
bookcase against the far wall. It looked as if the killer had
simply grabbed books at random and hurled them across the
room.

The dining room was unscathed, except for a broom on
the floor that she guessed had been used to smash the chandelier over the dining room table. Bits of glass sparkled
against the glossy wood of the mahogany table and studded
the pine floor.

She stared at the remains of the chandelier, at the way the
slivered vestiges fractured the light. She could almost hear
the chandelier shattering and bits of glass showering to the
floor, tinkling like wind chimes. *You took a swing at it like
it was a piñata that was going to rain candy, didn't you. You
enjoyed this. You loved it.*

Her shoes crunched over the glass as she continued into
the kitchen. Another adult had been found in front of the
sink; she guessed it was Jenny Michael. The chalk silhouette
enclosed bloodstains, as if to contain them. Blood also had
splattered across the cabinet doors, darkened the faucets, and
stood out in stark relief against the white of the refrigerator
door. The second child—*a boy, the judge had two boys*—had
fallen in the doorway between the kitchen and the hall.

Schoolbooks were piled on the round butcher-block table;

a yellow pencil marked a page in a math book. The door of the dishwasher was open, the top rack pulled out, stacked with glasses and mugs. There was a dishpan filled with dirty water on one side of the double sink. On the other side, the porcelain was stained with blood.

She was too close to it—the afflux of smells, the gloom, the vestiges of a fevered rage—and stepped back from it mentally, visualizing the room as though she were high above it, peering down. *The bird's eye view:* just like flying, she thought. She saw the kitchen as it must've been last night, Jenny Michael at the sink, probably rinsing and stacking dishes, and one of her boys at the table, doing his homework. The judge and the other boy were in the living room. It had been an ordinary Thursday evening in the life of an ordinary family until . . . *What?*

Mentally, she zoomed in closer now. She plucked a paper towel from the roll over the sink and used it to open the kitchen door. She ran her hand over the wood and lock; it hadn't been jimmied. But a streak of blood trailed across one of the planks to the steps that led to the driveway. She walked to the end of the porch, descended the steps, peered right, following the driveway with her eyes to the two-car garage. Then she drew her gaze back to the white concrete of the driveway directly in front of her. No blood. Why not? Why did the trail end right here?

To either side of her, along the edge of the house, were wide strips of grass and a bushy hibiscus hedge that bloomed with bright red and pink buds, and farther down, at the corner of the house, gardenia bushes. She knelt in the grass, in the scent of gardenias and jasmine, looking for more blood. She found it—thin streaks that vanished into the hedge.

She parted the branches with her hands and gorge surged in her throat. There, curled in a tight ball against the side of the house, partially hidden under an old plastic gray tarp, was a child. There was so much dirt and blood on the face that Aline couldn't tell if it was a boy or a girl, alive or dead. Clutched to the child's chest was a dead orange cat whose fur was matted with blood.

Aline leaped up, shoved her way through the hedge, and crouched down at the top of the child's head. A girl. Curly blond hair. Long lashes so blond they were almost white. *Please be alive.* Her hand trembled as she sought a pulse in the girl's neck. Her skin was cool, damp, but, oh Christ, she felt it, a faint, erratic pulse. The child, just like the lone figurine of the balloon woman, had somehow survived the slaughter. Aline threw off the tarp, unhooked the child's arm from the cat, and picked her up.

She raced along the driveway toward the front of the house, the girl's head hanging limply over the side of her arm, her mouth slightly open, her jeans and T-shirt stinking of blood and urine. As Aline rounded the corner, she spotted Doc Prentiss and the chief on the porch with two officers. Aline shouted; her voice pierced the breezy, February air, a supplication, a cry of hope.

2: KINCAID

I

He didn't hear the shouts in the yard.

Ryan Kincaid was upstairs, at the back of the house, in the master bedroom, where the air was as still and deep blue as the bottom of a lake. Everything in here was in perfect order. The king-size bed was made, spread folded down, pillows puffed up. The twin mahogany bureaus shone and were free of dust. The blue curtains at the picture window were closed, and the twin closets with the pine French doors stood ajar, but the stuff inside was neat neat neat. So how come there was a maroon towel hooked over the knob of the bathroom door? And why was the edge of the matching bath mat flopped over at the corner like a basset hound's ear?

He padded into the bathroom, glancing around, disturbed by something he couldn't name. The bathroom was huge, with inlaid Italian tile floors and a pair of eggshell-blue matching sinks with gold-plated faucets. A Jacuzzi and an adjoining bathtub dominated the far corner where the window jutted out and curved upward to a skylight. Plants billowed from clay pots along the windowsill and the back of the tub. At the other end of the bathroom was a shower. A pair of monogrammed gray towels were draped over the rack.

Kincaid opened the shower door with the hem of his T-shirt and squatted. His eyes moved slowly across the tiled walls, the floor, the faucets. The wall was dry, but moisture had beaded on the floor, near the drain. He yanked a piece of Kleenex from the box on the back of the toilet and touched the edge of it to a drop of water. The corner turned faintly pink. He pulled a couple more pieces of Kleenex from the box, looked through the medicine cabinet until he found a pair of tweezers, and returned to the shower. He plucked several hairs from the area around the drain—blond, brown, and black. Mrs. Michael and the judge had black and brown hair respectively. The boys both favored their mother. So who the hell did the blond hair belong to?

He set the hairs on the bed of Kleenex and carefully folded it into a neat little square. He reached into the box of Kleenex, removed the stack of tissues inside, and set his folded piece of tissue into the box. Next, he straightened the corner of the bath mat and stretched out on the floor, eyes roaming the surface for more hairs.

"If you're settling in for a siesta, Kincaid, let me suggest the bed," said a voice in the doorway.

"Hi, Bernelli." He didn't look around. With the tweezers, he lifted a blond pubic hair from the mat and placed it on another tissue.

Bernelli lowered herself to the floor beside him. "Forensics has already been through here."

"Not very well. The killer took a shower after he finished his business downstairs." He sat up, gestured toward the Kleenex box. "I'm placing bets the bastard is blond. Like you, kiddo."

Bernelli rolled her taffy eyes, pulled a pack of cigarettes from her shirt pocket, and lit one. "You aren't exactly a brunette yourself, Kincaid." She pulled her legs up and rested her head against the wall. "Aline found a little girl out by the side of the house. Still alive. She rode the ambulance into town, with Bill Prentiss following in his car. You're supposed to meet her at the hospital."

She said this so factually, it took a moment for the import to sink in. "Any idea who she is?"

"Nope. Prentiss said she's in shock. She was holding the Michaels' dead cat. It had been stabbed."

"How old is she?"

"Nine, ten, around there. A possible witness. They're going to keep it out of the papers." Bernelli's voice maintained that hard, factual edge—the voice of a seasoned cop. But the way she smoked her cigarette, with quick, almost urgent puffs, said she wasn't inured to any of it.

She was a thin, intense woman whom Aline had known

since junior high and with whom Ryan had had a brief affair about four years ago. Her skin was smooth and creamy, the sort of skin other women envied and sought through cosmetics and mud packs. She wore her curly blond hair very short, which set off her long neck, where the tendons now stood out like cords of rope. The four gold chains at her neck were tangled, and as she spoke, her fingers worked at them nervously, impatiently.

"Danny was going to spend the night here last night, Ryan," she said, referring to her fifteen-year-old son. "He and Paul Michael were good friends." She looked over at him, emotion swimming in her eyes, the fluorescent lights turning her soft, flawless complexion milk-white. "But he flunked a math quiz yesterday so I told him no way was he going to spend the night with anyone. Suppose he . . ." Her voice cracked then, and she pressed a hand over her eyes.

Kincaid gave her shoulder a squeeze.

"Don't," he said gently. "It didn't happen, so don't play the 'what if' game, Bernie."

Her hand fell away from her face and she stared at the far wall.

"Who took the call?" he asked.

"Me. A neighbor lady called the station. She and Jenny Michael were supposed to have breakfast this morning and then go shopping. When Jenny still hadn't shown up at eight, she called here, then came over. No one answered the bell, so she walked around back. The kitchen door was unlocked, and she came in and saw . . . saw Jenny and the youngest boy." She paused, flicked the ashes from her cigarette into her hand. "The bodies were hacked up, Kincaid. The judge's throat had been slit, he'd been shot in the knees, his hands were tied. Something had been . . . been stuck in it, I think. Paul, the older boy . . . I found him between the kitchen and the hall . . . the fingers on his right hand were . . . were gone. . . ." She leaned forward and dropped her cigarette in the toilet. It hissed as it went out.

"Did you talk to the neighbors?" he asked.

"Sure. No one heard anything. The houses are too far apart, and besides, it was hot last night and most everyone on the street had the air-conditioning on, windows closed up. The phones here were dead, too."

"C'mon. Let's get out of here. I'll buy you a cup of coffee or something."

"What I need," she said, "is a stiff drink."

"Fine. Then I'll buy you a stiff drink."

"We'd better take this bath mat with us."

"And the towel," he added.

"I'll find a garbage bag."

She seemed grateful to have something to do, and stood quickly. She found a package of short white garbage bags in the linen closet in the bathroom, and Kincaid folded the bath mat carefully and slipped it inside one of the bags. He did the same with the maroon towel and the bar of soap from the shower. He picked up the bags, and Bernelli, the Kleenex box.

"How well did you know the judge?" Kincaid asked as they started downstairs.

"Mostly through work. He presided over some of my arrests through the years. I actually knew Jenny better, because of our kids."

"Did the judge have any enemies that you know of?"

"What the hell, Ryan, you know as well as I do that judges always have enemies, and I think Henry Michael had more than his share because he was pro–capital punishment. But why ask me? You knew him. You worked for him from time to time, didn't you?"

Kincaid nodded. Henry Michael had been a friend—not a close friend, true, but a friend nonetheless, and he didn't feel like discussing the man's enemies here in the house where he'd been killed.

In the living room downstairs, they turned the goods over to Conchita Guzmán, the only Cuban on the forensics team and the only woman.

Kincaid set the bags on the floor beside her. "They missed some stuff upstairs."

Conchita rocked back on her heels and regarded him over the rim of her tortoiseshell glasses. Like Bernelli, she wore her chestnut hair short and had smooth, flawless skin that barely creased when she smiled. "My area's this room, Ryan, but I'll make sure it gets back to the lab. What is it, anyway?"

He told her. Conchita made a face. "We do our best, Ryan, but unfortunately, when you're dealing with a lunatic like this, the best sometimes isn't enough. I'll keep Aline posted.''

"Thanks."

As they headed toward the door, Bernelli said, "Were you working on something for the judge?"

"Why do you ask that?"

"Why else would you be picking hairs out of the shower, Ryan?"

"Curiosity?"

"Ha," she said with a snort.

Outside, the hot light had thickened, coating the front lawn like varnish. The sprinklers, hooked into an automatic timing system, had come on and twirled mindlessly, showering the marigolds and zinnias that bordered the edges of the driveway. The blooms on the proud and neatly trimmed hibiscus hedge at the front of the yard drooped as though they were weeping.

"C'mon, Ryan. Were you working for him?" Bernelli persisted. "On what?"

Bernelli, who was about nine inches shorter than he, impaled him with her eyes as she waited for an answer. Her tenacity was admirable, but he didn't want to go into it here. He wasn't sure he wanted to go into it at all until he'd had a chance to think about it. "We'll talk about it over that stiff drink I'm buying you."

"We should swing by the hospital first and pick up Al."

"Okay. Meet you there." He hurried away before she could call him back.

2

He followed the Old Post Road back into Tango, wondering what sort of statement the chief would give to the press. There'd be no mention of the girl, of course, although word might leak out. Gossip was ubiquitous on this island, and surely some of the gawkers had seen the child being put into the ambulance. He doubted that the chief, Gene Frederick, would mention the mutilations either. The statement would be far more succinct and vague than the judge's conversation

with Kincaid two days ago, when they'd run into each other
at the courthouse.

Kincaid had been over there checking the public records
as a favor to his first ex-wife, who was in the process of
divorcing her third husband and wanted to know about some
property he owned. Henry Michael had stopped him in the
hall and invited him out to the house over the weekend.

"Bring your suit and we'll take the boat out. I've got a
couple of things I'd like to discuss with you, Ryan."

"My parking tickets are paid up."

Michael had laughed. He was a short, good-looking man
in his late forties who had shared Kincaid's interest in traveling. When he'd been Tango County's star prosecutor, Kincaid had worked on a half-dozen cases for him, mostly culling
information. Kincaid couldn't stomach Michael's opinions on
issues like capital punishment, but he liked the man and
agreed to join him on the boat Saturday.

"So if this isn't about my parking tickets, then what *is* it
about, Henry?"

"I've gotten some rather disturbing phone calls and a note.
They may just be cranks, but I'd like you to look into it. It
wouldn't surprise me if they were connected to an old case.
I've got several possibilities as to the source."

"What kind of calls?"

"Threatening. Toward me."

"Male?"

"Don't know. There've only been two calls, and the person
always whispers. But here's the note." He'd reached into his
wallet and pulled out a 3-by-5 card. Typed on it was a verse,
signed with a deep green smiling-face sticker:

> *Death will come by night,*
> *a sharp and bitter bite*
> *which you & yours will fight*
> *& lose—against God's greater might.*

"Why don't you go to the cops, Henry?"

Michael had shrugged and folded the card, slipping it back
into his wallet. "Listen, Ryan, the police really don't have
the manpower to deal with something that might just be a
looney tune out there who's decided he's got a beef with me.
It's better like this. And I don't want Jenny to get wind of it,

because all she'll do is fret." He'd smiled. "My wife is a great fretter."

Then an attorney had interrupted them and Michael had handed Kincaid a check for $3,500, said, "That should cover your expenses for a while. See you on Sunday," and walked off with the other man toward the cafeteria. It was the last time Kincaid had seen him. He didn't doubt that the calls and the note were connected to the murders. And the $3,500 obligated him to at least find the connection, didn't it?

The Saab crawled the last four miles into town because the traffic was so bad. Every other license plate, it seemed, was out-of-state, and those that weren't were rentals. The snow-birds had swollen the island's population to almost 17,000 this year, and he knew it would get worse as Easter and spring break approached. Tourists pumped millions into Tango's economy, but they also strained every facility on the island—from the police department and hotels to things as basic as the water supply.

He blamed the snowbirds, in fact, for Aline's virtual absence from his life these last few months. She and the other detectives and officers in the department were putting in sixty-hour weeks. When she had a free day, she usually spent it in Whitman's, her bookstore, thus relieving her co-owner, who kept it running smoothly and efficiently six days a week.

Like so many people on Tango Key, Aline couldn't have lived here without the income from two jobs. The property taxes were the highest in the state; groceries cost twice what they did anywhere else in Florida; and basics like electricity, water, and gasoline were astronomical. If two could live as cheaply as one—and he wasn't entirely convinced that was true—then maybe the answer was for them to move in together. It would ease her financial problems and give them more time together. The problem, of course, was who would move where.

They both owned houses. One of them could rent for the season and make a tidy little sum—enough to cover the months when the house was unoccupied, with some profit left over. But again, which of them would rent? He didn't particularly like the idea of strangers living in his house and knew Aline felt the same way. The ideal would be to get married, sell both houses, and build one of their own. But Aline didn't seem to be in a big hurry to get married; he

supposed he had his lousy track record to blame for that. Two
marriages, two divorces: hardly the stuff stability was made
of.

So here they were—their free day together over before it
had barely begun, and the same old concerns swarming like
mosquitos around him: murder, mayhem, and the elusive
American dream.

3

He parked in back of the Tango Key Hospital and entered
through the emergency room. Aline wasn't in the waiting
area. He didn't know if that meant the girl had died—or been
moved. He approached the desk and asked the nurse where
Bill Prentiss was.

"With a patient, sir."

"A child?"

"Uh, yes. That's right. The little Jane Doe."

"There was a detective with them. Would you happen to
know where she is?"

"Oh. Aline. Sure. She's in the coffee shop."

Was there any local on Tango who *didn't* know Aline? But
then, she was a Fritter, born and raised here; he was just a
twenty-three-year transplant.

He walked down the corridor that smelled of Pine Sol and
wax to the coffee shop and saw Aline sitting alone at a table,
paging through the newspaper, a mug in front of her. Her
wavy cinnamon hair was gathered at the back of her head in
a loose ponytail that snaked halfway down her right arm. She
stroked the end of it, wrapped it around her index finger,
stroked it again. Then, as if sensing him nearby, she looked
up. Her eyes were the vibrant blue at the cool tip of a flame,
and they watched him intently, as if she could see right
through him. Her nose was long, slender. Her mouth was
one that begged to be touched, and it slid into a smile as he
neared. No one had a smile quite like that: it could've lit up
Pluto.

"You left me in Bernelli's clutches," he said, sitting across
from her. "How's the girl?"

"She's in shock, but not seriously injured physically. Bill moved her into intensive care. He said he'd be down in a couple of minutes."

"Who is she?"

Aline shook her head. "I don't know. I called the station and asked Roxie to run a computer check through the missing children's division in Miami. They're hooked up with the feds. Maybe that'll turn up something."

"How old is she?"

"Bill says she's between ten and twelve, but small for her age. Did Bernie tell you about the cat?"

He nodded. "Was it orange?"

"Yeah."

"Then it was probably the Michaels' cat."

"I should ticket you for speeding, Ryan," Bernelli said, coming up behind him. "For a stretch there on the Old Post Road you were doing eighty-five." She claimed the seat next to him. "You're lucky I've already had my coffee this morning, otherwise I'd be real grumpy and ticket you now."

"Mean, tough Bernelli."

She winked at him, signaled the waitress, and lit a cigarette. "Okay, now I want to hear about Judge Michael. What he hired you for."

Aline's brows lifted. "What? When?"

Bernelli stabbed a thumb toward Kincaid. "Ask lover boy here."

He explained and showed them the 3-by-5 card. Both women glanced at it; Aline rubbed her arms as if against a sudden, deep chill. "He didn't give you any indication as to who might have sent the note and made the calls?"

"No. But I got the impression he thought it was connected to a case he'd presided over."

"Where was the note mailed from?" Bernelli asked.

"He didn't say."

"It gives us a place to start," Aline said. "We can go back through the courthouse records to see which cases Judge Michael sat on."

Bill Prentiss strolled into the coffee shop and made a bee-line toward them. He was a lean six feet and had a handsome, kind face and curly black hair that was just as thick now as it had been ten years ago when they'd met. He didn't fit Kincaid's idea of a coroner; he looked more like a male model for BMWs.

As he sat down next to Aline, Kincaid connected them with a mental line; Prentiss had been Aline's first lover. He drew a second line between himself and Bernelli, since they'd also been lovers—however briefly—and a third line between himself and Aline. That left only the right side of this people square open, because he didn't know if Bernelli and Prentiss had ever been lovers. The odds said yes; life on Tango Key sometimes bordered on the incestuous.

". . . her vital signs are a lot stronger now," Prentiss was saying. "She has a nasty lump on the back of her head, and she's a bit dehydrated, but otherwise she's okay. The shock was brought on by a severe psychological trauma, probably from witnessing what went on in that house."

Bernie stabbed out her cigarette. "The chief wants a round-the-clock guard at her room, Bill."

"I hope to Christ he didn't release anything about her to the press."

"No. Nothing. His statement was pretty vague. But you never know what might get around on this island."

"When do you think she'll come out of it?" Kincaid asked.

Prentiss shrugged. "Hard to say. People react to shock in different ways. But she's in intensive care, where they can monitor her closely. As soon as she starts coming around, I want a child shrink to take a look at her. A woman I know in Miami who works with severely traumatized children has already agreed to donate her services. And the county's picking up the medical expenses, at least until her parents or guardians turn up."

"When will you have the autopsies done?" Aline asked.

"I'll get started this afternoon. But I don't think they're going to tell us anything we don't already know."

"But what I found in the master bathroom upstairs might." Kincaid told him about the stuff he and Bernelli had passed on to Conchita Guzmán. Prentiss didn't look too happy about the fact that his skeleton crew had been sloppy, but promised to have something on the hair samples by tomorrow morning.

"And since it looks like I'm going to be pulling an all-nighter, folks, I'd better get moving." Prentiss pressed his palms against the table as he pushed himself to his feet. "Oh, I almost forgot. Molly and I are going to have a barbecue real soon. Everyone's invited. It'll be informal, swimsuits and shorts.''

''Soon?'' Aline laughed. ''That's plenty vague.''

Prentiss grinned sheepishly. ''Depends on my schedule in the next week or ten days. Anyway, keep it in mind.''

''Molly,'' sniffed Bernelli when Prentiss had left, ''is an asshole.''

''She's a good student,'' Kincaid offered in her support.

''What?'' Bernelli burst out laughing. ''She's taking flying lessons from you? Jesus, she doesn't look bright enough to drive a car, much less fly a plane.''

Kincaid clicked his tongue against his teeth. ''Very nasty, Bernelli.''

''You got that right.''

''I like her life-style pieces in the *Tribune*,'' Kincaid said. ''And her column is good.''

Bernelli's mouth twitched. ''Yeah, Lois Lane, star reporter. Makes me gag.'' She glanced at Aline. ''See you back at the office.''

''Hey, Bernie, what about that drink?'' he called after her. But she didn't stop. ''I meant that as a joke.'' Kincaid watched her as she walked quickly through the door and out into the corridor.

''When it comes to Bill,'' said Aline, ''nothing is a joke with Bernie. They spent a couple of nights together before he started seeing Molly, and then he just never called her again. Bill's weird when it comes to women.''

Well, well. He mentally drew a line between Bernelli and Prentiss, completing his people square. Incest, for sure.

3: DIGGING

I

Aline spent six hours in the courthouse, combing through Judge Michael's cases for the eight years he'd sat on the bench. There were hundreds of them, ranging from speeding tickets to first-degree homicides. She weeded out everything less than a felony, then narrowed these to the harsher sentences he'd imposed—ten years and up, twenty-five years with no parole, life, and the death penalty. *If* he and his family had been slaughtered as some sort of vendetta, it didn't necessarily mean she would find leads in the more heinous crimes. To a lunatic, sixty days in the county jail might be grounds for a full-scale massacre. But she had to start somewhere.

By five that afternoon she had ten cases that seemed like good candidates for a vendetta. All involved violent crimes— rapes and mutilation, murder, child abuse. In three, she'd been the arresting officer.

It would take a little time to track down where each individual presently was in the criminal justice system and to request records. But she needed to know who had been paroled, who had escaped, who was on work release. She needed names and addresses of family members, relatives, wives, girlfriends, anyone on an inmate's visiting list.

She jotted down the case numbers and requested copies of the complete files for the ten cases. The clerk, a sweet young transplant from the mainland, cracked her gum and leaned into the desk. "You're kidding. That could take me the rest of the night."

"I'll pick everything up in the morning."

Another crack of her gum, a deep sigh, then: "Look, the cases are on microfilm and we've got copies. How about if you just check out the copies, Detective Scott?"

"I don't have a microfilm machine at home."

"I got one in the back room you can take. How's that?"

"I need one that makes copies."

A wide smile from the sweet young thing and a final crack of her gum: "This one's got a copier built into it. A dime a page."

Fifteen minutes later, the backseat of the Honda was loaded down and Aline putted through the navy-blue dark toward home. Her place rose from the hump of a man-made hill at the dead end of Hurricane Drive. Like so many homes at the southern tip, it was built on stilts. It was a knotty-pine beach house with vaulted ceilings, a sleeping loft, tile floors, wicker furniture, huge floor-to-ceiling windows: strictly island fare.

It had once been her family's weekend getaway, a refuge from Key West, where her parents had owned Whitman's Bookstore. When her father had died in 1978, she'd relinquished the apartment she'd rented on White Street and had moved in here. In 1980, she'd started a smaller Whitman's on Tango, which she now owned with her former manager, Mark Finley, who'd bought into it two years ago. Finley was also co-owner of the Key West store and was actually responsible for the profit both stores had earned last year, which they'd poured back into the business. Eventually, maybe by summer, she would have enough money saved to buy a new car. The irony was that if she'd been living anywhere else, her income would have been comfortable and she would've had that new car a couple of years ago. But if you chose to live here, you paid dearly for the privilege.

She carried everything into the den and set the microfilm machine on the floor while she cleaned off her cluttered desk. The room was decorated in peach and pale silver, two colors she found particularly soothing. Each room in the house was done in a certain color or combination of colors that emanated serenity and a sense of well-being. The refurbishing had been one of her domestic projects during the last year.

It had started when the chief had ordered all the cells in the jail to be painted pink because he'd read some convincing articles on how pink prison cells seemed to diminish violence. There had never been that much violence to begin with in the Tango jail, but she'd noticed that dispositions among the inmates had improved and they slept a lot more. The influence of the new palette on her own life was more subtle, but she couldn't deny that the pink and pale blue in the bedroom enhanced sleep and sex, and not necessarily in that order.

Wolfe, her pet skunk, padded into the den to see what the commotion was all about. His little nose worked furiously as he circled the machine. Once he'd determined it presented no threat, he nudged Aline's leg with his nose, asking to be picked up. She accommodated him, stroking his silky black and white fur, then set him down on the desk. He plopped onto a pile of papers, his tiny raisin eyes asking where dinner was.

"Stinko Delight coming up in a second," she promised. "Let me just get things here squared away."

Stinko Delight consisted mostly of raw eggs, raw chicken, and raw beef, supplemented with whatever mice and other goodies Wolfe caught on his own. Aline had found him four years ago, cowering behind a boulder where his mother had been killed. He'd been small enough to fit into the palm of her hand; now he was two feet long, with an eight-inch tail, and had the run of the house. Although he'd been de-scented eighteen months ago, it hadn't cramped his style in the least. He still came and went freely through the hinged panel in the back door that led onto the porch. From the porch, he could descend to the woods behind the house, where Aline suspected he now had a lady friend.

He hustled out of the way as she set the microfilm machine on her desk. The phone rang, startling him, and he slid over the side of the desk and landed on the chair to the right. Aline laughed and picked up the receiver. It was Ferret—her indefatigable source of information, friend, and bookie.

"Sweet Pea, Ryan and I are sitting down here at Lester's tipping a few and having dinner. How about joining us?"

"He fill you in?"

"What's there to fill in? I heard about it about an hour after Bernelli arrived on the scene."

She wondered how, but didn't ask. She never asked Ferret where his information came from; she was almost afraid to know. "See you in twenty minutes."

Lester's Bar was an island landmark. It dated back to 1947, three years before the bridge was built that connected Tango Key to Key West. It was snuggled into a copse of pines and shrubbery at the eastern periphery of the city park. It had once been a soda fountain and still boasted ornate spigots that had flowed with root beer and Dr Pepper, huge glass jars filled with beef jerky and hard-boiled eggs soaked in vinegar, and twirling stools at the counter. The movie posters on the walls were vintage Hithcock: *The 39 Steps, North by Northwest, Dial M for Murder.* The jukebox played no tunes recorded after 1960. Lester's existed in a permanent time warp.

Aline found the boys in Ferret's usual booth at the back. It was strewn with racing forms that Bino, Ferret's albino sidekick, was patiently perusing. "If you've got a five spot, Sweet Pea, I've got a sure bet at the dogs that can net you about fifteen hundred."

"I need about ten times that for a new car, Ferret. Got any hot tips on lottery tickets?"

"*Lottery* tickets? Please, Sweet Pea. There is no future in lottery tickets, not until you can start choosing the numbers yourself."

She slid into the booth next to Kincaid, who said, "See? I told you, Ferret. No small-shit bets for the lady." He patted her thigh, his huge hand lingering there, warming her skin through her slacks, stirring a kind of lazy desire. "What'll it be for dinner, kiddo?"

"The usual."

Kincaid signaled the waitress and ordered two roast beefs on rye with two mugs of Corona beer. "Ferret calls this stuff yuppie beer, you know."

"Is that you think we are, Ferret? Yuppies?"

He snorted. "Leave it to Ryan to screw up everything I say. What I said, Ryan, was that yuppies have made Corona second only to Heineken for popularity of imported beers and it's probably going to surpass Heineken this year."

"It's peasant beer, Ferret. A quarter a bottle in Mexico."

"Which just proves my point. Marketing is everything. Even in your biz."

Aline and Kincaid glanced at each other. *You get it?* asked his eyes.

She shook her head. "Nope."

Ferret looked from one to the other, then flicked his hand through the air, dismissing the whole thing. "What'd you find at the courthouse, anyway?"

"I narrowed it down to ten cases, but no guarantees." Aline shrugged. "And I've got a list."

Ferret's lips drew away from his teeth in that strange smile that always chilled her. "Lemme see it." He put on a pair of Ben Franklin glasses that tempered the thin hunger of his face. His black hair, which was short and slicked back, gleamed under the stained-glass lamp that hung over the center of the table. His skeletal finger slid down the list, pausing here, there. "Two of these are on work release in Big Pine Key." He plucked a pen from his pocket and printed WR next to the names. "One of them lit out from a work release center in Pompano Beach about two, three months ago, and the word is that he left the state. Two are still doin' time, three I don't know about, one got his throat slit at Raiford, and one's out."

"Who?"

"Woman named Sheila Reiner."

Aline remembered her. Sheila Reiner had been one of *the* social butterflies in the Cove and had allegedly poisoned her multimillionaire husband. Throughout the trial, which the tabloids had covered in as much detail as the regular press, she'd maintained that she was innocent. For some reason, Judge Michael had given her a break on her sentence. Instead of the twenty-five-year mandatory most people had felt she'd deserved, she'd gotten ten years.

"How long has she been out?"

"Couple of months. She stays pretty close to home."

"Right back into the Cove social scene, huh."

"More'n likely, especially now that she's got a couple mil to play around with."

"You think this is the right track?" Kincaid asked.

Ferret shrugged and smoothed a hand over his hair. "I figure anytime you got mutilation, it's revenge of some sort. You just gotta peg the whys."

"You make it sound so easy," Aline commented.

Ferret smiled; that chill worked its way back into Aline's

bones. When Ferret smiled, it triggered a primal center in her brain. She would see him on all fours, hunched over a corpse in a dark alley, gnawing at an arm or a nose or sucking blood from a jugular. She couldn't help it. Even though she'd known the man for years, and had come to him for information that had usually proven useful, she'd been unable to completely ignore his appearance. He resembled the predatory creature he'd been named after.

"Listen, Sweet Pea, that's all you gotta do in the beginning: listen to what you feel. Bino's real good at list'nin', ain't ya, boy?"

Bino, who'd said nothing until now, glanced up, tilted his sunglasses back into his white hair, and gazed at Ferret with his eerie pink eyes. "I'm bettin' the killer's jus' gettin' started."

"Why do you think that?" Aline asked.

"Cuz that's how it is."

Swell.

Bino turned back to his racing forms, and Ferret chuckled. "That's the boy's hunch for the day."

"Ayuh," grunted Bino.

"What about the kid?" Ferret asked. "Anything new on her?"

Aline shook her head. "Nothing showed up on the computer. Tomorrow I'm going to run a check with HRS on families who take in foster children. That might turn up something."

Their dinners arrived, and the conversation veered toward jai alai, the dogs, the lottery, the horses. Now and then Kincaid's hand touched Aline's thigh, sliding over it, an absent, distracted movement that nonetheless did nice things to her insides. She and Kincaid put up $350 apiece for a bet on Saturday night's jai alai. It would definitely hurt her budget for the month, but maybe she'd get lucky. Ferret was delighted they'd placed $200 over the five he'd recommended to Aline, but chided Kincaid for not putting down $1,500.

"Not this time. I'm conserving, Ferret."

"For what?"

"My pension."

Ferret threw his head back and laughed. "Your *pension*? Oh, man."

A corner of Kincaid's mouth dimpled. "Hey, it was a joke."

"You never joke about money, Ryan. Now come clean." Ferret waggled his fingers.

"Al and I are planning a trip."

It was news to her. "We are? Where?"

"I don't know. We'll spin the globe and see what happens."

It was tantamount to an official announcement that she could expect him to depart within six to eight weeks, whether she accompanied him or not. She should've known. She should've been expecting it. It had been a year since Kincaid's last trip—a five-week jaunt to Alaska. But that hardly counted, since his sojourns usually ran from five to eight months. His last *major* trip was to South America, not long after they'd met. That had lasted seven months, and she'd visited him twice—in the fall for two weeks in Buenos Aires and at Christmas, which they'd spent on the island of Chiloé. She'd footed her ticket for the B.A. trip, and he'd bought her ticket to Chile. But she had a feeling this particular trip was going to be a lot more expensive than her finances could sustain. Like to the Far East or the South Pacific.

God, it was a depressing thought.

3

"So when're you leaving? Next week?"

They were walking out to the parking lot, and the moment she'd spoken, she regretted the accusatory tone of her voice. After all, Kincaid had a perfect right to live his life the way he wanted. He didn't have to answer to her. Or to anyone.

He leaned against the Saab, arms crossed at the waist. His battle stance. She, in turn, leaned back against her Honda, which was parked alongside his car, and crossed *her* arms. The dim glow of the street lamp turned his face and beard a pumpkin color, and the light puddled against the ground between them, a poisoned lake of the heart.

"You make it sound like I've already got my ticket."

"Don't you?"

"No. I haven't spun the globe yet."

"Oh." She lowered her eyes to the ground, feeling foolish now.

"Besides, there's some things I wanted to talk over with you before spinning the globe."

"What kind of things?"

"About us."

Cool wisps of air slid along her arms, raising gooseflesh in their wake. She didn't want to have this conversation now, here, outside of Lester's Bar, but she didn't want to wait, either. Couldn't stand the thought of waiting. If this was going to be bad, she needed to know it right this minute. She needed to know instantly so that by the time she got home, her crying jag would be over with and she could concentrate on the microfilm reels.

"Kincaid, I'd appreciate it if you'd just say it, all right?" Her thoughts already had leaped into the turbid pool of possibilities: he was bored with their relationship, there was another woman, he'd actually been married all this time. Sure. That was it. His wife lived in Miami or Palm Beach and he'd bought the Cessna to facilitate the logistics of his dual life. The woman was probably a knockout—svelte, rich, independent. She appealed to the sojourner side of his personality, the side that sought diversity, the exotic. "Tell me the worst part first."

His frown brought his lapis eyes closer together. She desperately wanted to lean toward him and press her finger against the frown, flattening it out. "What worst part?"

"Of whatever you're going to say."

"Why do you always assume there's a worst part?"

"Isn't there?"

He sighed. "I was just going to suggest that maybe we should try living together awhile."

Aline burst out laughing. "I thought—"

"I know what you thought. Thanks. Three years and you're still thinking that maybe—just maybe—I've got a wife stashed away somewhere that I forgot to tell you about."

"Professional hazards." She shrugged. "Besides, Kincaid, we practically live together now."

"We play musical beds, Al."

"Whose place would we live in?" She shifted her weight to her other foot and let her arms fall to her sides. Kincaid's hands slid into his pockets. Now that a battle had been averted, their body language had changed.

"I don't know. That's one of the details we'd have to work out."

One of many. Whenever the topic of living together or getting married had arisen in the past, she'd treated it casually, as in, *It might be an interesting thing to do someday.* To her it had remained an abstract, a nice notion, a goal ensconced safely in the far future. She loved Kincaid, but the emotion frightened her.

Three years ago, they'd met during a homicide investigation, when her longtime relationship with another cop, Steve Murphy, was on the decline. Murphy was now dead, accidentally killed by the woman who'd been Aline's competitor. The story, even now, seemed rather dark and sordid to her, and although she no longer mourned for Murphy, that glutinous fear of losing someone you loved had clung to her the way the memory of hunger stuck with someone who'd grown up poor. Now Kincaid was talking concrete, day-to-day, intimate, mundane living, the sort of living where a cap left off a tube of toothpaste might be a big deal. It meant romance yanked from the clouds and pressed like dried flowers between the pages of ordinary life. It was a test they might both fail utterly and completely.

"What brought this on?" she asked.

Annoyance limned his features. "You're making it sound like a sinus attack, Aline."

She rocked toward him, her face inches from his, and growled at him. He didn't crack a smile. He pressed back against the Saab, pressed back so hard he looked as if he expected the car to part in the middle like the Red Sea. She growled again and tickled him in the ribs. His face broke loose as he laughed and grabbed her hands, pinning them behind her. He peered down at her, towering over her by half a foot, and kissed her quickly. His beard tickled her chin. He smelled of the wind, the night, of smoke.

"You're in big trouble, Allie."

"Promises, promises."

"We hardly see each other." He released her hands and slid his fingers through her hair, lifting it from her shoulders. "I guess that's what's behind it."

Fair enough, she thought. "Then let's go back to my place

and talk about it over Nightmare Chasers and the microfilm machine.''

4

Chamomile and honey with a touch of mint and eucalyptus— her mother's old recipe for chasing off nightmares. Aline made a pitcher of it and carried it and two glasses into the den, where Kincaid was studying the globe. She set the tray on the desk and walked over to the bookcase.

''Ready for the spin?''

''Spin away,'' she replied.

She closed her eyes and touched the tip of her finger to the globe as it spun. After a bit, it began to slow, and then it stopped and she opened her eyes. Her finger impaled the east coast of New Zealand; Kincaid let out a whoop of delight. ''Fantastic.''

And way out of my price range. ''I can't afford a trip to New Zealand.''

''You could if we lived together and split expenses.''

''I could?''

''Sure. I worked up some preliminary figures. I'll show them to you tomorrow.'' Then, quickly, he added, ''If you're interested.''

''It sounds like a business proposition.''

He sighed. ''Okay, forget it. Forget I said a damn thing.''

''I was kidding, Ryan. Just give me some time to think about it, okay?''

He smiled. ''I wasn't trying to pressure you.''

''Yeah, you were.'' She laughed. ''But it's okay. I'll think about it.'' She made an X over her heart. ''Really.''

Placated now, he asked if she had handy the list with Ferret's notations on it. She brought it out of her purse, smoothing it in front of him.

He studied it, then perused the case numbers on the microfilm screen. ''Any of these your arrests?''

''Three of them, including one who got the chair. Jimmy Ray Luskin. My first arrest.''

Kincaid made a face. "I remember that one. A double homicide. His sister and her lover, right?"

Not just homicide, she thought. Luskin had tortured them first with an electric cattle prod and burning cigarettes and had shoved crushed glass up his sister's vagina. Aline could still see him sitting beside his attorney, his beautiful face a study in repose as the prosecution called one damning witness after another.

The defense attorney's mistake was entering a plea of guilty by reason of temporary insanity. He had even put Luskin on the stand to describe his relationship with his sister and the physical abuse she'd subjected him to with her clients. He'd been twenty at the time of the trial and no more insane than she was. He was nothing but a bad seed, one of those people born without a conscience. Aline supposed his attorney had been hoping that Luskin's youth, his powerful physical presence, and the truth about his relationship with his sister would soften the jury. But the ploy had backfired when Luskin blew up on the stand under cross-examination by the prosecutor.

Luskin: no chance in hell she'd ever forget him.

Aline booted up her computer, hooked in the modem, and tapped in the code for the computer at the police station. Then she and Kincaid went to work.

5

Shortly after midnight, when they were sitting on the floor, stapling their material and labeling file folders, the phone rang. The answering machine was on, but immediately after the recorded message, screaming filled the room, a woman's scream, high and shrill, panicked. *"What're you doing? Why're you doing this? He's just a child, he hasn't hurt you, oh God, please . . . no, please . . . don't hurt him. . . ."*

The hairs on the back of Aline's neck stood on end; the voice belonged to Jenny Michael. "My God, what—"

A child's shrieks and wails shredded the air, then stopped quickly, suddenly. The two or three seconds of subsequent silence pulsed against the walls in Aline's den. She waited. She heard Kincaid swallow. She closed her eyes, knowing it wasn't finished, that even when it was, it would remain with her, a hideous echo.

A man's screech sundered the air, and then there was an audible click as the caller disconnected.

Aline leaped up, slammed her finger against the REWIND button, popped out the tape. It felt hot in her hands, alive. She stifled an irrational impulse to hurl it across the room, stomp on it, rip it apart, light a match to it. She set the cassette carefully on her desk and ran her hands over her arms as the silence carved a hollow in the very air she breathed.

4: FROM THE MORGUE

I

He smelled of formaldehyde. The stuff had worked into the wrinkles on his hands and fingers; the odor had permeated his shirt, his jeans, his hair. Bill Prentiss knew it wouldn't matter how many times he scrubbed or what he scrubbed with, the stink would remain until he sank his hands into mud, sank them up to the elbows.

He didn't know why mud absorbed the odor, liquidated it. Maybe it didn't. Maybe it was all in his head. Maybe it worked because he believed that it would, because he'd had a professor in medical school who'd told him mud would banish the stink of death. The Egyptians had used it, the professor had said, although Prentiss had yet to find any reference to such a thing, but he supposed it was possible. The Egyptians had been medical wizards.

He snapped off the latex gloves, tossed them into the receptacle, and finished hosing down the aluminum autopsy table. The four corpses rested on gurneys, inside body bags. They were leaving the same way they'd arrived—packaged, bundled up, dead. Tomorrow, someone from the funeral home would be by to pick them up, to embalm them. The caskets would be closed at the funeral. But even so, the morticians would work the kind of magic the Egyptians would've appreciated. They would arrange Jenny Michael's hair, her face, her makeup. They would restore Judge Michael's face so he would once again look like the dignified man that he was. They would stitch the boys' bodies back together again.

Prentiss scrubbed up in the aluminum sink and raised his

hands to his nose when he'd finished. Jesus, the stink was still there. He rummaged through his storage cabinet for a bar of Camay soap, found it, ripped it open, lathered his hands and arms with it. Another sniff: it hadn't put a dent in the stench.

Maybe some of Molly's bath oil would help. It certainly did wonders for *her* skin. But even without the bath oil, she always smelled faintly erotic. *Three in the A.M., good buddy, and you're thinking about bubble baths and sex.* He couldn't have gotten it up right now if his life depended on it. He knew some coroners who, after an autopsy, fucked all night, men for whom death was a turn-on. The only thing death and autopsies did for his libido was kill it and throw him into a blue funk that lasted until he'd distanced himself from it all: a few beers, a long run on the beach, a hard workout in the gym.

It hadn't always been like that. Now and then in medical school, when he'd been doing his pathology specialty, it had happened—impotence, a lack of interest in sex, but that had been mostly fatigue. It was only in the last five or six months that the situation had become critical. Or maybe it had been longer than that but he just hadn't noticed it because he hadn't been involved with anyone.

Except Bernelli.

No, that wasn't quite right. He hadn't been *involved* with Claudia Bernelli. They'd gone out a half a dozen times, slept together, had some laughs, but that was all. Things might've turned out differently, of course, if Molly hadn't come into his life. Yes, he would concede that much. Bernelli was the sort of woman who grew on you. But from the night six months ago when he'd laid eyes on Molly at the Pink Moose and had come on to her, there had been no one else.

It had been one of those hot summer nights when the cries of crickets echoed against the stillness and the humus scent of the island was thick in the air. He'd gone over to the Pink Moose for a bite to eat on his way home from work and she'd been standing alone at the open bar on the top deck, sipping beer from a bottle, tapping her foot in time to the music. He'd threaded his way through the crowd and claimed a spot next to her as he ordered. She'd glanced at him once, then again, and he said, "Yeah, I know, I look like someone you know, right?"

She'd laughed. "Actually, that's what people are always telling *me*," and she'd extended her hand and introduced herself.

She'd been in town two weeks, she said, having moved here from Tallahassee, where she'd been stringing for the Tallahassee *Democrat*, free-lancing, and completing a master's program in journalism. She'd filled a spot on the Tango *Tribune* vacated when one of their reporters had been killed in a car accident. They had talked for the better part of an hour, and when he suggested they go back to his place, she hesitated, then said no, she didn't think that would be a good idea. For the next month, he'd pursued her relentlessly—lunches, dinners, movies, sailing, and skiing.

One night on a beach off the Old Post Road, they finally made love, and her hunger was not so much for the act of sex itself as for the intimacy. She confessed she had left Tallahassee because of a man—*Bradley*, she said. *Isn't that a stupid name for a man?*—who was married.

After that, for the next few months they spent most of their free time together. They had practically nothing in common, but it had worked to their advantage. He introduced her to scuba diving, and Molly, who was born and raised in Vermont, introduced him to snow skiing when they'd hit Aspen for a week in December. She observed one of his autopsies, and he accompanied her on a series of interviews she'd done in connection with one of her life-style articles. He turned her on to old movies, and she got him interested in spy thrillers. And until two months ago, when they'd clashed over a homicide she was covering for the paper, things had been great.

The problem was that he had performed the autopsy on the homicide victim (a man killed in a dispute, police suspected, over a drug deal) and refused to give her the details because vice was keeping the lid on the case and had released only minimal information to the press. She'd taken umbrage at his refusal and hadn't spoken to him for a week. It wasn't until the case finally broke and Molly got her story through the usual channels that they mended the rift between them. But it had changed something essential for Prentiss. Now he consciously censored himself when he talked about work, even if it had nothing to do with what Molly was covering for the *Tribune*. It had diminished the spontaneity between them, but he couldn't help it. She had her job and he had his, and it was best to keep them separate.

But even this hadn't affected the chemistry that had drawn them together initially. He'd read in one of his journals that a Japanese researcher had assigned a specific musical note to each amino acid in DNA. The result was rather astonishing. When the tune of human DNA was played on an instrument, it sounded hauntingly like the music of the masters—of Chopin and Beethoven, Mozart and Bach—leading the researcher to believe that a propensity for music lay in the genes. The researcher had also used the musical assignments in reverse, analyzing diseases like cancer, diabetes, multiple sclerosis. And ironically, a funeral march in Mozart's Requiem mass equaled cancer.

The moral of the story, he supposed, was that most things, even attraction to another human being, were genetic predispositions. It rather spoiled his concept of free will, but held a kind of cosmic logic that deserved scrutiny.

And you, good buddy, would scrutinize your fucking toenail if you thought you could learn something from it.

Pick pick pick: all his life, he'd been a picker, an analyzer, a man who dissected things until they yielded their secrets. Perhaps that was why pathology suited him. If you dug deeply enough, you usually found answers, even if they weren't the answers you'd hoped for.

Like now, he thought.

The autopsies on the Michael family, for instance, had told him they'd been killed within ten or fifteen minutes of each other, starting about half an hour after eating a dinner of potatoes, chicken, green beans, and tossed salad. The older boy had been killed first, and the judge last. Unfortunately, an autopsy never revealed a motive.

But one of the pubic hairs Kincaid had plucked from the floor of the Michaels' shower had belonged to a woman between twenty-five and forty, who had O positive blood. The blond hair was dyed, to cover her gray—a rather weird predilection, he thought, but not the strangest he'd ever come across. Unless the Michaels had a maid who routinely used their shower or the judge was having an affair, then Prentiss was betting the stats fit the killer.

If so, then her only mistake had been to shower after the killings, because otherwise she'd left no traces whatsoever.

No fingerprints, no tissue samples under any of the victims' nails, nothing. She hadn't broken into the house, either, which indicated the Michaels might've known the woman or, at the very least, been expecting her. A salesperson who'd called ahead, for instance.

"Knock, knock."

Prentiss glanced around and saw Molly standing in the door, smiling, holding out two cups of coffee. "You finished communing with the dead for the night?"

He chuckled. "We dance down here when the sun sets." Prentiss walked over to the door, kissed her quickly on the mouth, and thanked her for the coffee. The first sip burned as it went down and rallied his tired blood. "What're you doing up so late?"

"Working. Too much distraction during the day, what with the phones and everything." She launched into a quick and funny story about the newsroom.

Prentiss had heard variations on this story before, but it didn't matter. He liked listening to her. He liked watching her face as she talked, the way her hands moved. It struck him that everything about her was excessive: her cloud-white complexion, her huge eyes that were as plump and blue as Concord grapes, the thinness of her lips, the softness of her straight honey-colored hair. Separately, her features were distinctive. But together, they created an asymmetrical quality to her face that made him think of adjectives like "striking," "unusual," "different," rather than "pretty." Which was fine with him; conventionally pretty women had never been his preference.

As she talked and he sipped his coffee, it occurred to him that as much as he would've liked to believe otherwise, it was the *Tribune* that had brought her here. She needed the inside dope on the Michael family murders.

"Guess what, Moll," he said when she finished.

"What?"

"I can't give you anything on the autopsies."

Disappointment flickered in her huge blue eyes, and she knew that he caught it, because she laughed. "I'm that obvious, huh?"

"Well, it *is* a quarter of four in the morning."

"Chip assigned me the goddamn story," she explained, referring to her editor, Chip Sonsky. "I told him I didn't want it, I hate covering crime stories, but he said tough shit. So that's what I was doing at the office, going through our files, looking for background stuff on Judge Michael."

"Well, the autopsies didn't tell us anything we didn't already know, except what they had for dinner."

She wrinkled her nose with distaste. "Gross. Let's get outa here, huh?" She rocked toward him and slid her arms around his waist, brushing her mouth against the side of his face. "I'm ready for breakfast. And the Tango Café is open all night starting yesterday through Easter."

He wasn't really in the mood for food, but he was definitely in the mood for Molly's company, as long as she didn't try to weasel information out of him. "Sounds good." He turned off the light in the morgue, but the phone pealed. "Let me get this. I'll meet you in my office."

"Right. Don't be long, huh? I'm starving."

He nodded and picked up the receiver. "Bill Prentiss."

"Bill, it's Bernie. There's still no change on Jane Doe."

He was tired and it took him a few seconds to remember that Bernelli had the midnight to eight A.M. watch on the little girl's room on the third floor. "Okay, Bernie, thanks. I'll be at home from about five on, so if there's any change, just call me there. I won't put the answering machine on."

"Fine. Hey, anything show up with the autopsies?"

"Our killer's female," he replied, and told her what information the blond pubic hair had yielded.

"Does Al know yet?"

"I was going to call her in the morning."

"Okay. See you later."

"Right."

His hand lingered on the receiver as he hung up. He always felt twinges of guilt about Bernelli. The last night they'd spent together had been three days before he met Molly, and he'd just never called her again. It had been cowardly on his part, and Bernelli deserved better. But now it was six months later, and to try to explain at this point would be absurd.

Yet it still bothered him because sometimes it seemed he dealt more fairly with the dead than he did with the living.

Kincaid lay awake in the dark, arms folded under his head. He could hear Wolfe's claws tapping against the floors downstairs, as he poked through the hinged panel in the door, the pound of the surf a block away, and next to him, Aline's soft breathing.

Breathing: something about the breathing on that tape.

There was enough starlight in the room to see the travel poster taped to the ceiling over the bed, a poster he'd put there for nights like this. The ceiling in his own bedroom was covered with such posters. But this one was special. It depicted a monastery in Kathmandu that he'd visited more than a decade ago. The starlight eddied over it, making the monastery appear almost luminescent, like a mirage that might sink back into the dark any second. After a while, he felt himself melting into it. He could smell the antiquity of its thin air, hear the soft, mellifluous chime of bells, and when he closed his eyes he saw the shadowed movements of the hooded monks, filing through the twilit halls as they chanted. Their voices mesmerized him, filled him like helium as he lifted up, up, and was borne along on the unbroken melody.

The breathing. Focus on the breathing.

He heard it now, a soft intake of air that laced the silence between those hideous screams on the tape. It meant something, but he didn't know what. He focused on the sound, waiting for the answer, but nothing came to him. He finally got up, climbed down the loft ladder, and went into Aline's den.

He needed a cassette recorder rather than the answering machine, so he could stop the tape, rewind it, play it at a lower speed. It should've been a simple thing, and would've been if he were at home. But Aline's concept of order wasn't even remotely similar to his. The den was tidy enough, and clean, and appeared to be an ideal working area—until you opened something. Inside the filing cabinets, those desk drawers, behind those French doors on the closet, lurked a disorder of appalling magnitude.

When he opened the closet, for instance, *things* sprang out at him: a framed photograph of the family dog with a five- or six-year-old Aline standing next to it; a pile of *Life* magazines from the 1940s; tax returns with stacks of receipts clipped to them; a first edition of *Lorna Doone*; an autographed, first edition of *The Old Man and the Sea*; an open box that spewed rusted paper clips that fell around him like rain. The *things* that didn't leap out had probably occupied their spaces on the shelves for decades. The dust that covered them was so thick, it looked like it had taken root and sprouted.

Christ, but it was depressing to realize it might take him all night to dig out a tape recorder. He could drive home and back fifteen times before he ever managed to excavate this mess. But hey, okay, he'd give it a shot, a wild guess. If *he* were Aline, rushing about, sweeping things off her desk to make room for the next onslaught of disorder, wouldn't he put the recorder someplace within easy reach? In other words, not on the upper shelf, but at waist level.

Kincaid glanced right, at a shelf midway down, and there, on a stack of bound book galleys, was the tape recorder. For a second, the galleys tempted him. A long time ago he'd run across a set of galleys in here to the third volume of Anaïs Nin's diaries. They were part of the rich heritage of the Key West Whitman's, of a childhood inhabited by literary luminaries. They'd intimidated him. No telling what these might be. He closed the door and walked over to the desk with the recorder.

Once he'd set it up, he popped the cassette into it and rewound it. Then he fixed the playback at half speed. He attached the earphones and fitted them over his head as he settled into Aline's gray leather chair. He hit the ON button.

Goosebumps fluttered across his arms as Jenny Michael's screams at half speed unfolded like a nightmare in slow motion. Each note of agony, of terror, elongated to an almost unbearable pitch. But then, in the interstices between the screams, he heard it—a long, slow wheeze, as though someone— *Jenny Michael? The killer? The son?*—had sucked in poisoned air.

Kincaid rewound to the same spot and listened to it at normal speed. Then at half speed again. A respiratory ailment of some kind. He was sure of it. He picked up the phone and dialed Bill Prentiss's home number.

Prentiss answered on the third ring, sounding drugged with sleep. "What is it, Bernelli?"

"It's Ryan."

"Oh. Shit. Ryan. God, what time is it?"

"About six. Sorry for calling so early."

"No problem." He yawned, and Kincaid could hear his bed squeak. "The killer's female, Ryan," he said, and explained.

"Did any of the Michaels have respiratory problems?"

"No. Why?"

"Then I think our lady does." He told him about the tape.

"Could be. Respiratory ailments can definitely be aggravated by stress and emotional disturbances. Or she may just have a cold or bronchitis or an allergy. How about dropping the tape by later today? Or having Al bring it over? I'll be in by noon."

"Will do."

"Don't be too optimistic about this respiratory thing. It might not be anything, Ryan. More than likely, it's an allergy. You'd be surprised by how many people have stuff like this. The high pollen count does it. Household dust. Animal fur."

"Well, listen to the tape and let me know what you think."

"Sure thing. Oh, one other thing. There were three weapons used—a hunting knife of some sort, a pin, and a .38."

"A pin? What kind of pin?"

"A long pin, maybe a needle. The judge's eye was punctured with it."

Kincaid winced. "Christ, Bill."

Prentiss sighed. "Yeah. Sometimes this business sucks, Ryan."

"Anything new on the girl?"

"Nope. Nothing. Tell Aline I'll call her or see her later today with the report."

"Okay. And thanks, Bill."

Kincaid spent a few minutes paging through the files he and Aline had compiled, and jotted down the address for Sheila Reiner. Then he pushed everything to the side and rolled a clean sheet of paper into Aline's typewriter. He thought for a few minutes. It had to be exactly right. A sales pitch with a touch of romance:

Personable man in late thirties seeking female companion to share bed, life, and expenses. I'm a terrific cook, don't leave the cap off the toothpaste, and I commu-

*nicate well with skunks. I would do the shopping and
cooking, if you'd do the cleaning. Your flying lessons
would be free. I already have someone to rent my place.
In a month, you would save $150 in utilities, $50 in
water, $250 in mortgage payments, $200 in food, and
so on. My body would be available as many times a
day as you desired it. I could be moved in by next week.
If this suits you, please respond below.*

He tacked it to the fridge in the kitchen and climbed the
ladder to the loft again.

Aline stirred. Heat radiated from her skin, as if she were
sunburned, and a sigh punctuated her sleep. Kincaid stroked
her hair and slipped his hand under the sheet, resting it in
the curve of her waist, where her skin was as soft as her hair.

He had known her, loved her, longer than he'd been married to either of his wives. His first marriage, to a pediatri-
cian, had lasted about a year. His second marriage, to an
economics professor at the University of Miami, had been
going along pretty well until he and his wife took a six-week
trip together through Central and South America. It was without a doubt the worst six weeks of his life, and they'd filed
for divorce three weeks after their return. A total of twenty-
six months for that marriage. There had been a number of
women before and since, but none that had gotten to him like
Aline. If she'd been so inclined, he would've married her
tomorrow.

But she wasn't inclined, so he would settle for second best.
Living with her.

Appalling closets and all.

Her leg brushed up against his as she rolled onto her back;
he caught the faint whiff of perfume from her hair, the nape
of her neck. The scent, rising from the aftermath of those
shrieks on the tape, filled him with an edgy eroticism that
had more to do with the affirmation of life in the face of death
than it did with desire. His hand slipped under her T-shirt,
into the fragrant warmth of her skin, and found a breast. A
peach, good enough to nibble on, which he did.

"I'm asleep, you know."

"I know. That's why I'm doing all the work." He insinu-
ated his thumbs under the waistband of her panties and drew

them off. Her arms came up and around him, urging him over on top of her.

"Let's be missionaries." Her tongue flicked his earlobe, the corners of his mouth.

He loved the drowsy smell of her, the scent that was specifically hers, the dampness that was hers, the warm smoothness of her belly, the taste of sleep on her mouth. Each of the separate details became a component of magic, something that transformed.

"I love you," he whispered. "And I'm a cinch to live with."

"I'm not."

"I'm easy enough for both of us."

She touched his beard, the sides of his face, and kissed him long and hard, with a kind of desperation. Kincaid stroked the inside of her thighs, where the flesh was warm, soft, and sensitive. His hands could pick out her legs in the dark, in a room filled with legs. They would gravitate to her particular damp heat, to her skin. He knew the topography of her body nearly as well as he knew his own, but there were always surprises—a curve he'd never discovered before, a new taste, a dimple, a quiver across the surface of her belly like a sand dune rippling in the wind.

He slipped his hands under her, lifting his hips as he moved inside her. It seemed that the pound of the surf got louder, but it was only his heart, thumping against his chest as Aline did something with her hips that drove him deeper inside her. Her hands kneaded his back. She moaned softly, her mouth against his neck as his strokes quickened and slowed. They found their rhythm, a beat orchestrated by the dark, by the surf, by the slide of wind through the branches just outside the window

A long time later, she began to shudder, her mouth opened against his shoulder, muffling her cry, and then Kincaid cut loose and soared.

5: JANE DOE

I

The phone pealed at nine on the button. Aline's arm snaked out from under the covers, grappling for it. "Hmm," she mumbled.

"Rise and shine, Al," chirped Bernie.

"Hmm."

"Little Jane Doe is conscious."

Aline's eyes opened wide, fixing on the Kathmandu poster on her ceiling. "And?"

"I think you'd better see this for yourself."

"I'll be there in half an hour."

Fifteen minutes later, she was in the kitchen, helping herself to a cup of coffee from the pot Kincaid had left brewing. She opened the fridge for cream and Wolfe's breakfast, then, frowning, closed it again and stared at the notes on the door. The first one said: *Spoke to Bill. Our killer is a lady. He wants you to drop tape by his office this afternoon.*

A woman.

Funny, but she hadn't pegged those murders as something a woman would do. So much for stereotypes.

She read the other note and laughed.

She read it a second time and felt the incipient flutters of anxiety deep in her gut.

A third time through and she fished for a pen in the drawer and across the bottom scrawled, *How about if you start moving in Sunday?* and hoped neither of them would regret it.

Jane Doe's room in intensive care was crowded: two nurses, Bill Prentiss, Bernie, and a tall brunette woman who Aline assumed was the child shrink Prentiss had mentioned yesterday. The girl was sitting up, papers and crayons strewn over the little table that swung across her bed. Her gold curls fell around her face as she scribbled furiously with a red crayon, her breath coming in quick, staccato bursts.

"Take a look at these, Al." Bernie drew Aline over to the window and picked up a stack of wild, erratic sketches. At first glance, Aline mistook them for typical kid stuff—stick figures with straw hair, a huge house created from four squiggly lines, trees that looked like a mass of wiggling worms. But then she saw all the red, deep reds, thick, as if the girl had been pressing down very hard with the crayon. She realized there were four stick figures, two in one section of the house and two in the other, and all were prostrate on the floor. A profusion of red grew around them, and it leaked onto what could've been overturned furniture. To the right of the house was a side door, and sprawled in it was a cat, streaked with blood.

"Christ, this is—"

"Exactly. This is what she saw. And right here . . ." She riffled through the sketches until she found what she was looking for, and smoothed it out against the windowsill. It was a stick figure sketch of a woman with dark, tangled hair. Everything in the drawing was exaggerated—the woman's huge dark eyes, the long sword she clutched in her hand, the hideous grin on her face.

"When did this start?"

"She woke up around five this morning, saw me, and went nuts, totally hysterical. Then I started talking to her, real softly, like I used to do when Danny was a kid and woke up from a nightmare. She stopped crying. I called Bill around seven, and he came over and took her off the IV and catheter and ordered some breakfast for her. When it came, I sat with her, watching her eat. She never said a word. Still hasn't. I'd brought along some of Danny's old crayons and coloring books, figuring that if she came to, I could get her to trust me. Well, she saw the crayons and dumped them out on the bed and started drawing on her pillowcase. I got some paper. That's when she did the sketches. Then she fell back to sleep for an hour or so, and in the meantime Dr. Stratton arrived."

"What's she think?"

"She hasn't said. So far, she's just been observing."

"You think we can take the coloring on this sketch as the real thing?"

"You mean the dark hair and eyes?"

"Yeah."

"Stratton says no. I asked her." Bernie explained about the analysis of the hairs Kincaid had found. If the killer was indeed blond, then perhaps she'd been wearing a dark wig when she killed the Michaels.

Aline looked back at the girl. She was now huddled over the table, the red crayon clutched in her fist as she bore down against the paper and drew the crayon back and forth, back and forth, faster and faster. The crayon snapped. She emitted a high-pitched wail and hurled the pieces across the room, then shoved the table away from her. It jerked back; papers flew. The box of crayons sailed off the table and struck the floor, catapulting crayons in a dozen directions. She pounded her small fists against her knees, then began pulling at her hair and kicking her legs, throwing off the sheets. Her wails broke into huge, gasping sobs. Dr. Stratton was at her side in a flash, talking to her in a calm, soothing voice, pulling her hands gently from her hair, urging her back against the pillow.

She screamed. She scratched. She bit Stratton's hand and tried to scramble out of the bed, but Prentiss restrained her while Stratton hurriedly pulled up the metal railings on the bed. A few seconds later, a nurse hastened into the room with a hypodermic. Prentiss got the girl turned on her stomach, and the needle sank into her small, white buttock. Her wails and shrieks gradually subsided to soft, pathetic sobs. Once, as if she were fighting the sedative, she gripped the bed railing, rattling it, and let loose with a final wail. Then she collapsed. Pathos washed through Aline; she wanted to brush her hands over the girl's cheek, smooth strands of damp hair from her temples.

"Is that how she's been when she isn't sleeping or drawing, Bernie?"

"Sometimes, yeah. C'mon, let me introduce you to Dr. Stratton."

Prentiss, who was gathering up the sketches and crayons from the floor, greeted her, then Bernie introduced her to Barbara Stratton. She didn't fit Aline's idea of a shrink, child or otherwise. She looked like a high-energy businesswoman in her late forties—slender and meticulously groomed, chestnut hair falling to her chin in soft waves, a sharp glint of intelligence in her blue eyes. Tiny lines of fatigue bloomed in the corners of her mouth as she smiled. Her handshake was strong, her palm smooth and dry.

"It's a pleasure, Ms. Scott. I understand you found our little friend."

Aline nodded. "What's your opinion about her?"

Stratton slid her hands into the pockets of her white cotton jacket. "The obvious. She's been severely traumatized. When I first started observing her, I felt she might be autistic, since there were periods in between the drawing when she didn't do anything but stare. But I think she's actually suffering a type of aphasia—motor aphasia, in which a person is incapable of expressing thoughts in speech or in writing, thus the frantic drawings."

"Is it permanent?"

"If the cause were physical, it could be. But in her case, it's psychological, from the shock of whatever she saw. She's trying to express it through the drawings. Do you have any leads on who she is? Where she came from?"

Aline shook her head, but Bernie spoke up. "Maybe." She looked over at Aline. "When nothing turned up in Miami, I decided to check with Tango Elementary and have them prepare a list of every fifth-, sixth- and seventh-grader who was absent yesterday. At the least, we can match the names with class photographs. I told the principal we're checking out absentees in connection with a vandalism case."

"Great. Let's get started."

"I'd sure like to speak to the parents when you find out who she is," Stratton said.

Prentiss, who'd joined them, remarked that he would like to see the parents declared unfit. Aline could tell by the tone of his voice and the pinched fatigue in his face that he was in a foul mood, and it wasn't just due to this case.

"She's been missing more than twenty-four hours. You'd think the least the parents could do is file a missing child report."

Stratton's smile was rueful. "Unfortunately, a lot of people who have kids, shouldn't. Even if the parents are found, I think she should remain here. For observation. For her own safety."

Bernelli said, "She's not going anywhere. She's the only witness to four homicides. We'll be moving her to a safe house once she's well enough. Another cop should be here within half an hour. If one of you is going to be here till then, I'm going to head over to the school with Aline."

Stratton said she would remain, and Aline accompanied Prentiss and Bernie into the hall. "Ryan said he told you about this." She handed him the cassette tape from her answering machine.

He slipped it into his pocket. "Did he and Bernie tell you about the autopsy and hair analysis?"

"Briefly."

Prentiss filled them in. Bernie said, "I still find it hard to believe the killer's a woman."

"Why the hell should that be any more surprising than a man, Bernie? Since when is homicide confined to one gender?"

"Oh, my, aren't we testy." She gave Prentiss a look that could've turned Lot's wife into salt, then spun on her heel. "See you downstairs, Al."

Prentiss jammed his hands in his pockets. "Shit, I have such a talent for pissing people off. Have you ever noticed that about me, Al?"

"You must've had a fight with Molly, huh."

"It shows?"

"Only to your friends." She hooked her arm through his, and they walked down the hall. "What'd you argue about this time?"

"This time? Do we have this conversation a lot or something?"

She shrugged. "It just seems that recently you two have been arguing a lot."

"Only when there's a case I'm working on that Molly's covering for the paper."

Aline looked at him sharply, thinking of Jane Doe. "You didn't—"

"Fuck, no." He pressed his thumb and index finger against either side of his nose. "But she really went at it over breakfast. I don't know, Al. Things with her were a lot different in the beginning."

"You two living together now?"

"We've talked about it."

Aline felt a weird something kick in her chest. She and Prentiss had both been born on Tango—same day, same year, thirty seconds apart. They'd grown through childhood, puberty, and adolescence together—first kiss, first date, first lover. There had been so many parallels in their lives that sometimes Aline had only to look at where Prentiss stood in his life to understand where her own was headed. This apparently wasn't one of those times.

"You and Ryan talking?"

"Yup."

"I knew it. And?"

"He's going to move in this weekend."

"Well, it's not going to happen with Molly. So there's one more difference for us, huh."

They pushed through the double doors, into the February heat. The sun quivered in the Tango sky like some sort of mutant beast, blistering the blue around it. Light struck the ficus and pine trees at either side of the hospital and seemed to suck the green from them. Aline slipped on her sunglasses as she and Prentiss started across the parking lot.

"What I'd like to know, Aline, is how come your life has been so stable the last three years and mine's been so goddamn frantic?"

"Must be that thirty-second lead you have on me."

Bernie's MG whizzed up behind them and screeched to a stop. The top was down. In her dark shades, she looked like one of the ta-ta ladies from Pirate's Cove who was out slumming in a sports car sorely in need of refurbishing. "I'm broiling, Al. C'mon."

"On my way."

Bernie cruised past Prentiss, wagged her fingers at him, and called, "We'll pray for you, Billy boy."

"Spare me," he murmured.

The elementary and junior high schools on Tango Key were in one large building shaped like an L. The enrollment stood at just over 400, and in the last two days 52 kids had been absent from grades five through seven. *Flu season*, the principal had explained. *Indifference*, sniffed her secretary. Out of that group, 24 were female.

The secretary had already pulled the files on the two dozen girls, and since photographs were included it took them only a few minutes to locate Jane Doe. Her real name was Renie Foreston, and according to the principal's secretary, her mother had called in yesterday morning and again this morning, saying her daughter had strep throat and wouldn't be in. "I can tell you that Renie isn't the sort of child who would be involved in vandalism. But the mother is *very* difficult."

"Difficult how?" Aline asked.

"An absolute witch who complains about everything," the woman said, peering at Aline over the rims of her bifocals. "And I'm sure that's contributed to Renie's absences from school this past year. She's still near the top of her sixth-grade class, but only because she's bright and perceptive."

"She's been ill a lot?" Bernie asked, turning the folder around so she could glance through it.

"So Mrs. Foreston reports. But her father is out of town quite often, and to be honest with you, I don't think Mrs. Foreston is capable of disciplining the child."

"Is she a problem here at school?"

"No. Just bored. And like I said, I just can't imagine her being involved in vandalism."

Aline nodded, pleased the woman had bought Bernie's story. "Is she an only child?"

"Yes. Adopted, I think. The Forestons are very . . ." She sought the right word. "Well, progressive parents, I guess that's what you would call them. They've encouraged her to be an independent thinker. That has its advantages, of course, until a child reaches puberty. Then all hell breaks loose."

"Is this their current address?" Bernie pointed at the address line in the folder.

"Yes, that's it."

It was about four miles from the Michaels' place.

* * *

The Foreston home was a strange, modernistic structure made of redwood—sleek, geometric lines, protruding windows, porches and decks that jutted out at various angles. The trapezoid-shaped front windows glimmered with sunlight and reflected the surrounding foliage and woods. Gardenias scented the air. Not a bad little haven, Aline thought as she parked behind the navy-blue Volvo in the driveway. It had a customized license plate on the back that said DOL-LARS.

"What's Daddy Foreston do for a living? Did it say in the folder, Bernie?"

"He's a developer. Mum Foreston writes children's books. And now that I think about it, I'm pretty sure Foreston's outfit has something to do with that new civic center that's being built downtown."

A maid in a white uniform answered the door. She had black eyes and thick black brows, and her voice, when she spoke, was slightly accented. "Yes? I may help you?"

"We'd like to see Mrs. Foreston," Aline said.

"The señora is working. If you will leave your name and number, she will call you back this afternoon."

"I'm afraid that won't do." Aline flashed her I.D. "We'd like to see her now."

The woman looked resigned, as if she had seen plenty of *policía* demanding ingress into private homes in someplace like Nicaragua or Cuba. It was a facet of Aline's job she disliked, and she felt compelled to apologize to the woman, to say something like, *Hey, I'm really not like this.* But it would only confuse the issue, so she said nothing at all.

They followed her into a stylized living room decorated in mauve, pink, and gray, where every piece of furniture echoed the future. There were net chairs that hung from the cathedral ceiling, a couch that looked as if it folded out of the wall, polyurethane tables shaped like teardrops.

"Please wait here. I will get her." The maid turned away, her shoes squeaking against the glossy tile floor.

Aline nudged Bernie and whispered, "Hey, look there." She gestured toward a family photograph on one of the end tables, where Daddy and Mum Foreston stood on either side of a lovely, smiling Jane Doe. "This is our girl, all right."

"And which girl would that be?" asked a voice behind them.

Aline glanced back. Carol Foreston was short, thin, and pretty—a China doll with shiny black hair that fell to her ears in a smooth wave, almond-hued eyes that seemed as glossy as the surface of the coffee table, and pale skin. She wore khaki shorts and a short-sleeve cotton blouse. Aline guessed she was in her late thirties or early forties.

As Aline introduced herself and Bernie, unease flickered in the woman's eyes and then crouched there, waiting. "What can I do for you?"

"Is that your daughter?" Aline motioned toward the photo on the mantel.

"Yes. Why?" The unease ballooned. Tiny gold flecks appeared in her almond eyes. A frown creased her brow. She glanced from Aline to Bernie and back at Aline again. "What's this about?" She withdrew a cigarette from a flat gold container on the end table. She had long, spidery-thin fingers with softly rounded nails painted coral. She lit her cigarette with a slender gold lighter monogrammed C.F. "I'm working against a deadline on a book, and I'd appreciate it if you just got to the point."

Aline didn't care for her attitude. "And your daughter's upstairs with strep throat?"

She combed her fingers through her black hair, looked down, puffed on her cigarette, glanced up again. "No." She whispered it. "No, she isn't upstairs." She lowered herself into the nearest net chair, lowered herself slowly, as though her body possessed enormous weight and mass. She crossed her slender legs at the knees, tugged at the hem of her shorts. "I don't know where she is. Has . . . has something happened to her? Is that why you're here? If that's it, just tell me. Please."

"She's alive, Mrs. Foreston, and she's safe," Bernie said. "Not that it seems to concern you enough to have called the police."

Carol Foreston ignored the gibe. "Safe where? Something *has* happened, hasn't it?"

Her face crumbled like old cake, and she started to cry. The tears seemed real enough and sincere enough, Aline thought, but a little late, considering the circumstances.

"Mrs. Foreston, if you could just tell us what happened, how long Renie's been gone. . . ."

"The . . . the night before last, we had an argument and she left. On her bike. She'd done it before . . . several times . . . and she always came back, you know. Always. She . . . she's very headstrong. But when she didn't show up yesterday morning, I . . . I started getting worried. I . . . I called my husband. He's in Miami, working on a building project. We . . . we agreed not to do anything. To give her another day or so to cool off and come home. I was going to give her until tonight."

She sniffled, reached into her shirt pocket, brought out a lovely lace hanky, and blew her nose. Aline wondered how many women in Tango's upper crust carried lace hankies when they wore shorts. Maybe it was a new fad, like Corona beer. "Why until tonight?"

"The police won't do anything in a missing persons case until the individual's been gone for forty-eight hours. Tonight it'll be forty-eight hours."

As though this exonerated her somehow, Aline thought.

"Please, tell me what happened."

So Aline told her, and omitted nothing. Halfway through the story, the woman began to cry again. Bernie rolled her eyes and sighed—heavily, loudly, a sigh that said, *This routine sucks an egg, Al.*

"When may I . . . I see her?"

"I'll have to talk to Dr. Stratton. Your daughter is in protective custody, Mrs. Foreston, as witness to four murders. So we'd appreciate it if you would keep this between you and your husband."

"Yes. Of course. Whatever you say."

Aline found her eagerness to please a little nauseating.

"What should I do about the school? What should I tell Renie's friends?"

"We'll talk to the principal," Bernie replied. "And as far as her friends are concerned, tell them she went to her grandmother's or something."

"Her grandmothers are dead."

Aline felt the heat of Bernie's temper radiating from her in a wave, but before she could say anything, Bernie exploded. "Mrs. Foreston, your daughter's been missing for almost two goddamn days, and you apparently haven't been too worried about what her friends might say. I'm sure you'll think of something clever."

"Don't you *dare* speak to me like that." Her spine had gone rigid. She stabbed out her cigarette and stood. "You have no right to judge—"

"I have *every* right. What'd you and your daughter argue about?"

"I don't remember."

"C'mon, Mrs. Foreston," Bernie snapped. "It could be important."

"I don't remember. I told you."

"Why would she go to the Michael home?" Bernie fired back.

"I . . . I really don't know. . . ."

"Did she know either of the Michael boys?"

"Maybe from school . . ."

"Maybe? You mean you don't know who your daughter's friends are?"

"I resent your tone, Detective Bernelli."

"And I resent how little you know about your own kid."
Aline threw Bernie a look: *Back off.*

She sucks as a liar, Bernie's eyes flashed back.

"So you don't have any idea why she'd be hanging around the Michael house?" Aline asked her.

"No."

"What time did she leave that evening?"

"I'm not sure. We argued during dinner. I had a lot on my mind. This deadline on my book, the . . . Anyway, around six, I guess it was. She huffed away from the table and said she was going to do homework. Usually when she gets like that I just leave her alone. Like I said, she's very headstrong. I did the dishes, then knocked on her door and said I had to run into town to pick up some groceries. When I got back, her bedroom light was off. I looked in on her and she seemed to be sleeping.

"The next morning when I went in to wake her for school, I realized she was gone. She'd shoved blankets under her covers. When I checked the garage, her bike was missing." She lit another cigarette, but more quickly this time, with far less polish, and her hand trembled just a bit. "Could you please call that psychiatrist now, Detective Scott? I'd like to see my daughter."

Aline made the call from the kitchen. There was nothing futuristic about this room—no chairs suspended from the ceiling, no oddly shaped appliances, no obvious thrusts out of the twentieth century. But the kitchen, like the living room, gleamed with light. It streamed through the wall of glass to her left, striking the white counters, the white refrigerator and stove, the pearled tile floor, white against white, brilliant and blinding. The excessive light was like a mirage, seductive, tricky, intended to efface or hide something about the Forestons, Aline decided.

If she could see beyond it or through it, she might be able to seize the shape of Carol Foreston's lie.

6: THE WOMEN

I

Kincaid's Saab rose through the Tango hills, where sunlight washed across the great muscular cushions of green. They were like supine giants stirring from a deep slumber that made the bright clusters of lavender periwinkles and the blankets of zinnias shimmer and dance.

The hills had always fascinated him. They were as anomalous as the people who lived here, and Kincaid had yet to hear a reasonable explanation as to their existence off a peninsula flatter than unleavened bread. The theories ranged from Tango as an Atlantean seaport that hadn't sunk with the rest of the continent to the island as part of the underwater chain of mountains that extended into the Caribbean.

Personally, he didn't give a damn about the whys. It was enough that the island possessed a mystique so consuming that it was sometimes easy to imagine that the world stopped at its borders. It was precisely this which spurred his need to detach from Tango every so often, to venture out like a medieval explorer to map the unknown.

New Zealand: the prize he and Al would collect before June.

He downshifted as the road dipped, then slowed as he approached Pirate's Cove. This was the rich man's Eden, a place every bit as spurious and unreal as Palm Beach and Beverly Hills, a bedroom community with an impressive marina. At one time it had been little more than a weekend haven for wealthy refugees from other parts of South Florida. But that had changed when the bridge between Tango and Key West had been built and an airstrip had been put in.

There was a small downtown area with several dozen exclusive shops. The only ordinary buildings in the area were several bars, offices, and the Publix supermarket on Treasure Isle. It looked like a monument to Art Deco, painted pink and pale blue, with a neon sign that boasted ten-foot letters. At night, the sign glowed purple.

Kincaid passed it and turned onto Doubloon Road. He parked in front of a plain brick building with a wooden sign on the lawn that said VIC XAPHES, ATTORNEY-AT-LAW. One of his least favorite people. Xaphes, in fact, was a royal pain in the ass, a man who defended anyone who could afford him. But he was an excellent source of information. Also, his name had appeared as defense attorney on four of the ten cases he and Aline had gone through last night, and in two of those, she had been the arresting officer. He supposed that—and the $3,500 the judge had paid him—was why he was here, why he would even consider fucking up his day like this with a visit to Xaphes.

The phone call had been bugging him. All right, so Aline was working on the Michael case. But so was Bernie, and *she* hadn't gotten a call from the killer; Kincaid had asked her earlier when he'd had lunch with her and Aline at the Pink Moose. And Gene Frederick, the chief of police, hadn't gotten a phone call, either. That meant it was significant that the killer had called Aline; it meant a whole lot of things he didn't particularly want to think about.

Of course, it was possible the killer had nothing to do with the ten cases Aline had chosen from all of the cases Judge Michael had presided over in eight years on the bench. It was even logical to assume as much. But his gut said to hell with logic. His gut had a mind of its own.

Xaphes's office was about what you'd expect for the Cove: glitzy. Colorful and weird abstract paintings adorned the walls, the floors were tile, and the windows boasted flower boxes brimming with ivy and soft lavender Mexican heather. Even his secretary looked the part: well-dressed, striking, a slick, practiced smile. He gave his name, and she asked him to please take a seat and would he like a cup of coffee? A soft drink? Anything?

Well trained, he thought. "Nothing, thanks."

She buzzed Xaphes's office, and he zipped through the door a few minutes later, his smile broad, affable, and as phony as the color of Ronald Reagan's hair. He was deeply tanned and not particularly handsome: his nose was too long, his lips too full, and his forehead too high. The last time Kincaid had seen him, his dark hair had been thin and he'd combed it to hide a bald spot. But today his hair was fully restored, the result of a follicle transplant, Kincaid suspected, or maybe a hair weave. In either case, the effect was humorous. Yet, despite all this, Xaphes exuded a powerful something that had earned him a reputation as one of the top defense attorneys in South Florida. And in the courtroom, where it counted, he shone.

He pumped Kincaid's hand and slapped him on the shoulder, Xaphes's equivalent of the Latin *abrazo*, or hug. "Goddamn, Ryan, but this is a surprise. It's good to see you. I figured you were in Mozambique or someplace like that."

Mozambique: now there was a thought. "Just holding down a job like the regular folks, Vic, and hoping I can chew your ear for a while."

"You bet. Sal, hold my calls," he told his secretary without looking at her. "C'mon back to the office. Sal, bring us two coffees."

Xaphes's office walls were covered with framed degrees, photographs of him with various Tango celebrities like F. Lee Bailey, who had a winter home here, and an Andrew Wyeth painting. An original Wyeth.

"So what can I do you for, Ryan?" Xaphes was still grinning as he settled in the black leather chair behind his teakwood desk.

"It's about the Michael family."

The smile went flat. His fingers laced together on the desk top, as though he were praying. "Worst damn thing that's happened here in a long time," he said quietly. "I liked Henry. He was a tough-as-nails judge, but he was fair. If you asked for a postponement and had a good reason, he'd give it to you. He didn't pull shit in the courtroom. When he put on those robes, it was like a physician going into surgery or a priest doing mass. It was . . . well, this is going to sound corny as hell, but I always got the feeling that he was one of those people for whom the law was sacred." He paused, his left thumb stroking a knuckle on his right hand. "But I could never agree with him on capital punishment. An eye for an eye is Biblical shit. It doesn't do a goddamn thing for civilization.''

It was quite possibly the only area where he and Xaphes concurred. ''A couple of days before he was killed he hired me to look into some threatening phone calls he'd gotten. We never got a chance to discuss it in any detail, but my impression was that it was related to a case he'd presided over. Aline went back through the cases he'd had when he was on the bench and nailed down ten of the worst. Out of those, you were defense attorney for four.''

''Everyone's entitled to a defense.''

Kincaid caught the defensive edge in his voice. ''That wasn't intended as a criticism, Vic. I'm just giving you some facts. Out of those four cases, Aline Scott was the arresting officer for two of them.''

''Which two?''

''Charles Sanborn and Jimmy Ray Luskin.''

Xaphes made a face. ''Jesus. You're dredging up bad shit, Ryan. Sanborn's doing twenty-five years without parole for holding up a convenience store and killing a cop with a sawed-off shotgun. I'm still wondering how come Henry didn't give him the chair. But he sure made up for it with Luskin. He fried six months ago.''

''Was either of them involved with someone who might be looking to get even?''

Xaphes sat forward. ''You saying what I think you are? That the Michaels were slaughtered by a woman?''

''Yeah. It hasn't been released to the press yet, so I'd appreciate it if you kept that to yourself.''

He thought for a moment, then punched a button on the phone and asked Sally Secretary to pull the files on Sanborn and Luskin. ''And could you get that coffee? . . . Thanks. . . .'' He hung up. ''She's pretty, but I think her battery's running low.'' He grinned as he said it, a good-ole-boy grin. Kincaid ignored it, and the grin didn't so much disappear as atrophy. Xaphes quickly returned to business. ''Offhand, I know neither guy was married when we went to trial, but both had girlfriends. Other than that, I can't remember too much, except that I lost the cases. The brain censors what it finds unpleasant, Ryan.'' Another grin, only this one had nothing commiserating about it. "And both men were fruitcakes. You know about Luskin?"

Kincaid nodded; he'd attended the trial, but Xaphes didn't need to know that.

He sat back and his chair squeaked. "Well, then you know how weird he was. No, weird isn't even the right word for Luskin. See, Sanborn was nuts. But Luskin was . . ." He paused. "Like Manson. He'd look at you and you would want to shrivel up and hide. He was *cold*, Ryan. The guy had ice water in his veins. All right, so his sister wasn't exactly a paragon of virtue, but no one deserves to die the way she did."

That Lenore Luskin hadn't been a paragon of virtue was an understatement. She was an erudite Wellesley graduate who became Tango's number-one call girl. At the peak of her infamous career she'd been pulling in two hundred grand a year and living in a suite at the Flamingo Hotel. She'd pissed the money away on boats and cars, clothes and jewelry and cocaine. Every few months, she and Luskin had left the Flamingo and stayed at the spavined house at the northeast tip of the island where they'd grown up. During one of those weekends, when Luskin was twelve, Lenore had seduced her brother, thus initiating a chain of events that had eventually ended in Luskin blowing her and one of her numerous lovers away with a thirty-ought-six. That her lover was a prominent South Florida politician hadn't done much for Xaphes's insanity plea, Kincaid thought, nor had the heinous nature of what had preceded the actual killings.

"Why'd you take the case?"

"His sister's attorney, Travis Feld, asked me to. Luskin wanted to hire him, but he felt it would be a conflict of interest, to say the least. So I took it, and I knew from the minute I met the man that I was going to lose. But hey, I gave it my best shot."

"How could he afford you? I thought his sister had spent her fortune."

Xaphes jerked a thumb toward the Wyeth. "At one time Lenore had a small fortune in art. That Wyeth and a couple of other paintings were Luskin's. He paid me with the Wyeth."

"What happened to the art collection?"

"I don't know. I guess it was auctioned off or sold, because when she died, the only pieces left were the ones Luskin had.''

The door opened just then and Sally Secretary walked in with mugs of coffee on a tray and the files tucked under her arm. She set everything down and left as silently as she'd entered.

Xaphes flipped open the file on Sanborn. ''Okay, let's see here.'' He studied it for a few minutes. ''God, how quickly it all comes back. Sanborn's parents are deceased, and he has an older sister who lives in Iowa. My last correspondence with him was about six weeks ago. He wanted to know what I was doing about his appeal.''

''You ever met the sister?''

''Nope. But I do know she's a paraplegic, Ryan. So you can discount her as a suspect.''

''What about Sanborn's appeal?''

Xaphes laughed. ''Yeah, that's exactly the point. There's no ground for an appeal. I've only told him that a hundred times. But Sanborn isn't too bright. Okay, let's see.'' He consulted the file again. ''Shit, I was wrong. No girlfriend. There was no one special at all in his life. So much for my memory.''

''What about Luskin?''

Xaphes slapped the Sanborn file shut, pushed it aside, and opened up Luskin's file. ''All right, there were two women in Luskin's life—besides his sister, that is. One was a ditzy broad in Pirate's Cove who had her own share of troubles. Sheila Reiner.''

Reiner: it was one of the names on the list, the lady who'd allegedly poisoned her wealthy husband. Kincaid mentioned this and Xaphes nodded.

''Yup. One and the same. Before we went to trial, I found out she and Luskin had been having an affair. I decided that bringing it out in court would do more damage than good, so I let the whole thing pass. Not too long after Luskin was found guilty, she did her husband in. Henry Michael sentenced her, and she's out now. So you may have a double revenge motive. The other woman he was involved with was a schoolteacher. Real spinster sort, even though she can't be more than thirty now. Her name's Louisa Almott. Teaches over at the high school.'' He closed the file and dropped it on top of the other folder. ''Since Luskin's dead, I can give you a copy of his file, Ryan. But it'd be a breach of trust to do the same with Sanborn, even though he's as good as dead. If you need any other information on him, though, just give me a call.''

''Thanks, I appreciate it.''

Xaphes buzzed Sally, and while she made a copy of Luskin's file he talked about the two passions in his life: skiing and women. He'd just returned from an Aspen ski trip—which explained his tan—and from the sound of it, the ratio of women to men had been better than Tango. ''I mean, Ryan, out there a man has *choices*. Many, many choices. These women are *hungry*, my friend, and they're all on vacation, so they've come to party.'' He then renumerated his various conquests during the week, and Kincaid thought about things like AIDS and wished him luck.

2

The strange and tragic thing about the criminal justice system, Kincaid thought, was that a woman like Sheila Reiner could do five years on ten for a murder rap and then return to the wealth she'd inherited and pick up her life where she'd left off as though nothing had happened.

Her home was several blocks from the downtown area in the Cove; Kincaid left the Saab in front of a health food store and walked the distance. Compared to most of the houses on the umbrageous road where she lived, Reiner's was large, set back on what he guessed was a two-acre lot. It was brick, with a pair of wide white porticos in the front, and a sweeping lawn landscaped with roses and zinnias. Four banyan trees kept the house in perpetual shade, and a warm but pleasant breeze whispered through the branches. Gracious and very southern, Kincaid thought, the sort of place you'd expect to come upon in Georgia.

A silver BMW stood in the crescent driveway, the trunk open. A woman was pulling packages out of it as Kincaid came up behind her. ''Excuse me, are you Mrs. Reiner?''

She glanced around, her short, light brown hair moving as she moved, a box from Lord & Taylor tucked under one arm.

She wore dark sunglasses, so he couldn't see her eyes, but he didn't have to see her eyes to know she was attractive. She was tall, five ten or so, slender, well dressed. She sure didn't fit his idea of an ex-con.

"Yes, I'm Sheila Reiner. Who're you?"

"Ryan Kincaid. A private eye. I'd like to ask you a few questions, Mrs. Reiner."

She tipped her sunglasses back into her hair. Her eyes were hot blue, fringed in thick, almost blond eyelashes that made him wonder if her hair was actually blond, not brown. *Or are you really prematurely gray, Mrs. Reiner? Do you dye your pubic hairs?* "A few questions about what?"

"Where you were the night before last between seven and eleven P.M."

She turned, pulled another box out of the trunk, this one from Neiman-Marcus, and shut the lid. "Why?"

"You read the papers?"

She faced him again. "Just get to the point, why don't you, Mr. Kincaid."

"I'm investigating the murder of the Michael family."

"What's that got to do with me?"

"Look, I know you did time and I know what you did it for, and I know Judge Michael sentenced you. So let's start all over again. Where were you the night before last between seven and eleven?"

Her eyes widened until they were as round as coins. "Excuse me, Mr. Kincaid, but I'm quite busy." And she brushed past him, hurrying up the walk to the porch, her high heels clicking against the brick.

Kincaid caught up with her. "You can either talk to me or the police." It was his standard line, and over the years had proven rather useful. He wasn't surprised that it worked with Sheila Reiner. She had been free only a few months; her memories of prison were apparently still vivid enough so that his mention of the cops made her a little more cooperative.

"Oh, all right." She sighed. "But we've got to make this quick. I'm already late for an appointment."

She unlocked the door, and, as it swung open, she slid her packages into the hall, then shut the door, turned, and leaned against it. Her hands slipped into the pockets of her skirt as she gazed at Kincaid. "The night before last, Mr. Kincaid, I spent the evening at home. Alone. That means I don't have an alibi. But just in case you're interested, I don't have a motive, either. I did my time and I'd like to forget about it. I like my freedom. So why would I kill Judge Michael just because he sentenced me? He could've given me twenty-five years, but he didn't.''

"It wasn't your sentence I was thinking about. It was Jimmy Ray Luskin's.''

Her hands came out of her pockets slowly, and she crossed her arms at the waist, as if for protection. Something—fear, perhaps, or suspicion or sadness—flickered across the smooth planes of her face. "In case you haven't heard, he got the chair in August.''

"Tell me about him.''

"Tell you what?''

"Were you in love with him?''

"Look, I don't think it's any of your business. That part of my life is over.''

He repeated his question, and implied in his tone was the threat of cops, of the unpleasant resurrection of her past, and she sighed and reached into her purse for a cigarette. "Yes, I suppose I was in love with him, although I don't have the vaguest notion why. When I met him, he was twenty-three years old and had just started selling real estate. I was thirty-three and married to a multimillionaire who was into everything but me. Jimmy Ray sold my husband and me this house. He was a real odd duck—charming in his way, very intense, and had a foul temper. I don't know what else there is to say about him. About any of it.''

"Did you hear from him after he went to prison?''

She tipped her head back and blew smoke into the air. "I went to jail shortly after he did, Mr. Kincaid.''

"That isn't what I asked.''

She looked at him again, eyes skewed with contempt. "I don't think I like you very much.''

"You don't have to like me to give me a simple yes-or-no answer.''

"Yes, all right. Yes. I heard from him. For a while, until I was busted, I was getting, oh, probably five letters a week from him.'' She let out a weird laugh. "Can you imagine? Five letters a week. After my own arrest, the letters stopped. Then about a year before I was released the mail started coming again. Here to the house. My attorney used to bring it

with him when he visited. It was strictly against the rules, of
course, but"—she shrugged—"that's prison life for you. The
rules are there to be broken." Her smile was quick, almost
smug, as though she prided herself on having gotten away
with it. "He said he had a pretty good deal at Raiford. He
was working in the library and someone was helping him
write a book about his life." Another weird laugh. She flicked
her cigarette away from her; it sailed inches past Kincaid's
ear and over his shoulder, landing in the driveway. "Like
anyone could've given a good goddamn about Jimmy Ray's
life. So. That's about it, Mr. Kincaid. Now if you don't mind,
I've got things to do." Without another word, she hurried
inside.

Kincaid heard the click of the dead bolt as she turned it.

3

He walked back into town, where he'd left his car, and ducked
into the health food store to replenish a couple of items in
Aline's supply of herbs. But most of the merchandise was
twice as expensive as it was anywhere else on the island.
Only the produce was reasonably priced, and none of it was
wrapped in cellophane. In fact, the display was a veritable
carnival of color: thriving dark red strawberries, deep purple
Chilean grapes, plums as red as a baby's cheeks, bananas the
color of canaries.

"Ryan, hi."

He glanced around and smiled at Molly Chapman, standing behind a cart loaded with all sorts of delicacies. Her
honey hair was drawn back with a pink and lavender silk
scarf. She wore jeans and a lavender halter top with a pink
print blouse thrown over it. On anyone else, the outfit
would've looked garish. But somehow Molly pulled it off so
well that the overall effect was one of panache, that peculiar
and eccentric flair he always associated with her. He could
see her tooting into the Cove in her jeep, the top off, her hair
flying, eyes on the street drawn to her like a magnet. "Hi,
yourself. Since when do you shop in the Cove?"

"Oh, I'm buying stuff for the barbecue Bill and I are having, and this is the only place on Tango where I can find all the herbs and spices I need. I was going to call you tonight about scheduling for another flying lesson.'' She spoke quickly, as though she were rushed. But everything Molly said or did was like that. It was just her way, and the one strike against her as a student pilot. If you were in a hurry in the air, your margin for error increased.

''Mornings are pretty clear for me, and the weather's usually good then. So any morning this week would be fine.''

''You think I'm ready to practice some stalls?''

Kincaid chuckled. Every student he'd ever had always asked this question in exactly the same tone of voice. ''A stall isn't different from any other maneuver.''

She wrinkled her nose. ''Ha. You go straight down, Ryan, that makes it *real* different.''

''You'll do fine,'' he assured her.

She still didn't look convinced, but she evidently decided to take his word for it. They walked over to the register together. ''How come you're up here?'' she asked.

''Business. Judge Michael hired me a few days before he was killed to look into some threatening phone calls he'd gotten.''

''Really?'' Interest flickered in her huge blue eyes, and he suddenly realized she was probably covering the story for the Tango *Tribune*. ''What've you found out?''

''Nothing yet. You covering the story?''

She nodded and looked down at her hands, curled around the cart's handle. ''I wrote one story, but my editor thinks Gene Frederick hasn't released some things, so now I'm supposed to be a *real* reporter, right?'' She laughed and looked up. ''You know, an *investigative* reporter. What Chip doesn't realize—my editor, Chip Sonsky—is that this story's creating some *serious* conflicts of interest for me.''

''With Bill, you mean.''

''Yeah. With Bill.''

''Things'll work out.''

''I'm not an optimist by nature, Ryan, but it's nice to know you are.''

Actually, he wasn't. Some people were born with optimism coursing through their blood, a genetic blessing. Other people had to work at it; he was one of them. But he didn't bother saying it. He told Molly to give him a call when she was

ready for her lesson, and scooted into the express lane with
his bag of fruit.

4

Kincaid reached the Tango Key High School at three on the
button. He found Louisa Almott, who taught ninth- and tenth-
grade math, in her homeroom, sitting behind a desk, eating
an apple as she graded papers. It was such a typical pose for
a teacher that if he'd had a camera with him, he would've
snapped a picture. But then she glanced up, brows coppled,
and destroyed the image.

She didn't look like a teacher; she looked like an Iowa farm
girl. Sturdy. Hardy. The sort of woman who could till the
land from breakfast to supper and have energy remaining to
feed and bathe four small children, read them all bedtime
stories, and still have something left for her husband. Her
eyes were as dark as fertile soil, and she had shiny hair the
color of acorns that fell softly around her face, almost to her
shoulders. There was an open freshness about her face that
startled him; he hadn't expected anyone who'd been involved
with Luskin to seem so . . . well, innocent.

"You're a little old to be a student here," she remarked
with a smile.

Kincaid introduced himself and stepped into the room. It
even smelled like a high school classroom—of chalk dust, old
floor wax, and books. "I'm a private investigator, Ms. Almott and I'd like to ask you a few questions."

"A real private eye?" Her smiled widened. "I thought
they were obsolete. You know, that they'd gone out with
Dashiell Hammett and Raymond Chandler."

He laughed. "There're still a few of us around."

"So what's this about?" She tossed the apple core into the
basket and leaned forward, arms folded parallel to the edge
of the desk. "What dire and terrible things are you investigating, Mr. Kincaid?"

Like it's a TV movie, he thought. "Jimmy Ray Luskin."

Her affable smile was sucked away. Her dark eyes turned
darker. The seams of her jaw tightened. The transformation

was so sudden and so complete it astonished him. "I have nothing to say to you. Please shut the door on your way out." She looked back down at her papers, dismissing him.

"If you don't talk to me, you'll be talking to the cops."

She moved her head slowly, and her eyes impaled him, zapped him. "Then I guess I'll just have to talk to the police, Mr. Kincaid. Good-bye."

It was as if a door had slammed in his face. And because he'd been in the business long enough to know when further rhetoric was useless, he left.

5

Kincaid drove north again along the Old Post Road, headed toward the northeast tip of the island—the cat's right ear. If he remembered correctly, Lenore and Jimmy Ray Luskin's family homestead had been located somewhere off Papaya Drive. It was a fancy name for a dirt road that, almost five years ago, had bordered a planned development that was touted as "rural island living." He had made a $10,000 deposit on a six-acre lot where he and his second wife intended to build a home—and patch up their failing marriage. Not only had the marriage fallen apart, but he'd also lost the ten grand when the developer had gone bankrupt.

It hadn't been a happy period of his life, and there was a lot about it that he'd forgotten. But one thing stood out with absolute clarity: the double murders that had taken place there one hot June night that summer.

June 10: Kincaid knew the date because it had been his ex-wife's birthday. That morning, she flew down from Miami, where she taught economics at the U of M, and they went back to the house they shared three days a week. They spent much of the day in bed, he remembered, then went to the Hibiscus Inn for dinner. He presented her with the receipt for the down payment on the property—and the blueprints for the house. She was so delighted, she wanted to drive out to the property and walk around it. So they had.

Kincaid could still recall the quality of the air that night— the thick humidity, the almost preternatural stillness, the

sharpness of the stars against the utter blackness of the sky.
He remembered how solid the ground had felt beneath his
feet as they strolled across the land—*their* land. He could
taste the sweet desire that had swelled in his throat when Nan,
laughing softly, had gotten down on her hands and knees,
patting a soft, loamy patch of earth and whispered, "Here,
Ryan. Let's make love here."

And it was while they were making love that they heard
the shrieks. The sounds had leaped from the quiet dark,
piercing it, shredding it, then seeming to echo for several
long and breathless moments, paralyzing them. Then it had
ceased. Just like that, it had stopped, and the pulse of the
silence had enclosed them again.

Two days later, after he'd watched Nan's plane climb into
an impossibly blue sky, he'd bought a newspaper and learned
about the double murders. The electric cattle prod. The tor-
tures. And he knew what they had heard, and had never spoken of it to anyone. But he'd followed the investigation and
had sat in on Luskin's trial.

In some dim corner of Kincaid's mind there remained the
visage of Jimmy Ray Luskin in the courtroom, seated next to
Xaphes. Luskin in a three-piece suit, handsome, composed.
His occasional smile said he was bored, said this had all been
some gross, bureaucratic mistake that would be rectified when
the trial was over. During the psychiatrist's testimony—which
had supported Xaphes's argument that Luskin was temporar-
ily insane when he'd committed the murders—the young man
had sat at the front of the courtroom, picking at his fingernails, as sane as they come.

He slowed as he passed the turnoff for the bankrupt development. Papaya Drive should've been less than half a mile
beyond it. But there were numerous dirt roads that angled off
into the trees, and no street signs. When the odometer said
he'd gone a mile past the development, he turned around. He
hung a right at the remains of a sign that said TANGO ACRES:
A NEW CONCEPT IN ISLAND LIVING.

The asphalt road was crumbling. The vegetation had gob-
bled up, for the most part, the once clear delineations of lots
and tracts of land. Ivy snaked up power line poles that had
never been strung with wire. Birds nested on empty trans-
former boxes. Now and then he came upon entire blocks with
sidewalks and curbs, fire hydrants and hedges, driveways and

green, paint-chipped street signs with names like Paradise
Alley written in white letters. Blocks without houses, blocks
waiting for people, for families and kids and pets. A kind of
unreality swirled around him. He felt like he'd stumbled
through the thin membrane between dimensions, into a probable neighborhood, a place that might've been—a way of life
he'd glimpsed, and lost.

He made his way through the trees, on a dusty road no wider
than a footpath, and eventually reached a small clearing. The
Luskin house was set back in a holt of trees and shrubbery. It
was a humble place wih a sagging porch and boarded-up windows, an attestation to Luskin's dark beginnings.

Kincaid got out of the Saab and walked through the dap-
pled shadows toward the house. The plank that had been
nailed across the front door had been knocked to the side and
hung like a pendulum from the wall to the left of the entry.
Someone had been here, all right.

Kincaid opened the door and stepped into the gloam of the
kitchen; the dank smell of the place made him sneeze. Everything was layered in three inches of dust and roach shit.
But even so, there was sufficient evidence of Lenore Luskin's
expensive tastes. Brocade furniture, now faded, satin curtains
draped like fabric in a coffin, hardwood floors, peach walls
with lighter areas where paintings had hung.

In the bedroom, he flung open the rotting curtains and
gazed at the huge canopied bed. Right there. It had happened
there. The canopy was gone, and so were the sheets, of
course, but the blood wasn't. The blood had seeped into the
mattress and stained the wall behind it. The blood was an
old river that had twisted this way and that, connecting the
past and the present.

The air was still and hot, and sweat sprang across his back,
his forehead, and his cheeks as he neared the bed, frowning
at slash marks in the mattress. Stuffing oozed from them.
Upon closer inspection, Kincaid decided the slashes were re-
cent. He took out his Swiss Army knife and cut around one
of them, excising it from the mattress. A long shot, but maybe
Prentiss or one of his people would be able to tell what had
been used to make the gashes.

On his way back through the rooms, a dark miasma
grew inside him like a fungus or mold. It was as if something
of what had happened here remained in the air and he was

inhaling it. Now and then the memory of the hideous screams echoed in his head. The violent despair of Lenore Luskin's final hours—and those of her lover—became almost palpable to Kincaid. He started to imagine things—cold spots in the room, shapes that flitted through the shadows, as elusive as butterflies, noises. By the time he was in the kitchen, his miasma was bone-deep.

He trotted down the steps and toward the Saab faster than necessary, spooked by something he couldn't name. *Luskin is at the heart of it. I know it. Luskin is the reason the Michael family is dead.* Now all he had to do was prove it.

And find who was behind it.

7: THE DOCK WORKER

I

Long shadows shot across the road and filled the spaces under the awnings as Whitley stepped out of the building. He paused on the stoop, lit a thin black cigarette, and drew the smoke into his lungs. It was his first butt since his break at three that afternoon, and Christ, but it tasted good. Ever since the word had come down from the higher-ups that smoking would be permitted only on the docks and not in the administrative buildings, his habit had plunged from two packs a day to about half a pack.

Okay, so his throat didn't feel like shit in the morning, but he'd put on seven pounds. Jean said she liked him with the extra weight, that he'd been too thin before, but hell, his clothes were starting to get tight. Pretty soon, if he didn't watch it, he'd have a paunch like Tinker, his boss. Tinker's shirts bulged at the buttons, and he was always patting his midriff like he was checking to see if any of the blubber had bled off overnight. Tinker was supposedly on a new diet, but just this morning Whitley had walked in on him in the lunchroom, chowing down a package of macaroons and guzzling a carton of buttermilk. *Way to go, Tinko.*

Thirty-five years Tinker had been toiling at the docks. He'd started at the bottom, unloading boats, and had worked his way up. Now he was in charge of three dozen men in the management division, and he would probably drop dead of a coronary in another couple of years. Tinker was an asshole, yeah, but he also symbolized everything Whitley was afraid of becoming: *Fifteen years I've been here: time to move on.*

But on to what?

He flicked his cigarette into the street and stood on the stoop a second or two longer, watching the smoke curl up from it. Then he started down the steps and headed toward his jeep on the other side of the street. A couple of beers at Rover's and a bite to eat and then maybe he'd feel like going home. *To what? The tube? The cat?*

He and Jean were supposed to have had dinner tonight at that ritzy inn up in the Cove, but her boss had asked her to stay late and do an inventory. It was probably just as well. He liked Jean okay, liked sleeping with her, liked her company, but he didn't love her, and didn't want to marry her. He supposed that sooner or later he was going to have to cut things off. She was already getting real clingy and possessive, calling him when he hadn't called her for a couple of days, or dropping by the office to see him on her break. She worked in shipping and he was in receiving, so it wasn't like Tinker would get on him about it, since there were legitimate reasons they might need to talk. But it bugged him. It bugged him to see her cute, hopeful face in the doorway, to hear her soft, breathy voice say, "Hi, Bob, got a minute?" Or, "I'm on my way to the lunchroom, want to join me?"

Jean was like him: she'd found a good job and would stay until they retired her. Thing was, he didn't want to be like that anymore. He wanted something new. Something different. He wanted something exciting to sweep into his life—an adventure, a woman with spunk, a woman like that weirdo chick Madonna played in *Desperately Seeking Susan*, a big win in the lottery.

The lottery had only started last month, but he'd already blown a hundred bucks on tickets and had won only fifteen. Goddamn thing was rigged, he decided, but knew he'd keep on buying, just like half the guys he worked with, because everyone was looking for excitement and just the possibility of winning a million bucks was almost as good as payday.

I need excitement, he thought again as he slipped the jeep into reverse and backed out of the lot.

Be careful what you ask for; you just might get it. That was Jean's standard response to people's gripes and complaints. *So what?* he thought. What could possibly be so bad about meeting some weird chick and taking her home for the night?

He headed toward Rover's Bar. He'd shoot some pool, have a couple of beers. Hell, maybe he'd even get lucky and meet a woman who didn't know Jean (who seemed to know everyone) and they'd go back to his place and . . .

Bob Whitley smiled. *It's gonna be a good night. I feel it.*

2

A flock of green parrots squawked overhead, winging their way through the dusk, as Whitley parked the jeep. The front door of Rover's was open and music pounded through it, music and smoke. Nothing special about the place, except that the beer was cold and a lot of the dock crew came here after work. Whitley took a quick glance at himself in the rearview mirror. *You look like shit, man.* He smoothed a hand over his dark hair, ran his finger under his mustache. *How're you going to meet a classy chick if you look like shit?*

He debated going home to shower first and put on clean clothes, but Christ, between here and his house were five miles of rush-hour traffic. Forget it.

The place was jammed with people, a lot of them snowbirds who'd probably heard Rover's had the cheapest booze on the island. You could always spot a snowbird. The women usually had bad sunburns, and the men, if they were older, wore floral-print shirts. He found an empty stool at the end of the bar and ordered a Miller. Fuck the Lite beer and the seven pounds he'd gained, he thought. The stuff tasted like horse piss, anyway.

He shot the breeze with the bartender awhile, had another Miller, this time with a tequila chaser, and was starting to feel real good. He played a game of pool with a fellow who worked in supplies at the dock, beat him, and played another, which he lost. He cruised toward the jukebox, beer in hand, his eyes roaming the room, checking out the women. Some of them he knew; most he didn't. Usually it was the other way around; he decided it was a good sign.

Whitley fed three quarters into the juke and punched out a number by Whitney Houston (he wasn't sure who she was, but he liked her name) and two tunes by Madonna. He definitely knew who *she* was. Someone bumped into him from behind, and as he turned, he smacked right into a woman, knocking her purse out of her hand. Things spewed from her handbag, and when her wallet hit the floor, change tumbled out, clattering across the floor.

"Jesus, I'm sorry," he said loudly, over the din of the music, and hurriedly crouched to help her pick things up. He plucked a knife in a leather case from the floor—a hunting knife, judging from the size of it—and held it out. "I wasn't looking."

"It's my fault," she stammered, dropping the knife hastily in her purse. They looked at each other, and Whitley liked what he saw. He liked it very much.

She had short auburn hair, a quick smile, and the greenest eyes he'd ever seen in his life. She wore perfume that was guaranteed to give him a hard-on within the next five seconds, an awesome fragrance, expensive.

". . . they're mostly pennies, anyway," she was saying.

"Like my piggy bank," he replied, and they laughed, even though it wasn't funny. "Look, the least I can do is buy you a drink."

"Okay, thanks. That'd be great."

"Hold out your hands."

She did, and he poured change into them. She funneled them back into her wallet. A few minutes later they were seated at the end of the bar, and he was thinking, *Be careful what you ask for, because you just might get it*. Well, hey, nothing too shabby about this.

Her name was Rebecca. She was from upstate New York, she said, but in graduate school at the University of Miami, working toward a master's in business administration. Brains: good, he liked that. But even if she'd been dizzy in the brains department, it wouldn't matter, because she had a terrific body, lean and graceful, with curves in all the right places.

She matched him drink for drink as they talked, and pretty soon he realized she was as loaded as he was. She giggled as she lifted her glass and said, "Hey, aren't we doing this backward? Isn't it supposed to be tequila with beer chasers instead of beer with tequila chasers?"

Flummoxed, he shrugged. "I don't know."

Then they both cracked up with laughter.

By the time the hands of the clock over the bar had started

to blur, he was trying to figure out a way to discreetly suggest they leave. But it had been a long time—*very long*, he reminded himself—since he'd picked up a woman in a bar, and he wasn't sure what his approach should be. Direct? As in, *Let's go fuck?* Or something more subtle like, *Let's go back to my place.*

In the end, though, she made the first move. She touched his thigh and whispered, "Let's go someplace quieter, Bob."

He replied by touching her chin and kissing her, a soft and gentle kiss. "My house is quieter."

Outside, he pulled her against him, kissing her again, her back against the side of the building. His hands locked at her hips, his tongue slid between her lips, her tongue tasted of tequila. She ground her hips against him and groaned as his hands moved up her ribs to her breasts, cupping one through the fabric of her shirt. She wore no bra, which excited him enormously. Jean always wore a bra, and it was always the last thing she took off, as though her breasts were sacred.

He flicked his thumb across Rebecca's nipples; she drew his lower lip between her teeth and murmured, "God, that feels good."

"I'll drive." His mouth cruised along the curve of her neck to her shoulder.

"I'll drive," she said.

They looked at each other and laughed again. "We'll both drive. It's not far. I'm in the jeep."

"Okay."

Be careful what you ask for, because you just might get it. Christ oh Christ.

3

His place was on a dirt road, tucked back in a niche of pines. He'd bought it twelve years ago, and although it was small, it was comfortable. "How about Charlie Byrd?" Whitley asked as he stood in front of the stereo.

"Great. God, I haven't heard Byrd in ages."

He put on the album, then checked the fridge for beer. All gone. Jesus, he was going to feel like shit in the morning if he switched to something else after tequila and beer. "You like Bailey's Irish Cream?" he asked, checking the bar.

"Love it."

When he returned to the living room with the Bailey's, she was reaching into her purse, and for a wild, drunken moment, he thought of that hunting knife. Then she held up a joint and he nearly exploded with laughter at his paranoia. "Best stuff there is for preventing a hangover," she said.

One puff on the grass and he was soaring. He had no clear memory of getting to the bedroom or what had preceded it. But now she was peeling away her clothes, and he left his where they fell on the floor and walked over to the bed, pulling back the spread. The Byrd album was still playing in the living room, and he liked the sound of it back there, sweet and romantic, the way he imagined music in Brazil.

He left the gooseneck lamp on. Jean would only do it in the dark, and for once, Whitley wanted to make love to a woman and see her face. He slipped under the sheet, watching Rebecca as she crossed the room, the light playing across her skin. She dropped her purse at the side of the bed, and he wondered why she hadn't left it in the living room. Maybe she had her diaphragm inside it or something.

"Move over," she said, smiling, which annoyed him a little. Why couldn't she just go around to the other side? But he slid to the left and she slipped in beside him, her skin cool and fragrant, her mouth seeking his, her breasts brushing his chest. His hands traveled slowly up her spine, over the flare of her hip, across her buttocks. He shifted so she was on her back now and he was raised above her, his mouth in a hot slide across her skin, the scent of that perfume a tightening net around him. He wanted to take it nice and slow, but he didn't think he was going to be able to. She was stroking him, nibbling at his ear, and as his hand slipped between her thighs, she whispered things to him, dirty words, telling him to touch her this way or that, things Jean never would have thought of, much less uttered.

But the way Rebecca said them aroused him. The words became pictures, and the pictures became real, and suddenly he was doing these things to her with his fingers, his mouth. Her nails sank into his shoulders as she shuddered against him and emitted a low, broken cry. He shifted again to move inside her, but she moaned, "No. Wait. Just a second." She sat up, swinging her legs over the side of the bed, and reached for her purse on the floor. "We've got to use something. I don't want to get pregnant or anything." Her hand vanished inside her purse, and for a second he tensed, thinking of the knife. But the sight of her back distracted him.

He drew his finger down the length of her spine and she murmured that it tickled. She reached back, holding out a condom. Whitley tore open the package and started rolling it on. When he looked up, Rebecca was bent forward, her vertebrae standing out in stark relief against her skin, and muttering something about how everything had fallen out of her purse. Her hair in the back had parted, and he touched his mouth to the nape of her neck and something weird happened to her hair. It seemed to shift on her head like a . . . *a wig. Christ, she's wearing a wig.* Cancer, he thought. She had cancer and the chemotherapy had made her hair fall out. No wonder she suddenly turned off the light. But he wished she hadn't. It was too much like Jean.

But the way she touched him wasn't. She shifted around, reaching for him, easing herself down over him so he was now inside her. She was tight and hot, and one of her cool hands was flat against his chest as she moved ever so slowly. "You know, Bob, you never should have found him guilty. I mean, he *was* guilty, he *did* kill her, but what else was he going to do? She abused him. Lenore made him do things for her clients. He told me. He told me all of it, and if I'd . . ."

Her voice reached him in the dark as if from a great distance. He didn't know what she was talking about, and it didn't matter, the only thing that mattered was the way she moved. He was going to explode, he was going to . . . *Lenore, something about Lenore. Who's Lenore? Why's that name familiar?*

Her hand slid slowly across his chest, his belly, and she kept moving, talking to him, her breathing odd now, ragged, like a wheeze, and he couldn't hold back anymore, he couldn't, he grabbed her at the hips, and she grunted as he thrust hard, pumping—

She cried out, clutching at him, and an instant later, they collapsed against each other. He stayed inside her, his heart still pounding, blood still rushing through his veins. But a part of him was puzzling through what she'd said about him, her voice a murmur, her hands cool against his shoulder, her . . .

Something burst in his chest, a pain so deep, so pervasive, that every muscle in his body convulsed, as if to thwart the source of the pain, to close it out. He couldn't scream, and now he couldn't breathe, he was gulping at the air, trying to draw it into his lungs. The air gurgled and hissed, and he felt blood pumping from the hole in his chest, felt his heart thudding, skipping beats, and, oh sweet Christ, the pain, the pain. . . .

The light winked on.

Rebecca was standing over him, smiling, her wig askew, blood smeared on her cheeks, her breasts, her belly, so much blood. *My blood my blood that's my blood.* His hands jerked toward his chest, and he looked down at himself, at the protruding knife. He tried to draw in air, but there wasn't any. His vision blurred a little, and the finger Rebecca was shaking at him seemed thinner than a pencil; it was fuzzy at the edges. *I hurt oh God how I hurt think about the hurt do something about it don't keep looking at that goddamn finger. . . .*

"It was wrong to find him guilty, Bob. It really was. Everyone has to pay for it. Now this is going to sting some, okay?" And she yanked the knife out of his chest.

Blood spurted. He lurched forward, hands pressed to the wound *the phone, get to the phone*—and his legs swung around, but he couldn't feel them. He stumbled to his feet, the room blurred now, and he heard Rebecca laugh, a soft, soft laugh. "Over here, Bobby boy."

He tried to turn, oh God, how he tried, but his muscles refused to obey, his muscles had gone soft and loose, and he toppled. His last thought was: *Be careful what you ask for; you just might get it.*

8: THE SECOND BODY

I

It had rained long and hard during the night, and was still raining the next morning. Aline awakened in her hammock to the tap of rain against the windows, the sound of it rushing through the pipe outside, the pound of rain against the roof. She sat up, swung her legs over the hammock, and opened the window all the way. A gust of wind blew rain into her face, rocked the hammock, and rattled the glass. The sweet scent of the rain ballooned with the humus smell of wet grass, leaves, the seemingly endless fecundity of an island that yielded mangoes and papayas, oranges and grapefruit, tomatoes, green beans, coconuts, and innumerable types of trees and flowers. It was also home to several panthers, wild green parrots, iguanas half the size of a cat, alligators that proliferated in the Tango Inlet. It seemed that the rain, the smell of it, contained all of these things and more. But it still irked her. She had a lot of running around to do today. Her Honda always leaked when it rained, and the car struggled for purchase on the wet roads because two of the tires were bald.

"We working on forty days and nights here?" she mumbled, supplicating the gray, pendulous sky with her eyes. "Is that it? Should I be getting ready to board the Ark?"

The storm responded with a clap of thunder, and under the hammock, Wolfe scratched at the floor. "Hey, don't do that with your claws, boy," she grumbled. "It messes up the wood."

He peered up at her with those tiny black eyes. *Feed me,*

90

change my box, amuse me, let me sleep, demanded those eyes. As her feet touched the floor, he rubbed up against her ankle, then nipped at her big toe—not hard, not hard enough to break the skin, but hard enough to get his message across.

"Mind if I take care of myself first?"

Wolfe evidently minded very much, because he padded after her as she strolled into the bathroom to shower and brush her teeth. He sat in the doorway, watching her as she turned on the water, his black eyes flicking this way, that, his tail raised and quivering with displeasure.

Aline showered and got dressed, then carried Wolfe down the loft ladder with her. She fed him, grabbed the umbrella from the hallway closet, and hurried out to the end of the driveway to retrieve yesterday's mail. She was always forgetting to pick up the mail. Maybe when Kincaid moved in, that could be one of *his* things to do. He was good about stuff like that.

She felt echoes of panic at the thought of him moving in, at the thought of her space shared—*violated*—by anyone. She'd lived alone too long to have another person around her day and night, over and over again, ad infinitum. They would get on each other's nerves. They would argue about her disorderliness and his precision. He would become critical; she would get mean. Things would go haywire.

Aline sprinted the last few yards to the porch, heart thudding in her chest—not from the sprint, but from anxiety. Her cheeks felt flushed as she skidded through the front door. *It's Kincaid, Aline. Kincaid.*

Right. Of course. Kincaid, whom she'd known for three years. Kincaid, whom she loved. It would be okay. Sure. It would. It would take some readjustments, but it would work out just fine.

She dropped the mail on the counter, then made herself a cup of hot tea and a bowl of oatmeal for breakfast. As she ate, she went through the mail. Bills, mostly bills. But a plain white envelope, with just her name typed on it, caught her eye. No address: just her name. She opened it.

> Eight fat crows
> All in a row
> Two knocked down,
> And six to go

Beneath it was a bright orange smiling-face sticker, the same kind that had been on the verse Judge Michael had gotten and given to Kincaid. A chill sped up her spine. She grabbed the phone and dialed Bernie.

"Hmm? Hullo?"

"Bernie, wake up. It's me. Allie."

"What time is it?"

"Seven."

"Goddamn," she grumbled. "Four hours of sleep. Al, I'll call you later."

"No. Wait. Did you get anything in the mail yesterday, Bernie? Anything weird? A verse with a smiling-face sticker at the end of it?"

"Al, what're you talking about?"

"Nothing, I'll call you later."

Kincaid was right. It's one of my arrests. But which one? Luskin? Sanborn? Or one of the cases she didn't pull? Maybe something as simple as a speeding ticket that went to trial under Judge Michael. No. Christ, no. It had to be something more than that. Had to be.

She went into her den and rifled through the folders she and Kincaid had put together. She found a copy of the Luskin file he'd gotten from Vic Xaphes and opened it. *Here. The answer's in here. I'm sure of it.*

The phone pealed; it was Bernie. "I'm awake now. Will you please tell me what you're talking about?"

She explained, but before she'd finished, she heard a click on the line that indicated she had another call. "Bernie, hold on. Let me get this other call. . . . Hello?"

"Al, it's Roxie. I just got a call from a woman who's pretty out of it. Seems there's been a murder over near the docks. Take down this address. . . ."

Two down and six to go.

"Call Bill Prentiss." She hung up and tapped into Bernie again.

"What's wrong, Bill?" she whispered.

Prentiss rolled away from Molly, ashamed and disgusted with himself. Things had been going along rather nicely for the last ten minutes or so, and then suddenly, for no reason at all, he'd lost his erection.

Wrong, good buddy. There's a reason. You were thinking about the puncture wound to Judge Michael's eye.

The same thing happened last night. They'd met at the Pink Moose for a beer around midnight, when they'd each left work, and had come back here and started to make love, and then . . . nothing. Not only had he lost his erection, but his desire had left him as well.

He gazed up at the ceiling, where the opaline light swirled and eddied against the wood, and hooked his hands under his head. "It's not you. It's me."

"It's that goddamn job of yours, you know." She lifted up on an elbow, her hair falling along one side of her face. He reached out and slid his fingers through it, and let his hand rest against the back of her neck. "How can you spend all day with dead people and then expect to have a normal sex life, Bill? Or any kind of normal life?"

"Look, I've been doing this for damn near ten years, Molly. It's not the job, it's just . . ." *Henry's eye, the woman stuck a needle in his eye.* ". . . facets of it."

"The Michaels, you mean."

"Yes."

The radio clicked on, and an old Blood, Sweat and Tears tune floated through the room. Prentiss sat up, swung his legs over the side of the bed, and gazed through the open porch doors at the far end of the room. The rain was coming down in sheets, blurring the pines in the yard. The wind whipped the tops of them, causing them to sway, and whistled along the eaves of the house. His eyes moved slowly around the room, over the old pine dresser, the closet doors, past the bookshelves, the cluster of potted plants. He looked and thought about how Henry Michael's sight in his right eye was destroyed in a matter of seconds.

The refraction and bending of light rays so they could focus on the retina and be transmitted to the optic nerve were accomplished by three structures: the aqueous humor, a watery substance between the cornea and lens; a crystalline structure just behind the iris; and the vitreous humor, a jellylike substance filling the space between the lens and the retina.

The lens of the eye, unlike the lens of a camera, focused on an object in two ways. If the object was in the distance, muscles pulled the lens, stretching it until it was thin and almost flat, so the light rays were only slightly bent as they passed through it. When the object was close, the muscles relaxed and the elastic lens became thicker, bending the light rays and focusing them on the retina.

In the retina, there were two different sets of nerve cells, the cone-shaped and the rod-shaped. They covered the full range of adaptation to light: the cone-shaped were sensitive in bright light, and the rods in dim.

The needle had entered the sclera of Henry Michael's eye, the white part. It had penetrated through to the choroid, the middle layer of the eyeball that contained blood vessels, and into the retina, which contained rods and cones. At that point, if the judge had still been alive—and Prentiss believed that he was—he would've been blinded. The pain would've started the moment the needle penetrated and grown steadily worse as the penetration deepened. The aqueous and vitreous humors would've started to leak almost immediately, and—

Cut. No more.

But he heard himself say, "The woman who killed them stuck a needle into Henry's eyeball. She hacked up Mrs. Michael with a hunting knife. She . . . she mutilated one of the boys. . . . She has type O blood, and she dyes her pubic hair blond, and so help me God, Molly, if this appears in the paper, I'll sue." He shifted around, looking at her. "I mean it."

She sat up. Color suffused her cheeks. "I'm not the monster you think I am, for Christ's sakes."

"I never said you're a monster."

Her look was bitter. "You didn't have to." An uneasy moment ticked by. His head ached. His eyes burned from lack of sleep. He wanted desperately to erase what had just been said and start over again. But Molly couldn't leave it alone. "The killer's female?"

"That was off the record." The words escaped through clenched teeth, in a sibilant breath.

"Hey, I'm asking you as a matter of curiosity, Bill, okay? Not as a reporter."

She looked hurt, and he immediately felt guilty. He knuckled an eye. "I'm sorry, it's just—"

"I know. It's just the same old thing with us, isn't it? You think I'm always after a story. You don't trust me. I'm the bitch on wheels. Shit." She threw up her hands. "I can't win, can I? We can't talk about your work anymore because you don't trust me, and our sex life has gone to hell because you cut up dead bodies and I'm supposed to sit here and reassure you that I understand the difference between what you say to me in bed and what you say to me as a coroner." She threw off the covers. "Fuck it."

She stood and marched off to the shower, and Prentiss stared at her receding back, the soft white globes of her buttocks, the slight sway of her hips. *Things are falling apart here, good buddy, sinking down the tubes fast.*

The phone rang, the sound too shrill in the silence, startling him. *Don't answer it. Take care of business first. Tell Molly things are on hold with you two until this case is finished. You can't trust her not to print what you just said. And you can't trust yourself, good buddy, to keep your mouth shut when you feel like this.* But when the phone rang a second time and then a third, he answered it.

It was Roxie, the dispatcher at the station, and as he listened, his head began to throb and his throat went dry.

3

Prentiss was the first person on the scene, which—considering the weather—meant Aline had probably had car trouble. A young woman with short, flaming red hair and a dusting of freckles on her cheeks stood on the porch of the little bungalow, hugging her arms against her as he darted through the rain from his Mercedes, his black bag smacking his thigh.

"In there." She tilted her head toward the open door. "He's in there."

"The police will be here shortly. I'm Dr. Prentiss, the coroner."

She ran her hands over her arms in short, jerky movements. "I'm Jean Stills. Bob's . . . Bob's girlfriend."

She started to cry and Prentiss just stood there, his temple thudding, an inchoate something clawing at his throat. He suddenly wished he was sequestered in the morgue, where the dead didn't cry or mourn, where the dead didn't do anything but offer up their secrets to his scalpel, his drills, his relentless probing. He moved toward the young woman woodenly, and touched her shoulder. "Is there anything I can do for you until the police get here?"

She bit at her lower lip and shook her head.

"I'm going to take a look inside. Just wait out here."

Softly: "Okay."

The drum of the rain against the windows was exacerbated inside the bungalow by the stillness. A fluffy chocolate and white cat was preening on the couch as he passed and didn't even look up. He paused in the doorway of the bedroom, the stink of death like a physical barrier. The man was lying on the floor, head at an awkward angle against the edge of the nightstand, blood crusted on his chest, his belly, smeared on his shoulders, his cheeks. One eye was open; the other was bloody, and Prentiss winced, knowing he would find a puncture wound to the eyeball.

It means something. The eye wound means something. A metaphor? That the judge and Whitley didn't see something? But what? What's the connection between Henry Michael and Whitley?

The lamp was on and cast eerie, butter-yellow circles of illumination against one of his shoulders and arms. Pale light from the window struck his feet and ankles. The rest of his body was shadowed, and it wasn't until Prentiss squatted beside him that he saw the condom on Whitley's withered penis.

"Good Christ," he whispered, and quickly opened his bag. He snapped on a pair of latex gloves and carefully peeled off the condom. If they'd been having sex when she killed him, then the vaginal secretions would tell him a hell of a lot more than one lousy pubic hair had. He sealed the condom in an airtight container, set it back in the bag, and touched his fingers to the man's chest, feeling for the wound.

There. His index and second finger slipped into the wound—half an inch, an inch. He could've penetrated more deeply, except that he already knew what the blade had hit:

the aorta and the pulmonary trunk. The man either bled to death or suffocated, depending on how much he moved once he'd been stabbed. A copious amount of blood had stained the sheets, so Whitley had apparently stumbled out of bed after she'd stabbed him, then fallen back onto it or been lifted onto it. *And the aorta would've been pumping frantically and he'd be sucking at the air, trying to draw in oxygen, and . . .*

Prentiss stood, wiped his fingers on tissue from his bag, and looked around the room. Very tidy. But next to the bed was a pile of clothes. Whitley had been in an awful hurry to hit the sack.

From his bag, Prentiss removed a magnifying glass whose circumference was as large as his hand. He went into the bathroom and opened the shower stall door. No beads of water: either the woman hadn't showered this time or she'd wiped down the walls and floor with that sponge in the soap dish. He picked up the sponge by a corner and examined it through the magnifying glass. Half a dozen hairs. Good. But they were all the same goddamn color. Like Whitley's hair. Bad.

But just the same, he carefully sealed the sponge and the bar of soap in a baggie, inspected the drain in the shower, then moved on to the sink. It was drier than a bone. He flipped back the lid on the toilet and smiled as he looked down into the bowl. A cigarette butt floated in it.

You paused for a smoke just like in the movies, huh. Nice going, lady. Beautiful. From the bag, he withdrew an instrument he'd designed himself that resembled a pair of tweezers, only it was a foot long, made of lightweight aluminum. He picked out the butt. The damn thing was waterlogged, but the word "Marlboro" was still visible on the white filter.

"Bill?"

"Back here, Al," he called.

Aline hurried into the bedroom with the police photographer, Clicker, tight at her heels, and behind him, Bernelli and Conchita Guzmán, from his skeleton crew. He gave them a quick rundown on what he'd found so far.

"Did this guy smoke?" he asked.

"I don't know," Aline replied. "But I'll ask. He worked at the docks, in management. He'd been there fifteen years. That was about all I could get out of his girlfriend before she started crying again. You have anything I can give her, Bill?

Something to calm her down, but light enough so she's still able to talk?''

"Yeah." He peeled off his gloves and reached into his bag for a vial of Librium, shook a tablet into his hand, and snapped it in half. "Two and a half milligrams. Real light."

Aline left with the Librium, and as though her departure were some sort of signal, everyone else in the room sprang into action. Bernie started marking off the area where the man had fallen. Conchita Guzmán began dusting for prints. Clicker got out his flash and went to work. Prentiss finished up in the bathroom and wandered into the next room, to Whitley's den. He poked around in the desk drawers, in the storage closet, only dimly aware of the footfalls on the porch and the arrival of the ambulance.

"Bill?"

He looked up at Bernelli. She stood in the doorway, lit from behind by the hallway light, hands in the pockets of the jumpsuit she wore. Light seemed to radiate from the top of her head like an aura, turning her blond hair almost white. He felt a funny twitch in his chest, and an image of her rose, unbidden: Bernelli poised naked at the edge of his swimming pool at night, her skin wet, as pale as light, arms over her head, then swinging down as she dived.

"Yeah?"

"His eye."

"I know."

For the beat of several seconds, neither of them spoke. Then she broke the silence. "Aline said to tell you Whitley didn't smoke Marlboros."

She turned, but Prentiss said, "Hey, Bernie, how about if we have breakfast some morning at the Tango Café?"

He didn't know why he'd said it. He hadn't intended to. He hadn't even been thinking about it. And he knew she was going to tell him to fuck off, and hey, he couldn't blame her, considering the way he'd treated her, never calling again and all. But to his utter surprise, she said, "Breakfast? Yeah, okay. But it'll have to be on my day off."

"When's that?"

"I'm not sure. Gene hasn't finished the scheduling. Give me a call," and she left.

Hey, good buddy. She just tossed the ball back in your

court. Now what're you going to do about it? He sat back, smiling. He would call, of course.

Despite everything, his day had just taken an upward swing.

4

Aline and Jean Stills sat on the back porch of the bungalow in a pair of rusted aluminum chairs. It was away from the activity inside the house, and from here she wouldn't see Whitley's body being carted out to the ambulance. Jean was calmer now, although Aline attributed that to the placebo effect of the Librium rather than the Librium itself, because it hadn't had long enough to work yet.

She asked the woman all the usual questions: how long had Jean known Whitley (two years, since she'd started working at the docks); what was their relationship (lovers for the last year); when did she last see him (yesterday at lunch). "We were supposed to have dinner last night, but my boss asked me to work late. I . . . I called Bob around eleven, I guess it was, when I got home, but there wasn't any answer. I figured he'd either gone to bed early or had gone over to Rover's for a beer. I came by here this morning because sometimes we have breakfast together before going to work."

"Rover's the bar?"

"Yes. It's not too far from the docks."

Aline nodded; she knew where it was. "Was Bob seeing anyone else that you know of, Jean?"

"No." She whispered it; raw pain brimmed in her eyes.

"So he's been faithful to you for the year you've been together?"

She hesitated, worrying her hands in her lap. "Well . . . no. Once he was going through this stage about me . . . me being possessive, and there was someone else, I think. Someone he met at a bar. She was a tourist. He didn't even know that I knew. A friend of mine saw them leave together."

"In the past couple of weeks, did he get any threatening phone calls or notes?"

"No. Not that I know of. He would've mentioned it, I

think, if he had. But he did say one thing that was kinda weird.''

''What's that?''

''That sometimes he felt like he was being watched or followed or something. But his boss, Tinker, was always watching him. Watching everyone. He's a hawk, you know, and after a while, that makes you pretty paranoid.''

''That's all he said about it?''

''That's all I can remember. I didn't pay too much attention to it. I just figured it was related to work. To Tinker.''

Aline paused, glancing through her notes, seeking the thread, the common denominator that would tie a dock worker to a judge. She took a wild stab. ''Did Bob ever work in a legal capacity of any kind?''

''He's been working at the docks since he was twenty.'' She frowned a little. ''He once did jury duty. Would that count?''

You bet. ''Yes, that definitely counts. When was it, do you know?''

''Before I knew him.''

''And you knew him two years, right?''

''Uh-huh.''

''Do you know what kind of case it involved?''

''No. It's like just something that sticks in my head.''

It didn't matter; she could check back through her files. The important thing was that she had a lead now. She'd found the connecting thread.

5

When Aline left Bob Whitley's bungalow, she drove out to the garage on the outskirts of town that Ferret and Bino owned. The Honda stalled en route—the fourth time that morning, and the reason Prentiss had beat her to the bungalow—and died with a terrible shudder as she pulled into one of the vacant stalls.

Bino shuffled over, his bleached white skin partially covered by denim coveralls, his dark shades snug against his nose. "Morning, Ms. Scott. Guess you want me to take a look under the hood, huh?"

"I'd really appreciate it, Bino."

"Sure thing. Just got to finish putting oil in Kincaid's car." He gestured to the last stall, where the white Saab stood, looking as new as the day Kincaid had driven it off the show-room floor. Enviable, she thought, to have a dependable car. "He's upstairs with Ferret."

"Thanks."

The two-story building that housed Ferret's base of oper-ations was a bastion of Art Deco. It was celery green with lemon trim, and on the second floor it had four beautiful arched windows. The stairs that led to Ferret's office were on the north side of the edifice and climbed steeply upward, almost like a fire escape. A window air conditioner clanked and clattered at the top of the stairs and dripped steadily enough to mark time by. The wind burst loose across the stoop, nearly soaking her as she rapped on the pane of stained glass in the door. A moment later Kincaid opened it. He was so tall he seemed to dwarf the doorway.

"My favorite cop."

"Wet out here,' she said with a grin, and rolled onto the balls of her feet to kiss him quickly hello.

"No smoochin' on my porch," Ferret grumbled, slam-ming down the phone as she stepped into the office.

"Bad day at the tracks," Kincaid remarked.

"No no no, Ryan. One has to maintain a level of optimism in this business," Ferret corrected. "We say this is a day of momentary setbacks. So what're you doing here, Al?"

"Having Bino look at my car. It's been stalling."

His lips drew away from his teeth in that chilling smile. "Want my opinion, you oughta trash that thing. Ryan's got something for you."

Kincaid reached inside his windbreaker and brought out a bundle of bills. "That three-fifty apiece we invested paid off. There's fifteen hundred here."

Her eyes lit up. "That's great."

"*Great*, the lady says. Not *terrific*, not *Thank you, Ferret*, just *Great*," griped Ferret.

"There's been another murder." Aline tapped the folders. "A guy named Bob Whitley. A dock worker. Before I left his place, I looked through Jimmy Ray Luskin's file. Whitley was on his jury.''

6

Eight black crows . . . Two down . . . six to go: the verse on the note Aline had shown him kept rolling through Kincaid's head as he studied the list of names they'd compiled from Luskin's file.

In *The People v. Jimmy Ray Luskin*, there had been a six-member jury, equally divided between men and women. They'd ranged in age from twenty-six to sixty-eight, and represented a wide spectrum of professions and backgrounds. Judge Michael had presided, and Aline had been the arresting officer. Vic Xaphes was the defense attorney, and a man named Lloyd Watkins had prosecuted. He'd left public work two years ago and had become a corporate attorney in Key West, although he still lived on Tango. Presumably, since the killer had gone after the judge, she also intended to hit the attorneys and the cop, as well as the members of the jury. But that was a total of ten people, not eight. A quick check of the Tango phone book told him that two of the six jurors were no longer listed. Either they'd left the island or had gotten unlisted phone numbers.

"Aline, can you check with the phone company to see if these two jurors have unlisted numbers?"

"I already called," she said, turning away from the windows where she'd been gazing out into the rain, and glancing at the slip of paper Kincaid held. "They have. But does the killer know that? And if not, then who are the eight she's marked? Are the attorneys included? Is the arresting officer?"

Kincaid knew she didn't expect an answer; she was just thinking out loud. She looked over at Ferret and asked if he had a car she could use until Bino was finished with hers.

"I s'pose we can cough up something, sure."

"I'll drive you back to the station," Kincaid said.

"Actually, I wanted to swing by Rover's Bar first."

"Okay, no problem."

"And then I want to visit this schoolteacher who was Luskin's girlfriend."

"Fine."

"And pay a visit to his Cove mistress."

"Let's roll, then."

A funny look crept across her face, and Kincaid thought: *She reads you loud and clear, pal.*

"I don't need protection, Ryan." She smiled as she said it, but he detected the chilly edge in her voice.

"I didn't say you did."

"You didn't have to."

Ferret held up his hands. "Hey, time out." He looked over at Aline, smoothed a palm over his slick hair. "Don't make safety a feminist issue, Sweet Pea."

"What?" She laughed.

"Turn the tables. If Ryan was on some killer's list, how would you feel?"

Her mirth vanished. She glanced from Ferret to Kincaid, then walked over to the desk and closed the folder. "Let's go," she said.

9: CRUISING

I

Every city had its eyesores, the neighborhoods on which it had turned its back, thought Kincaid, and the area around the docks was Tango's.

In the gray light, the buildings looked surreal, on the verge of collapse, like sets in an old movie that had never been disassembled. Even the air here didn't smell quite right. Despite the clean sweep of rain, there was an oppressiveness about it, an almost greasy texture to it that stirred a desire to shower—and fast.

Rover's Bar fit the neighborhood. It was old and rough, the sort of place he liked to seek out when he traveled. There were maybe a dozen people at the bar when he and Aline entered, and four people shooting pool. Behind the bar, perched on a shelf in the corner, were a TV and a VCR, where a Clint Eastwood movie was showing.

"What'll it be?" asked the bartender, a short, beefy man with graying hair, a thick white mustache, and a Brooklyn accent.

"A Michelob on draft," Kincaid replied, and glanced at Aline.

"Iced tea."

"No iced tea, ma'am."

"Coffee?"

"Not after twelve."

"Water," she said. "Just water."

"Coming up."

When the man returned with their drinks, Aline, whose

mood darkened by the moment, said: "You know a man named Bob Whitley?"

"Yup." He lit a cigarette and skewed his wrinkled eyes against the smoke. "Sure do."

"Was he in here last night?"

"Why?"

She reached into her purse for her I.D. and dropped it on the counter. "Because he's dead and I want some answers, that's why."

"Dead?" The man's expression was so blank, it was as though he didn't know what the word meant. Then comprehension leaked into his face. "Bob's *dead*?"

"That's what I said. Was he here alone last night?"

"When he got here, he was alone. When he left, he was with a woman with brown hair."

"Brown? You're sure?" Kincaid asked.

"Yeah, yeah, I'm pretty sure. Sort of reddish brown hair."

"Which?" Aline snapped. "Brown or red?"

"Auburn, I guess. You know, brown hair with reddish tints to it. Like that."

"How tall?"

"Hard to say, she was wearing heels."

"How was she dressed?"

"Nothing fancy. Slacks, I think."

"Thin? Plump? What?" Kincaid asked.

"Nice body."

Aline sighed. "Nice how? Could you be a little more specific?"

"Look, Detective. We was real busy in here last night. I can usually tell you what people drink, if they're regulars, but I don't know what color their eyes are or what they're wearing. Only reason I noticed the woman at all was because she and Bob bumped into each other by the juke there, and then they came over here and started drinking. He was drinking beers and tequila before he ran into her, and then they was both drinking beers and tequila. By the time they left, he was pretty shitfaced."

"Was she?" Kincaid asked.

"No. She'd been dumping her drinks in that potted plant there, see it?"

The plant he referred to was a four-foot-high rubber tree

with leaves as muddy brown as the Amazon River. "You didn't think that was odd?"

The bartender laughed, puffed once more on his butt, stabbed it out. "Mister, people do all sorts of strange things in bars. Let 'em, that's my rule, as long as they don't make no trouble for me. The only thing I thought was kinda peculiar was that Bob wasn't with Jean, the lady he sees, and I was wonderin' if they busted up."

"About what time did they leave?" Aline asked. "Do you remember?"

"Not exactly. But it was early, I know that. Before ten."

"You said they bumped into each other at the jukebox," Kincaid went on. "What do you mean, exactly?"

The bartender pointed. "Bob was standing there punching buttons. The woman must've been on her way to or from the rest room. They bumped into each other."

Or she bumped him from behind. Not exactly an original way to meet the man you've marked, Kincaid thought, but what the hell. It had worked.

"Did you notice anything at all about her besides the color of her hair and that she had a nice body?" Aline's voice quivered with annoyance.

"She wasn't wearing no wedding band, no jewelry at all on her hands."

"Did you happen to see what kind of car she was driving?"

"No."

Aline looked over at Kincaid and flicked her damp hair off her shoulder. "I guess that about wraps it up here, huh," and she tipped her glass of water to her mouth, drained it, and walked toward the door.

Kincaid remained where he was. His glass was still half full; no sense in wasting it just because Aline was pissed at the world. "What's *her* problem?" the bartender grumbled, gazing after Aline.

"Bad day. Whitley's body was just found this morning."

The man shook his head and leaned into the bar. "Back when I first came here, in 1945, this island was paradise, my friend, paradise. The bridge to Key West hadn't been built yet, the town just had a couple of stores, and there was hardly any houses at this end. Pirate's Cove was just a bunch of weekend places, with a little harbor that had maybe two dozen slips. Now look at the place, will you? Tourists pouring in here every day, so much traffic it takes a man nearly an hour to get from end to end, a loaf of bread costs nearly three bucks, and our water and electricity cost more than anywhere else in South Florida. On top of it, we got murder. Hell, up till 1952, there had never even *been* a murder here.''

The lament was a familiar one, and for the most part, true. And because there was rarely anything that could be added to or argued with in this kind of truth, Kincaid merely nodded. "That's progress. How much for the draft?"

"Two bucks."

"For a *draft*? C'mon."

The bartender smiled. "Like you said, friend. Progress." Kincaid dropped two bills on the bar and left.

2

"Pull around back, Kincaid."

"Aye-aye."

Aline detected annoyance in his voice, and hey, who could blame him? "I'm in a lousy mood, Ryan. I don't mean to take it out on you."

"New Zealand, Al. When things get bad, think about New Zealand."

"I can't even *afford* a trip to New Zealand, so what's the point in thinking about it?"

"We each just cleared over a thousand bucks on a three-fifty investment. Two more of those and we'll have air fare. Three more and we'll have food and part of our lodging."

She laughed. She felt as if the lid of her gloom had been blown off by Kincaid's weird optimism, and the effluvium was hissing into the rainy air.

Kincaid poked the Saab into a tight parking space in the employee lot behind the high school, reached into the back-seat for an umbrella, and passed it to her. "I'll wait."

"Okay. If she's in class, I'll get her called out."

"Hey, Al. One more thing. That crack you made about what's the point of thinking about New Zealand if you can't afford it?'' He clicked his tongue against the back of his teeth. ''That's negative programming.''

''It's a fact, Kincaid. At this point in time, I *can't* afford the trip, and it seems stupid to think about it until I've got the money.''

''That's what I mean. Subconsciously, you've already set yourself up for failure in advance.''

What an absurd place for a conversation like this, she thought, and all because she'd just been stating a fact. ''Oh, c'mon.''

If you repeated something enough times, he said, your subconscious began to accept it as true and acted accordingly. People tended to draw experiences to themselves that reflected what they believed. She supposed it made sense *if* you bought Kincaid's premise that everything began with the mind. It was an eighties version of Descartes' adage, ''I think, therefore, I am,'' but with a New Age twist. It reminded her of the children's story, The Little Engine that Could, in which a small red train engine struggled valiantly to chug up a steep hill, huffing and puffing, ''I think I can, I think I can.'' Its power ebbed until it changed the chant to ''I know I can, I know I can,'' and then it sped up the hill to the crest. That was the moral of Kincaid's lecture.

''What's this discourse *really* about?''

He scratched at his beard. ''It's about finding a killer.''

''Program for success, right?'' She smiled.

''Now you've got it.''

''Kincaid, finding a lunatic isn't even remotely similar to telling yourself you'll win enough money on the horses or jai alai to go to New Zealand.''

He sighed. ''It is if you believe it is.''

Belief is everything: why not? She had nothing to lose.

Kincaid was right: Louisa Almott really did look like an Iowa farm girl. *A nice body*, as the bartender had put it: yes, she definitely had that. And she was pretty in a rural sort of way—pink cheeks, lashes so thick they'd probably never been touched by mascara, an oddly sensuous mouth. Even her hands were a farm girl's hands—square, strong, with sensible nails. The only thing that didn't fit the farm girl image was that she was smoking—a Marlboro Light, Aline noted.

They were in the teachers' lounge, which was empty. It

was her free period, and there were papers spread out in front of her, her grade book was open, a red pencil rested over her ear. She was more cooperative with Aline than she had been with Kincaid, but kept glancing at the clock on the wall, obviously resenting the intrusion into her free period.

". . . I don't know that there's a whole lot to say about Jimmy Ray and me, Detective Scott. That was a long time ago."

She said it as if "long" meant several decades.

"Did you correspond after he went to prison?"

"Yes." Her gaze dropped to her cigarette, whose tip she rolled against the inside rim of the ashtray. "Up until he was executed, but not on any regular basis, really."

"How often, would you say?"

Her eyes flicked to Aline again. "I guess I'm a little unclear on what Jimmy Ray has to do with anything, Detective Scott. He's dead."

"And so are some people who helped put him on death row. Judge Michael and his family and another man. You *do* read the papers, don't you?"

She smiled, but it was no farm girl smile. It was tight, a little ugly. "Of course I read the papers. But just because the judge and his family were killed, why would I automatically associate that with Jimmy Ray?"

"Where were you the night of February second, Ms. Almott? And where were you last night?"

She did the unexpected: she laughed. It was a quick sound, light, fluted, almost mocking, the way Aline imagined that an elf would laugh. "I can't believe this. Am I a suspect just because I was involved with Jimmy Ray? Jesus, if that's true, then law enforcement is *really* in bigger trouble than I thought."

"Jimmy Ray is *the* connection between the judge and the man who was killed last night. Now just tell me where you were on the second between, oh, seven and eleven, and last night between eight and one this morning." She didn't know what time Whitley had been killed, but judging from what the bartender had said and the time Jean Stills had called him, this range seemed safe enough.

Almott dug in her purse and brought out a brown appointment book. She flipped through the pages and stopped on February 2. "Okay. Here we go. I was at school until four.

I picked up my dry cleaning on the way home and I came back here around seven that evening for parent-teacher conferences, and I think I got home about the same time The Tonight Show came on.''

"You can prove that?"

"Ask in the office, Detective Scott."

It bothered Aline that everything on the second was spelled out in the appointment book in a neat little list. Almost intentional, she thought. "And last night?" *C'mon, let's see the entry for yesterday, Ms. Almott.*

"It was a school night. I graded papers for a while and went to bed early."

"What's your blood type, Ms. Almott?"

"This is absurd," she burst out. "Now, unless you've got a warrant for my arrest, Detective, then please excuse me. I've got a ton of papers to grade before my next period."

"I thought you graded papers last night."

Exasperation leaked into her voice. "I did. These are different papers."

"Tell me something. Were you in love with Jimmy Ray?"

"That's really none of your business. But yeah, I was. So was that glitzy mistress of his up in the Cove. Have you talked to her? To Sheila Reiner? You *do* know about Sheila, don't you, Detective?"

Farm-girl wrath: this is what it looks like. This was the sort of anger that would wring a chicken's neck if it didn't lay its quota of eggs. *Vengeful.* "Yes, I know about Ms. Reiner. Is there anyone else I should know about?"

"Yeah. Lenore Luskin, Jimmy Ray's sister. Everything that happened to him, everything he did, was her fault. From the time he was twelve until the night he killed her, she corrupted him, twisted him."

"But you loved him, right? So he must've had some redeeming quality?"

"He was good to me." She uttered it so simply, that at first Aline thought it must've been a line she'd heard in a movie or read in a book. *Bring on the violins. Make we weep.* But as the seconds ticked by, she realized the words were sincere. They hinted at a dark underside to the woman's life, some event in childhood, perhaps, that had irrevocably scarred her, left her vulnerable to someone like Luskin.

"Good to you how?"

"He cared."

"Even though he was seeing someone else."

"What's that got to do with caring?"

Aline ignored the question and asked her again what her blood type was.

Almott sighed and lit another cigarette, even though the one in the ashtray hadn't burned out yet. "It's O. I'm the universal donor. That's what we O's are."

Aline smiled. *I believe, Kincaid, I believe.* "I've taken up enough of your time. Don't leave the island, Ms. Almott, until you check with me first."

She laughed—that same elfin laugh. "Oh, brother, you must watch a lot of detective movies."

The remark struck Aline the wrong way and became just one more thing she found offensive about this woman. She leaned into the table, narrowing the space between them. "You leave without notifying me first and you're busted, lady. That's a promise."

Louisa Almott regarded her with those implacable dark eyes, those Iowa farm-girl eyes. The corners of her mouth twitched into a small, triumphant smile that said she knew she'd gotten to Aline and it was a very satisfying feeling, yes, indeed, it had made her day.

In the office, Aline inquired about the parent-teacher conferences on the second. Yes, said the principal's secretary, there had been conferences that night. When she checked Almott's schedule, however, her last appointment was at 7:45, and most of the meetings lasted only fifteen minutes. Were the teachers allowed to leave once they'd finished their appointments? No, the secretary said, they were supposed to stay at school until eleven. But was it possible to leave without anyone knowing? Well, yes, the secretary hemmed, no one signed in or out, because the principal assumed all of the teachers were professionals, and so on.

Thank you very much, Aline told her with a wide, bright smile. That was all she needed to know.

The Saab sped through the Tango hills, negotiating the tight twists, the turns, the wet road with obscene ease. It hummed, it didn't chug like her Honda, and the wipers whipped efficiently back and forth, back and forth, in a clean, even rhythm. If they won any more of the bets they placed with Ferret, she thought, common sense said she should spend the money on a down payment for a new car, not blow it on a trip to New Zealand. But there was a part of her that said to hell with common sense, she needed a vacation to someplace *very* distant from Tango, someplace exotic. *Sheep and volcanos. Towns with names like Christchurch and Auckland.*

Christchurch: what kind of name was that for a town? Was it on the north island or the south? *Does it matter?*

"Yeah, it matters," she muttered. "I believe. I believe. I believe."

She downshifted into third as the road dipped, and at the bottom of the hill, coasted into the downtown area of Pirate's Cove—what little of it there was, anyway. Expensive boutiques, shops that equaled those on Worth Avenue or Rodeo Drive, and lots of classy cars idling at the curbs, chauffeurs at the wheels.

At the stop light, she glanced at Sheila Reiner's address, which Kincaid had jotted on a slip of paper. He'd offered to pick up her car at Ferret's garage, so she'd dropped him there when they'd left the school. The move, she suspected, was Kincaid's way of telling her he knew she could take care of herself and that contrary to what she thought, he hadn't been trying to *protect* her.

To guard, to shield, to defend: no matter how you defined the word, it was associated with some degree of violence— ordinary household violence from which a mother tried to shield her child, or the larger variety, like murder. *Or revenge. This woman's out to nail you.*

She thought of Judge Michael and his family. Of Bob Whitley. She thought of

Their eyes, this looney punctured their goddamn eyes with a needle

the blood, pints and pints of it, and of Michael's slit throat, his head at such a terrible angle. She thought of

She made chopped liver of Jenny Michael

the judge's shattered eyeglasses, and suddenly jerked the wheel to the right. The Saab bounced up onto the shoulder of the road and she slammed on the brake. She turned off the engine and sat there clutching the wheel, blinking into the rain smearing like spit on the windshield, sweat beading on her upper lip, the *deliberateness* of the punctured eye and the shattered glasses and the tape recording—*she stood there recording it, for Christ's sakes*—seeping through the pores in her skin like a toxic gas.

After a moment she unhooked her fingers from the steering wheel, tendons stiff with tension, aching with it, and reached into her purse for her notepad and a pen. Her hand trembled as she fixed the pad against her thigh and scribbled:

—*Shattered glasses, rendering Henry blind*

—*Punctured eyeball while Henry still alive*

—*Mutilations to one of boys while Jenny Michael watched*

—*Killed Whitley as they were making love*

—*Showers after killings*

—*Followed Whitley, observing him, before she killed him*

—*No jimmied doors: so the Michaels either knew her or knew she was coming*

—*Dyes her pubic hair blond: does that mean we're looking for a blonde? Between 25 and 40 years old, type O blood, connected to Jimmy Ray. Who next next next*

She stared at the list, the writing lopsided, quivering, as though the words had been written by someone afflicted with a nervous disorder. She was overcome by a sense of heat, hopelessness, fear. She began to tremble. She hugged her arms to her waist, biting her lower lip, squeezing her eyes shut, her head sinking into the headrest at the back of the seat. The rain drummed on the roof of the Saab. The windows started to fog on the inside. The center of her chest burned and burned and started to ache, a fierce and terrible ache. *I'm having a heart attack.* Oh Christ, the irony. *Cop Dies of Cardiac Arrest en Route to Suspect's House. Cop Targeted by Killer Dies of Fear*: a caption to one of Molly Chapman's stories, she thought, and started to laugh.

She laughed and laughed until tears coursed down her cheeks, until her belly ached, until the laughter snatched her fear and hurled it beyond her, into the rain, the grayness. She sat there for another few minutes, listening to the tap dance of the rain, waiting for her life to pitch forward again, waiting for some internal mechanism to snap into action. It did finally, reluctantly, and she reached out and turned the key in the ignition, the skin on her back of her hands white and tight, the tendons standing out.

I'm going to beat her.

4

Aline finally caught up with Sheila Reiner at the Cove Women's Club. She didn't know what the woman looked like, but the hostess at the door pointed her out. From a distance, she could've been a clone of the three other women with whom she was playing bridge—chic, attractive, late thirties (which made her Luskin's senior by eight or ten years), a woman whose very demeanor whispered, *Money money money.*

It seemed surprising to Aline that Reiner's stint in prison hadn't made her a social pariah among the in-set in the Cove. But on the other hand, maybe it imbued her with a certain mystique, created a kind of seductive aura around her that the Cove ladies found vicariously titillating. Or perhaps it was simpler than that, nothing more than the fact that a couple of million could make you overlook a lot about a person.

Aline approached the table and stood silently for a few moments, ignored so completely by the four women that she might've been invisible. If there was one thing she couldn't abide, it was being ignored by anyone. So rather than waiting *politely*, she butted right in.

"Mrs. Reiner?"

Sheila Reiner drew her gaze slowly from her bridge game to Aline, her eyes hard with a cold disapproval that said, *Don't you hired help know your place?* "Yes, what is it?"

Fuck you, bitch, she thought, and introduced herself. "I'd like to speak to you for a few minutes."

That word, "Detective," stirred the ladies from their haughty torpor. The other women all looked up at Aline; Sheila Reiner seemed to turn five shades of purple. The air felt tight and weighted, the way Aline thought air would be inside of a balloon. "Uh, certainly, Detective." Her lips cockled as she spoke, and the words came out softly, with a sibilant hiss at the end. "Count me out for this hand, ladies," Reiner managed to say with a smile, her voice less terse. "Be back in a jiffy."

She whisked past Aline, who followed her out into the hall. The moment they were free of the dining room, Reiner whipped around, her blue eyes blazing with anger. It wasn't a seething anger like Almott's; this was a rich bitch's fury, quick and heated, the equivalent of a spoiled brat's tantrum. "*That*, Detective Scott, was incredibly rude."

"Sorry, but I don't have all day, Mrs. Reiner. Where were you last night between eight and one?"

She exhaled loudly. She rolled her eyes toward the ceiling. She shifted her weight from her right foot to the left. She acted like Aline was the maid who'd just done something unforgivable like toss a bag of garbage without binding the ends tightly enough. *Go on, lady, provoke me a little more and I may slug you.*

"Christ. Last night. All right, let's see. Last night I was having dinner with a very nice gentleman named Granger Mallone. He owns the one-hundred-and-fifty-five-foot yacht now anchored at the marina. I was there from, oh, around seven I would say until"—now she smiled beautifully—"until about seven this morning."

"What's the name of his yacht?"

"My dear," she sniffed, "it's the only one-hundred-and-fifty-five-foot yacht in the marina."

"And the night of February second, Mrs. Reiner? Do you remember where you were then?"

"Do you, Detective?"

"Do I what?"

"Do you remember where you were on February second?"

"Yeah, as a matter of fact I do." *I was at home fretting about my first flying lesson.* "But I'm not a suspect in two murders, Mrs. Reiner. You are."

Her eyes narrowed. "That Ryan Kincaid fellow. He came around asking me the same question, and I'll tell you what I told him, Detective. I was home alone. And yes, I was having an affair with Jimmy Ray, and yes, I did time, and yes, it was for allegedly poisoning my husband. But like I told him, that part of my life is over, do you understand? Over. O-v-e-r."

Oh God, spare me, Aline thought. *A speller.* "Mrs. Reiner, what's your blood type?"

"Why?"

"Because we know the blood type of the woman we're looking for."

Another sigh of exasperation: "An O. I'm an O."

Terrific. It wasn't called the universal blood type for nothing, Aline thought. Fifty percent of the population in the country were type O.

"Now do you mind, Detective Scott? I have a bridge game to get back to."

So she told Sheila Reiner the same thing she had told Louisa Almott—not to leave the island without checking with her first. She was sick to death of hearing herself say it, sick of type O's, of the rain. She watched Reiner stroll back into the room with the huge windows, to her clutch of women, her bridge game.

Aline walked back outside to Kincaid's car, opened her wallet, and dug down deep inside. She brought out a joint that looked like it had been through the wash and sat there toking on it and listening to the rain.

5

The one-hundred-and-fifty-five-foot yacht Reiner had mentioned was a Chris-Craft, a beauty of a vessel with mahogany trim, chrome that gleamed even in the rain, and an interior that smacked of European drawing rooms, royalty, unimagined wealth. Aline had seen larger yachts, but never had she been inside of one so elegant.

The onboard butler showed her to a living room at the bow of the yacht to wait while he notified Mr. Mallone that she was here. Would she like anything to drink? To eat? Iced tea, she said, would be great. Herbal tea? Yes, yes, wonderful. He walked over to the bar trimmed in brass and prepared a glass of Chinese tea for her. Mr. Mallone, he said, was a big tea drinker and had an impressive collection of teas from all over the world. One of the Chinese teas was his personal favorite, a gift from Chiang Kai-shek, who Mr. Mallone had met during a trip to Taiwan in the early seventies.

"What is it, exactly, that Mr. Mallone does?" she asked.

"Does?"

"His work."

"He's retired from the diplomatic corps." While the tea steeped, the butler went to fetch Mallone.

She'd expected a man who was a cross between Luskin, the lowlife, and Reiner's dead husband, the wealthy businessman. But the man who entered the room a few minutes later was a different breed altogether. He was tall, sinewy, white-haired, and dressed like a character out of *The Good Earth*. He might've been fifty or a hundred and fifty. He was soft-spoken and polite to a fault, pressing his palms together as he gave a small bow. Then he gestured to the sitting area near the window and the butler brought them tea—iced tea for Aline and hot tea for Mallone.

He drew his legs up into a yoga position that would've had her muscles screaming in seconds. "How may I help you, Detective?"

"I'm trying to verify an alibi for Sheila Reiner, Mr. Mallone. I understand she was here with you until seven this morning, is that right?"

"She was here last night, but I'm afraid I didn't see her after, oh, nine or ten o'clock in the evening."

"Then she didn't stay?"

"Her room was slept in, so she definitely stayed. I just can't vouch for what time she left."

Aline frowned. She'd been under the impression that Reiner and Mallone were lovers. "I thought . . . I mean . . ."

Mallone suddenly laughed. "Ah, I see Sheila didn't explain what our relationship is. I instruct her in yoga and meditation. Once or twice a week we meet here for several hours, and after I retire, she practices on her own, and is free to use my library and the other facilities onboard. She comes and goes as she pleases."

"Would your butler know when she left?"

He called the man into the room. "Carl, do you know when Mrs. Reiner left the yacht?"

"She was at breakfast this morning and left shortly after that."

"Would it be possible for her to leave the boat and then come back without your knowing it?"

"Of course."

She thanked Mallone for his time and started to get up, but he said, "What is this all about, Detective?"

She told him.

Mallone untangled his legs; his slippered feet sighed as they touched the floor. "The old Sheila is dead, Detective Scott. The woman she is now is incapable of murder. Believe me."

"Prison rarely changes people *that* much, Mr. Mallone."

"I'm not referring to prison. I'm referring to an elevation in Sheila's consciousness."

From murderess to disciple. "Well, thanks again, Mr. Mallone." She appreciated his opinion, but she just wasn't buying it.

10: CLOSE CALL

I

Kincaid hadn't intended to come out this way. But once he was on the Old Post Road, test-driving Aline's Honda, he just kept on going, moving steadily toward the northeast tip where the old Luskin homestead was.

The rain had finally let up, and the dusky light gleamed against the dampness of everything. The road looked lacquered, and the verdant pines that rose on either side of him sparkled like Christmas trees. The windows were down, and the clean, sweet scent of the woods wafted through the car. It reminded him of another island, Chiloé, off the coast of Chile, where the air smelled sweet enough to bring an ache to your chest.

Kincaid felt a sudden nostalgia for the place, for the color of the sky there, for the simplicity of the life. He longed to stand on the Ancúd beach at dusk, watching fishermen haul their day's catch into shore in huge nets. He thought of the kid who'd come up to him, lopped off the top of a sea urchin, squeezed lemon juice over it, and held it out for a taste. The stuff inside was the color of melons, soft and sweet. Kincaid could still taste it. He could still see the rolling green hills where sheep grazed, the cobblestone streets, and the harbor that was supposedly haunted by a ghost ship called the *Caleuche*. He thought of the fog, of the legends of mermaids, of himself and Aline traveling by bus to one of the smaller towns where everyone drove old American cars and wanted to know if it was true that all gringos were rich.

But most of all, Kincaid thought about how the worst crime

in Ancúd, the largest town, was the occasional theft of a chicken or a rickety fishing boat. Murder was virtually unheard of. An anomaly.

This time he had no trouble finding the turnoff for the old Luskin homestead. The melaleuca, pine, and ficus trees through here were so tall, so thick, that over the years the continual buffeting by the wind had bent many of them in over the road. Branches had knitted together, creating a canopy of green that blocked out what little light remained. The Honda putted through the aphotic gloom, bouncing over potholes in the muddy road. Twice, the tires spun for purchase and he had to shift into reverse and drive along the edge of the trees, where the wet ground was blanketed with leaves and pine needles.

The headlights swam against the tree trunks and struck puddles of water. Spectral shapes shifted amorphously across the windshield. Water dripped from the branches. He turned on the wipers, but all they did was smear the grime that had accumulated on the glass. Once, through the branches, he thought he glimpsed a flicker of light in the direction of the old house. But there were no street lamps out here, no houses, and he figured it must've been the reflection of his headlights against the dripping branches.

He was relieved when he finally came into the tiny clearing. But the moment he turned off the engine and killed the headlights, the blackness pressed in around him. His relief gave way to a thick, grumous unease. Crickets chirred in the stillness. Something rustled in the brush to his left. The Honda's door squeaked as he opened it and stepped out. The moon hadn't risen yet, and clouds hid the stars. The unrelieved blackness disoriented him. He looked toward the house, barely able to make out its shape in the dark. His eyes skipped across the trees and brush at either side of it.

Something's not right. . . .

The back of his neck prickled, the surface of his skin bristled and itched, as if he'd stumbled into a nest of ants. He was being watched. He felt the eyes, zeroing in on him, impaling him, but didn't know if they were animal or human. They watched, these eyes, as he crouched and fished for the flashlight under the driver's seat. They watched as he quietly shut the Honda's door and moved around the back of the car.

He suddenly wished he had his gun, but it was in the Saab's glove compartment.

Kincaid paused at the rear of the car, leaned into it, and shut his eyes for a moment. He cleared his head. He took deep, even breaths, first through one nostril, then the other, then both. He continued the breathing until he heard that internal click that meant his mind had shifted into a kind of hyper-alertness. The pores in his skin opened like craters; along his arms and across his palms, the flesh tingled, sensitized to the slightest change in the air. Adrenaline poured into the muscles of his legs. He moved toward the old house, gripping the flashlight in his right hand but not turning it on. His vision had adjusted to the dark, and he moved through it as if through his element, certain now that the eyes watching him were human.

It's her. She's here.

(Then where's her car?)

Hidden, like she is.

His arrival had surprised her. Trapped her.

At the foot of the front stairs, Kincaid paused, listening. The crickets had stopped their relentness chirring. The only sound was the rush of water through the rainpipe at the side of the house. The steps creaked as he ascended. He switched on the flashlight and let the beam slide across the front door. It stood partially ajar, a wedge of thick blackness that yawned at him. He turned off the flashlight and stood to the right of the door, back against the wall, listening again. He heard another sound now, a clawing, a scratching. If it was a rodent, then it was a mighty *big* rodent, he thought, and slid around the doorjamb, into the black. The clawing was coming from the back of the house. *In the bedroom.*

Kincaid crept farther into the dark, testing the floor to make sure it didn't creak before he put his full weight on it. The clawing sound continued, and just as he decided that maybe it *was* a rodent, a crash reverberated in the silence. *The planks over the bedroom window: she got them loose.* He tore into the bedroom, and just as he burst through the doorway, he made out a figure shimmying through the torn screen.

A woman.

He lunged toward the window.

She didn't stop, didn't look back, and vanished through the hole seconds before Kincaid reached it. He heard her grunt as she smacked the ground, and then she was up and racing into the dark. He scrambled through the window and crashed into the trees after her. For a few moments he could hear her running—the sharp snap of twigs under her feet, the crackle of dry leaves. But he couldn't tell in which direction she was moving because sound echoed in the tunnel of trees. He stopped, backing up to a tree trunk, his senses straining for the slightest noise.

There was nothing except the hoot of an owl.

She stopped. She's listening, just like I am.

Kincaid let his eyes close, started the deep breathing again, cleared his mind, and tried to focus on her, to get a fix on her. *She's close.* He could feel her presence, could feel her as though an invisible wire connected them in the dark. Her propinquity to where he was caused a tingling sensation along his arms again. The skin across the back of his neck tightened even as he stood there, as though the flesh were flash-drying in an August sun and about to crack. He barely breathed. He blinked, squinted his eyes, trying to penetrate the absolute pitch-black of the air. He lifted his hand to rub at his neck, and his elbow creaked like a rusted hinge. The noise, quick and soft as it was, seemed to ring out in the stillness. He knew she'd heard it. He sensed that she was moving, but didn't know if it was away from him or toward him.

Kincaid clutched the flashlight more tightly in his right hand and turned his head slowly to the right, then the left. He stepped away from the protection of the tree, leaving his back exposed, and sidled to the right, his footfalls silent, his heart thudding.

He felt a ripple in the air. As he spun, he glimpsed a dark shape rushing toward him, and then something cold and sharp lanced through his windbreaker, his shirt, and ripped into his upper shoulder. The pain was sudden, intense, and white-hot. It oozed and throbbed from his shoulder to his arm, zipping back and forth, up and down, deeper and deeper. It robbed him of breath, but not of consciousness, and his right leg shot out, struck home, and he heard the woman gasp. Something whistled past his ear. *The knife, Jesus, she still has the knife.* He feinted. It was so dark he could barely see two inches in front of him, but he swung blindly with the flashlight and hit something. The flashlight flew from his hand, the woman cried out, a muffled cry, and Kincaid whipped left, toward the sound. But it was too late, she barreled into him like a tsunami, like a collapsing wall, knocking him to the ground.

He landed on his wounded shoulder and nearly passed out from the pain. Black dots exploded inside his eyes. He lay there for a moment, trying to catch his breath, his cheek flat against the leaves. The deep, pervasive smell of the earth and the stink of his own blood thickened in his nostrils. He heard her sprinting through the trees, fleeing. He tried to scramble to his feet to follow her, but he was already weak and lightheaded from loss of blood, and barely had the energy to sit up.

It was another few seconds before he could get to his feet. Blood seeped through his windbreaker and oozed down the inside of his arm. As he made his way carefully back through the trees and the Honda, he heard the screech of a car in the distance and knew it was her.

By the time he reached the Honda, his arm was throbbing terribly. Fortunately, he'd left the key in the ignition. He used it to unlock the trunk and dug out the first-aid kit Aline carried in the back. Once, a long time ago, he'd poked fun at her for carrying the damn thing. *Just shows what* you *know, asshole.*

Inside the car, he peeled off the windbreaker, and oh sweet Christ, did it hurt. He turned on the light, grimaced when he saw that the sleeve of his shirt was soaked in blood, and set the first-aid kit on the dash. He removed the items he needed, then began cutting away his sleeve. There was too much blood to tell how deep the wound was, but he didn't think it had damaged any muscles because he could still move his arm.

He soaked a sterile pad in hydrogen peroxide and pressed it against his shoulder. The stuff fizzed, and a second later it started to sting, and then it burned so badly it felt like someone was holding a branding iron against it. He finally tipped the bottle to it and just poured the peroxide directly into the wound. His eyes teared. He bit down hard on his lip to keep from crying out and finally just opened his mouth and bellowed.

With the blood cleaned away momentarily, he could see how deep the gouge was. He nearly puked. He quickly ripped open the package of gauze with his teeth. The bleeding was from damaged veins, he thought, not an artery, but unless he did something to stem it, he'd be unconscious before he made it to the hospital. *Where's the pressure point for venous bleeding? Think, man. C'mon.* He struggled through the fuzz that was rapidly impinging on his consciousness, and started wrapping the gauze around the wound. A part of his mind detached and fluttered back to Kathmandu, to a woman he'd met there, a local healer.

Kincaid could see her soft, round Oriental face, her long black hair, the impossible white of her skin. He could even hear her mellifluous voice, speaking to him quietly, patiently, as though he were a small, ignorant child.

The pressure points for arterial and venous bleeding are exactly the same, only on opposite sides of the body, Ryan. She lifted her shirt then, drawing it off over the head, so she was naked from the waist up. She lifted her right arm and touched her fingertip to a spot just under it. *Against the highest rib in the armpit is the pressure point for bleeding. Right side for venous bleeding, left for arterial. Moderate finger probe.*

Kincaid tied the gauze tightly enough to keep it on, but kept it loose enough so circulation in his arm wouldn't be cut off. He took the remainder of the roll of gauze, placed it over the pressure point above the highest rib, and held it in place by lowering his arm. He started the car but had trouble shifting, because when he moved, the wad of gauze slipped a little. He got the Honda pointed in the right direction, shifted into second, readjusted the gauze, and pressed his foot against the accelerator.

Okay, you piece-of-shit car. Get me back to Tango.

2

There was very little traffic on this stretch of the Old Post Road. Most of the cars coming over the bridge from Key West turned south, toward town. Normally, Kincaid liked the road for that very reason. But tonight he would've welcomed the sight of traffic. A scythe of clouds covered the slivered moon, so it was almost as dark here as it had been in the woods.

He put on the brights, but they struck the sides of the steep hills and diminished his visibility.

Easy does it, Kincaid. Go slow, real slow.

At first he kept the Honda in third gear, rather than shifting every time he hit a perilous twist in the road. But at one point the car skidded on the wet asphalt and he slammed the gear into second, tapping the brake lightly, and the wad of gauze slipped out from under his arm. It was another three hundred yards before he could pull onto the shoulder to fix it, and by then the bleeding had started again.

The spot where he'd stopped was on the inside of a curve, about fifty feet above a precipice that ended on a carpet of rocky beach. He could hear the hiss and pound of the surf breaking over the rocks as he adjusted the pad of gauze under his arm once more. The smell of blood and sweat that rose from his skin was bad enough to choke a horse, and he was still weak and dizzy. But it wasn't much farther to the turnoff for town, and after that it'd be a breeze. He no longer thought he would bleed to death, but this would be the last time he ventured anywhere without a weapon.

Headlights suddenly burst through the rear window. Kincaid glanced in the side mirror. Some jerk with his brights on was speeding toward him, rounding the bend at what looked like 60 miles an hour or faster. Kincaid skewed his eyes against the brightness, waiting for the driver to make the turn. But he didn't. The car was headed straight toward him.

He threw open the door and leaped from the Honda, his long legs gobbling up the dirt between the road and the edge of the precipice. His head jerked around once to see how close the car was. It was almost on top of him. The bright headlights impaled him. The only thing that registered was the height of the headlights from the ground. A jeep, he thought, or a van, something that sat higher off the ground than a car. Then he was sliding over the lip of the cliff, his feet scrambling for purchase, knocking loose rocks and pebbles. He clawed at tufts of grass and sea oats to stop himself, dug in the heels of his running shoes, saw the dark waters rising toward him, and there, the black shapes of jagged rocks that would chew him to bits.

His heels slammed into a rocky ledge, and he tottered for an instant, weaving like a drunk thirty-some-odd feet above the rocks. He sank the fingers of one hand into the dirt and grabbed hold of a prickly bush with the other and held on.

Above him, there was a tremendous crash, and a moment later Aline's Honda sailed over the edge of the precipice. Its headlights arched through the black, winking on and off. For the space of a single breath, it seemed to hover, suspended like some antediluvian bird, and then it dipped forward and dived into the jagged rocks, exploding on impact.

A ball of fire flew upward. Tongues of flames clawed at the air, lighting up the water, the beach, the side of the hill where Kincaid clung like a spider. Plumes of greasy smoke whooshed past the flames, drawing them up in a chute, higher and higher. The smoke stung his eyes, making them tear, and he could feel the heat of the flames as he pressed back against the hill, an arm flung across his face. He started to cough. He could barely breathe.

He moved his right foot along the rocky ledge, testing it, then his left, then he was inching steadily to the right, away from the fire, the smoke, around the curve in the hill. When the ledge ended, he was far enough away to draw fresh air into his lungs. He smelled smoke on his clothes, in his hair, smoke mixed with sweat and blood and a fear that had struck him to the bone.

He turned his head slowly to the left, looking for a way back up the hill. The saffron light washed across its jagged face. He could see the path his heels had cut through it, the torn clumps of brush and sea oats. He might've made it up if he'd had the use of both arms and hadn't lost so much blood. But Kincaid knew his limitations; Rambo he was not.

For what seemed a long time, but couldn't have been more than a few minutes, he peered below at the flames and smoke still leaping from the ruins of Aline's Honda and lost himself in them. A part of him seemed to rise up, up above the lip of the precipice, seeking the perpetrator, shouting for help. When his mind clicked forward again, his left foot was slipping, a rock was rolling down the incline, and he had to slide another inch to his right to keep from falling.

Then he heard the shriek of tires in the distance and closed his eyes, waiting, holding his throbbing arm against him, praying it wasn't her again. If it was, he would be dead.

Believe, he heard himself telling Aline, and he started to laugh, but it hurt too much. *You cracked a rib: good going.*

Another rock worked loose.

He listened to it tumble down the hill.

He was now at the very end of the ledge. The only place to go was down. *Please don't let it be her.*

Thirty feet down.

Could he survive a fall of thirty feet?

Yeah, no problem if there was something soft at the end. Spongy sand. Rocks made of cotton. Water.

He nearly laughed again, but caught himself.

Don't burp, don't sneeze, don't even scratch your goddamn nose. . . .

Once, in Santiago, he'd gotten caught in the middle of a street battle between Pinochet's henchmen and a group of dissident students. He'd flattened himself against a wall, try-ing to make himself invisible as bullets whistled past him, as rocks sailed around him, as a man bleeding from the head had fallen at his feet. Panic bloomed in his gut, brighter than a new penny, and seconds before it erupted, he inched into a doorway and started deep breathing. It had kept him from doing something stupid, like bolting for cover, and had saved his life.

Deep breaths. C'mon. Deep, even breaths even if it hurts, even if it feels like your chest is on fire. Inhale: one . . . two . . . three. . . . Exhale: one . . . two. . . . Good, keep the rhythm going, that's right. . . . Nice, even breaths. . . .

After a while, the breathing worked its magic. The throb-bing in his shoulder diminished some, the ache in his side wasn't nearly as bad, and his fear had receded, shrunk to a tiny, hard ball, a marble that rolled around the edge of his mind.

A van or a jeep, some sort of vehicle that sits higher off the ground than a normal car.

He heard brakes now, nearly on top of him. He could see the reflection of headlights. *It's her, oh Christ, it's her.* He tried to hunker down, tried to press back into the shadows, but there wasn't room. He craned his neck, struggling to see something over the lip of the cliff, but he nearly lost his bal-ance.

She sees well in the dark.

He heard someone shouting. *Her. Jesus. It's her.*

He squeezed his eyes shut. *She knows those woods. She was waiting for me.*

"Hey! Hold on, buddy. We'll get you outa there!"

Not her. Christ oh christ, hurry.

A man's face appeared over the edge of the precipice. Kincaid shouted back; the beam of a flashlight struck him, warmed him. He nearly wept with relief.

She thought Aline was in the Honda.

PART TWO

11: OMENS

1

Everything about Lloyd Watkins, thought Aline, said he was an attorney: his clothes—casual, because today was Saturday, but expensive nonetheless—his dark good looks, the shiny Mercedes he drove. It was inherent in the way he moved, the tone of his voice, the things he spoke about. He wore his profession like a medal of honor, and Aline found it somewhat nauseating. But despite that, she liked him, and liked him best at moments like now, when he shucked his *I am a lawyer* routine and was simply himself.

They were sitting in a back booth at the Tango Café, finishing up breakfast, and Watkins—who had prosecuted Jimmy Ray Luskin—was telling her about his vacation out west. ". . . so here we were in East Podunk, Utah, Allie, on a road so empty it was like everyone in the state but Samantha and I had died. I've got no jack in the rental car and a tire so flat it's concave. But hey, no reason to get uptight, right? We've got a bottle of Scotch, a cooler filled with mixers and food. So we made ourselves a great little dinner there by the side of the road and waited a couple of hours. Sure enough, a trucker eventually comes by. The moral of the story is patience. That's what I learned on my vacation." He sat back, and his smile slid into gloom. "And now that I'm back, it's gone."

"Well, this may try it a little more. I guess you know about Judge Michael and his family?"

"One of my partners called me out in Utah with the news. Is it your case?"

Aline picked her way through the murder of the dock worker and then moved farther back in time to Jimmy Ray Luskin again. Watkins didn't interrupt. The frown between his bushy brows deepened. When she was finished, he asked if she'd talked to everyone else connected with the case.

"Two of the jurors are no longer living on Tango. Claudia Bernelli and I split the other names. With you crossed off my list, I've got two more to go. One of the jurors and Vic Xaphes."

The corner of his mouth turned down at the mention of Xaphes. "That horse's ass should never have defended Luskin in the first place. When was the dock worker killed?"

"A little over two weeks ago. Nothing's happened since."

"And the girl? Has she remembered anything?"

"Nope. She's at a safe house now. We've got two suspects, Lloyd. Sheila Reiner—formerly of Broward Correctional Institution, where she did five years on ten for poisoning her hubby—who was Luskin's mistress, and—"

"Yeah, I remember her," he interrupted. "I bet the other one is Louisa Almott, right? Luskin's girlfriend?"

"Yes."

"I cross-examined her. I wanted to cross-examine the Reiner woman, too, but Judge Michael ruled against me on that one—much to Xaphes's relief, I think."

"There's something else." Aline told him what had happened to Kincaid.

The furrow between Watkins's eyes deepened. "Is Ryan okay?"

"He is now. But he had to have about twenty stitches in his shoulder."

"I don't suppose anything was left of your Honda."

She laughed. "Hardly. The insurance company is paying for a rental until we settle. The car was old, though, so I doubt I'm going to get much out of it."

"So what're you suggesting I do, Aline? What precautions should I take?"

"I don't really know, except"—she smiled—"don't go home with any strange women."

"If I did, the woman would have more to worry about from Samantha than from me," he said with a laugh. "My wife would quarter her. As far as security measures at the house, we've got an alarm system, I keep a weapon in the nightstand,

and our Doberman would rip apart anyone he didn't know."
He shrugged. "Part of the reason I got out of prosecution
was because prosecutors are so damn unpopular."

"Look, Lloyd, all I'm saying is keep your eyes open, okay?
And the same goes for your wife."

"Right." He sat forward, his thick fingers curled around
his coffee cup. "You know, of all the cases I was assigned to
in the prosecutor's office, it figures that Luskin would be the
one to come back and haunt me. We had some real scum
come through the courts during those years, but Luskin was
star scum, Aline. He was shit through and through."

"Hey, I arrested him, remember? You don't have to convince me."

"The shrink on the case thought differently. He blamed
Luskin's personality on his environment—namely his sister."
Watkins gave an indignant snort. "Environment, my ass. It
was genetic. He was born with pieces missing. That day I
cross-examined him and he lost it on the stand—I remember
thinking that I hoped to Christ I never ran into the guy in a
dark alley. Not once did he ever give any indication that he
felt remorse about what he'd done. Not once. Frankly, I
breathed a lot easier the day they pulled the switch on him."
A wry smile touched his mouth. "For all the good it did."

"Is there anything you can think of offhand about him or
his life that might point to someone other than Sheila Reiner
or the schoolteacher?"

He sat back, sipping at his coffee, his pensiveness aging
him around the eyes. "There is something, but I don't know
whether it's significant in terms of all this stuff. When Luskin
was around twelve, he and Lenore supposedly left the island
for a while. We heard about it through a street source. Supposedly they left because Lenore was pregnant and wanted
to have the baby off the island. We weren't able to verify any
of it, but if I were you, I'd ask Vic. Maybe he knows more
about it." Watkins smiled. "In fact, I'd lay a ten-spot that
he does. The only other thing you might look into is to find
out if Luskin was friendly with any of the prison employees.
Or if he corresponded with any women through the chaplain's
office at the prison. Maybe he met a prison fly, Allie."

"I already checked."

The way he'd uttered *prison fly*, as if he'd bitten into something distasteful, pretty much summed up her opinion on

prison flies—women who were attracted to or fell in love with incarcerated men. The phenomenon was surprisingly common, and Aline had heard various psychiatric explanations for it over the years. Generally, the women seemed to share certain characteristics: an inability to sustain a satisfactory relationship with a man on the outside; a need for a dominant purpose or mission in life; and romantic idealism that created a hero of the inmate, who the woman, naturally, believed was innocent of the crime for which he'd been incarcerated.

She had checked on prison flies and prison employees, and had gotten nowhere. Her calls to the warden at Florida State Prison had been transferred down the pecking order to a half-dozen employees, none of whom could tell her anything. Out of Luskin's records she'd pulled the name of his classification officer and his college tutor. The first had nothing elucidating to tell her, and the second, Joe Waldo, was no longer associated with the prison system. When she called the junior college where Waldo still worked, she was told he was on vacation in Europe and not due to return for several weeks. She had left her number and asked that he call upon his return. Dead ends, all the way down the line.

"You know how Luskin paid Xaphes, don't you?"

"Yeah, Kincaid told me. With an original Wyeth. Not bad. He said the rest of the collection was sold."

"Supposedly Lenore got a bee in her bonnet at some point and decided she needed the money."

The waitress came over and asked if they wanted refills on their coffee. Neither of them did. Watkins consulted his Rolex and said, "I should get going pretty soon. Samantha and I are taking the plane up to Miami. We thought it'd be a change of pace to spend the night in the Grove."

Watkins owned two planes—a slick twin-engine that seated six and an aerobatic number that Kincaid had coveted since he'd first laid eyes on it. "Hey, that reminds me. I heard up at the airport that you're taking lessons from Ryan."

"I just soloed a couple of days ago."

"It's great, isn't it?" And for the next ten minutes they talked shop.

It was a wonderful feeling to talk about flying as if she were already part of the same spirit that had produced Earhart, Lindbergh, and Saint Exupéry. It diminished her guilt at having spent so much of her free time in the air the last two weeks. But Kincaid had urged her to log hours in a compressed period, rather than spreading it out over several months, so she had. And always, the instant the plane lifted, her disposition improved, and things fell into their proper perspective. Some of Kincaid's irritating quirks, for instance, ceased to bother her when she was flying. It was only when she was confronted with them again on the ground that her annoyance returned.

Like this morning.

This morning she had fixed breakfast and he was supposed to clean up. But Kincaid's version of "cleaning up" consisted of rinsing the plates and leaving them in the sink, instead of putting them in the dishwasher. He didn't bother wiping off the counter, either, or sweeping the floor, both of which went along with KP. Okay, so these were small things. But when *he* cooked, which he did most evenings, and *she* cleaned up, the dishes went into the dishwasher, the counter was wiped down, the floors were swept, and most of the time she also took out the garbage.

Small things: he griped about how leftovers *always* got shoved to the back of the fridge, like it was *her* fault entirely, like she stayed up nights devising intricate plans on how to sabotage the order in the refrigerator. She usually countered that with a reminder that *he* used a clean towel every time he showered, and couldn't he please cut that number by at least half as long as she was responsible for the laundry?

He took issue with the number of books piled at random around their bed; she resented the travel posters that now covered the ceiling *over* their bed. It came to a head one night when Kincaid stubbed his toe on the foot-thick *Random House Dictionary* on the floor and threatened to put up a travel poster for every book of hers on the floor. Even though he uttered it softly, in that tight *I really don't want to argue* voice, she heard the deadly tone only Kincaid could pull off, and blew up.

In the two weeks since he'd moved in, their relationship had plunged like the stock market before a recession. In the pocket calendar where Aline had always jotted a small red L every time she and Kincaid made love, the L's had diminished lamentably, even though bed was one place besides the cockpit where they still got along well.

It could be worse, chided a small, niggling voice at the

back of her mind. *Kincaid could've died that night in the woods. He could've gone over the cliff with the Honda.*

Perspective, she thought.

As she and Watkins were leaving, they ran into Bill Prentiss and Molly. The two men already knew each other, but Aline introduced Molly to Watkins, then the four of them stood outside the café for a few minutes, talking. Or rather, three of them talked; Molly just stood there, obviously bored out of her mind. Aline sensed she and Prentiss were in the midst of an argument and that Molly was anxious to pick up where they'd left off. As usual, she was dressed fashionably.

This morning she wore an outfit Aline had priced at the Banana Republic only a week ago—$165 for khaki slacks with a matching blouse worn over a pale pink T-shirt. Not exactly *gracious* attire, but certainly suitable for Tango and definitely flattering to her particular figure. As someone—probably Bernie—had remarked, *With a body like that, who cares what her face looks like?*

Actually, contrary to what Bernie was always saying—and Bernie's opinion in relation to Molly didn't really count, because she was always bad-mouthing her—Aline thought Molly was rather pretty. She hailed from Vermont, and had that open, fresh look about her that Aline associated with people from New England. It was a snow skier's face, innocent of makeup, with a salubrious glow in her pale cheeks and a quick brightness in those huge blue eyes.

"Bored?" Aline whispered, leaning toward her.

Molly smiled, then laughed. "Yeah, I am, as a matter of fact. Hungry, too. Want to join me for coffee?"

"I just finished breakfast, but I'll keep you company till they finish."

They claimed the booth in front of the one Aline had just vacated. It made her feel like a character in an existentialist play, something similar to *No Exit* or *Waiting for Godot*. In this play she was a woman trapped forever in a café, condemned to eating eggs and home fries, paying for the meal, rising to leave, and begin accosted in the doorway by people she knew and then having to repeat the whole scene again. And again.

"We're having an argument," Molly announced as their coffee arrived, her hands sliding around the mug.

"I figured as much."

"Aline, you've known Bill most of your life. Has he always been so pigheaded?"

"About certain things, yeah."

"He's been so goddamn moody. I feel like I don't know how to talk to him anymore."

Aline nodded. It was how she'd been feeling about Kincaid the past few weeks. "Have you two moved in together?"

"No. That idea's on hold." She curled strands of her shiny, honey hair behind her ear. "It's different with you and Ryan. You've known each other a lot longer. Bill and I have only known each other six months. I think it'd be a mistake for us to move in together at this point."

Aline hadn't been aware that her living arrangements were a worthy enough item for the Tango grapevine. It irked her a little that Prentiss had apparently mentioned it to Molly, but then, why shouldn't he? *She*, after all, had told Kincaid that Prentiss and Bernie had had breakfast together a week or so ago. It was the sort of island intrigue that was tossed back and forth over meals, drinks, cards.

"It'll work out, Molly." She felt like a hypocrite saying it, because she doubted very much that anything would work out with Prentiss and Molly. She hoped, in fact, that Prentiss would get his act together and do what he should've done six months ago—pursue Bernie with a vengeance.

"I don't know. Things would have a lot better chance if my editor would take me off this goddamn story, Aline."

A small alarm shrilled in the back of Aline's mind. The story, of course. That was why Molly had suggested coffee. She was still digging for facts, prodded on fiercely, no doubt, by Chip Sonsky, the editor of the *Tribune*. "Why's Chip bothering? The last murder was two weeks ago. Nothing new has turned up."

"Wrong, Aline. He heard from one of his sources that there was a witness to the murders of the Michael family. One of the neighbors apparently saw someone being carried to the ambulance."

Aline's blood turned cold. The ubiquitous island grapevine had scored again. "I'd certainly question my source if I were Chip."

"So there isn't any witness?"

"If there were, Molly, don't you think we'd have the killer by now?"

"I hear it's a woman."

Christ, Aline thought. "Another one of Chip's sources, I suppose."

"Actually, that came from Bill. Off the record, of course," she added quickly.

"Great."

"Don't worry. I know the difference between off the record and on, Aline."   •

"But Chip might not."

"I haven't said anything to him. Right now he's relying on his sources, and usually they're pretty accurate. He did some digging on his own, too, and made a connection between Judge Michael and that dock worker. The connection is Jimmy Ray Luskin. He thinks the killer has marked everyone who was involved with the Luskin case."

I don't need this. "Really? That's fascinating. Did he mention a motive?"

"No. But his theory is that once you figure out what it's about, who gives a shit about motives?"

"Typical Sonsky. If he's so sure about everything, then why hasn't there been a story on it?"

She shrugged, and her blouse slipped off her shoulder, revealing a patch of skin smoother and whiter than a pearl, the sort of skin, Aline thought, that had never been marred by sunburn or zits. "I guess he's not so cocksure of everything, and I haven't told him anything Bill said off the record. But he still dumped the whole thing in my lap, and—"

"And then you pump Bill for information and he gets aggravated."

She flashed a charming but sheepish grin. "Yeah, something like that."

"Molly, a bit of advice. If you don't want things to fall apart with Bill, then don't ask him questions he can't answer."

She sat back, her soft, pretty hands cupping the mug again. "Yeah, I guess that about sums it up, huh."

"Yeah, I guess it does."

"But if I want to keep this job, I'm going to have to start digging at night with asshole Chip."

"Good luck."

Molly laughed. "Luck? I need more than luck when dealing with him. I mean, I asked him the same thing you just said, that if there'd been a witness to the murders, how come the cops hadn't caught the killer yet? He didn't have an answer for that, but he sure had a lot of theories."

Yeah, I'll bet. "Like what?"

"Oh, that the witness is a deaf-mute. . ."

Close.

". . . or blind . . ."

Not bad.

". . . or injured and in a coma . . ."

Getting better all the time.

". . . like that."

Just then, much to Aline's relief, Prentiss joined them. A few minutes later she was able to duck out politely, the perfidy of her conversation with Molly tagging along beside her like a shadow, a dark omen.

2

The last juror Aline had to speak to, Peg Perkins, was a social worker in her early thirties. She was a short brunette, on the chunky side, with the kind of cute, innocent face you might see advertising low sodium and high fiber. She'd been laid up with the flu since yesterday, she explained with a sneeze, when she'd returned from a three-week Christian retreat in North Carolina.

"Would you like something to drink?" she asked as they settled in a bright, sunny room at the back of her duplex.

"No, thanks. I'm fine."

Peg, clutching a small packet of Kleenex in her hand, sat at the edge of the couch, the tip of her nose a strawberry red. With her other hand, she nervously fingered the bright gold crucifix at her throat.

"Does this have something to do with those horrible murders?"

Aline nodded. "We have reason to believe that the people connected with the conviction of Jimmy Ray Luskin may be in some danger, Ms. Perkins."

She whispered, "I knew it," and sneezed again, a small,

dainty sneeze. She blew her nose. "During the retreat, I had a vision. God told me I was going to be tested."

Wonderful. She was here to talk about precautions, and this woman was talking to God. "We're asking people who were connected with the case to be cautious. We think the killer is a woman who stalks her victims first. Do you work nights?"

"Yes, sometimes."

"Then it might be a good idea to curtail the night hours for a while, if possible. Or to make sure there's always someone else in the office."

Her beatific smile was another bad omen; it hinted at divine protection—and intervention—and filled Aline with dread. "Detective Scott, my belief is that if you're right with Christ, there's nothing to be afraid of."

"That's exactly the kind of attitude that could get you killed."

"I'm sorry you feel that way. It's—"

"Listen to me, Ms. Perkins. This woman has already killed a family of four people and nearly killed a fifth person. She punctures her victims' eyes with a pin. She mutilates them. She's real. She's not a test from God, she's not something dreamed up on TV."

She looked a bit paler, which Aline thought was a good sign. At least she'd caught the woman's attention. "Have you gotten any crank calls? Anything through the mail?"

More color leaked from her face. Her thumb was now stroking the crucifix, as if to draw something from it. Strength, perhaps. "Uh, well, as a matter of fact, I got a couple of calls last night. The person never said anything, but there was this heavy breathing. I hung up."

"What kind of heavy breathing? Panting?"

"No, not exactly. It was . . ." She considered it a moment. "Well, like a wheeze."

The wheeze of a respiratory ailment, of allergies, a cold.

"Look, if *anything* at all unusual happens. Ms. Perkins, I'd like you to call me." She jotted her home number on the back of a business card. "Either one of these numbers, okay? And any time, day or night."

"All right. Sure."

The most encouraging thing Aline heard from Peg Perkins was the sharp click of the dead bolt as she left.

The county owned two cottages on the island that were ordinarily used to accommodate visiting politicians or businessmen. This was one of the few times Prentiss could remember the place being used as a safe house.

The larger of the two houses, where Renic Foreston had been staying, was located in the woods on the northeast side of Tango. It was made of Florida pine, had almost 3,000 square feet of living space, a full basement, four bedrooms, and three bathrooms—which made the word "cottage" something of a misnomer. There were only three ways to reach it—by air, by scaling the 75-foot precipice it backed up to, or by the dirt road that led to the guardhouse and the front gate.

A sergeant from vice directed Prentiss through the iron gate and onto the grounds. He swung his Mercedes into the half-moon driveway. Judging from the number of cars, it looked like a party was in progress: Bernelli's rusted MG, Dr. Barbara Stratton's rental, Carol Foreston's station wagon, and, next to it, Frank Foreston's Volvo. All for a twelve-year-old kid who was missing some vital memories.

A breeze rifled through the surrounding trees as he started up the walk. The air here smelled of salt and sea, sweeter than anything you'd find in town. Dried leaves tumbled across the gravel driveway. The song of a cardinal floated up through the branches, toward the patch of hot blue sky. A peaceful spot, better than summer camp, unless you stopped to consider why Renie Foreston was here, he thought.

Bernelli answered the door. "The good doctor. You're just in time for a Molly Ringwald movie."

He laughed. "Which one?"

Bernelli rolled her taffy eyes. "*The Breakfast Club*, what else? I've already seen it twice. It's one of Danny's favorites."

He jerked a thumb over his shoulder as he stepped into the house, and lowered his voice. "Mama and Papa Bear are both here. How'd that happen?"

"Papa Bear has to leave for Miami tonight, and he wanted to spend some time with his little girl." She touched his arm and leaned closer. "He'll be leaving soon. I hope."

Prentiss wasn't sure whether it was the scent of Bernelli's perfume or the way she leaned into him or just that when she'd answered the door it had struck him how much he genuinely liked her. But he caught her arm, stopping her before they reached the end of the hall, then touched her chin, lifted it and kissed her.

Her mouth tasted faintly of chocolate. Her lips were cool. Her tongue curled around his, and his hands slid from her shoulders to the small of her back, her tiny waist, the slender flare of her hips. He felt her heartbeat against his chest. Or maybe it was his own heart. It didn't matter. This was the first time in weeks he'd felt desire for anyone.

She stepped back, a small frown working its way between her brows. *What was that about?* asked her eyes.

"I don't know," he replied out loud.

They both laughed, and she gave his hand a quick squeeze. "C'mon, we'll miss the movie. Renie's making popcorn."

The hall led into a spacious living room with sliding glass doors that offered a breathtaking view of the sea. There was a desk that jutted out some fifteen feet over the edge of the cliff. Sunlight poured into the room, shot across the dove-gray rug, the wicker furniture, and struck the black iron banister of the spiral staircase to their right. Bernelli started down the staircase first, and Prentiss smiled at the funny sway of her hips—not a practiced sway or anything, just a Bernelli sway. She felt his eyes on her and glanced back, a hand still on the railing.

"You coming?"

"I'm admiring."

Her cheeks flushed with color, and he laughed. "It's not funny," she said. But her eyes asked, *What's with you and Molly?*

"Want to talk about it over dinner?"

"How come I get the feeling that you keep reading my mind, Bill?"

"Does that mean yes to dinner?"

"I may still be here."

"Then we'll have dinner here."

She smiled and gave the barest of nods and continued on down the stairs.

The basement was a wonderful room with cedar-paneled walls and tropical-colored furniture. It was capacious enough so you didn't notice the absence of natural light, and it would've made a great pool hall, Prentiss thought. There was a small kitchen adjoining it, as well as a half bath and a bedroom, where Carol Foreston had stayed several nights. She, her husband, and Barbara Stratton were sitting in front of the TV, chatting, the picture on hold, while Renie finished popping corn in the kitchen. Prentiss greeted everyone, poked his head into the kitchen, and said hi to Renie.

"Hey, Dr. Bill," she chirped, the freckles across the bridge of her nose seeming to slip and slide as she grinned. "I was hoping you'd show up."

"How's the corn doing?"

She wrinkled her nose. "I burned the first batch. This time I used the microwave stuff."

"Need any help?"

"Nope. Be finished in a second." She crooked a finger at him and he leaned closer. "Guess what," she whispered. "Did you know there's a secret passage in the basement bathroom, Dr. Bill?"

"No kidding. Where is it?"

She giggled. "If I told you that, it wouldn't be a secret anymore. Now go sit down, okay?"

"Righto, boss."

But before he reached the couch, Frank Foreston had gotten up and come toward him. He had a drink in his hand. The only other time Prentiss had talked to the man, he'd also been drinking. "Could I talk to you for a second, Dr. Prentiss?"

"Sure. What is it?"

They moved away from the door to the kitchen, and were far enough from the couch so the others couldn't hear them. Foreston smoothed a hand over his salt-and-pepper hair. It was longish, stylishly cut. Everything about Foreston was stylish, from his designer pastel shirt and slacks to his Rolex watch to his healthy tan. He looked as though he hailed from California, and was into exercise, sushi, and success. But then he posed his concern and Prentiss realized that even though Foreston looked like a progressive thinker, he was just a home boy at heart, hung up in the mainstream.

"Dr. Stratton would like to try hypnosis on Renie, and I was just wondering what you, uh, thought about it."

"Hypnosis isn't something I have a need for in my line of work, Mr. Foreston, but I trust Barbara's judgment."

"I understand it can be dangerous."

"Really? How?"

Foreston's expression was blank. It was the look of a man for whom the adage *a little knowledge is a dangerous thing* fit like the proverbial glove. "Well, my understanding is that it leaves you wide open for—"

"For what, Mr. Foreston?" *Possession by spirits? Mind control? What're you* really *afraid of?*

"I'm, uh, not sure. I guess what I'm trying to say is that under hypnosis, a mind can be tampered with."

"I doubt it. All hypnosis does is bypass the conscious mind. And that's where your daughter's memory block is. In her conscious mind. She's made tremendous strides in just two weeks. She's able to speak again, to function, to do schoolwork. But the block's still there. She has nightmares. She wakes up screaming. What she isn't remembering could cause her a lot of problems as she grows up. I think Dr. Stratton has your daughter's interests at heart, and the hypnosis is a good shot. Does that answer your question?"

Foreston smiled, but it wasn't very convincing. "Yeah. Yeah, I guess it does. But my wife and I would like to be there when this takes place."

"I don't see any problem with that." It was a lie; Prentiss saw the potential for *big* problems. But rather than debate the issue now, here, with Renie in the next room, he let it pass. "Now let's go watch the movie, okay?"

"That sounds like an excellent idea," Foreston said, and tipped the glass to his mouth, draining the rest of his drink.

12: SATURDAY AFTERNOON

I

The general aviation building at the Tango Key Airport had been built in the late thirties and refurbished when the Art Deco craze hit the island in the early eighties. It was blue and pink with plum trim and had large arch-shaped windows on both floors and all four sides. It was crowned by a glass bubble observation deck that provided a magnificent view of the entire airport and the hills to the west.

Most of the second floor was taken up by classrooms for ground school and offices for the several general aviation outfits and two cargo companies. The weather office was also on this floor, in a tremendous room that fascinated Kincaid because of the maps. The maps had been etched onto plexiglass panels that were mounted into the walls and lit from within.

The east wall, for instance, was a map of the U.S. that indicated general wind currents and velocities, storm systems, temperatures, and barometer readings for every major city in the country. The west wall was the same map, but divided into sections by South and Southeast, Northeast and Midwest, West, and Southwest. It gave the same information but in more detail. By tapping the appropriate code on one of the twelve computer terminals in the room you could also obtain a six-hour projected weather forecast for a particular area.

The north wall, where Kincaid was, included a detailed map of Florida, the Bahamas, the Gulf, and the Caribbean. A section of it showed an enlarged Tango Key. Here, the present weather was shown as hot and sunny, with temperatures ranging between 80 and 85, a barometer reading of 28.6, winds out of the north-northwest at a steady five knots, and visibility a perfect 15 miles. The six-hour forecast called for light showers by four P.M., with gusts up to twelve knots out of the south, visibility diminishing to three miles. From six to eight P.M., skies would be partly cloudy with winds at a steady eight knots out of the south-southeast, and temperatures in the mid-seventies.

What all of this meant to Kincaid was that from now until four, the weather would be ideal for practicing stalls and spins with Molly. He'd already had three other students today and, given his druthers, would've cancelled the lesson with Molly and taken the plane up by himself. But when he'd called the paper, she'd already left the office.

"Hey, Ryan."

He glanced up and saw Lloyd Watkins, a canvas flight bag over his shoulder, sunglasses riding on top of his head. "Lloyd, nice to see you. Looks like you're off for the weekend."

"Just to Coconut Grove. A little change of pace. I saw Aline earlier today and she filled me in on everything. Sounds like you had a pretty rough time of it there for a while."

Kincaid laughed. *Rough time:* yeah, he supposed that fit as well as anything. "A bit. I'll tell you one thing about this woman. She sees a hell of a lot better than I do in the dark. Who owns the old Luskin homestead now, do you know?"

"The county. There wasn't much left to Lenore's estate when Luskin killed her. She spent the money as fast as she earned it. As far as I know, the only thing she ever invested in was art, and she sold off most of that a long time ago. On my way over here, I was thinking about all this, and it occurred to me that you should talk to Travis Feld. He was Lenore Luskin's attorney all those years."

Feld: Xaphes had mentioned the man, too. "He's not practicing anymore, right?"

"No, he's retired. Lives in a palace up in the Cove. He's a crotchety old fart, but he probably knows as much about the Luskin family as anyone."

"Thanks, I'll make a point of talking to him."

Watkins tapped his Rolex. "I've got to get a move on. I'm already running late."

"You taking the Pitt?"

"No way I can get Samantha into it." Watkins chuckled. "She's afraid I'll trick her and do a loop or something. We're taking the twin-engine. But how about if I give you a call next week and you and I take the Pitt up?"

"Barnstorming over Tango. Now *there's* an attractive idea. That'd almost be worth having the FAA on us about it."

Watkins laughed. "My sentiments exactly."

They walked downstairs and outside together, where they parted company. Kincaid scanned the parking lot, looking for Molly, but didn't see her. She was already fifteen minutes late, which was typical. She had yet to be on time for a lesson, despite his requests to the contrary. But Molly was one of those people who evidently thought *her* time was more valuable than anyone else's. So let her wait, he thought, and started toward the Cessna, looking forward to some solitary flight time.

He untied the plane and started his preflight check. As he reached inside the cockpit and hit the master switch to check the fuel quantity indicator, however, he saw Molly through the window. She was scrambling across the parking lot from her Bronco, long hair flying behind her, purse bouncing against her hip. "Ryan," she called, waving.

He ignored her, made sure the ignition switch was off, that the fuel valve handle was on, and turned off the master switch again. He then removed the control wheel lock.

When she reached the plane, he was crouched at the front tire, checking the pressure. She was out of breath, stammered an apology, and started to give him her usual song and dance about traffic, but Kincaid stood, and his glare silenced her.

"You're twenty minutes late," he snapped.

She seemed surprised that he was angry. "Hey, I said I was sorry. There's a lot of traffic. Snarls of it."

"Yeah, and you always get caught in it."

He turned his attention to the propeller, running his hands over the blades, checking for nicks, dents, anything that might impede the airflow. She just stood there, breathing hard, watching him. He disregarded her presence and moved around to the wing, understanding completely why her relationship with Prentiss was so rife with discord. He drained a cupful of gas from the tank, inspected it for water, tossed the gas out. She followed him with small, urgent footsteps, waiting for him to tell her to finish the check, but he had no intention of letting her off the hook so easily. She finally said, "So you want me to finish the check?"

Kincaid looked over at her. She wore acid-washed denim jeans with a matching jacket, and under it, a tank top with no bra that probably had the male reporters in the newsroom salivating like rabid dogs. "What I want, Molly, is for us to understand each other. Either you're on time for our next lesson or you can find another instructor."

"It's only twenty—"

"I don't give a goddamn whether it's five minutes. I'm always here at the time we agree on, so you can be, too. And if you can't make it, then I expect a phone call at least two hours ahead of time so I can schedule another student in the slot."

She bit at the inside of her lower lip as if to keep back what she *really* wanted to say. "All right," she muttered, and opened the passenger door, tossed her purse inside, and finished the preflight without another word.

When they were in the cockpit and taxiing toward the runway, she said, "We going to practice stalls and spins?"

"If you're up to it."

"I psyched myself for it last night."

She had soloed more than a month ago, and had mastered every technique except stalls and spins. Once he signed her off on her three solo cross-country requirements and she took the written exam, she'd be done. And truthfully, he'd be glad to be rid of her. Although she was bright, learned quickly, and had an innate feeling for aviation, she was too self-absorbed. She wanted to do things her way, on her terms, even if it wasn't strictly by the book. It was an attitude that could get you into big trouble in the air.

Her takeoff was smooth as butter, and her ascent was perfect. "Okay, take her up to four thousand feet, Molly, out over the ocean. I'll do the first stall, then we'll take her up again and you do one."

"Power-off stall?"

"Yes."

"Shit."

"We don't *have* to do it. Don't force yourself."

She glanced at him, her mouth set in a hard, thin line, her

brows arched, her eyes hidden behind her sunglasses. "I never force myself to do anything, Ryan."

At 4,000 feet, Kincaid took over. He started easing back on the throttle. "We're going to do it with flaps up, and twenty degrees of bank."

"What speed does it stall at?"

"That depends on the weight, the bank, whether or not you're using flaps. With our specs, it'll stall around sixty-five. You'll feel a slight buffeting just before it stalls, and five to ten miles an hour before, you'll hear the stall horn. It'll keep blaring until the nose returns to straight and level flight."

He banked twenty degrees and pulled the throttle all the way out; the engine died. The wings started to buffet. Molly groaned. He began raising the nose. The stall horn blared. To a neophyte, it was one of the most terrifying sounds in the world, the call of death, the bellow from the void. But to Kincaid, to anyone who'd logged as many hours as he had, the sound was exhilarating. It underscored the fundamental seduction of flying: when you were up here alone, your life depended solely on your own ability.

The nose turned down. The buffeting grew stronger. The ground 4,000 feet below rushed toward them as the Cessna plunged. The stall horn kept blaring; it sounded like a sheep in excruciating pain, a bull charging full speed ahead. Gravity pressed against Kincaid's chest, plastering him to the seat. He glimpsed the swirl of blue that was sky, that was ocean, melding into a single expanse of blue. Seconds before the plane would've twisted into a spin, he nudged the throttle in and slowly brought the nose flush to the horizon, parallel to the sea. The stall horn fell silent. The propeller spun rapidly again.

"That wasn't too bad, now was it?"

Molly was absolutely white. She still clutched the edges of the seat, her eyes fixed straight ahead. She turned her head slowly, almost painfully, toward him. Her sunglasses had slipped forward on the bridge of her nose, and he could see her eyes—bright, feverish, with a sheen like sweat. He thought she was either going to puke or pass out. Instead, she smiled, clapped her hands once, loudly, and threw her head back and laughed. She reminded him of a kid who'd been scared shit-less by her first roller coaster ride and was now cruising in an adrenaline high, anxious for more.

"Again," she said breathlessly. "Let's do it again. No, let's do a spin. I want to see what a spin's like. Then I'll do both, okay? Is that okay? Can we do it that way?"

Kincaid had taught forty-nine students since he'd gotten his instructor's license, and none had ever reacted this way to a stall. Never had a student gone into a stall and then requested to do a spin. Usually, they wanted to go down, that was all, just down to hard-packed earth under their feet, back to what was known, stable, safe.

"You sure?"

She grinned. A kind of rapture swept over her face. "Yes. Now." Then she added, "Before I lose my nerve completely, Ryan."

Okay: that was something he understood.

He took them back up to 4,000 feet and put the plane into a stall. But this time, instead of pushing in the throttle to bring them out, he allowed the Cessna to begin its turn into a spin. The pressure against his chest seemed to double, triple. The wind shrieked as the plane spun toward the painted sea. Kincaid watched the altimeter, ready to retrieve the plane from the spin at 2,500 feet.

But Molly suddenly moaned, a racheting, anguished sound that burst into a scream. In his peripheral vision, her arms blurred as they jerked up, toward the control wheel. *"No!"* he shouted. "Don't touch anything!"

But her hands clutched at the wheel. She grappled with it, trying to pull it back, battling a gravitational pressure one and a half times what it usually was.

Kincaid's arm shot out, and he bore down with his thumb and index finger, pinching the exterior thoracic nerve in her neck. *The old Mr. Spock trick:* she passed out, slumping against the door.

The first flutters of terror fanned his throat. His shoulder, where the stitches had been removed only two days ago, ached fiercely. *Large pitch, small radius. Play the rudder pedals. Do not panic. Hand on throttle. Fuck oh fuck. There: steady, slow. Okay, reversing now, pressure easing up, altimeter at 1250. Christ . . . the ocean . . . just look at the ocean . . . I can see the whitecaps. . . . Nose up, good, very good. . . . Power on . . . 1800 RPM . . . 2100 . . . nice and easy.*

Kincaid leveled out at 925 feet, his insides like Jell-O, his lunch in his throat, the back of his shirt so damp with sweat it stuck to the seat. As he headed back toward the island, Molly stirred and came to. She said nothing; neither did he.

Kincaid slipped into the traffic pattern, and only when they touched down did she say anything. "I . . . I'm really sorry, Ryan. I . . . I panicked. I . . . my mind just went blank."

He nodded.

When they reached the tie-down area and he'd shut down the plane, he turned to her. "If you want to remain my student, don't ever do that again."

"I thought—"

"I know what the hell you thought. And what I'm telling you is that you could've gotten us both killed. Believe me, I wouldn't be up here if I didn't know what I was doing, and I sure as hell wouldn't be taking people up there with me if I didn't know what I was doing. You're either going to have to believe that or find another instructor."

She'd been staring at her hands, and now her head snapped up, she tilted her sunglasses back into her hair, and into the intensity of her gaze leaped an emotion so savage, Kincaid thought he was imagining it. It was that strange, feral look women sometimes got that shouted about issues like dominance and subservience, sex and power, but it was extreme, grotesque, almost a parody of itself. She opened her mouth as if to say something, then seemed to change her mind and nodded.

"You're right. You're absolutely right. It's a matter of trust, isn't it?" She smiled then, and it dispelled whatever he thought he'd seen in her face. "I've got a cross-country scheduled for next week. Could you take a look at my flight plan? Maybe at Bill's tomorrow afternoon?"

It took him a moment to remember that she and Prentiss were having a barbecue at his place tomorrow. "Okay, sure, tomorrow would be fine."

He would've preferred not dealing with it at all, but he'd come this far with her, and, despite everything, he felt an obligation to see her through to the end. "Sure, I'll take a look at it." If she heard the reluctance in his voice, she gave no indication, and a few minutes later he watched her hurrying back across the tarmac, beneath a sky that promised rain.

Aline looked down at Bernelli's lap, where she was carefully unwrapping a Big Mac with everything on it. The goop dripping and sliding from the bun was nauseating. "Are you really going to eat that?"

Bernelli licked at her fingers as she looked up. "Any reason I shouldn't?"

"Yeah. High sodium, high chemical and preservative content, and no telling what's in that disgusting stuff oozing out of it."

"God, Al, sometimes you're such a killjoy." She brought the bun to her mouth and bit into it, smacking her lips for effect. "Hmm. Delicious. Really. Want a bite?" She held it out, and several drops of goop plopped against the seat. "Oops." Bernie swiped at it with her napkin.

"I'll pass, thanks."

"A French fry, then, Al. McDonald's has terrific French fries."

The fries, jammed into a little container, glistened with grease and were so overcooked they looked like shriveled fingers. "No, thanks."

Bernie shrugged. "Suit yourself."

The smell of the burger and the greasy fries stank up the inside of the Buick the insurance company was paying for, but Aline kept her mouth shut and cracked the window. It had started to rain, and she could barely see the front of Louisa Almott's house now. Not that it mattered much. Nothing had changed in two hours, since Aline and Bernie had relieved the surveillance cop from vice who'd been watching the place since last night. Almott's van hadn't moved from the carport, and her mail was still sticking up out of her mailbox. The vice cop said she was definitely home, because he had followed her to the grocery store and back about an hour before Aline and Bernie had arrived. So what did a single schoolteacher at home alone on a Saturday afternoon do all this time? Grade papers? Clean the house? Rearrange furniture? Nap? Gab on the phone? What?

Plan murders, she thought.

She switched on the wipers; leaves and bits of twigs flew off with the water. They were parked under an overhang of branches in the park across the street from the schoolteacher's. Aline supposed she could see them as clearly as they could see her house, but doubted she would think much of it, since the Buick wasn't the only car in the lot. There were at least a dozen other vehicles that belonged to picnickers and joggers, all of whom had gotten rained out. Now these refugees huddled under the shelters or were closed up in their cars, waiting for the storm to pass.

"Bill and I are having dinner tonight," Bernie said, shoving the refuse from her meal into the McDonald's bag it had come in.

"Now *that* sounds like progress. But I thought Stratton was going to try a preliminary hypnosis tonight."

"We all still have to eat. Why don't you and Kincaid come up to the house too?"

"We'll cook, you guys clean."

"Sounds fair. I think he's interested, Al."

"I don't think he ever stopped being interested. He was just diverted for a while."

"It doesn't mean Molly's out of the picture, you know."

"Sounds to me like she's on her *way* out, though."

Bernie smiled and lit a cigarette. "Yeah. It does, doesn't it?" She cracked her window and blew smoke through it. "What worries me is that she's the type who, if she found out Bill and I were having dinner, would get even by convincing the *Tribune* editor that they should write the story even if all the facts aren't in, based on what Bill told her. And then we'd all be in deep shit."

"Even Molly wouldn't stoop that low, and I don't think Sonsky's going to print anything just on hearsay. He's a jerk, but he isn't stupid. And why should Molly care who Bill sees, anyway? I've always gotten the impression she was with him just because he happened to be the most interesting game in town at the moment."

"Maybe. But I still think she's the vindictive type. And she's lucky, Al. Look how she got the job at the *Tribune*. I mean, there hadn't been a vacancy at the *Tribune* for—what? Three years? Then that other reporter gets killed in a car accident, and two days later she's sitting pretty in his job. My ex is like that, but with money. I mean, he could blow five grand at the track and still come home with five grand of winnings in his pocket. Good karma."

"Oh, so good karma is the reason for Molly's success, huh."

"I wouldn't go so far as to say she's successful—just lucky. Hey, look." She pointed toward Almott's house. "Our little lady has a visitor."

A shiny black VW Jetta had pulled into the driveway, and a tall, bookish-looking man was getting out. He wore jeans and a striped shirt and had long, quick strides that carried him quickly through the rain. He didn't ring the doorbell; he let himself into the house with a key.

"I thought she lived alone," Aline said. ·

"That was my understanding."

Aline reached for the binoculars in the glove compartment and focused on the Jetta's license plate. On the bumper was a sticker that said *I'd Rather Be Flying*. "Let's run a check on the license." She read off the number, and Bernie picked up the car phone and dialed the dispatcher. About ten minutes later, Roxie buzzed back.

"The car belongs to a Jack Cranaski, thirty-six years old, married, one kid, a son. He teaches science at the high school. He lives on Southwest Twelfth Street. One speeding ticket in the last three years, doing seventy on the Old Post Road. His wife is a nurse at Tango Hospital, works the three-to-eleven shift."

So *that* was how Louisa Almott filled her Saturdays, Aline thought.

"Anything else?" Roxie asked.

Aline had been holding the phone out so Bernie could hear, and now they looked at each other, both of them thinking the same thing. "Nothing else for now, Roxie. Thanks." She hung up. "Looks like little Ms. Schoolteacher has herself a married lover, Bernie."

"Shore does."

"How come we didn't know before now, though?"

"This is one of those nookie-at-school affairs." Bernie could speak with some authority on the topic, since she'd spent a long time as a science teacher before becoming a cop. "Besides, we've only had her under surveillance nights and weekends. What d'you say?"

"Let's give them fifteen minutes."

They waited, and fifteen minutes later Aline started the Buick. She pulled out into the street, then across it to Almott's driveway, and parked behind the Jetta. In the rear window was a second sticker: *Join the Mile High Club*. "What's the Mile High Club, Al?"

"Making love a mile up."

Bernie's eyes widened. "Yeah? And who's driving the plane?"

Aline laughed. "I don't know. I'm not a member." She wondered if Kincaid was.

"A ten-spot says she won't answer the door," Bernie said.

"A twenty says she will if we pound loudly enough."

"You're on."

For about two minutes, it looked like Bernie had won the bet. But then Aline pressed on the bell and didn't let up, and about thirty seconds later Louisa Almott answered the door. She was wearing *very* wrinkled navy-blue short shorts and a *very* wrinkled halter top, and her shiny acorn hair was *very* mussed. Her Iowa farm-girl face looked neither innocent nor fresh; her cheeks possessed a deep flush. She had a piece of Kleenex in her hand and sneezed into it before she said, "You make house calls now, Detective Scott?"

What's the sniffle from, missy? Coke? Tears? Maybe a cold? "This is Detective Bernelli. Mind if we come in for a few minutes?"

She obviously wanted to say that yes, she minded, but the wind was blowing rain under the awning, preventing them from talking on the porch. So she sighed, a cloying, exasperated sigh, as though Aline and Bernie were kids selling Girl Scout cookies and she'd been roped into buying. "All right, but I'm really quite busy."

Yeah, I bet you are.

She sneezed again as she shut the door.

The inside of the house was nicely furnished. But it was so . . . well, pristine: everything in its place, no dust, no clutter. *No character.* Almott suggested they talk out on the back porch, but Aline, noticing the closed door just inside the hall, said, "This won't take but a minute, Ms. Almott."

Her eyes flickered nervously to the closed door, then back again. She smoothed her hands over her shorts. "We'll, uh, be more comfortable on the porch."

Aline went on as if she hadn't spoken, her voice loud enough to carry through the closed door, her mind fastening on an image of the dock worker. *His eye* . . . "I checked with the office, as you suggested, about the hours of the parent-teacher conference the night of February second. The secretary dug out your schedule and said your last appointment was at seven forty-five. That means you were finished by eight. What did you do after that?''

"I stayed at school. That's what we were supposed to do. Mingle.'' She folded her arms at her waist; her sturdy farm-girl chin lifted defiantly until it was slapped back down by another sneeze.

"Well, if you mingled, then there must be someone who can vouch for you, right?'' asked Bernie.

She sniffled, blew her nose. "Look, Detective, there must've been five hundred parents there that night. I don't know who all I spoke to, so how's anyone else going to remember talking to *me*?''

Aline shrugged. *Did you stick a needle in the dock worker's eye, Ms. Farm Girl? Did you attack Kincaid? Ram my car over a cliff?* "You'd better remember, Ms. Almott. Because right now, you don't have satisfactory alibis for either homicide, your blood type is the same as the killer's, and you were Jimmy Ray's lover.'' *And if you've got gray pubic hairs you dye blond, you're really in a world of shit, lady.* "So I suggest you think about it real hard.''

The seams of her jaw had tightened, and she'd lost color in her cheeks just in the few minutes they'd stood there. Now her arms dropped to her sides and her hands slipped into the pockets of her shorts like ships seeking safe harbor. "I, uh, I'll think about it. I'll try to remember. But as I said, there were so many people there that night and—''

Bernie interrupted her. "Just one more question. Do you color your hair?''

"What?'' She laughed, but it was a laugh of disbelief, of astonishment.

"I said, do you color your hair?''

"I know what you said, Detective, but I just think you've got a lot of goddamn gall, barging in here like this on a Saturday and—''

"Oh, cut the horseshit, lady. Yes or no.''

Aline winced. Bernie had never been known for her tact, and now Almott looked as if she were on the verge of apoplexy. "I do *not* color my hair, not that it's any of your business. Now if you don't mind, I prefer not spending my day talking to the police.'' She moved toward the door, but neither Aline nor Bernie budged.

You believe her? Bernie mouthed.

No. You? asked Aline's eyes.

Nope. Bernie shook her head.

Aline looked toward the closed door in the hall and said, ''Both cars in the driveway yours?'' *Did you catch that, Mr. Cranaski?*

''No, just the van. The Jetta belongs to a friend. I'm keeping it for her for the weekend, while she's out of town.''

Right.

She held the door open. ''I hate to be rude, but . . .'' She was interrupted by another sneeze.

''Cold?'' Bernie inquired, leading the way to the door.

''Damn pollen.'' She blew her nose on the now tattered piece of tissue.

''Well?'' said Aline as she and Bernie hurried back out to the car.

''I like the way this is adding up. The blood type is right, she's got allergies, her alibis suck, she was in love with Luskin. That fact alone makes her a suspect in *my* book. But she doesn't dye her hair.''

''So she claims.'' And that was minor, Aline thought, because during their little visit, she'd made an important quantum leap. Now she could easily imagine those sturdy farm-girl fingers working a needle into an eye. She could visualize those strong, square hands driving a knife into Whitley's chest as that farm-girl body straddled his in a parody of lovemaking, as that fresh, almost innocent face gazed down at him and smiled.

13: THE CRYSTAL CITY AND AFTER

I

Just beyond the edge of the safe-house deck there was nothing but blackness—and stars. They blanketed the sky, stars so sharp, so bright they looked like chips of illuminated glass that had poked through the ebony skin of the heavens. The moon hadn't risen yet, but close to the horizon Aline could see its wash of mango-colored light.

She leaned into the wooden railing, listening to the din of the surf over the rocks seventy-five feet below, and turned her face into the breeze. The air was almost cool enough for a sweater, thanks to the cold front that had swept in on the heels of the rain this afternoon. Between the air and the good meal Barbara Stratton and Bernie had cooked for supper, she felt like curling up in the lounge chair with a mug of Nightmare Chaser and a good book.

She heard Kincaid laughing inside. He and Renie Foreston were playing a space game on Stratton's fancy computer setup. They had hit it off almost instantly, and over the course of dinner, Aline had glimpsed a side of Kincaid she'd never known existed. But then, in three years, there had never been an occasion when she'd seen him with a child. She liked what she saw, a gentler man less driven to escape through travel, through flying, a man whose laughter was deeper.

So you're thinking about marriage and kids now, Al? Is that it?

No. Of course not. It was just an interesting observation, that was all.

"Okay, we're nearly ready in here," Prentiss called.

Aline went back inside. She, Bernie, and Kincaid claimed spots on the couch. Prentiss slid behind the computer terminal. Renie Foreston made herself comfortable in a recliner that looked like a cross between a dentist's chair and something on *Star Trek*. Stratton began connecting electrodes to her scalp, her arms, her chest.

"Now if at any point you feel like stopping," Stratton told her, "just say the word."

"Right." Renie gathered her shiny hair at the back of her head and secured it with a rubber band. She wore turquoise shorts, a red top with a dinosaur embroidered over the breast pocket, and sandals. With all the wires trailing off her, she looked terribly small and vulnerable. But she flashed a big smile, a winning smile, Aline thought, as Stratton instructed her to get relaxed, close her eyes, take several deep breaths.

"We ready over there, Bill?" she asked Prentiss.

"Just about." He fiddled with a dial on the console and glanced at the computer screen. The only thing Aline understood about the computer system was that it was state of the art and on loan from the hospital. It was supposed to monitor Renie's vital functions as well as her brain waves as Stratton regressed her hypnotically to the night of the Michael family murders. The evidence, if any turned up, would not be admissible in court. At the very least, Aline hoped it would provide them with a few leads and a clearer picture of what had happened that night. Renie had asked that her parents not be present for this preliminary session, which had suited everyone. It made Aline uneasy, though, because if something went wrong and the Forestons found out about it, Frank Foreston was the sort of man who would sue with a vengeance.

Prentiss flashed a thumbs-up, and Stratton got down to business. She talked the girl into a deeply relaxed state, then asked her to imagine a TV screen. "Just like we've been practicing, Renie. An ordinary TV, but the kind with a really big screen. It has knobs you can use to adjust the picture if it blurs or to turn the TV off and on, or to fix the sound. Can you see the knobs, Renie?"

"Uh-huh." Her reply was soft, languorous.

"I want you to look at them and make sure you know which knob has which function. Okay?"

"Okay," she replied after a few moments.

"On the screen, Renie, is a fantastic city, a city like you've never seen before. It's made of crystals. Red and green and blue crystals, gold and purple and yellow, all sorts of colors. Can you see the city?"

"Hmm. Pretty."

"Can you see the buildings?"

"Yes."

"One of the wonderful things about this screen is that it's magical. You can actually walk into the picture if you want. All you have to do is say *In*, and you'll be inside it. If you want out, then you just say *Out*. I'd like you to venture into the city, Renie. I want you to notice how clean the air smells, how people look, the colors, everything. Can you do that?"

"In," she whispered.

"Just walk around the city for a while, getting used to it. You'll find a plaza, Renie, with a huge clock tower made of pink crystal. Tell me when you've reached the plaza."

A minute passed. Two. Renie remained perfectly still, her eyeballs beneath her lids flicking rapidly back and forth, back and forth, as if she was in REM sleep and dreaming.

"I see the plaza. I see the tower."

"Very good, hon. Now on this tower is a clock, like I said. As you're watching, the clock's hands start moving backward in time. Can you see it happening?"

"Uh-huh."

"Beneath the face of the clock is a panel with the date on it. As the hands of the clock go backward, the calendar panels are also going to flip back in time until they reach the day of February second. Can you see the hands moving, Renie?"

"Yes. Back. They're moving backward."

"And the calendar panels? Can you see those?"

"Uh-huh."

"I want you to tell me when the panels stop on February second."

Silence: it filled with the hum of the machine, the susurrous song of the wind, and, more distant, the pound of the surf.

"Okay," Renie said.

"Where are you?"

"Outside a building."

"What kind of building?"

"A crystal house."

"Did you walk to the house?"

"Took my bike."

"What's the house like?"

"It's real light blue. When I look up close and put my hands at the sides of my face to block out the light, I can almost see through the walls."

"Are you doing that now?"

"Hmm."

"What do you see?"

"A boy. He's on the floor, watching TV. A man is in a rocking chair, reading. It's a real nice house. Pretty. I like it better than our house. . . ." Her voice suddenly grew tight and frightened. "I . . . I want to leave now."

"Just say *Out*."

"Out."

"Now it's just a picture on the screen, Renie. Can you still see it?"

"Yes."

"Are the man and boy still there?"

"Yes."

"I want you to turn up the knob for the sound, so you can hear what's going on in the house. Can you do that, honey?"

"Sure." A pause, then: "The TV. And the doorbell's ringing. I hear a lady say, 'I'll get it.' "

"Can you see the lady?"

"No."

"I want you to adjust the picture knob on the TV until you can see the lady, Renie."

A tiny frown creased her brow. She didn't say anything.

"Have you adjusted the picture?"

Whispered. "Yes."

"Can you see the lady who's answering the door?"

"Uh-huh. A cat is following her. An orange cat."

"Who's outside, Renie? Who rang the doorbell? Can you see the person's face?"

The frown deepened. Her eyeballs flicked back and forth so fast under her lids, it was as though they'd become detached from her head. She whimpered. She started to squirm.

Stratton glanced at Prentiss; he nodded, consulted the screen, scribbled something on the legal pad to his right. "Switch the channel on the TV, Renie."

The girl's frown vanished.

"Did you switch?"

"Yes."

"What're you watching?"

"*Star Trek.*"

Stratton smiled and signaled Prentiss again, who nodded and jotted something else on the pad. "I'd like you to switch back to the picture with just the man and the boy, Renie, can you do that?"

"Uh-huh."

"Can you hear them talking?"

"Yes. The man says, 'Who is it, Jenny?' And someone says, 'It's the . . .' " And then she threw her head back and screamed and screamed, her mouth wide open, her eyes squeezed shut, her arms flying upward toward her face, snapping loose some of the electrodes.

Before any of them had moved, Prentiss had leaped up, a hypo in his hand, and had sunk the needle into the girl's thigh as Stratton held her down. Renie kept screaming, bucking in the chair as though she were having an epileptic seizure. Bernie and Kincaid had jumped up, but neither of them seemed to know what to do, so they hovered like giant dragonflies around the recliner. Aline just remained where she was, paralyzed with horror as it dawned on her just what had happened. Renie Foreston had seen the slaughter from the beginning. *It's the . . .*

The what? *The Avon lady? The teacher? What?*

The screaming diminished by degrees. Renie stopped bucking. Her arms fell to her sides and her head slumped against her chest. Her soft moon face gleamed with sweat. One of her sandals had fallen off, and the other hung on her little toe, then slipped and slapped the wooden floor. No one spoke. The wind blew into the room, the computer hummed, insects chirred in the nearby woods. It was as if a frame in a movie had frozen, but the sounds continued.

And then, slowly, Stratton straightened up. Prentiss snapped the needle from the syringe and set it and the hypo on top of the computer. Kincaid removed the electrodes from Renie's scalp and chest. Aline felt herself coming loose from the edge of the couch and thought: *Lawsuit. If the Forestons had been there, we'd already be knee-deep in a lawsuit.*

Bernie was the first one to speak. "I need a cigarette," and she walked out onto the porch.

Prentiss picked up Renie. "I'll put her in her room."

Dr. Stratton walked over to the computer terminal and tapped the keyboard. The screen went blank, then scrolled with information. "That first time, when she started whimpering . . . look at this." She pointed at a set of figures on the screen. "Her pulse shot from 62 to 128. Her blood pressure went from 65 over 116 to more than twice that on both systolic and diastolic. And brain waves . . . Jesus . . . she was borderline theta and delta—deep sleep—and lunged right into beta. Full consciousness."

"I think you'd better make sure she doesn't mention this to her parents," Kincaid said. "I've got a feeling Frank Foreston would go for your jugular."

Stratton smiled. She no longer looked like a crisp, efficient businesswoman, Aline thought, but her smile remained self-assured, confident, and fully cognizant of what Kincaid was saying. "Frank Foreston, Ryan, would go for my license. But I think we made good strides tonight. I've got to work with her on developing more distance from what she sees. Two weeks ago, the memory would've been too deeply buried to get at through hypnosis. She's making progress."

Aline suddenly wasn't so sure if progress—at least this way—was such a good idea. But she kept her opinion to herself.

2

Aline and Kincaid had left, Stratton had gone to bed, and Renie was still asleep. It was just the two of them, himself and Bernelli, sitting on the wide deck with tall glasses of Stolichnaya vodka with a dash of soda water. The moon was suspended within a cluster of stars, grinning. *The joke's on you, good buddy*, it seemed to be saying.

". . . so I imagine her science teacher friend had a lot of questions after we'd left," Bernie was saying, referring to what had happened at Louisa Almott's house earlier.

"Maybe she was with him the night of the Michael murders."

Bernelli looked over at him. "Then why not come out and just say so, for God's sakes?"

"He's married, that's why not."

"Hey, if it's save-your-ass time, Bill, then you cough it up and the hell with the guy's marriage."

"Is everything always so black and white for you, Bernie?"

"Is that how you think it is for me?"

"That's how it seems."

"Oh, brother." She tipped her head back against her chair and blew smoke into the air. It curled up into the moonlight. "Only with some things."

"What things?"

She thought about it. She flicked her cigarette out over the railing. It sailed past the tips of her shoes, which were resting on top of the railing, and arched out through the dark, a bright orange spot of light that seemed to hover for a second, then vanish. "Right and wrong."

"Are we right? You and I?"

She turned her head, looking at him. "That's a loaded question, now isn't it?"

"Yeah." He grinned.

"That isn't the kind of right or wrong I was talking about."

"I know."

"Maybe I should be asking *you* that."

Ha-ha, chuckled the grinning moon. *Joke's on you, good buddy.* "Things aren't that clear-cut for me, I guess."

"Oh, I think they are. You're a picker. Like me. Things for pickers are always clearer than they should be. That's the problem."

Hey, guess what, good buddy, whispered the moon. *She's got your number.*

The wind rattled the glass doors; it carried the bark of the police dog at the guardhouse. A chill fanned out across his spine that had nothing to do with the cool air. *What's there for a dog to bark at up here?*

Well, hey, that was easy. A rodent. A Key deer. Maybe even a panther. Sure. The world was a logical place; it was only human beings that didn't cut it.

"You feel guilty about Molly, is that it?" Bernelli asked.

"Have you always been so blunt?"

"Whenever I can get away with it."

Prentiss laughed, leaned toward her, slid his hand across the back of her neck, and drew her face toward his. He kissed her, tasting the vodka, the soda. Her skin smelled faintly of perfume and smoke; he felt the ineluctable heat in his groin.

"Can you stay?" he asked.

"Can you?" she countered.

"You first."

"Danny's spending the night with a friend."

"Molly's working late and isn't expected."

"Then I guess I can stay."

He kissed her again. For an instant, he worried that he would be impotent, that he would mess things up like he had the first time. Barring these first two things, he fretted that he would fail in some other way, fail utterly and irrevocably.

They remained on the porch for a while longer, then descended the stairs to the basement and went into the bedroom. He turned on the lamp and pulled back the covers and closed the door. Bernelli looked around the room and shook her head.

"I feel like I'm in a bomb shelter or something. Is there another bedroom we can use?"

"One upstairs."

"Do you mind?"

"No. No, that'd be better. You can hear the ocean from there."

On their way back upstairs, he grabbed a bottle of wine from the kitchen and two glasses. He opened the windows in the bedroom and the wind puffed out the curtains like sails. Moonlight spilled across the floor and struck the foot of the bed. He popped the cork on the wine, filled the glasses, and Bernelli sat on the bed beside him.

"What're we drinking to?" she asked him as he passed her a glass. "Success? The year? What?"

"To clarity," he said.

"To clarity." She smiled and clicked the edge of her glass against his. "That sounds like a good beginning."

He laughed, a quick sound that seemed to release him from his own skin, and he slipped his arms around her and buried his face in the curve of her shoulder. "Christ, but I've missed you, Bernelli."

She let her tongue glide across his lower lip, as though memorizing its shape, and whispered, "Ditto, friend."

He wasn't impotent. He didn't bungle anything. He didn't fail.

3

The fierce yapping of the guard dog roused him from a doze. Then it stopped. Beside him, Bernelli stirred, whispered, "You awake?"

"I am now. You hear that?"

"Yeah. The pooch probably smells a deer."

"You been awake all this time?"

"Sort of. I've been wondering something."

"What?"

"What went wrong the first time? With us, I mean? Last summer."

Bernelli's voice seemed disembodied in the dark, distant, as though he'd been blinded

Needle in the eye

and was clawing through the blackness, trying to seize the light. He reached out, and his palm touched the cool skin of her belly. A breast. The curve of a shoulder. Then he realized his eyes had been closed

It's okay okay

and they fluttered open and he lifted up on an elbow, gazing down at her. "A few days after that last night we spent together, I met Molly at the Pink Moose. I guess I was . . . hell, I don't know. Ripe for it. I couldn't muster the nerve to call you after that."

She slipped her slender leg between his as she turned on her side, her hand resting against his hip. "What's the attraction?"

Her bluntness, he thought, would take some getting used to. "Nothing now. But in the beginning, I think it was her differences from me."

"What kind of differences?"

He tucked one arm under his head and closed his eyes again, thinking about it, his hand stroking her soft skin. The differences were subtle ones, but important. Molly had grown up as the youngest of four children; he was an only child. Her father was a language professor at Middlebury College in Vermont and her mother was a concert pianist. His father owned a restaurant here on Tango and his mother was a nurse. Molly didn't get along with her family; he'd never had any problems with his. She was a doer and a pusher, aggressive, often singular in her purpose; her mentality was northern. He was an islander, more laid-back, passive.

"Fire and air." Bernelli shifted her hips, and his hand slipped into the damp heat between her thighs. For a long moment she didn't say anything. She made a sound in her throat, like a cat purring. "She burns her paths, you think them through. Like that." Pause. "God, that feels good."

"Fire and air. That simple, huh," he whispered, his mouth cruising up her neck, to her throat, where a pulse beat steadily against the tip of his tongue.

"I'm a reductionist."

"I thought you were a picker."

"That too." She moaned and opened her mouth against his, drawing him down against her, against the sharpness of her hip, into the fragrance of her skin, a scent so different from Molly's skin, muskier somehow, earthy. She stroked him with her hands, but he was already hard, hard despite the neon pulse of that image in his head that wouldn't go away, that stink of formaldehyde that had lodged permanently deep inside his sinuses. The wind was suddenly silenced as he slid into her, and the curtains snapped back against the window as if something had sucked the air from the room. A long, baleful howl of the guard dog rang out in the quiet, a dark, uneasy sound that made Bernelli shiver against him and prickled his arms with gooseflesh. Then the animal started that frantic yapping again and hands flattened out against his back, holding him still. She whispered, "That dog. Something's wrong with the dog, Bill."

Prentiss rolled away from her, and they both got up, pulling on clothes. He started to switch on the lamp. "No," she said. "Don't. I've got a flashlight." She grabbed for her purse and a moment later pushed a flashlight into his hand—and a weapon. "It's automatic. All you have to do is flick off this . . . and start firing."

"I've never shot a goddamn gun in my life."

"But you've treated gunshot wounds, so you aren't likely to shoot without reason. That's good."

He started to question her logic, but decided the hell with it. She plucked another weapon from her holster on the chair and they slipped out of the bedroom.

The house quivered in the silence. It felt like some huge, impatient beast, prepared to spit them out at the slightest provocation.

They passed through the kitchen, into the utility room. Prentiss tapped a code into the security system, turning it off, and the door clicked open. The pelagic smell of the air rushed in. Moonlight streamed though the trees just beyond the fence.

Prentiss clutched the flashlight like a weapon, and he and Bernelli inched along the side of the house, their backs to the wall. The dog's howls had stopped, but his unease had shifted into something greater, into a kind of distress, as though his blood chemistry had run amok.

As they reached the corner of the house, he paused, and Bernelli peeked around his right side. He could see the iron fence that surrounded the house, and beyond it, the pumpkin glow from the guardhouse. Through the windows, he saw a shadow. *One shadow: there should be two.*

"Something's wrong." He started forward, but Bernie caught his arm.

"Wait. Along the fence over there. And keep low, below the concrete foundation if you can."

He nodded, and they sprinted the distance between the house and the fence and hit the ground. Leaves and twigs poked his cheeks. His throat felt like he'd swallowed ground glass. *I'm a doctor, not a fucking commando,* he thought, and lifted his head. He peered over the edge of the three-foot-high concrete foundation. He saw nothing. Heard nothing except a whisper of the wind returning.

They slipped at a crouch through the moonlight and reached the front gate seconds later. Now he could see the guard clearly through the window. His back was to them; he was on the phone. A second later, the phone in the house pealed. The sound galvanized them both. They leaped up and raced toward the gate. "Hey, Tom!" Bernelli shouted. "Unlock this thing!"

The cop glanced back, hung up the receiver, and the elec-

tronic gate slid open. "Someone's out there in the woods.
Dick and the dog went to investigate," he said, stepping out
of the guardhouse. "It might just be a rabbit or a deer or
something, but I don't think so. The dog went nuts, practically tore his chain outa the wall."

"I'll go have a look," Bernelli said.

Prentiss handed her the flashlight and off she went. By
now, Barbara Stratton had come out of the house, her robe
flapping in the breeze as she hurried through the gate.
"What's going on?"

Prentiss explained, and anxiety seized Stratton's features.
"Do you think—"

"It was probably just an animal." He said it quickly, as if
to reassure himself as much as Stratton.

He heard the dog again, and voices, and Bernie and the
other guard came out of the trees, the German shepherd
bounding along in front of them.

"Whoever it was is gone," said Bernie.

"Probably poachers," said the second cop, Dick, as he
filled the shepherd's bowl with fresh water from the hose.
"There've been a few of those in the past year, hunting Key
deer. Crockett picked up the scent, didn't you, big boy?" He
patted the dog on the head. "But lost it at the road."

"You hear a car?" Prentiss asked.

"Nope," Bernie replied.

"Probably wouldn't with poachers," Dick said. "They
generally come in on foot."

Bernelli nodded in agreement. But when she glanced toward Prentiss, her eyes whispered, *I'm not buying it*.

And neither was he.

14: THE BARBECUE

I

Kincaid stood at the edge of the pool crowd in shorts and a T-shirt, sipping from a glass of lemonade and wishing he hadn't come. *A few people,* Prentiss had said. *Some friends.* Instead it looked like half the populace of Tango Key was here, yukking it up, rapidly depleting the well-stocked bar, swimming in the fat, kidney-shaped pool, spilling through the sliding glass doors into the yard. A bartender and two waitresses flitted through the crowd, refilling drinks, offering tidbits from trays of hors d'oeuvres while Prentiss cooked up ribs on the grill.

Be sociable.

But he remained where he was, irritated that he was so utterly lacking in the art of cocktail chatter, and worse, that he had no desire to change. Given his druthers, he'd be flying, or down at Lester's, chewing the fat with Ferret and Bino. In fact, the more he thought about it, the better an imminent departure looked. He threaded his way toward the house to find Aline and let her know he was leaving. He murmured hello to people who addressed him, but didn't pause long enough to become a part of any group. His head ached from the heat, and the brattle of the music worked under his skin like a thorn. But none of it was the source of his foul mood; he blamed the argument he and Aline had had before leaving the house for that.

Today's disagreement, interestingly enough, had started with his observation that during her landing when she had soloed several days ago, she'd crabbed into the wind when she should've come in straight. A small detail, but vital. He should've called her on it as soon as she'd gotten out of the plane that day, but her euphoria had been so great he hadn't wanted to spoil it. When he finally mentioned it this morning, her response was that she was sick and tired of his criticisms about everything she did. From there, the conversation had rapidly deteriorated to the usual issue: equitable division of labor.

But at the heart of it lay two simple truths: you really didn't know a woman until you traveled with her—and lived with her. The first truth had ended his two marriages, and it looked like the second was going to murder his relationship with Aline.

So much for truth.

"Ryan?"

A hand brushed his shoulder and he looked back. Vic Xaphes grinned, Xaphes in his deep tan, decked out in designer shirt and jeans, holding a tumbler with a lime straddling the edge. "Vic. I was hoping you'd be here."

"Yeah? You got legal problems or something, Ryan?"

Kincaid chuckled. "Not yet. Actually, I wanted to ask you something about Luskin."

"I figured. I heard about the dock worker. He was one of the jurors at Luskin's trial."

"I know." Kincaid nodded.

"Aline was talking to Lloyd Watkins and he mentioned something about Lenore Luskin having a child."

"Oh. *That*." Xaphes rolled his eyes and sipped at his drink. "Hell, it was probably just another one of Jimmy Ray's lies. The guy was a pathological liar, Ryan. *Incapable* of telling the truth. But one kick he got on was this story that when he was twelve, thirteen years old, Lenore sent him to military academy for a year and she moved to Miami to have the baby of one of her clients. I verified the military thing, but I never got to first base on Luskin's claim that Lenore had a child or that she'd stashed away money for it. That was the part Luskin was interested in, see, since he was pretty broke at the time, except for a few paintings. He figured he could claim the money."

"What was she supposed to have done with the child?"

"That depends on which of Luskin's stories you want to believe. Let's see. One version was that she had an abortion.

Another version was that she miscarried. The third and fourth versions were that she left it on the steps of an orphanage and gave it to her sister to raise.''

"They had a sister?"

"No. That's exactly my point. Luskin couldn't even keep his lies straight. Did you talk to Travis Feld?"

"Not yet. I was planning on going up there tomorrow."

"I hope you didn't call ahead, because he'll refuse to see you if he knows you're a dick."

"I hadn't planned on giving him any advance notice at all."

"Good. And I'm pretty sure he'll be able to answer your questions about Lenore." His eyes were flicking here and there now, roaming restlessly, looking for some sweet young thing he could charm. He leaned toward Kincaid. "Don't look now, but *here* comes a body, Ryan."

Kincaid followed the man's eyes and laughed. The body he'd referred to belonged to Molly Chapman, who slipped through the hot late-afternoon light as if through her element. She wore a skimpy black bikini with the bottom partially covered by a flowered wraparound coverup slit along one side. "Your tongue's hanging out, Vic. Besides, she's taken."

Sort of, he corrected himself. There had definitely been sparks flying last night between Prentiss and Bernie, and he knew she'd stayed at the safe house because she'd called the house this morning and had told Aline about The Incident. *Poachers:* the chief said *maybe,* and doubled security around the house.

"Taken or not, Ryan, any woman can be tempted. You just have to tell her what she wants to hear."

His insufferable arrogance made Kincaid laugh and brought a smile to Molly's mouth as she stopped and greeted them. "So what's the joke, guys?"

She was flying high—Kincaid heard it in the way she spoke and saw it in the way she carried herself. "No joke. Vic's got a theory that any woman can be tempted. You think it's true?"

She tilted her sunglasses forward on her nose and regarded Xaphes with a look that was both sensual and coy. "I guess that would depend on what the temptation is."

Xaphes grinned. "Illicit sex."

"Then it depends on the man." She deliberately let her

eyes drop from Xaphes's face to his groin, then up again. She shook her head. "Sorry, Vic. You're not my type."

Xaphes laughed—a quick, embarrassed laugh—and then he excused himself and slipped away into the crowd. Kincaid chuckled. "Beautiful. You just stripped him of a week's worth of arrogance."

"Lawyers are parasites." She stared after Xaphes as she said it, then looked back at Kincaid and touched his arm as she smiled. "And flight instructors walk on water. Could you take a look at my cross-country route? I brought the map."

"Sure." He followed her into the house and in the family room, she dug into her flight bag and brought out the map. She kneeled on the floor and spread it open on the coffee table. Kincaid, seated on the couch, leaned forward, studying the route she'd laid out. It would take her from Tango to Vero Beach, west to Fort Myers, and back to Tango. She'd calculated her fuel consumption and flight time based on tomorrow's weather forecast. She'd even copied down the flight plan she would file. "Looks good."

"I reserved a plane with Av-Tech. The only thing that could foul it up would be the weather."

To keep down his insurance premiums, Kincaid's students flew his plane only when he was in it; for solo work, they rented from one of the aviation outfits. "You might want to fly into Fort Pierce Airport rather than Vero. It's not as busy."

"It's got to be at least a hundred miles between each stop, right?"

"If you land in Fort Pierce, it'll only cut off ten miles from your route. It'll still be over a hundred miles. And Molly, don't practice any stalls, okay?"

She turned those huge blue eyes on him; they crinkled at the corners as she laughed. "Don't worry, I won't." She sat back on her heels and folded the map carefully, meticulously. "I figured tomorrow is a good day to be off the island, see, because the first of my articles on the homicides is coming out. There're going to be some people looking for my head."

"I thought the *Tribune* had been covering the story all along."

"This is more in-depth."

Here we go, Kincaid thought. This was going to be the inevitable shit-hits-the-fan story they'd all been expecting but hoping against. "In-depth how?"

"Alluding to a cover-up in the police department. That was my editor's contribution," she added quickly.

"A cover-up?" Kincaid laughed. "There hasn't been any cover-up, Molly."

"Ryan, I realize you live with Aline, but I'm sure she doesn't tell you everything."

"Believe me, I'd know about a cover-up. There're details the police haven't released to the press, yes, but that's because of the investigation, not because of some cover-up conspiracy."

She slipped the map back in her flight bag and sighed. "I'm sure Nixon thought the same thing, Ryan."

"Look, we're not talking Watergate here. This is an investigation into five brutal murders that seem to be a vendetta. There are a number of other people involved who—"

"Ryan, people have the right to know what's going on in the place they live."

"Not if it endangers others, they don't."

She laughed—and he heard inebriation. "That's bullshit."

She's goading you, Kincaid. She's trying to piss you off enough so you'll spill your guts.

It might've worked, too, except they were interrupted by someone who came into the room to use the phone. Kincaid seized the opportunity to escape.

He found Aline in the kitchen with Prentiss and some people he didn't know. He caught her eye and she came over, her mood light, playful; she'd already forgotten their earlier disagreement.

"I thought you'd been abducted." She poked him in the ribs.

"Who would have me?"

"Aliens?"

He laughed. "I doubt it."

She slipped an arm around his waist and they walked into the hall. An old Creedence Clearwater Revival tune—"Bad Moon Rising"—was playing in the next room, and she had to lean close to hear him when he spoke. She smelled good: Shalimar, he thought. The scent stirred the tired beast in his libido, and he touched her shoulders and kissed her.

Her hands locked at his waist. "I'm sorry," she said. "About before."

"Me, too."

She grinned at him; her finger traced the shape of his mouth. "Want to leave?"

"You read minds?"

"Only yours." She smiled, and they left.

2

It was a clear, almost cool night. Stars burned against the black sky, growing brighter and brighter as they ascended into the Tango hills and the city lights fell away behind them. Kincaid took the long route toward the airport, along the Old Post Road to the west of the island. It was quite a distance from the spot where he'd been the night Aline's Honda had been rammed, but he still felt twitches of unease out here. There was very little traffic, and there were no street lights.

They stopped to pick up a bottle of wine, and at the bend in the road where the expanse of the Gulf spread out before them, Kincaid turned down a dirt road. It meandered through trees and came to a dead end at the edge of a cliff. They got out of the car and sat on the Saab's hood, backs against the windshield as he opened the wine. They passed it between them, gazing out across the protracted slate of sea rippled like aluminum with moonlight.

"I spoke to Molly at the party. She said that the first of her articles on the homicides is coming out in tomorrow's *Tribune*."

"Swell." She shrugged. "I guess it was inevitable. I'll have to warn the chief, so he doesn't have a coronary when he opens the paper tomorrow morning. Did she say whether she'd mentioned a 'mysterious witness' in the article?"

"She didn't say that specifically. But it wouldn't surprise me."

"She just couldn't keep the lid on what Bill told her in confidence," she said, and changed the subject. She dropped her head back and stared up into the belly of the star-dusted sky. "What's that one, Ryan?" She pointed, and he followed her finger.

"The real bright one?"

"Hmm."

"Venus. And there. . ." He lifted his hand. "Orion."

"Think the Southern Cross is visible in New Zealand in June?"

"I don't know."

"What?" She looked at him. "I think that's the only time I've asked you a travel-related question that you haven't known the answer to."

"That's astronomy, not traveling."

She laughed. "Ha. It's one point for me, that's what it is."

The more they drank, the looser they got and the harder they laughed, and the more he wanted her. He touched her chin, turning it toward him, and kissed her. Her mouth was cool and damp. They slid off the hood to the ground, and she laughed as he pressed her up against the side of the Saab, his hands moving under the shirt, seeking the ridges of her spine, her ribs.

"There's traffic on the other side of those trees, you know." She breathed the words against his neck. "And suppose a car pulls in here?"

"No one pulls in here but people who've got the same thing in mind." He was concentrating on the zipper on her jeans, which had gotten stuck. He finally gave up, reached through the Saab's window and pulled the beach towel from the backseat. He spread it on the ground next to the car.

They made love in the cool, damp scent of grass, her cinnamon hair a fan against the towel, then a curtain at the sides of her face as she moved on top of him. It was the best thing that had happened to Kincaid in days. The best thing until he opened his eyes and over Aline's shoulder saw the unmistakable whirl of lights that was a small plane in trouble about 2,500 feet up.

Big trouble.

A spin.

And then the high-pitched whine of the plane's engine filled the air, a sound like an animal in terrible pain, the din of a hundred fingernails scraped across a blackboard and amplified. They scrambled apart, adjusting their clothes as they craned their necks toward the sky, following the plane with their eyes. It slammed into the shoals five or six miles to the south and exploded.

A fireball leaped fifty or sixty feet in the air and blazed against the dark like an alien sun. Then it plunged from orbit, breaking apart until there was only a bright orange rain of burning shards.

By the time the Saab hit the pavement and barreled south, Kincaid was cold sober.

15: AFTERMATH

I

The sun pushed up out of the sea like a huge but timid creature, spilling bright shoots of rose and lemon light across the water and the sand. It hurt Aline's tired, bloodshot eyes. She slipped on her sunglasses and glanced over her shoulder at the trail of footprints she and the chief had left in the wet sand. The prints weaved like a drunk. Sandpiper birds pecked through them, scurrying forward when the water receded, then back again as the wave broke and eddied across the straw-colored slice of beach.

Lloyd Watkins's twin-engine plane had crashed about three hundred yards offshore, in a deserted half-moon cove. Parts of it had washed onto the beach—mangled blades from the propellers, a seat, a suitcase, pieces of the tail, a wing. Half a dozen cops and representatives of the FAA were sifting through the debris. Four men in scuba gear were combing the area underwater, looking for Watkins's body.

According to his wife, they were on their way back from Miami when Watkins started having trouble banking the plane. They landed on Tango and he checked it out, couldn't find anything, and decided to take the plane up just once more to see if he could determine the problem. She had stayed on the ground.

She'd told the FAA inspector that her husband felt the problem was in the ailerons. Kincaid had agreed. He said he could tell from the sound of the engine and the position of the wing lights that Watkins couldn't turn the plane properly. He'd stalled, gone into a spin, and couldn't pull out. Aline didn't

178

think they would recover enough of the plane to determine if it had been sabotage. But there was no doubt in the chief's mind—or her own—that it had been. The question, of course, was where had the sabotage happened? On Tango before the Watkinses had left on Saturday? If so, then why hadn't he noticed the trouble en route to Miami? Kincaid thought the most probable scenario was that the sabotage to the aileron had entailed trimming the cable a little and trusting that at some point during the flight it would snap. It hadn't made much difference to the killer *when* it happened, so long as it did.

As they neared the debris, the stink of gas clung to the air like a stubborn, wind-borne virus. "If that plane had come down in the middle of the island," said the chief, "we'd be looking at carnage right now, Aline."

She nodded. Gene Frederick was puffing on one of his putrid cigars, and the smoke made her cough. She waved her hand in front of her face and Frederick glanced over at her. "Oh, sorry."

He was a thin, intense man with hair whiter than laundry detergent. He was often difficult, hot-tempered, and demanding, but she couldn't imagine working under anyone else. When Aline had started out as a cop, Frederick had been chief of homicide. About two years ago he'd become chief of police for Tango County. Although it meant he had less to do with the streets now, he'd been at the scene within fifteen minutes of the crash, barking orders, coordinating everything, and running interference with the FAA.

"We've got to make some decisions. These people deserve protection, Aline."

"I can tell you right now that the social worker thinks she's under divine protection, and that Xaphes is probably going to tell you he'll hire his *own* protection. I don't know about the others."

"What about you?" His blue eyes narrowed against the sunlight.

"What about me?"

"You think you're under divine protection?"

She looked at him, a corner of her mouth turning down. "Yeah, sure, Gene. I'm one of God's chosen."

Frederick lowered himself to the sand, stretching his thin legs out in front of him as he leaned back on his hands. Aline settled next to him and watched a plump seagull in a freefall toward the sea. "I want you staying at the safe house. After what happened up there Saturday night, that's the most secure place on the island."

She laughed. It sounded like an eighties version of *Rapunzel*. "Forget it."

"I'm not giving you a choice."

Her laughter died. "Then I'll be giving you my resignation."

Frederick puffed urgently on his cigar, then stabbed it out in the sand and left it there. The spent cheroot protruded from the sand like the atrophied stump of a plant. She waited tensely, certain he was going to call her bluff. It wouldn't be the first time she'd resigned. Frederick was progressive in many ways, but still held some old-fashioned ideas about women. She quickly calculated the loss of income from her job and was grateful she still had the bookstore.

"I don't know why you and Bernelli have to be so goddamn difficult sometimes," he groused.

Aline slid her feet through the sand, pulling them toward her, and hugged her knees. "Look at it this way. If I were a man, would you order me sequestered in the safe house?"

"It's not the same—"

"Not the same thing?" She smiled. "But it is. The only difference is that I'm female. So what?"

He didn't say anything. He plucked the cigar from the sand and relit it. It wasn't until he changed the subject that she knew for sure she'd made her point—and won this round. "What do you think about this Sheila Reiner, Al?"

"I don't know. Her alibis have holes. Since Judge Michael sentenced both her and Luskin, she has a double motive. She's also got the right blood type."

"And the schoolteacher?"

Aline considered it. "I think she's our best bet. She's been under surveillance nights and weekends, so the only way she could've sabotaged Lloyd's plane was by ducking out during school hours, when we weren't watching her. On top of it, the guy she's involved with is a pilot. I checked. That means she could easily find out what she needed to know."

"Then we'll beef up surveillance on her and put the Reiner woman under surveillance as well."

"We're not going to have the manpower, if any of the jurors request protection."

"The jurors and the girl come first, and we have enough men to cover them. I'll see if I can get some help from Monroe County." He ground out his cigar again. "As for you. . ." His eyes skewed again, and before he could speak, she interrupted.

"I'll resign, Gene. I mean it."

"You're too pigheaded for your own good, Aline."

A definite win.

As the sun slipped higher in the sky, Aline told him about Molly Chapman's article that was due to appear in today's *Tribune*. Frederick didn't seem too surprised. "That goddamn Chip Sonsky has been on me ever since I issued a statement about the Michael murders. Right from the start, that horse's ass has been accusing me of withholding information. So I've been thinking about playing the game his way."

"Sure, Gene."

He grinned. "We'll feed him some false information. I've just got to come up with the right story, and the timing has to be perfect. We'll play it by ear."

"You really think Reiner or Almott can be lured like that?"

"Don't know." He shrugged. "Won't know until we try." He stood, held out a hand that she grasped, and pulled her to her feet. They continued walking toward the scabrous landscape of refuse that glistened in the hot lights of the rising sun.

2

The radio clicked on, and Prentiss awakened to the disc jockey at WPQR-FM saying, ". . . six thirty this Monday morning, the temperature outside is already like August, a balmy eighty and rising. To get you moving this Monday morning, here's a golden oldies tune." The Mamas and Papas' "Monday, Monday" floated through the bedroom, a mournful tribute to the sixties. Prentiss started to sit up, but felt Molly's cool hand against his back. He winced as it slid over his hip to his belly, nails stroking lightly, seductively, a touch that had once lit up his insides and now made them shrivel.

He had not wanted her to stay the night, had intended to tell her things were over. But she'd been so blasted after the barbecue she'd passed out on the couch, and he'd just left her there. Sometime during the night, he'd heard her stumbling into the bedroom, and he'd thought, *Tomorrow, I'll tell her tomorrow*. Now it was tomorrow, and he couldn't very well do it right this minute because he would be late getting to the hospital.

So he sat up, felt her hand fall away, and switched off the alarm. "Did I do or say anything unforgivable last night?" Her voice was husky and hoarse.

"I don't know; did you?"

"I can't remember." She spoke to his back; it seemed he could feel each of the words' letters slapping his skin, softly, like tiny hands. "God, my head hurts."

"There's aspirin in the kitchen." He stood and started toward the bathroom.

"You hung over?"

"No."

"Then what's bugging you?"

He stopped in the bathroom doorway and turned. She was raised up on her elbows, her honey hair tangled against her shoulders, her eyes wide and bloodshot. "Things with us aren't working out, Molly." He blurted it; he didn't just say it. "I feel like every time we're together, it's because you're trying to dig information out of me for this story."

She sat straight up now, frowning. "I must've said something to you last night, huh."

Something, he thought, and nearly laughed out loud. Yeah, she'd said *something*, all right. *There really* is *a witness, isn't there, Bill? What kind of needle was used, Bill? What kind of knife? C'mon, you can tell me. . . .*

"Yeah, you said a few things. I realize you were blasted, but that doesn't change what was said. I just think it would be better if we called it quits and parted friends."

She rubbed at her temple and spoke softly. "Why is it okay for you to think of yourself first all the time, but when I do it, it's unforgivable? I mean, we haven't had sex in weeks because *you* haven't been able to get it up, Bill. But that doesn't mean I blow everything out of proportion and suggest we end things."

"I've got to get ready for work. Let's talk about this later."

"Later." She threw off the covers and swung her legs over the side of the bed. "Forget later." She stood, and his eyes followed her up. Her body against the opaline light struck him as utterly perfect, flawless—not just her smooth, taut skin, the flare of her hips, the lift to her breasts, but the bones beneath it all, the way the muscles were stitched to them, the way the tendons and joints fitted together. He watched her stroll toward the door and knew that she knew he was watching her. He knew she believed the sight of her nudity would trigger some sweeter memory that would cause him to say, *Hey, Moll, I didn't mean it.*

Instead, he walked into the bathroom and shut the door and switched on the shower.

You blew it, good buddy. You should've told her to leave. She would have understood that.

The hot needles drummed his shoulders, his head. Steam filled the stall. He felt a ripple of cooler air and knew Molly had opened the door. He heard the toilet seat thud as she flopped it forward. "Bill?"

"Yeah?"

"Could you turn off the water for a second?"

"I'm almost finished."

She suddenly yanked back the shower curtain, and water splashed over the edge of the tub, onto the floor and the bathmat. "I want to talk now," she demanded, her cheeks bright red.

"I don't," he snapped, and jerked the shower curtain closed again, so angry he could barely see. He finished showering and glanced once to his left and saw her shadow against the curtain. When he was finished, he switched off the faucet so hard, the pipes clattered. He swept the curtain open and reached for his towel, wrapping it around his waist, not looking at her. She moved off the mat as he stepped out of the tub, then hovered in the doorway, watching him in the mirror as he shaved. She was still nude. He knew she was waiting for him to say, *Well, what is it?* But he refused to give her the satisfaction.

"There's someone else, isn't there?" she said finally.

"That isn't the issue."

"I want to know."

"No, there isn't anyone else," he lied.

"Then I don't understand," she whispered, and began to cry.

Prentiss stared at her, at her hands covering her face as her shoulders shuddered, and her sobs wrenched at him. *Don't cry, please. Christ.* He went over to her and touched her shoulders. "Molly, I'm sorry, I didn't mean to hurt you." He pulled her gently against him, and she burrowed her face against his shoulder and her arms went around his neck, holding on tightly. He stroked her hair and murmured, "Ssshh, sshh," as though she were a small child with a skinned knee. He felt miserable and mean and guilty, and when she lifted her head, her mouth seeking his, he didn't stop it, didn't push her away, didn't say anything. "Please, Bill, please," she whispered, her blue eyes watery with pain as she tugged on his hand, moving back toward the bed. "Please love me, please."

The bright light in the bedroom was as viscous as butter. His legs felt weighted, his feet dragged with each step, words clamored in his throat, but nothing came out. There was an inevitable quality to the whole thing, as though he were a character in a movie acting out a part that had been written for someone else. They fell back onto the bed and she pressed up against him, her whispers sliding through the air around them, desperate, pleading. Now she was lifting up, hovering over him, her cheeks damp, her hair tangled around her face and brushing his chest as her mouth moved down his body.

His arms jerked up. He grabbed hold of her shoulders and moved her away as he sat up. "This isn't going to solve anything."

She began to cry again, her hair fanned out across the pillow as she knuckled her eyes like a two-year-old. His head throbbed fiercely. *Nice going, good buddy.* He smoothed strands of hair from her temples, her cheeks, stifling the urge to flee. Her hands fell away from her eyes and sought the sides of his face, drawing him down to her, whispering, *Give me a chance, Bill, please.*

But in the end, it worked no better than it had for weeks. He felt nothing, and his body faithfully followed the dictum of his emotions despite the urgent heat of Molly's hands, her mouth. He thought of Bernelli, of how easy it had been with

her, of how her skin had tasted, and suddenly he gripped
Molly's wrists, pushing her back against the bed. He thrust
his hand between her legs, angry now, wanting to hurt her,
to be rid of her, stroking her roughly, stroking until she
writhed, trying to break free. She sank her nails into his
arms. She bucked against the weight of his body. She struggled. But he held her down, impaling her against the bed as
she shrieked, "Stop it! Let me go!"

"Isn't this what you want, Molly?" he hissed. "Isn't it?
You want me to fuck you, don't you, Molly? *Don't you?*"

She jerked an arm free, and her palm slammed across his
cheek. He straddled her, grabbing both wrists before either
connected with his face again, and trapped them against the
bed, at the sides of her head. Her eyes gleamed like chips of
steel. Sweat pimpled her face, her heaving chest. She didn't
move. And then, quietly, a smile sliding over her mouth, she
said, "You're hard, Bill."

And in that moment, he hated her. She had goaded him,
he'd fallen for it, and he hated her.

He let go of her arms and moved away from her, his anger
a hot, dry wind that swept up his spine. "I'm going to work.
Lock up when you leave."

For the rest of the day, the incident clung to him, sticky,
thick, oppressive. But it wasn't until he saw her article in the
Tribune that his anger gave way to rage—and loathing.

3

Aline parked her rental Buick in the alley between Whitman's
Bookstore and the Tango boardwalk and got out. A warm,
humid breeze licked at her face and arms. The sharp tang of
salt burned through her nostrils and stung her bloodshot eyes.
She stood for a moment, facing the ocean, watching a few
joggers along the beach, their dark silhouettes against the sky
moving up and down, up and down, like ponies on a carnival
carousel.

Closer in were people on bikes, pedaling down the boardwalk. Only a few of the shops were open; eight A.M. was a
little early even for the hard-core sunbathers. But by ten the

beach would be festooned with brightly colored towels and the snowbirds would be greasing up for a day of deep tanning. The boardwalk would be crowded with shoppers, people sipping espressos at the outdoor cafés, spring breakers chugging down beers. A regular festival.

She knuckled her burning eyes and turned away from the boardwalk to unlock the rear door of the bookstore. She should've been home in bed, she thought, but a part of her felt the need to touch base with her old self, to taste the life she might've been living if—what? If she'd never become a cop? If she'd never met Kincaid? If her parents were still alive? Was there really just one event that had nudged her life in a different direction? Or had there been several? She didn't know.

Aline stepped into the cool hall, this morning's *Tribune* tucked under her arm. The scent of the air here was sweet and thick with the past. The matrix of her childhood closed around her, protective, asking nothing, demanding nothing. Her parents hadn't lived long enough to see this Whitman's. But something of them had endured here, she thought, among the books and within her own memories of that lost time.

In the front room, she wandered up and down the rows of books, deferring the moment when she would have to open up the paper and be confronted, again, with the present. She paused at the displays her manager had set up, admiring them, nodding to herself, pleased. This store wasn't as large as the Key West Whitman's—and lacked the patina of legend her parents had so carefully nurtured in it. But this place possessed an intimacy that suited her. Books crowded in on every side, climbing from floor to ceiling. The spiral staircase twisted upward like an exotic vine; she climbed it to the second floor and stepped into the browsing area.

A couch, chairs, a long, low table with a coffeepot on it. There was always fresh coffee here—free—and if you arrived early enough, you'd find pastries from the shop next door. It was a Whitman's tradition that her manager had continued and embellished on. On weekends, Mark Finley made sure that even the pastries were replenished and that there were three or four copies of *The New York Times* around.

Aline sighed as she sank into the couch and lifted her feet onto the table. She unfolded her paper and the headlines literally jumped out at her: POSSIBLE WITNESS TO MULTIPLE MURDERS.

As she read through the article, her heart hammered. Anger clawed at the backs of her eyes. Certain phrases shouted at her: . . . *child was seen by three neighbors being carried from the yard of the Michael home on the morning of February 3.* . . . *Speculation that one of the Michael boys survived the slaughter and is being sequestered.* . . . *Possible connection to the five-year-old case of Jimmy Ray Luskin, who was executed in the Florida electric chair on August 1 of last year.* . . . *Detective Aline Scott, one of the investigators in the case, denies any knowledge of* . . .

"Christ," she whispered. That morning in the Tango Café, Molly had been telling her about the conclusions her editor had reached and Aline had replied with a simple, *Really?* and that had been twisted into a denial. There was similar "evidence" attributed to "Tango County coroner, William Prentiss" about the killer's blood type, the dyed pubic hair, the needle used on the judge and the dock worker, the hunting knife as the probable weapon, the shower the killer took after the murders. All of it was stuff Prentiss had inadvertently blurted to Molly off the record. About the only thing she hadn't included was the names of the other people connected with the Luskin case.

Aline shut the paper and let her head drop back on the cushion. She closed her eyes and massaged her aching temple. The air conditioner clicked on; cool air whispered through an overhead vent, making her shiver.

Go home. Get some sleep. It's done, the damage is done, there's nothing you can do about it.

But when she opened her eyes, she noticed something stuck to the pillar about six feet up. She frowned and sat forward. It was a red smiling-face sticker with wide eyes fringed in lashes, a heart-shaped mouth, and brows like tiny hills. It gazed down at her with its laughing, cartoon eyes, and as she looked at it, that little mouth seemed to move, to quiver, to hiss, *Ha-ha, guess who?*

An icy shudder that had nothing to do with the air conditioner zipped along her spine, her arms, propelling her to her feet. She reached up, her nails clawing at the sticker, tearing it off the pillar. An eye came away, a brow, now part of that grotesque mouth, the lips still whispering, *Ha-ha, guess who who who?* And the words reverberated in the tight, silent air, pursuing her as she fled.

16: TRAVIS FELD

I

The man who had been Lenore Luskin's attorney lived in Pirate's Cove, two miles from the marina. His home was built into the slope of a hill that offered a magnificent view of the Gulf and the Atlantic and would take the full brunt of a hurricane, if and when one churned up Florida's west coast, Kincaid thought. But he guessed Feld had so much money that if he lost his home in a hurricane, he would just build another one.

When he rang the bell, a dog inside started barking. Definitely not a poodle. This was the sound of a *dense* dog, a muscular shepherd, for instance, the kind of dog mailmen avoided. It pawed at the floor inside, snarling and growling, then someone said, *"Sit, Benjamin. Sit. Be quiet."*

The silence was immediate. A well-dressed, dignified woman—in her late sixties, Kincaid guessed—opened the door. "Yes? May I help you?"

A pit bull was sitting close to her heels, drooling. It was the largest bull Kincaid had ever seen, with paws the size of his hands and a body that must've weighed sixty pounds. "Is Mr. Feld at home?"

"Is he expecting you?"

"No."

She smiled. "He's home."

Weird, Kincaid thought, and introduced himself. "I'm a private investigator."

She held out her hand. "I'm Winnie Feld. Please come in. Travis is in the pool." She opened the door wider, but the pit bull emitted a low, mean snarl, lips drawing away from its fangs, eyes sinking into the folds of its face. *"Quiet, boy,"* she demanded, wagging a stern finger at him. The snarling stopped; Winnie rewarded him with a pat on the head. "He won't bother you, Mr. Kincaid. He's quite well trained."

That's supposed to be comforting? What was the dog well trained for? Assassination? Defense? Bill collecting? He stepped into the hall, and the pit bull thumped its nub of a tail against the floor. It sounded like a drumbeat, the prelude to a voodoo ritual.

"Heel, Benjamin," Winnie said, and the dog padded along beside her as they walked down the hall. But every now and then it turned its ugly head back toward Kincaid. Its lips drew away from its fangs without growling, without making any noise at all, a clandestine grin just to let him know who was *really* running the show.

They emerged in a backyard with a resplendent view, a jungle of plants, and, in the center, a long swimming pool. Inside of it, doing laps, was an older man with a perfectly bald head, a Kojak head. His breaststroke was strong, fast, and smooth. He appeared to be totally absorbed in his swimming and gave no indication of having noticed them. But when he reached the shallow end of the pool, he stopped and looked over. Only then did his wife speak, as if his acknowledgement of their presence was her permission to do so.

"Travis, this is Ryan Kincaid. He'd like to have a word with you."

"Talk away, Kincaid." Feld pushed back from the side of the pool in a fluid, powerful backstroke. His position in the water revealed a tanned, hirsute chest, broad shoulders, long legs, a sinewy body honed by exercise. "You can walk along the side there."

Thank you, bwana.

Winnie Feld made a soft, disgusted sound and walked away. Feld watched her as he continued to swim, watched as if he were remembering something about her. Then his gaze flicked to Kincaid. "You're a dick, aren't you?"

"Right."

"It shows."

"I feel the same about lawyers." Kincaid laughed, just to show there were no hard feelings, but he already knew he didn't like Feld.

"Good. Then we understand each other." Feld had reached the other end of the pool and hoisted himself out. He reached for a towel on a nearby chair and hooked it around his neck. "Have a chair, Kincaid." He gestured toward a shaded aluminum table on the grass, near a garden lush with bromeliads, ivy, and ferns. A telephone weighted down a stack of papers on it, and to the right of the papers was a pair of sunglasses, which Feld reached for and fit over his bald head.

"Something to drink?"

"Water, thanks."

"Water?" Feld smiled. "I thought all dicks started drinking by ten."

"Only in the movies."

Feld dialed a number, and Kincaid heard the peal of the phone in the house. "Winnie, could you bring out a glass of Perrier for Mr. Kincaid and some of that lemonade for me? . . . Well, send the maid with it." He replaced the receiver quietly, and his fingers lingered against it with a deadly sort of deliberateness. "You married, Kincaid?"

"Twice divorced."

Feld grinned; he had very white teeth. "Smart man." He slid the towel back and forth across his shoulders; it reminded Kincaid of a dog trying to scratch a stubborn itch by rubbing up against a tree trunk. "So what can I do for you, Kincaid?"

"I need some information from you about Lenore Luskin."

Feld's expression remained the same: implacable. "In relation to what?"

"The murder of Judge Michael and his family, a man named Bob Whitley who worked at the docks, and the death of Lloyd Watkins."

"They're connected?"

"Yes."

As Kincaid explained, a maid in a white uniform appeared with their drinks. She was young, remarkably pretty, and something about the way she avoided Feld's gaze told Kincaid her role in the household went well beyond servant. Feld admired her retreating figure with an avuncular lust that was both amusing and pathetic.

"What is it you want to know about Lenore?" Feld asked when he'd finished. "I don't quite understand."

"Jimmy Ray is central to these homicides. I need to know

if there was anyone in his life or his sister's who would vindicate his death sentence by knocking off the people who were involved in the case."

Feld lifted the glass of lemonade to his mouth, sipped, and then destroyed his genteel image by turning his head and wiping his mouth on his shoulder. "That's pretty specific."

"So is murder."

"Do you know about Sheila Reiner and the insipid schoolteacher, oh, what's her name? . . ."

"Louisa Almott."

"Right. Anyway, they're the only two people I can think of offhand who would've had a motive. The Reiner woman even more so, really, since she had a double whammy against Judge Michael."

"How long did you know Lenore?"

He laughed and brought his hands together as though he were praying. "Too long. Too damn long. Oh, she was a good client. But she was one crazy lady and a hell of a lot of trouble."

"Did Lenore and her brother leave Tango for about a year when Jimmy Ray was twelve, thirteen years old?"

A nod from Feld. "I don't remember exactly when it was, except that it was more than a decade ago. Yeah, I'm pretty sure of that."

"Where'd they go?"

"She went to Miami and he went to military school. In Tennessee, I think."

"Why Miami?"

Feld's eyes narrowed. "Get to the point, Kincaid."

"Did Lenore have a child when she was in Miami? Is that why she left Tango?"

Feld's laughter rang out a shade too loud, and came a heartbeat too late. "What? Where did you ever hear such a thing?"

"From Vic Xaphes."

"Oh. Well." He snorted. "No wonder."

"It's not true?"

"Certainly not."

You're lying, you prick. Kincaid leaned toward Feld, into his personal space, his breathing space, and the attorney drew back a little. "Then maybe you can clear up a little riddle for me. It's my understanding that Lenore's art collection was auctioned off, presumably to pay for property and estate taxes and whatnot.''

"Right. So? What's there to clear up?''

Just one small detail, which he'd stumbled on this morning. ''The fact that neither of the auction houses on the island has any record on it. And their records go back twenty years, Mr. Feld.''

Feld, who wasn't easily ruffled, slurped noisily at his lemonade. ''That's because there wasn't a public auction. A number of years before Lenore was killed, she sold all but two pieces to friends. When she died, Jimmy Ray inherited an Andrew Wyeth painting, which went to his attorney, and I inherited an original Picasso print.''

''The sales must've entailed a substantial amount of cash.''

''Several million. I don't remember the exact figure.''

Just then, the pit bull bounded out of the house, the pretty young maid calling after it, clapping her hands; the dog ignored her. Feld whipped his towel off his shoulder as the dog neared and snapped it toward the animal. Benjamin grabbed hold of it and pulled. Feld pulled. The dog pulled back. Kincaid watched as man and dog moved away from the table, closer to the garden. He sipped at his Perrier and looked over at the maid, who stood a short distance away, hands on her shapely hips, smiling as she watched Feld and the dog. Kinciad had the distinct impression that the little show was for her benefit.

Her gaze connected momentarily with Kincaid's, and she turned away and walked toward the house. Kincaid tilted back in his chair, his free hand grasping the underside of the table so he wouldn't tip over backward. But as his fingers closed over the curled strip of metal, something pressed against them. He let his chair touch the ground again, and now his fingers defined the object. Small and round, hard and cool. Metal. Lightweight metal. He worked the thing loose and looked down at the electronic bug in his hand.

Guess what, hotshot?

Kincaid slipped the bug in his shirt pocket as Feld and Benjamin worked their way back toward the table, still playing tug-of-war. Feld suddenly let go of the towel, and the dog, snarling, pounced on it and proceeded to tear it to shreds. Feld looked on like a proud father. Prickles of fear raced up Kincaid's arms. *Give me a skunk any day,* he thought.

"Goddamn good watchdogs." Feld tipped his glass to his mouth and gulped down the rest of the lemonade. "Anything else?"

"I don't think so. But thanks for your time." Kincaid stabbed a thumb over his shoulder as he stood. "You lost your audience a few minutes ago."

"What audience was that?" Feld's eyes narrowed, and Kincaid smiled.

"Guess you'll have to figure it out for yourself."

Since the sliding glass door that led to the kitchen was closed, Kincaid started around the side of the house. He was sure now that Lenore Luskin had given birth to a child the year she moved to Miami. But why would Feld lie about it? What possible difference could it make now that the Luskins were both dead? And what relevance, if any, did it have to this case?

Money. Several million. The money from the auction was the connection. He didn't know how, not yet. But he would.

He'd reached the deep shade at the side of the house before he became aware of the chill kneading the back of his neck. He looked over his shoulder and the chill burst across his back and made his wounded shoulder throb: Benjamin was trotting along behind him, lips drawn away in that clandestine grin again. Kincaid stopped. He turned slowly. The dog also stopped and sat back on his haunches, waiting.

In a quiet, friendly voice, Kincaid said, "I guess hotshot gave you the signal, huh, Ben ole boy?"

Benjamin emitted a low, mean growl, and Kincaid slowly moved his hand to his waist and then around to his back and under his shirt. His fingers brushed the cool, hard metal of the .38. He kept talking to the animal in a quiet, atonal voice.

"Now I really hope we can discuss things, turkey, because otherwise I may have to fill you with holes, and I really don't want to do that, Ben. I'm not partial to pits, but I've never shot an animal in my life. You supposed to injure? Maim? Kill? What?"

The dog began to shuffle his rear paws; his fangs were showing. Kincaid flicked the safety off the gun and began to inch backward through the shadows. There wasn't any breeze here. The air was tight and hot, like the inside of a coffin baking in ninety-degree heat. He kept speaking quietly to the dog, no longer aware of what he was saying. His awareness had shrunk to nothing more than the dog—those burning eyes, the ugly face, the paws, the power quivering in those leg muscles, the teeth, white and wet with saliva, the pink gums.

Belief, Kincaid. It's all in what you believe. Isn't that what you told Aline?''

Okay. He believed. He believed he was going to get out of this without being maimed—and without having to shoot the dog. But damned if he knew how he was going to do it.

Benjamin's growls were louder now, feral, matching the primal burn radiating from his eyes. Kincaid's finger tightened against the trigger.

Belief.

He inched back.

The dog crept forward.

He raised the gun slowly.

The dog's eyes impaled him.

"No farther, Benjamin. Lie down,'' demanded Winnie Feld, her voice coming from behind Kincaid.

The animal whimpered but obeyed.

"Just keep moving back very slowly, Mr. Kincaid. I would prefer that you not shoot Ben.''

"So would I.''

But he kept the gun aimed on the dog. Heat struck his back as he emerged from the shadow of the house. He heard the crinkle of paper as Winnie Feld unwrapped something and told Ben she had a little goody for him. Ben's ears twitched as a sizable chunk of raw liver landed millimeters from his nose. He went to work on it, and Winnie approached him slowly, talking to him, and snapped a long leash on his collar. She then wound the end of the leash to the faucet at the side of the house. She tied it with a double knot, and Ben, oblivious that he'd been tethered, went on with his feast.

"You sure that's tied tightly?''

"Absolutely.'' She turned her back on the dog as if to convince him, her hands laced together in front of her. Kincaid put away the gun, and he and Winnie Feld rounded the corner of the house. They stopped at the porch and she turned. She shaded her pale blue eyes with her hand—a manicured hand with two diamonds on it the size of walnuts, he noted.

"I'm awfully sorry about that, Mr. Kincaid.''

"Sorry wouldn't have been much of a consolation if I'd been attacked. He learn that trick at assassin school or something?"

She smiled, but the only thing Kincaid saw in it was sadness—deep, impenetrable, a sadness she'd absorbed so completely it had become a permanent part of who and what she was. "Benjamin has been a wonderful watchdog, but he's quite old now and gets confused."

"Right. Confused." Kincaid reached into his pocket. He held out his hand, the electronic bug a dark smudge against his palm. "I'm afraid I've got the same problem as ole Ben, Mrs. Feld. I'm so confused at the moment that I may just have to turn this over to your husband."

She reached for it, but his fingers closed over it. "I need some answers first."

She stared at his fist, as though willing it to open. *Demanding* that it open. When it didn't, she raised her eyes, but slowly, reluctantly, as if with remorse. "About what?"

"If this baby works"—he held up his fist—"then I think you already know about what."

Her long, elegant, diamond-laden fingers slid through her salt-and-pepper hair as she studied the ground. When she looked at him again, he saw compliance in her sad eyes. "Yes, I suppose I do." She stole a nervous glance over her shoulder as Ben started yapping. "Give me a place and a time. I'll bring you what you need."

"Tonight at—"

"No. I can't tonight." She cast another anxious look back as her husband's voice rose in the still heat, silencing the dog. "It'll take a little time."

"How much time?"

She twisted one of the rocks on her fingers. "Tomorrow. I'll meet you somewhere tomorrow."

"With what?"

"With what you need, Mr. Kincaid."

"Okay, I'll meet you at Lester's Bar." It wasn't the kind of place that someone of Winnie Feld's social station was likely to know about, so he gave her directions. "I'll be there at noon."

"Noon. Yes. All right. Noon."

Feld came around the side of the house then, Benjamin trotting along a foot in front of him. Kincaid slipped his hand—and the bug—in his pocket. "Oh, Kincaid. I thought you'd left."

Fuck yourself, pal. "A problem with the pooch. Your wife rescued me."

The dog leaped up, barking, snapping at the air, drooling, and Feld yanked so hard on the leash the animal jerked back and fell to the ground, whimpering with pain. *"Play dead!"* Feld hissed.

Kincaid barely resisted the urge to sink his fist into Feld's self-satisfied face as the dog rolled on his side and closed his eyes, chest heaving, tongue lolling from his mouth, the tiny, sharp metal spikes on the inside of his collar drawing blood. "Thanks again," he said, his gaze momentarily connecting with Winnie Feld's.

Then he turned and walked toward his car, the skin on the back of his neck shriveling with every step, the muscles in his arm tightening, preparing to reach for his gun, his injured shoulder aching fiercely.

But nothing happened.

The dog didn't leap on his back.

Feld didn't shoot him with a bow and arrow.

There was only the sun, and the hot blue sky, and then he was in his Saab, the doors locked. The Felds didn't move from their spots near the porch as he pulled out of the driveway, and Benjamin, bless his loyal, fearful heart, was still playing dead.

2

Kincaid drove as far as the Cove Marina. From a pay phone, he called the SPCA with an anonymous tip.

One of the advantages of living on an island where the taxes were the highest in the state was the allotment that went to those who could not adequately protect themselves. Children. The elderly. And animals. The tip would be checked out. If Benjamin was still wearing the spiked collar, he would be removed from the home, and it wouldn't make any difference to the folks at the SPCA who the hell Feld was. He'd face a stiff fine for cruelty to animals and ninety days in jail.

What a fitting postscript for a retired attorney.

17: THE SOCIAL WORKER

1

They were the island's Invisible People, and Peg Perkins loved them all. They were young, old, and middle-aged. They were single mothers with small children, families who had fallen on hard times, widows and widowers eking out an existence on Social Security. Some of them were transients who migrated south like birds during the winter and lived in abandoned warehouses near the docks, in parks, or even in the woods at the northeast tip of the island. Most of them were black, white, or Hispanic, but over the years, she'd also had a handful of refugees from Southeast Asia, as well as Russian Jews.

It made no difference to her what color they were or what language they spoke. She did what she could to help them, often bending the HRS regulations to do so. Her job was in Applications, which meant she interviewed people to determine if they were eligible for aid, and if so, what kind of aid. Food stamps? Medicaid? Emergency housing? A monthly stipend?

Transients were the most difficult to help, because the HRS rules usually required a three-month residency on the island. There was an emergency fund that could be drawn on until the three-month requirement was met, but this money had been raised exclusively by the Cove Women's Club and was supposed to be used sparingly. Still, whenever Peg couldn't fit a transient into one of the other programs, she slipped him or her into the Cove Fund, as it was called. She'd already approved three people today for the fund—which was two

199

short of what she allowed herself for an entire week, and this was only Monday. But she suspected she was going to have to use the fund again for the woman seated to the left of her desk: she was definitely a transient. Over the years, Peg had become deft at recognizing them.

The woman had long copper hair, wore a faded blue shirt, old jeans, dark sunglasses, and black high heels. She was chewing gum. Her legs were crossed at the knees, and she kicked the right foot forward and back, slowly, rhythmically, answering Peg's questions in a soft, hesitant voice. She seemed nervous, which was natural, and smoked one Marlboro Light after another. Her name was Zelda McClellan.

Peg guessed she was in her late thirties, although it was difficult to tell sometimes because poverty aged you. She said she'd been waitressing up north and had come to Tango Key because she'd heard how good the tourist season was here. But so far she'd been unable to find work, and now she was running out of money.

From the wire basket on her desk, Peg brought out a stack of forms. "I think I'll be able to help you, Ms. McClellen, but we've got to go through a list of questions first."

The woman's eyes sought the clock on the wall behind Peg. "Don't you close at five?"

It was ten of. "Don't worry about the time. It won't be the first time I've worked late."

Zelda picked at her thumbnail. "I . . . I could come back tomorrow if—"

"Really, it's okay." She tapped the stack of papers against her desk, stuck the end of her pencil into the electric sharpener, and got started.

Fifteen minutes later, the man with whom she shared her small office, Rich Jeller, peeked around the side of the Japanese screen that separated their desks. "Hey, Peg, some of us are going over to the Flamingo for drinks and dinner. When you finish here, why don't you join us?"

"How long are you going to be there?"

"Probably eight or so." He tilted his head toward Zelda McClelland and mouthed, *How much longer? I miss you already.*

Color rose into her cheeks. "I'll see you around six."

He grinned and flashed her a thumbs-up and was gone, entering the flow of traffic in the hall, where the building was being abandoned like a disabled ship. She and Rich had been seeing each other off and on for several months now. They had become lovers over the weekend, and she still wasn't sure what she felt about it. He wasn't a Christian, and what she'd done was wrong because they weren't married, but how could something that felt so good and so right be wrong?

She'd stopped by the church on her way to work this morning, intending to speak to her pastor about it. But before she reached the front door, she lost her nerve because she knew what he would say. That it was wrong, period, end of story. He would have flipped to the verses in the Bible where it talked about fornicators. He would have told her to pray for the strength to resist temptation again and to ask Jesus for forgiveness. She would've left feeling more guilty than she already did.

She had tried to pray as she drove to work, but instead she thought about how she was thirty-five years old and not getting any younger, and how she wanted very much to get married and have a family of her own. She had started to cry. By the time she reached the office, Rich was already at his desk, and he looked at her in that special way when he saw her. During lunch, they had gone back to his place, and instead of eating anything, they had made love and showered together and were half an hour late getting back.

How can it be wrong?

She turned her attention back to the application. "Okay, Ms. McClellan. We've gotten up to 1985. What jobs did you hold that year?"

"Listen, I can come back tomorrow if you want to leave. I—"

"It's okay. We can whiz through this paperwork in about half an hour, then all I have to do is fit you into one of the programs. Oh, and tomorrow you'll have to bring back the proper I.D. before you can pick up anything. I'll need copies of the I.D. for your file."

By 5:40, the bulk of the five-page application form was completed, with Peg's recommendations dutifully noted. *Client eligible for two-week emergency aid (Cove Fund) & one month of food stamps.* All she needed to do now was fill out a food stamp slip. But she couldn't find one in her metal basket. "I'll be right back. I've got to get another form."

The building was quiet; it always was after five. At least

three nights a week she was here until eight, and sometimes as late as nine. It depended on how many clients she'd seen during the day and how much paperwork she had to finish. She had never minded in the past, but realized she minded plenty right now. She wanted to be at the Flamingo with Rich. Peg didn't know if she would spend another night with him. But just the thought of this afternoon left her a little breathless, with a strange and wonderful feeling in the pit of her stomach.

It isn't wrong.

In the Food Stamp Office, she turned on the light and opened the bottom drawer of the filing cabinet. It was filled with folders that contained nothing but forms. FS4567, FS1346, FS1920 . . . it was worse than the IRS, she thought, and slammed the drawer with annoyance because the one form she needed wasn't where it should've been.

She walked over to the messy desk and started going through the junk piled high in the wire mesh basket. She thought she heard something behind her, and glanced back quickly. Nothing there. *Of course not. You're spooking yourself.* Then she saw Zelda McClellan leaning against the door.

"This place is sort of creepy after everyone leaves," she said.

"Yeah, I guess it is."

"You work late a lot, huh?"

Peg turned her attention back to the stuff in the basket. "Yes."

"You get paid overtime for it?"

She laughed. "No."

"At least with waitressing, you get tips," Zelda remarked.

"Hmm. I'll be along in a second, as soon as I find this blasted form. You can go back to my office if you want."

"I'd rather stay right here."

"Actually, you're not allowed in here. Ah. Great. I found it." She wagged the form as she turned around. "You'll bring this back with you tomorrow morning, and once you present it, you'll get your food coupons."

Zelda smiled. She was standing with her hands behind her back, and there was something about her expression that Peg didn't like. That scared her a little. *Something unnatural.*

"Why don't you sit down, Ms. Perkins."

"This isn't my office. I—"

"Sit down." Zelda was still smiling, such an odd, twisted smile, and now her hands slipped out from behind her back and Peg stared at the knife in her right hand and the roll of masking tape that enclosed her right wrist like a bracelet. "I said sit down, Ms. Perkins, and please don't scream because then I'll have to cut your tongue out before we have our little talk."

Peg's mouth opened, but nothing came out. Her fingers went to the cross at her throat. A wall of sweat swept across her back. *Jesus is testing me because of Rich, because I slept with Rich, Jesus is showing me His power, He . . .* Zelda stepped toward her, light glinting from the tip of the knife, and Peg moved back until the edge of a chair pressed up against her legs. She fell into it, her eyes still on Zelda's face.

"Money? Do you want money? Is that it?"

"Money?" Zelda laughed, and it warbled in the air, high and shrill, and was somehow more terrifying than the knife. "No, I don't want money, Peg. I want . . . let's see. What's a good word for what I want? Vindication. Yes, I guess you could call it vindication. You remember that old TV show, *The Avengers*? Well, that's sort of what I am. An avenger." She touched the end of the knife to Peg's throat. "I keep it quite sharp, Peg, so please don't make any sudden movements, all right?"

"I . . . I don't understand." But she was beginning to, oh dear God, she was beginning to understand. She remembered the detectives who'd come by the house. She was thinking of the call she'd gotten this morning from the chief of police, offering her round-the-clock protection, and how she'd thanked him but said no, she really didn't need it. She thought of the article she'd read in the *Tribune* this morning . . . *Needle in the eye* . . .

Jimmy Ray Luskin: that's what this was about.

"Well, I guess I'll just have to explain it to you, Peg, now won't I? But right now, you put your arms on those little old armrests . . . that's a good girl, Peg. I like people who know how to follow directions." She kept the knife at Peg's neck, the tip pressing in against the skin, pressing in hard enough to almost draw blood. With her teeth, she yanked a length of the masking tape from the roll and tore it off. With her free hand, she wrapped the tape around Peg's arm and under the armrest, securing it. She repeated this with her other arm. "Stretch out your legs and cross them at the ankles."

"Please. You don't have to do this." Peg spoke calmly, but her voice quavered. "I. . ."

Zelda tapped the flat edge of the blade against Peg's cheek. She was still smiling. "And I thought you were such a good girl. That you could follow directions." The blade slid upward toward Peg's eye. "Now do it, hon, I won't tell you again."

She extended her legs, crossing them at the ankles, and now Zelda—*What's her real name?*—bound Peg's ankles with the masking tape. Tears burned in the corners of her eyes, threatening to spill. *Please, God, tell me what to do, guide me,* she prayed silently.

"There. Very good, Peg. Now I think we can have our little chat." Zelda paced back and forth in front of her, slapping the flat edge of the blade against her palm as she spoke. "You remember Jimmy Ray Luskin?"

"Y-yes."

"You remember how you and the other folks on your jury found him guilty?"

"Y-yes."

"Did you think he was guilty, Peg? In your heart?"

"He pleaded guilty by reason of insanity."

"That's lawyers' jargon, Peg. I'm talking about what *you* felt."

If she told the truth, she was going to die. If she didn't tell the truth, she would probably die, anyway, so what was the difference? "I . . . I believe he killed her. But there were extenuating circumstances. She . . . his sister provoked him. She had abused him. I thought the charges should've been dropped to manslaughter."

Zelda glared at her. For a long moment the only sound in the room was the *slap, slap* of the blade against her palm. "The way your hands and ankles are bound now, Peg, that's how it was for Jimmy Ray when they strapped him in the chair. Only it was worse, much worse, because there were people around. He was practically naked. And bald, he was bald, too. They shave your head before you go to the chair, did you know that, Peg?" She leaned close to her, so close Peg could smell the faint tinge of sweat and perfume, a stale perfume.

Tears were streaming down Peg's cheeks now. Her bladder ached with fullness. She kept trying to pray, but she no longer knew how.

"Did you know that?" Zelda hissed.

"Y-yes."

"Are you scared, Peg?"

"Yes," she whimpered. "Oh God, please. . ."

"Jimmy Ray was scared, too. Now you know how *he* felt, Peg. Everyone's going to know how he felt." She removed something from inside her purse. She held it up. It was a long hat pin with a red bulb at the end. "You know what this is, Peg?'

She screamed. She screamed so loud, it bounced against the walls, echoing, shredding the quiet. Zelda rushed toward her and slapped her across the cheek, nearly knocking her senseless, killing the scream. Then she pressed a strip of masking tape across her mouth.

"You shouldn't have done that." She peered into Peg's eyes, her face so close to hers it was blurred. "I don't like screamers. I don't blame you for being afraid; I would be, too, if I were in your place. But really, Peg. I expected you to have more dignity." She moved away, pacing again, slapping the knife against her palm. "On second thought, though, why should you be any different from the others? In the end, they were all nothing but screamers. The judge was the worst, you know."

Peg squeezed her eyes shut, sobbing deep in her chest, her nose stuffing up so she could barely breathe. Her bladder had let loose, and she felt the warmth seeping through her skirt and into the chair.

"Do you believe in capital punishment, Peg?"

She opened her eyes. The woman had stopped moving and just stared at her, slapping the blade against her palm, sharp, quick slaps.

"Do you?"

Peg sniffled and shook her head frantically. *No, no, I don't believe.* It was true; she didn't. When the other members of Luskin's jury had wanted to recommend the death penalty, she'd spoken up. She'd been overruled. She kept shaking her head. *No, no.*

"No? That's curious. Then how come the jury recommended the electric chair, Peg? Hmm?" She let the tip of the hat pin trail over Peg's arm. "And how come you, as the foreman of that jury, got up and stated to the judge that the jury recommended the chair?"

I had to. I was overruled, Peg grunted into the gag, and Zelda smiled.

"Very tough to reply with tape over the mouth, isn't it, hon? But that's how it is on death row. Did you know that? When you're on death row, no one hears you." She let her eyes drop to the hat pin, which had paused on the back of Peg's right hand. The woman slowly poked the hat pin into the skin between two knuckles. At first it stung. It was like a bee bite, maybe not even as bad. But as the woman worked the hat pin deeper and deeper into the skin it struck something, and pain exploded in her hand and she screamed into the gag, screamed and watched in horror as blood oozed around the pin. When it poked out the other side of her hand, the woman twisted her wrist, so she could see it, and smiled. "Bet that smarts, huh? I bet you're wondering why I use a hat pin. I bet the police are wondering, too." She grinned. "And guess what? There's nothing dark and secretive about it. A hat pin is just easy to hide." She laughed and worked the hat pin a little more.

Peg sobbed into the gag, sobbed and tried to pray, sobbed and thought about Christ's hands nailed to the cross. Pain radiated up to her wrist, her hand throbbed, she stared at the hat pin as the woman began to remove it, slowly. Blood streamed from the puncture wound and soaked into the arm-rest of the chair. The woman wiped the pin on Peg's skirt and set it aside, on the desk. From her purse, she brought out a pair of scissors.

"What we have here, Peg, is an ordinary pair of house scissors." She snapped them inches from Peg's face. "You have a boyfriend, Peg?"

Her head bobbed up, down, up and down. *Please God, let someone show up. The janitor, make him show up early, before seven, please oh please God.*

"I bet he enjoys your cute little figure, doesn't he." The woman snipped away the buttons on Peg's blouse and hummed as she worked. When all the buttons were gone, she folded open the sides of the blouse and looked at Peg's breasts, cocking her head to one side, then the other, like she was trying to figure out something. "A white cotton bra. Cute, real cute, Peg.'' She laughed. ''Those damn things went out fifteen, twenty years ago. I bet you even wear white cotton panties, don't you?''

''Nuhnuhnuh,'' she grunted into the tape.

Now the woman, Zelda—*Your name, what's your real name?*—slid one of the blades of the scissors up under the bra in front, and cut it loose. It fell away. She stood back again, cocking her head once more. ''Not bad, Peg. How does your boyfriend turn you on, anyway?''

She was weeping again. The tears blurred the woman's face, the scissors, the room, everything. She turned her head to the side, fighting back a surge of vomit in her throat as the woman brought a hand up under Peg's breast. *You'll suffocate if you throw up. Suffocate. Choke to death. Stop oh stop please . . .*

''Like this? Is this what he does?'' She flicked her thumb over the nipple, and it went harder than a pebble, and the woman laughed and laughed and kept doing it, over and over again. ''Jimmy Ray liked women with fuller breasts. Like mine.'' She stood and thrust out her chest. ''Nice, huh. I don't think he would've been too crazy about your trainer bra, either. Or your hairstyle. In fact, I think we need to do something about your hair, Peg.''

The woman moved around behind Peg, ran her fingers through her dark hair, and started snipping away at it. Hairs fluttered to Peg's shoulders. Great chunks of it fell to the floor. *Snip, snip,* went the scissors, and hairs floated into her lap, down the front of her chest. ''Oh, this is going to look very nice, Peg. A real punk hairdo.'' *Snip, snip.* ''If there was time, I'd even color it for you. I like changing my hair color from time to time. When I knew Jimmy Ray, I was a redhead. He was partial to redheads. That's what he said, anyway. We used to meet in this room at the prison. I had some connections, see, and it was just him and me. He loved me, you know. He did.'' *Snip, snip, snip.* ''A couple of times we even did it in that room. Standing up.'' She giggled. ''All kinds of things you can get away with in prison, Peg. Except busting him out.'' *Snip, snip.* ''That was the one thing I . . . I couldn't do.'' Her voice cracked. *Snip.* ''So I promised him I would get even. I always keep my promises, Peg. You have to. You give your word, then you gotta keep it. It's a matter of honor.'' *Snip.*

"There. All finished, Peg. I've got to scoot, because the janitor is going to show up. That's what you've been hoping for, isn't it? But see, I did my homework, hon. I always do. If you do your homework, you don't get caught."

She ran her hands through Peg's hair; bits of it rained around her. Tears stung her eyes again, but she blinked them back. If she cried anymore, she wouldn't be able to breathe. Peg grunted.

"What was that?" The woman came out from behind Peg's chair. "Got something to say, hon?"

Another grunt.

"I'll let you say your piece. That's only fair. Even Jimmy Ray got to say something before he fried. You know what he said, Peg?"

"Nuhnuhnuh."

She brushed at the hair on Peg's chest. "Nasty stuff doesn't come off too easy, does it?" she wheezed. "It's the sweat. You're sweating a lot, Peg. You nervous?" And she grinned. "Can't imagine why." She wheezed again, and stepped away from Peg for a moment, fanning her hand in front of her nose. "Christ. You pissed on yourself, Peg. How awful for you. I guess we should get rid of that nasty skirt, shouldn't we? The skirt you peed in. Poor Peg. Incontinent already, and the best hasn't even happened yet."

She wheezed more deeply now as she began to cut up the front of Peg's skirt. "Oh, what Jimmy Ray said right before they pulled the switch. That's what I was going to tell you, wasn't it?"

Snip, snip.

Peg stared as the scissors worked up the center of her skirt, cutting carefully. She grunted again, but the woman ignored her and kept cutting, telling her what Jimmy Ray had said.

"He said, 'I forgive all of you.' Isn't that something?" She brushed the pieces of the skirt off Peg's thighs and burst out laughing. "White cotton panties. God, I knew it. I just knew it." She reached into her purse and brought out a compact, which she flipped open. "Just one more thing, then we can get on with it, Peg. Well, two more things actually. First. . ."

She reached for the hat pin. Peg screamed against the masking tape as her eyes widened, watching the woman pinch the red bulb at the top of it between her thumb and forefinger. "Where should be put this little ole hat pin, sugar?"

Peg squeezed her eyes shut and screamed again and again as the woman drew the tip of the pin lightly between her breasts, down, down to her navel. Now the pin circled there. "Hmm, right about here, I think," she wheezed, and the hat pin slipped in.

Peg passed out.

2

"You weren't supposed to pass out on me like that, sugar."

The voice reached her as if from a great distance. Peg's eyes fluttered open. Her body ached. It shouted with pain. She was no longer able to tell exactly where the pain was coming from, but it didn't matter. She didn't want to know. The woman was wheezing very badly now. Spicules of sweat dotted her upper lip, her brow, even her throat. Peg swallowed, but the inside of her mouth was so dry, it hurt to swallow. Then she realized the masking tape had been removed from her mouth; her jaw seemed to creak as she opened it.

"I always keep my word, Peg. I told you you'd get a chance to say something. So start talking."

"Kill me," she hissed. "Just kill me."

"No one tells me what to do, Peg, or when to do it."

Peg shrieked, and the woman slapped her, shook her finger at her. *Nonono*, she said. *Badbadbad*, and then she twisted the hat pin and Peg squeezed her eyes shut and sobbed as she repeated the Twenty-third Psalm. She was dimly aware of the woman wheezing as she laughed, but after a moment, even this sound dimmed. The words of the psalm soothed her, comforted her, deafened her to everything but the voice of God. She was being lifted, transported. She was rising out of her body, out of her bones, rising like a cloud of smoke, and she could see herself below, see her shorn hair, the hat pin sticking out of her navel, the blood crusted over the knuckles on her hand, her hair blanketing the floor. But she felt no pain. Angels had kissed away the pain. She watched the woman in the chair—herself but not herself, not anyone she knew, not really, not anymore.

And from her perch high above the room, she could hear the woman in the chair scream again as Zelda McClellan slid the knife across her throat. But the scream was brief, and then there was only the dark, warm and eternal.

PART
THREE

18: PRISON FLIES

I

Aline reminded herself that snowbirds pumped millions into Tango's economy each year, created jobs, and enabled the year-round residents to enjoy a quality of life second to nowhere in Florida. But this evening, none of these reminders pacified her.

It had taken her nearly an hour to shop for the week's groceries because the aisles were jammed with snowbirds. On top of it, she had to wait twenty minutes in line to get anywhere near the cashier, and *then* the tape on the machine ran out. She stood there another five minutes while the cashier changed it. As if this weren't enough, she got out to her rented Buick and realized she'd locked the key inside. She had to go back into the store and ask for a hanger at the office register, where you cashed checks, returned bottles, and filed complaints. The woman who waited on her was the Publix Sourpuss. She was plump, with salt-and-pepper hair, and had a prissy little mouth that never smiled. She seemed to think customers were pariah, with God knew what sort of diseases, because whenever she returned change, she never dropped it in your hand. She slapped it on the counter. Aline asked for a hanger and explained why she needed it, and she said hangers were in household goods. Aline pointed out that the hangers in household goods were all plastic; she needed a wire hanger.

"Try the drugstore next door," she said.

"Where's your manager?"

"He's not here."

"Then I'd like to talk to your assistant manager."

"He's not here, either."

But just then the assistant manager came through the double doors to the left of the register, and Aline, who knew him casually, said she'd locked her keys in her car and did he happen to have a hanger she could use? Sure thing, he said, and looked at Ms. Sourpuss, who glared at Aline, then reached under the counter, and brought out a hanger, which she dropped on the counter.

By then, Aline was livid. "You ought to smile once in a while. It'd help your constipation," she told Sourpuss, and walked away.

It took her ten minutes to work it through the window and hook it around the lock. Then she got into the car and it wouldn't start because she'd left the headlights on. A bag boy tracked down jumper cables and used his own car to get hers going.

Now here she was, chugging up Hurricane Hill in the dark, wondering if the ice cream had melted, if the milk had soured, if anything else would go wrong with the loaner car before she pulled into the driveway. She should've stayed in bed when she'd awakened this afternoon at four, after six hours of restless sleep. Thank God it was Kincaid's night to cook, because if it had been up to her, they'd be having yogurt and fruit.

The car made it to the driveway. The trunk even opened. She hadn't forgotten her house key. Kincaid was home. Things were definitely looking up.

She found him in the kitchen, at the stove, stirring one of his mysterious, delectable sauces. He wore the bib apron with a red pitchfork on the front that said I GOT FRIED ON TANGO. Steam drifted up around his face, into his beard.

"More packages in the car?"

"A bunch."

"I'll get them if you stir." He gestured toward the wooden spoon sticking up out of the pan. As she took hold of it, he kissed her quickly. "You home for the night?"

"Definitely. You?"

"Yes. I've got some stories, Al." He grinned, and she laughed.

"Boy, is *that* ever a lascivious grin."

"We're making progress," he said, and went out to get

the groceries. Aline wondered if he meant the two of them were making progress or if he was referring to the investigation. As they were unpacking the groceries, she asked what he'd meant. "If you're asking, that must mean you don't think you and I are making progress."

"I think we are. I just didn't know if you felt the same way."

He reached across the paper bag that separated them and kissed her again. Not a quick kiss, not perfunctory. This was a serious smooch, the kind that made her toes curl, a prelude to something else. "I haven't stubbed my toe on the *Random House Dictionary* for a week. That's progress."

"But it's not what you were talking about."

"No." As he finished unpacking the groceries and Aline set the table, he told her about his visit with Travis Feld— and his appointment with Feld's wife tomorrow. "I don't know what she knows or what it has to do with any of this, but it's worth checking out."

"So maybe Lenore had a child. So what?"

"I don't know. Not yet. But the leads have trailed to Feld, and maybe whatever his wife knows will push us toward the next lead and that one will get us on to the next and so on."

Until they either ran out of leads—or ran into the answer. That was how it worked in theory, anyway.

But theories rarely behaved the way they were supposed to when put into practice. One of Aline's homicide investigations had dragged on for eight months. Another was still unsolved. Another had been cracked in three days. There were no assurances that A automatically led to B and resulted in C; there were no hard-and-fast rules that applied uniformly to every case, every investigation. Homicides, perhaps more than most crimes, were as individualized as the people who committed them. The trick was in finding a particular killer's imprint and figuring out how to decode it.

An investigation was a bit like sex, she thought. The basics were the same for everyone, but it was what you did with what you knew that made the difference.

"What'd you do in that monastery?" Aline lifted her arm and pointed straight up.

"Played tourist."

"C'mon, really."

They were lying in bed, shoulders touching, the heat of their lovemaking lingering in the loft. He lifted her hand, spreading the fingers against the starlight that fell into the room through the window, lifting it higher and higher until she could see the poster through her own splayed fingers. "What I did in the monastery was listen to the monks chat, meditate, and freeze my ass off." He brought her hand back down, resting it against his chest.

She laughed. "No women in Kathmandu?"

"That was years ago."

"That means you don't remember?"

She turned on her side, lifting up, head resting in the palm of her left hand while her right stroked his beard. The best parts of Kincaid's travel stories were about the women; they fascinated her. She would try to imagine him traveling with these women, loving them, leaving them. Sometimes she would think about the stories afterward, wondering what the women looked like, how they talked, whether they still thought of him. She would see herself trekking through the Himalayas or the Alps and meeting Kincaid on a train or in a bus station. A different Kincaid, a sojourner whose connections with people were transitory, momentary. Probable selves, she thought. "C'mon, Ryan. What was she like?"

"Oriental."

Ah, now they were getting somewhere. "Black hair?"

"Sure."

"Thick, long hair?"

"Too cold for anything but that."

Her hand slid over his beard, to his chest. "Did she speak English?"

"I sure didn't speak Kathmandese."

"What?" She burst out laughing. *"Kathmandese?"*

"She spoke English. She'd studied in Europe."

"What else?"

His fingers wound through her hair, drawing her mouth to his. Her legs slipped between his; her hipbones rubbed against his. "Like that?" She pulled back. "She kissed like that?"

He laughed. "Okay, she initiated me into the mysteries of the *Kama Sutra*. How's that?"

She poked him. "You lie like hell."

He smiled and traced the shape of her mouth with his fingertip, and she wasn't so sure he was lying. "All right, the truth.'' He folded his arms under his head and gazed at the poster. ''The truth is that her mother was from Nepal and her father was French and she really was educated in Europe. We spoke French most of the time. The summer I was in Nepal, she was in Kathmandu studying with one of the monks.''

''Studying what?''

''To be a healer. A Zen healer. We stayed in this run-down hotel with no heat, and for about six weeks she showed me Kathmandu, taught me a little about Zen, about acupuncture, about meditation. Then we left and traveled to Paris together, then to southern France, then I never saw her again.''

Now *that* had the ring of truth, she decided. ''What was she like?''

He turned his head, and in the dim light she saw that his eyes were laughing. ''Like as a person? A tour guide? What?''

''What was she like in bed?'' Aline asked.

''Like this.'' His hand trailed down her spine.

''Like this? How?''

''She asked me the same kind of questions you do. She wanted to know what it was like with American women, if it was like in the movies.''

''What'd you tell her?''

''I didn't. I showed her.''

''Show me.''

He did, and midway through, the phone rang.

''Goddamn,'' he muttered.

She felt as though she'd been swimming through cool, thick water and was now surfacing for air. ''It's a wrong number.''

''Right.''

But on the fourth ring, his hand shot out and grabbed for the receiver. ''. . . Uh, Bernie. Hi. . . . What?'' He sat up. ''When?'' He swung his legs over the side of the bed. ''Yeah, we're on our way.'' He hung up and stood, reaching for his clothes.

Aline shivered as she stood. ''Who, Kincaid?''

''The social worker.''

The HRS building was one of the ugliest on Tango—a low, squat, concrete building that looked like an abandoned World War II bunker. Except for the twin panes of glass at either side of the front door, there were no windows. Blue and red lights swirled in its front parking lot, ghostly specters she had come to associate with violent death.

As she and Kincaid got out of the Saab, she saw Bernie talking to a man who was leaning against the paramedic truck, obviously distraught. She guessed he had found the body. There were the usual gawkers who, drawn by the lights, the sirens, the promise of blood, had clustered at the periphery of the property and spoke in hushed tones among themselves.

Just inside the door, in what appeared to be a small waiting room, she ran into Gene Frederick. Perhaps it was the light, but his white hair had a yellow tinge, like nicotine, and so did his face. "I'm bringing in the Reiner woman and the schoolteacher for questioning."

"Weren't they under surveillance?"

Frederick looked ill. "I pulled the men and put them on the two jurors who wanted protection. Perkins didn't want help; I spoke to her just this morning."

"Who found her?"

"The guy who shared her office. Richard Someone. I got the impression they were more than just co-workers. She was supposed to meet him and some other people at the Flamingo for dinner and drinks, and by seven when she didn't show, he called the office. No one answered. He figured she was on her way. When she still hadn't shown by half past, he got worried and drove over to see what was what. The janitor had just arrived; he was in the lobby and hadn't even seen her yet.

"According to the boyfriend, there was a redhead with the woman when he left at five. He just saw her from the back. Her name on the receptionist roster is Zelda McClellan. We already ran a check on the address she gave: it's bogus. Bill's back there now. I've seen enough."

Aline stared after him as he pushed through the double doors into the night air. *I've seen enough:* not once in five years had she ever heard Frederick make such a statement.

She made her way down the hall, past silent offices, to where Clicker, the police photographer, stood in the hall, loading his camera with film. He nodded when he saw her; she nodded back. "Her throat was cut," he said. "But that's not even the worst of it."

She paused in the doorway, where Prentiss and one of his skeleton crew were working. She looked at Peg Perkins, slumped in the chair near the desk, and her fingers tightened against the doorjamb, gripping it as her legs went rubbery. *I've seen enough:* she understood. She closed her eyes for a moment, but inside them, the image burned, dimmed, burned again. A huge pressure built in her chest. It felt as though a cold, clammy hand were squeezing her heart, robbing it of blood, of oxygen. She opened her eyes and stepped into the room and looked to make sure she'd seen what she thought she had.

Between Peg Perkins's breasts, just above the hat pin in her navel, was a smiling-face sticker, apple green, with peaked black brows and little slits for eyes.

3

"Clicker, didn't you work in a prison for a while?"

"Yeah," the photographer replied. "A medium-security place in Vero Beach. Why?"

"What'd you do there?"

He and Aline were standing at the end of the hall, where he'd opened the door. The night air was much warmer than the air in the hall, but it was fresh. Clean. She inhaled it deeply, trying to get rid of the stink in her nostrils that was as much the fetid odor of death as it was of fear. Her own fear. Clicker exhaled a pother of smoke, and even that seemed sweeter than this other smell.

He was older than she was by perhaps ten years, in his mid-forties, but tonight he looked sixty. "I was a classification officer. Basically that means I set up inmates' schedules—their jobs, education, everything they did in prison."

"Ever have any contact with prison flies?"

"Sure. Why? You think a prison fly did that?" He jerked his thumb back, indicating the office.

"I don't know." Was Louisa Almott a prison fly? She'd been on Jimmy Ray Luskin's mailing and visitors' list, and had admitted being in love with him. But those things alone didn't make a prison fly. Had Luskin become her sacred mission? Had she moved close to the prison after his incarceration, uprooting herself from Tango, to be near him? Maybe.

"For about a year, Allie, we had this female psychologist on staff. She was a dynamite-looking woman, bright and very innovative. She got results. Then I heard she was banging inmates. So one night after she'd left, I checked her office and discovered that she'd disconnected her intercom system. I hooked it up again and for the next few days eavesdropped on her sessions. The intercom was a kind of Big Brother device where you could listen in anywhere on the compound without anyone knowing it. Sure enough, she was screwing guys there in her office."

"Wonderful," she drawled.

Clicker turned and flicked his cigarette out the door. It trailed an orange arc through the dark, a miniature comet, a shooting star. Then it hit the ground and sparks flew away from it. "It was a power trip, Al, although I didn't realize that then. I didn't really understand what she was about until I'd been there a lot longer and had seen prison flies come and go. They're about power. Here's another example. A seventeen-year-old kid on my caseload attempted suicide. Turns out the assistant superintendent—a man—was taking this kid and a half-dozen others who had outside grounds detail to his trailer some afternoons. Ostensibly, they were supposed to be working on the prison vans. Instead, he was screwing them, and in return they got favors—better job assignments, the promise of early parole, whatever. Whenever a free person messes sexually with someone who *isn't* free, the only thing behind it is a need for power."

"But prison flies don't have sex with these men usually," Aline said. Instead, they married the men and the marriages were never consummated. Instead, they pledged they would wait for the men until they were paroled or maxed out their time. Instead, their lives revolved around a two-hour visiting period once a week.

Clicker adjusted the camera strap around his neck. "The

promise of sex is there, at some unspecified time in the future,'' he continued. ''The woman—who usually can't make a go of it in a relationship with a man on the outside—now has a man who needs her, who maybe even loves her, and best of all, he can't be unfaithful to her, unless it's with another man, and that doesn't really count, does it, because he has to get his rocks off somehow.''

''So she's a loser.''

''In her *own* eyes.''

''You think it's possible for a man on death row to be involved with a prison fly?''

''It's tougher, but, Al, you can get anything in prison if you've got the dough—or the connections. Anything.'' He closed the door and they walked up the hall and then down the other hall. ''So yeah, I think it's possible.'' They stopped in the doorway to Peg's office. ''That was her desk.'' Clicker gestured toward the other side of the Japanese screen that separated the two desks. Aline walked over to it, into the small space that had constituted the social worker's professional life. She noted the framed photograph of a Persian cat, stretched out on top of a TV; the desk calendar; the clock on the wall; the wire basket stacked with forms; and the crucifix dangling from a chain that had been hooked over a corner of the basket.

That about summed it up: the end of a life that had barely begun.

4

The last time Aline had seen Sheila Reiner was that day at the Cove Women's Club. This woman hardly resembled her at all. Her arrogance had abandoned her. Fear had tightened the tiny lines around her mouth, at her eyes. She wasn't wearing any makeup. Her pretty light brown hair was disheveled. Her eyes were rheumy from crying, and the tears had left trails like ditches against her cheeks, which aged her. She had bummed cigarettes from Frederick and smoked them at a frantic pace, one after another, as he and Bernie fired questions at her. Aline sat in a soundproof room, behind a one-way mirror, watching.

The problem with Sheila Reiner was that her answers were consistent—not pat, not practiced, but consistent. Also, between five and eight that evening she'd been at the Women's Club, playing bridge; half a dozen witnesses had verified her alibi. She might've murdered the Michael family, Whitley, and perhaps she'd tampered with Lloyd Watkins's plane, but she didn't kill the social worker. Either someone else had—*Louisa Almott?*—or this was the work of a copycat killer, the result of Molly Chapman's article in the *Tribune*.

She rubbed her eyes, swiveled in her chair, and peered through another one-way glass, watching Louisa Almott. She'd been brought in half an hour ago, and for the most part she'd done nothing except pace, sneeze, and page through the stack of magazines on the table. She was sitting now, legs crossed at the knees, those sturdy farm-girl fingers restlessly drumming the table. Now and then she glanced toward the glass, aware that she was being watched. Once, she even smiled and waggled her fingers like the whole thing was someone's idea of a bad joke but, hey, she could be a good sport about it, see?

Her alibi—*again*—wasn't much of an alibi: she was at home grading papers. But her lover was a pilot, she seemed to have a perpetual case of allergies, and she had a motive.

The chair squeaked as Aline got up. She was tempted to throw the intercom switch and hiss into it, startling Almott from her phlegmatic complacency. Instead, she went next door. The schoolteacher didn't even bother looking up as Aline stepped into the room, and Aline didn't speak or move any closer.

Farm-girl hands, strong hands

Her heart fluttered like a moth in her chest.

Hat pin

Her hands dampened. Her knees felt as if they'd been injected with Novocain. *Allergies . . . She loved Luskin . . .*

Almott dug into her purse for a pack of cigarettes and lit one. *Marlboros.* The butt Prentiss had fished out of Whitley's toilet was a Marlboro Light and these were regular, but it was close. Close enough to bring a chill to the base of Aline's spine. *Do I want to be alone with this woman?*

"You took your sweet time getting here, Detective Scott,"

she said. And only then did she look up, smiling her sweetest farm-girl smile. So innocent, so guileless, Aline thought dimly, a slow dread scratching its way up her legs, her arms, prickling the back of her neck. "But as a teacher, I've learned patience." She was doodling on the magazine, the pen standing almost rigid in her left hand. "So?"

"You have an attorney?"

Some of her hubris left her. "No. Why? Am I under arrest?"

"You may be before we're finished."

She drew in smoke, tipped her head back, blew it into the air. "I doubt it. You've been asking me for alibis. I have them."

"Being alone at home isn't an alibi."

She smiled, and this smile was triumphant. "I lied."

"Why?"

"Because I've been seeing a married man." She twisted the cigarette between her fingers, watching it as though it were made of gold. "And I was lying to protect him." She stabbed out the cigarette and sat forward in the chair. "And now I've decided to hell with protecting him. It's my turn to be protected. His—"

"Yes, I know. Jack Cranaski. He teaches science. He's married and has a child. He lives—"

"I know where he lives," she snapped, annoyed now. "And you don't have any goddamn right, spying on me like—"

Aline exploded, suddenly hating this woman with her farm-girl face and her sturdy hands, hating the way the fresh innocence camouflaged the woman in front of her now, a woman growing old on her bitterness. "We have every right. You haven't given us one straight answer since the beginning. And since I suspect your lover boy may be in on this with you, I'm going to bring him in for questioning unless you start talking."

She looked stunned. Then contrite. Then frightened. And then she began to talk.

5

The air in the morgue was so cold Prentiss had to wear a sweater under his lab coat, and when he exhaled, he could almost see his breath. He flicked on the lamp over the aluminum autopsy table. It swung for a moment, casting shadows where there shouldn't have been any, the light gleaming against the wall of metal drawers. It spooked him. In fact, everything about this room spooked him tonight—the quiet, the cold, the lights, his solitude, the body on the table.

He looked down at Peg Perkins. Except for her color and the blood crusted at various spots on her body, she might've been asleep. The dead always looked asleep, he thought. Until you cut them open. During his first autopsy in medical school, he'd been convinced that the man they were about to work on wasn't really dead and that any second he was going to bolt forward and scream. He'd been so sure of it that the moment the physician had pressed his scalpel against the sternum, he had passed out.

That was how he felt now. Only the Perkins woman wouldn't bolt forward. Her eyes would just open slowly, as though against an ineffable weight, and her lips would move, and he would have to lean closer to hear her whisper something. *A name. She'll give me a name and this horrible mess will be over with.*

A Japanese horror movie, he thought, chiding himself, and lifted her injured hand. He cleaned the wound and examined it. The recorder was on, and he spoke into it as he worked, moving from her hand to her navel, where the hat pin still protruded. With gloved fingers, he slowly pulled it out and held it up to the light. A moiling unease seized his gut, and it worsened by the second until he thought he was going to puke. *Four inches, four goddamn inches. This went into the judge's eye, the dock worker's eye, oh sweet Christ, four inches. . . .*

He quickly set the hat pin aside and moved on to the slash at her throat. He cleaned away the blood and examined the wound. Same type of weapon, he decided, that had been used on the judge and sunk into the dock worker's chest. It . . . *Jesus, how did I miss this before?*

He straightened so fast he bumped his head on the edge of

the lamp, knocking it sideways. It swung again, light glinting here, there, as he hurried over to the computer terminal. He tore off his gloves, booted up, tapped in his code, and accessed the file on Judge Michael.

There. Incision begun just below right ear, severing carotid artery. His *right* ear. Just like the Perkins woman. The killer was left-handed.

He reached for the phone and dialed the station.

19: AROUND TOWN

I

Kincaid sat in a back booth, sipping coffee and paging through *USA Today*. Whenever the door opened, he looked up, hoping to see Winnie Feld. But it was only another regular, wandering in from the streets with his thirst and his tall tales. Every so often he'd hear a grunt or a murmur from Ferret, who was seated across from him, studying racing forms. He was alone today; Bino was minding the garage.

"I think Winnie Feld is standing you up, Ryan." Ferret tipped his head toward the clock on the wall. "It's already half past twelve."

"She'll be here."

"Yeah?" Ferret sat forward, his long, spidery fingers sliding together in an attitude of prayer, lips drawing away from his teeth in one of his weird, eerie smiles. "You feel sure enough about that to place a bet?"

"Is there anything you *don't* bet on?"

"Yeah. The weather. You feel sure enough or not?"

"Okay."

"How much?"

Hey, that was easy. "The price of a new car for Aline."

Ferret laughed. It was the same sound a fussy parrot made. "I love to gamble, Ryan, but I'm not an asshole."

"You asked."

"True." He drew his finger around the rim of his coffee mug. "Feld's not a man to fuck with, you know."

Kincaid shrugged. "You know much about him?"

"No."

"But enough to tell me not to fuck with him."

"Yup."

"You want to be a little more specific, Ferret?"

"Things you hear, that's all."

"What kind of things?"

"That he and Lenore Luskin had such a nice professional relationship that whenever he needed dirt on a defense attorney or a local politician, Lenore indulged him. She apparently had the dope on just about every hotshot on Tango, and if she didn't, one of her hooker friends did. And we're not talking low-life hooking here, Ryan. We're talking high-class shit. Two thousand bucks for a night. The kind of woman a man dreams about. The kind of woman a man will tell things to."

"I get the picture, Ferret."

"Yeah, but the problem with you, Ryan"—and his dark eyes narrowed—"is that you may get the point, but then you go ahead and do what you were going to do, anyway. That's how come you nearly got your ass smeared that night up on the cliff."

Kincaid ignored the observation. "Maybe Feld fathered this child she supposedly had."

"Maybe, but I doubt it. My impression of the man is that sex was never a big deal for him; power was."

Kincaid thought of the cute little maid in the Feld household. "He's retired now. He has time for women."

"Runaway" blared from the juke; Kincaid checked the time. She was thirty-five minutes late. Either she was the sort of Cove woman who was always fashionably late for her appointments or she simply wasn't coming. He turned his attention back to the newspaper again, but he couldn't concentrate. He kept thinking about Prentiss's left hand conclusion and the irony of a democratic system. Even though Louisa Almott was left-handed, had type O blood, and had allergies that could result in the sort of wheezing that had been on the taped call Aline had gotten that night, they couldn't arrest her. Her married lover had vouched for her for all three nights of the murders. It was likely that he was lying, possible that he was involved, but nothing had been proven. If he *wasn't* involved, then perhaps he'd vouched for her because she'd threatened to go to his wife, maybe because he believed in her, maybe for another reason altogether. But the point was, she now had alibis, and there was nothing they could do about it.

Except watch her and wait.

"Hey, Ryan. Your date's here." Ferret picked up his forms and knocked his knuckles against the table. "Just think. I coulda been out the price of a Honda. Must be my lucky day."

Kincaid looked back as Ferret slid out of the booth and saw Mrs. Feld standing in the mouth of the hallway. She seemed small and uncertain, and from the way she was dressed, she could've passed for a woman in mourning: black tailored slacks and a pale pink silk blouse on her surprisingly youthful figure, black pumps, a large black handbag hanging over her shoulder.

She spotted him and came over. Kincaid stood as she slipped into the booth across from him and apologized for her tardiness. "I had a little trouble finding the place."

"Not exactly the sort of place you hang out at," he said, and she laughed.

"Not for at least forty years."

He asked if she would like something to drink or eat, and a small smile touched the corners of her mouth. Coffee, she said, would be just fine. She seemed uptight and out of place here, and he felt a pang of regret for her as he went up to the bar for her coffee and another cappuccino for himself. Once he was seated again, she got right to the point.

"After you left yesterday, Mr. Kincaid, I decided that you aren't the sort of man who uses blackmail to get what he wants. Once I'd reached that conclusion, I almost didn't come."

"What made you change your mind?"

She cupped her hands around the mug; one of the diamonds on her fingers caught the light, spalling it. "Several things, really. The first was a visit from the SPCA." She paused, her eyes seeking his, eyes that might've been amused or angry, he couldn't tell. "I don't suppose you know anything about that."

"Nope."

"Anyway, it was a relief. Travis has abused Benjamin for a long time, despite my efforts to thwart it. In a sense, you did me a favor." She smiled just to let him know his denial about the SPCA wasn't fooling her one bit, and he smiled back. "I felt I owed you something for that." Although her voice was soft and measured, behind its calm Kincaid detected a surfeit of emotion, and suddenly knew that her reason for coming here was central to her life. It was something that had been festering in a back room of her mind for years and the suppuration had finally burst loose. "Then there was that article in the *Tribune*, which I didn't see until last night, and the murder of the social worker. I assume her death is connected to the other murders?"

He nodded. "Everything keeps coming back to Jimmy Ray Luskin."

"How does Lenore fit?"

"I'm not sure. I'm just following leads, Mrs. Feld. Your husband was Lenore's attorney. I thought he might be able to confirm some things for me."

"Like about whether she had a child?"

"Yes, that was one thing."

She stirred her coffee. "Runaway" ended; "Palisades Park" came on. She leaned forward so he could hear her. "Well, she did have a child. She gave it up for adoption. For a long time I suspected Jimmy Ray was the child's father and Lenore had given it up because it was . . . was an abomination of some kind. Severely retarded, perhaps, or handicapped."

She lifted the mug to her mouth, sipped, set it down, and stirred it again with slow, rhythmic motions. "I would think of backwoods incest, the faces you see sometimes in small towns in the North Carolina mountains. But then I realized that if Lenore had known the child she was carrying was her brother's, she would've had an abortion. So that meant there was either some question in her mind or she knew who the father was. I think she knew." She paused. Sipped. Stirred. The light from the stained-glass lamp over the table spilled into her salt-and-pepper hair and glinted off the glasses nested there. The diamonds on her fingers shone and shone. "Then I naturally thought of the obvious. That the child was my husband's."

"Were he and Lenore—"

"I don't know. It's possible. They were very close. At the time all of this was going on, Travis and I were on the verge of divorce, so this became something of an issue. Oddly enough, it also brought us back together. For a few years, anyway. In retrospect, it seems unlikely that Travis or Lenore ever mixed business with pleasure. But perhaps that's only what I want to believe.''

The song had ended. Silence settled through the room like a mist, coating everything. Then, gradually, he became aware of the ping of the cash register, a peal of laughter from the bar, the scraping of a stool against the floor as someone got up. ''Then who was the father?''

Her shrug strived for nonchalance, but didn't quite cut it. ''I don't know. But I can offer you two leads.'' She reached into the side pocket of her purse and brought out a sheaf of papers clipped together. ''These are copies of bank statements from an account in the Caicos, Mr. Kincaid. The trustee is a nun. She receives money from the bank, she sends it to Travis, he disperses it.''

''A *nun*?''

''Sister Mary Joseph. Her name's on the account, and she sends Travis copies of the statement.''

''Who does he disperse the funds to?''

''I don't know.'' She dropped the papers in front of him. ''These statements cover only two years. As you can see, withdrawals are made quarterly and are quite substantial.''

Kincaid glanced through the papers. The ''substantial'' withdrawals she referred to amounted to enough to travel for at least ten years, maybe fifteen if you watched expenses: $150,000 a year. It was interest from an initial investment of three million. ''So this is why Lenore sold off her art collection.''

''It appears so. The statements go back twelve years, which is about when Lenore's child was born. I presume the money goes to the child. I have no way of proving that, of course.''

''I gather your husband doesn't know you know this.''

Her laughter was genuine. It burst from her, without a trace of cynicism or bitterness. It rang out with acceptance of whatever hand she and her husband were playing out. ''Heavens, no. The only reason I know anything at all is because once a year Travis receives about $75,000, which he claims is from 'investments.' Well, I've been the banker in the family for almost as long as we've been married. Although I haven't done the actual investing, I *do* know what investments we have. This $75,000 is unaccounted for.''

He'd been right about one thing. Her reason for being here

was definitely central to her life: she wanted to know the truth about her husband's relationship with Lenore Luskin. "The nun is now a mother superior at the Immaculate Conception Church in Miami. Before that, she was in charge of a Catholic hospital. She's an Ursuline nun, and traditionally that order has been focused on nursing and teaching."

"So you think Lenore had her child at the hospital this nun was in charge of? Is that what you're saying?"

"Yes."

"Wouldn't it be simpler just to go to her yourself, Mrs. Feld, instead of going to all this trouble to pretend you're here out of a benevolence you don't really feel?"

He expected her to take umbrage at the remark; she didn't. She just smiled. "I'm glad we understand each other, Mr. Kincaid. This information is important to you for *your* reasons, and the answers you find are important to me for *my* reasons."

"That doesn't really answer my question."

She stirred her coffee again, the spoon clinking against the sides of the cup. "If I go to the nun, my husband will hear about it. I would prefer that he didn't. I would rather use this as, well, a surprise."

Kincaid thought of the pretty maid and the electronic bug. "As ammunition, you mean."

She shrugged. "Yes. Since my husband retired, he has been mixing business with pleasure quite often. Certain, hmm, facts have come to my attention about my husband's relationship with our cute young maid. And I intend to use the answer you find as leverage."

Couldn't happen to a nicer guy, Kincaid thought. "May I keep these bank statements?"

"Oh, I don't think that would be a very good idea." She tapped the stack against the surface of the table, straightening them, and slipped them back in her purse.

"Not a very good idea at all."

"If you want your answers, Mrs. Feld, then I may need these statements to get them."

"You might also take them to my husband."

Kincaid handed her the electronic bug, which she dropped in her black purse.

"That doesn't prove your intent, Mr. Kincaid."

"No offense, Mrs. Feld, but if I saw your husband bleed-

ing in the middle of the road, I'd have to really think twice
before stopping. So why would I go to him and snitch on
you? All I'm interested in right now is finding a killer.''

After a moment, she nodded and slid the statements across
the table. ''When you have your answer, Mr. Kincaid, give
me a call, hmm?''

She slid out of the booth and was gone before Kincaid
could reply.

2

Island News & Things in downtown Tango occupied a space
barely larger than a closet. There was hardly room to breathe
in the shop, much less browse without bumping into a display
rack. But it was the only place at this end of the island where
you could get out-of-town newspapers and cigarettes that un-
dercut the competition by a third. Kincaid, however, wasn't
interested in either newspapers or cigarettes. He was looking
for information.

He wended his way to the back of the shop and knocked
on the open office door. Marge, the proprietor, was on the
phone, but she glanced over and smiled when she saw him.
A long time ago, between marriages, Marge was one of a
half-dozen women Kincaid had gone out with. It was during
a period of his life when women were amusing diversions and
nothing else. The moment he got too interested, or the woman
did, he was gone. His tryst with Marge had lasted about a
month, and they'd remained friends.

''. . . look, just call me back when you've checked the
computer, okay? I can't wait all day. Right. Thanks.'' As she
hung up, she stabbed a thumb toward the phone. ''The computer goes down and there are no answers, Ryan. That's the
technological age we live in. Ain't it fine?'' She combed her
fingers through her auburn hair and shook her head. ''So
how've you been?''

''No complaints. How's business?''

''Great. I love snowbirds.'' She leaned against her desk
and lit a cigarette. Amid the clutter of papers and piles of

books, she seemed serene, as if the mess rooted her. "Now, about you. What's today's question?"

Kincaid laughed. "Am I that transparent?"

"As long as Al's in the picture, I know you're not here to ravish my bod."

"Not to mention that you're married."

"Minor point. Let's hear it."

From his pocket, Kincaid drew out the note Aline had received several weeks ago, shortly after the murder of the Michael family. He folded it so just the smiling-face sticker showed. "Got any idea where someone would buy a bunch of these?"

"Hey, my niece collects those. Stickers are the rage in elementary school, you know. You check the toy shops?"

"Yeah." He and Gene Frederick had checked toy stores, novelty shops, even the local printing shops and hadn't turned up anything. Marge frowned, bit at her thumbnail, then snapped her fingers. "Hold it. Somewhere around here . . ." She rummaged through the wire mesh basket on her desk, lifting items, dropping them, then opened the bottom drawer and pulled out a pile of papers. "Ah. Okay. Take a look at this." She held up a cellophane packet. "A *Highlights* promotional thing left over from Christmas."

"What's *Highlights*?"

"A magazine for kids." She slid a sheet of smiling-face stickers from the packet. There must've been two or three dozen on the sheet in various colors, each face wearing a different expression.

"May I have this?"

"Sure. You developed some sort of fascination for these or what, Ryan?"

"You know what a signature is? In a homicide?"

"The killer's mark or something, right?"

"Yeah. That's what these are."

"If I were you, I'd get their mailing list for Tango Key subscribers. It'll probably cost you an arm and a leg, but what the hell."

"Thanks, Marge. I owe you."

Sunlight glinted off the hoods of passing cars, shoppers strolled the sidewalks, people on lunch breaks hurried through the heat, joggers cut into the park and vanished in the cool shade of the trees. Outside, it was life as usual, Aline thought as she stood at her office window. Then she looked down at the note in her hand and the comfort of the ordinary world deserted her.

> Eight fat crows
> All in a row
> Four knocked down
> & four to go

There were several things about this note that were different from the one she'd received previously. The smiling-face sticker at the end of it had been colored black with a felt-tip pen. The note had arrived through the regular mail, instead of being left in the mailbox, and it wasn't typed. It had been hand-printed very neatly, in block letters. She suspected the differences were significant—especially the black-painted face of the sticker—but significant how?

Simple, Al. It means you're the next mark.

She reached for the phone, dialed the number for Monroe Junior College, and asked for Joe Waldo, the man who had been Jimmy Ray Luskin's tutor on death row.

"He isn't expected back for a few days, ma'am, but if you'd like to leave your name and number, I'll—"

"I was told two weeks ago that he'd be back today. This is Detective Scott on Tango Key."

"Oh, right. Detective Scott," the woman said. "I have your message for him right here. I'll be sure to have him call you as soon as he's back in town."

It may not be soon enough, she thought, but thanked the woman and hung up. She pressed the heels of her hands into her eyes, fighting back a tide of deep unease. The feeling had washed through her at odd intervals for the last few days, as if an invisible hand were turning the adrenaline spigot off and on. It had gotten worse since the death of the social worker last night, the fear sometimes surging when she least expected it. In the shower this morning, for instance, she'd started shaking like a leaf under the hot spray, teeth chattering like old bones. And later, over breakfast, as she'd been paging through the newspaper, an image of that hat pin in Peg Perkins's navel had drifted into her head. Her mouth had dried in a flash, her temple pounded, and that terrible cold squeezed at her heart again.

Once she'd found the note when she'd left the house this morning, her paranoia worsened. Now that the woman's fevered obsession had rooted in her, infected her, she was imagining things—noises, voices, hidden messages in what people said to her, the creepy sensation that she was being followed on her way to work, that she was being watched, that even as she sat here, Louisa Almott was somewhere outside this building, waiting for her, that fresh Iowa farm-girl face smiling. *Smiling.*

A while ago, when she was in the rest room washing her hands, she looked into the mirror and saw a hat pin protruding from her eye, saw it clearly, saw it so clearly, in fact, that she'd nearly screamed and her hands had fluttered up to her face and the pressure had broken loose from her chest and she'd started to weep.

You're losing it, Al.

"You sick or something?"

Her hands dropped away from her eyes, and she smiled thinly at Bernie. "Only in the head."

Bernie plopped into the nearest chair, lit a cigarette, and brought a small portable ashtray from her purse. "Ryan's in with the chief. He got a lead on those stickers, Al." And she explained.

A kids' magazine. "I suppose the school subscribes."

"Yeah, they do. I checked. I figure it's just one more strike against Ms. Iowa Farm Girl. Wouldn't be too difficult for a teacher to lift them, now would it?"

"It's still not enough to arrest her. Not as long as lover boy is her alibi."

"I don't think lover boy was involved in the murders, Al, but I think he lied for her." Bernie tapped her cigarette against the edge of her little ashtray. "But anyway, the chief is going to set her up."

"How?"

"He—"

"By using the *Tribune*. Like we talked about before, Al," finished Frederick, who stood in the doorway, stinking up the air with one of his cigars. He came into the room and claimed the chair next to Bernie. She held out her little portable ashtray and he laughed. "Has it gotten that bad around here for smokers?"

"Only for us peons, Gene," replied Bernie.

"You give her shit about smoking?" he asked Aline.

"Whatever gave you that idea?" She opened the bottom drawer of her desk and plucked out an aerosol can of air freshener. Two quick squirts and the air smelled like Christmas. "I don't discriminate against smokers."

Frederick made a face and stabbed out his cigar. "Very funny, Aline."

"Tell me about the setup," she said eagerly.

"This evening, Chip Sonsky and I are having a drink. I'm going to verify that there *is* a witness, who's under police protection, and tell him we expect to make an arrest within the next two to three days."

"You're not going to name her, are you?"

"Of course I'm not going to name her. I'm moving Renie off the island. I don't want her anywhere near Tango when this story breaks."

"You going to tell Sonsky about the jurors being under protection?"

"Yup."

"When do you think the story will run?"

"Hopefully, as soon as possible. But if I press Sonsky about it, it'll look too obvious. So I'm going to tell him you'll talk to a reporter about the case. If you're game, Aline."

She smiled. "I'm game." *And the sooner the better.*

20: CRYSTAL CITY REVISITED

I

The dark licked at the glass in the kitchen. The wind whipped up the sides of the cliff from the sea and whistled along the window's cracks and beneath the eaves. Kincaid noticed that the noise grated on Frank Foreston's nerves. He pushed away from the butcher block table where he'd been sitting with the rest of them and started to pace. Now and then he glanced back at the blank video monitor in the center of the table, then strolled over to the door, pushed it open, and peered into the next room.

"What's taking them so long, anyway?" He addressed the question to no one in particular.

"It takes time to check out the equipment, honey," replied Carol Foreston. She was as uptight as her husband, Kincaid thought, but disguised it better. "Dr. Prentiss will let us know when they're ready to start."

Both of the Forestons wore yuppie regalia—the expensive casual look, as Aline called it. Kincaid had the impression that, through their clothes, their demeanor, they were trying to make some sort of statement about who and what they were and the type of environment they had provided for their daughter. *We are caring, loving parents*, whispered the pink warmup suit as Carol Foreston moved to the doorway beside her husband. *We are progressive parents*, said the Pierre Cardin label on Foreston's shirt, *who have allowed our daughter to make her own choices*.

Kincaid wasn't sure whose benefit this statement was supposed to be for. Maybe for Stratton as Renie's psychiatrist, or for Gene Frederick, who was outside at the guardhouse, or for Bill Prentiss, who had treated Renie initially. Perhaps for all of them. Regardless of who it was for, Kincaid knew that the act—from the clothes to the orchestration of their movements to the things they said or didn't say—was intended to vindicate their action, or lack of it, the night Renie hadn't come home. After all, if the events that night had turned out a little differently, Renie wouldn't have ended up at the judge's house, and none of them would be here.

The video camera had been Renie's idea. She'd told them she didn't want anyone watching her during the hypnosis, because it distracted her. Although she'd said "anyone," she had meant "my parents." But Foreston, who didn't know about the first hypnosis or what had happened during that session and wouldn't have consented to this one if he had, insisted on being present. So here they were.

The video screen suddenly flickered to life, and Renie's parents returned to the table. Foreston fiddled with the knobs until the snow was gone, and turned up the volume. Aline glanced at Kincaid across the table.

These bozos are going to screw things up, said her eyes.

Relax, replied his shrug.

On the screen, Stratton was talking Renie into a deeply relaxed state. Bernie, who was operating the camera, occasionally zoomed in on the girl, zoomed in close enough so the dusting of freckles across her cheeks was visible. Most of all, though, the closeups told the rather simple truth of a young girl, of her vulnerability, of her trust in the adults who had been her only companions the last few weeks.

Stratton's voice was soft, fluvial, a mesmerizing voice that was probably capable of putting a hysterical child into a deep sleep in minutes. Kincaid's own body responded to it—muscles loosening, eyes beginning to feel heavy, a pleasant heat infusing his bones. His skin felt as though warm butter were being rubbed across it. Even Aline looked like she was about to nod off. The Forestons, however, seemed immune.

Carol worked her hands against the table. Foreston was poised at the edge of his chair, frowning, body tense, his eyes never straying from the screen. "I'm still not convinced that hypnosis is the way to go with this," he said suddenly.

His wife's hands paused in their fretful movement. "It's a little late for that, Frank."

"Not if we stop this right now." He spoke as though Kincaid and Aline weren't present.

"I think this is best for her," Carol replied.

"I don't."

Carol Foreston's pretty China doll face darkened, and Kincaid sensed there was more behind this exchange than the welfare of their daughter. "Renie chose to do this."

"She also *chose* to leave the house that night, Carol."

"And *you* chose not to be at home," she countered, and for some reason, this silenced him. He turned back to the screen.

". . . You're in front of the TV now, Renie, tuning into the magical crystal city. Can you see it?" Stratton asked.

A sleepy, dreamy response: "Hmm. In front of me."

"In the lower right-hand corner of your screen you'll see a digital calendar. It has today's date on it. As I talk, that date is going to change, moving backward in time to the late afternoon of February second."

"I must've missed something," Foreston said, fiddling with the Rolex on his wrist. "What's this crystal city stuff?"

"It's just a technique," Aline replied. "The city is an imaginary place where Renie feels secure. Through the screen, she can control what she sees."

Only Foreston's eyes moved. "How would you know what my daughter feels, Detective Scott?"

Aline refused to be goaded. "I asked her."

Which is more than you've done: the unspoken words might as well have been spray-painted on the walls, and had the desired effect on Foreston. He slipped into a tight, moody silence.

Now Stratton was moving Renie slowly back in time. Yesterday. Two days ago. Four. Eight. Back to the afternoon of February 2. "What's on the screen now, Renie?"

"The kitchen at home. I'm looking in the fridge for something to eat. Mom's upstairs; I can hear the computer keys. She comes downstairs just as I'm getting some cookies from the jar and tells me it's too close to dinner for a snack. It makes me really mad when she does that. She—"

"When she does what, Renie?" asked Stratton.

"Tells me not to do something. I mean, half the time she and Daddy are telling me I have to make my own decisions, and then the rest of the time they act like I'm three years old."

"I told you that's how she felt," said Carol, glaring at her husband.

He didn't say anything at all. He just continued to sit at the edge of his chair.

"Did you tell your mother that?" asked Stratton.

"Yes. And I eat one of the cookies anyway and she says she's going to tell Daddy when he gets home and I start screaming at her. She grabs me by the shoulders and shakes me for talking back to her. 'Your father's going to be very disappointed in you, Renie,' she says."

"And what do you say?"

"That Daddy doesn't care. Daddy's never home. She . . . Mom . . . says he has to work a lot, but I know that isn't all of it."

"What do you mean, Renie?"

"At night sometimes, when Daddy's out of town, I hear Mom crying. One night . . . one night she was talking on the phone with a friend, and I heard her say she found something on Daddy's shirt. When I asked her about it the next day, she acted like she didn't know what I was talking about and screamed at me for eavesdropping."

This elicited a dark look from Foreston, which his wife ignored.

"Let's move ahead a little, Renie. What're you having for dinner?"

Her eyes flicked rapidly back and forth under her lids. "Chicken. A baked potato. Broccoli. I'm not hungry. I don't like broccoli. Mom tells me if I don't eat the broccoli, I can't watch TV. I don't care. There's nothing on TV, anyway."

"Do you argue about it?"

She frowned. It deepened when Stratton repeated her question. "I . . . I don't know. We argue, but I don't know about what."

Kincaid heard Carol Foreston suck in her breath; when she expelled it, it hissed through clenched teeth.

"Renie? Can you see yourself and your mother on the screen?"

"Uh-huh."

"Then turn up the volume a little so you can hear what

you and she are arguing about." Pause. "Can you hear now?"

"No."

She's blocking something, Kincaid thought. But what?

"Okay, you're at the table still. Do you finish your dinner?"

"No. I leave the table. I just get up and leave."

"Why?"

Whispering, "She lied. Mommy lied to me."

Carol Foreston's face was marble-white.

"Your mother lied?"

"Uh-huh."

"About what?"

"Can't tell. It's a secret. No one can know."

The camera zoomed in on her face, then panned the room, showing Prentiss at the computer terminal and Stratton moving away from Renie toward the open porch doors as she talked her into an even deeper relaxed state.

Aline looked at Carol Foreston. "What'd you lie about?"

"My daughter's very mixed up."

"I think we'd better stop this whole thing right now," Foreston said, and started to rise.

"What're you afraid of, Foreston?" snapped Kincaid.

He was standing now. "*I'm* not afraid of anything. It's my daughter I'm afraid for."

"If that's true," piped up Aline, "then you'd better sit down, Mr. Foreston, because right now this is your daughter's best chance for a normal life again. Has she told you about her nightmares? Has she told you how she sometimes wakes up screaming at night? Ask her about those things, Mr. Foreston."

"*This*," burst Foreston, stabbing a finger at the screen, "is for the *cops'* benefit, not for Renie's. This—"

"Shut the fuck up, Foreston." Kincaid stood. He was taller than Foreston by four inches, and the homicidal look on his face made the other man pull back slightly. He reached for a brown envelope on the counter, opened it, and dumped the contents. The police photographs taken at Judge Michael's house spilled across the table. "Now tell me this isn't also for Renie's benefit. This is what's locked up in her head."

Carol made a harsh, choking sound. Foreston looked like he was on the verge of getting ill. He shoved the photos back into the envelope, and his body seemed to fold up as he sat down. "That was uncalled for, Kincaid." But his voice lacked conviction, and Kincaid ignored him and turned back to the screen.

2

"Your mother has left the house, Renie. What're you doing now?"

Giggling: "Stuffing pillows under the covers on my bed."

"Why?"

"So she'll think I went to sleep."

"You're going somewhere?"

"Yes."

"Where?"

The frown reappeared, burrowing down between her closed eyes, a little black mole of distress. "There."

"Where?"

"I'm on my bike . . ."

"Focus the knob, Renie, and tell me the name of the street."

"Grapevine. It's Grapevine Boulevard."

The Michaels' street.

"What do you see now?"

"A cat, a pretty orange cat that's stumbling around on this porch."

"What porch?"

"Of a house."

"A house on Grapevine?"

"Uh-huh."

"Whose cat is it, do you know?"

"Here, kitty, kitty," she whispered. "C'mere."

"What does the cat do?"

"It . . ." She whimpered. "It fell over. I pick it up. The kitty's all bloody. The kitty's hurt. I'm going to take it home. I'm going . . . but I hear someone screaming. Inside the house, someone is screaming. I hear it. I hold the kitty tight and run to the window. I look in. I . . ." Tears rolled out from under her eyes. "I . . ."

"Renie, the picture is only on the screen. Nothing in the picture can hurt you. All you have to do is change the channel or turn the TV off."

A full minute ticked by. Renie stopped crying.

"What's on the screen now, Renie?"

"A lady. She's on the kitchen floor. She's screaming." She winced, but it was just an *oh, gross* wince, as though she were watching a horror movie. "There's another lady blocking the way, so I can't see very well."

"Can you see the other woman's face?"

"Uh-uh. Just her back."

"What color hair does she have?"

"Black. Long, black hair."

A wig, another goddamn wig.

"Why is the lady screaming, Renie?"

Her mouth twitched. Bernie pulled back with the camera, panning the room, so Kincaid could now see Prentiss, jerking his thumb up and down in the air, indicating that Renie's pulse and blood pressure were rising.

"The picture can't hurt you," Stratton repeated. "You're just watching a movie. If something you see disturbs you, all you have to do is turn the set off."

Thirty seconds ticked by. Sixty. At the two-minute mark, Prentiss turned his thumb down. Stratton proceeded. "What's on the screen now, honey?"

"The lady isn't screaming anymore. There's . . . there's stuff all over the floor."

"Where's the woman with the black hair?"

"Living room. She . . . she . . . she has a knife . . . she's kneeling over someone . . . a man . . . she . . ."

Another signal from Prentiss, and Stratton said, "I want you to turn off the TV set now, Renie."

" . . . the man is screaming. The man . . . she's doing something to the man . . . she . . ." And then she shrieked, *"His eye, she's stuck something in his eye, his eye . . ."* She bolted forward from the chair, tearing the electrodes from her scalp, her chest and arms. The image on the screen tilted, then it went blank and the Forestons were both up and running, with Kincaid and Aline close behind them.

In the living room, Renie was curled up in a ball on the couch, arms covering her head as she sobbed. Stratton was speaking softly to her, but every time the doctor touched her,

Renie jerked away and shrieked. Frank Foreston rushed toward his daughter, but Kincaid caught his arm, holding him back.

"They're going to sedate her. Hold on, just hold on."

Foreston yanked his arm free, spun, and struck out with his fist. Kincaid saw it coming, threw up his arm to block the blow, and sidestepped, but not far enough. Foreston's fist sank into Kincaid's shoulder, into the same spot the woman's knife had penetrated two weeks ago. It hurt like a son of a bitch and snapped the last thread of Kincaid's patience. He spun, focusing his strength in his right leg, and kicked; it was swift, deadly, and caught Foreston in the ribs, throwing him off balance and knocking him to the floor.

By the time Kincaid caught his breath, Prentiss had sedated Renie, Carol Foreston was hovering over her, alternately cooing and sobbing, and Prentiss was helping Foreston to his feet.

"That does it!" he exploded, brushing his hands over his Pierre Cardin shirt and his designer slacks. "We're taking her out of here tonight."

Carol's head snapped up. When she spoke, there was no trace of hysteria in her voice, nothing but a determination like steel. "She's staying here and I'm staying with her and when Chief Frederick gives the word, we're moving her off the island and that's the last of it."

Foreston looked like he'd swallowed his tongue. "Suit yourself." He turned and hurried out of the room. A moment later, the front door opened and slammed.

In the silence that followed, Kincaid heard the dark pressing in against the safe house like a hot, hungry, and poisoned wind.

21: THE MOTHER SUPERIOR

I

Clouds hung over the island like sagging pockets of old gray skin. The winds were gusting out of the south between ten and twenty-five miles per hour, and visibility between Tango Key and Miami was about eight miles. Not the greatest flying weather, Kincaid thought, studying the maps in the weather room at the airport. But it could've been worse. Squalls were expected by early afternoon, but with luck, he and Aline would be back well before then.

He walked outside. The hot wind did little to alleviate the mugginess in the air, the oppressiveness. The humidity bothered his shoulder, creating a dull ache where Foreston's fist had struck last night. *Where the knife sank in.* He wondered if, over the years, the injury would become one that foretold rain, like an old broken bone that throbbed with every change in the barometer. A lot of the travelers he'd met seemed to have some old injury or another that portended everything from changes in the weather to changes in fortune and in love. If the worst happened, and he and Aline didn't have the money for round-trip tickets to New Zealand, they could buy one-way fares and work their way around the country as fortune-tellers.

Funny, how his mind kept skipping over what lay directly in front of them—*it's dark, it's unknown, it's scary as hell*— and leaped into the more distant future. But whenever he tried to visualize how Frederick's setup would work, he came up with a blank. Sonsky was evidently suspicious of Frederick's intentions. He wanted an in-depth interview with one of the

245

cops who'd been investigating the case (which fell right in with Frederick's plans); verification from the coroner on what had been found (Frederick said he couldn't speak for the coroner); and he wanted to talk to the witness. Frederick had nixed the witness part of it, and said he would get a statement from Prentiss. The interview was scheduled for tomorrow, and the piece would run the following day.

But the whole thing bothered him. There were too many missing pieces to bridge the gap with an assumption that Louisa Almott was their killer. All right, so the specs seemed to fit. And she had an apparent motive. But something about her wasn't right.

Then who did it, hotshot?

He had reached the gas pumps, where the Cessna was parked. As he was topping off the tanks, he saw Molly strolling toward him from the parking lot, moving across the tarmac, her blond hair a whiskey river in the light. "Hi, Ryan," she called.

He lifted his hand in greeting and went back to what he was doing, hoping she wouldn't stick around, that Aline would show up on time, that they wouldn't get a late start. But of course she stopped at the plane. "You going to get in some flying today?" he asked.

"Just some practice landings and takeoffs. Nothing fancy like stalls." She gathered her hair at the back of her head and wiped her neck with her hand. "But now I'm having second thoughts. These winds are a little more than I bargained for."

"It'll be good practice." He started his preflight check and she followed him around the plane like an obeisant puppy. "Just remember to crab into the wind," he told her.

"Right. So where're you off to, Ryan?"

"Miami for a few hours. Did you get the cross-country done?"

"Yeah, and it went without a hitch. I'm laying out the route for my second one. Could you take a look at it when I'm finished?"

"Sure thing."

He drained some gas from the right wing, checking it for condensation. There was none, and he tossed the gas out and crouched to check the pressure in the tires. Molly's shadow fell across him. He sensed she had something to say, so he rocked back on his heels and peered up at her. The light was at her back, and when she moved slightly, the sun struck him in the eyes. It blinded him enough so that the only thing he saw of her was a dark silhouette, hovering like a giant bat. It spooked him. When she spoke, her voice seemed to float free of her, and that spooked him, too. These days, everything spooked him, he thought.

"Have you, uh, seen Bill?"

"Just briefly, last night. Why?"

"I think he's pissed about the article."

Kincaid blinked and tilted his head to the right, out of the sunlight. He stood, and her face swam into focus. Now they were gazing at each other across the top of the wing. Over her shoulder rose the hazy bruise of the Tango hills. "You're surprised?"

"He hasn't even given me a chance to explain. I figured he might've said something to you." She looked down at the ground and kicked at a pebble, sending it skittering across the concrete. "I mean, since you two have known each other so long."

"He didn't mention it." It was a lie; Prentiss had not only mentioned it, he'd raged about it last night when they'd left the safe house.

"Oh." She shrugged. "I guess I don't blame him. Not really. Not for that." She looked at him again. "But I don't think he told me the whole truth, Ryan. I think there's someone else."

Very good, Moll oh Moll. "Why do you think that?"

"Intuition." She smiled. "And intuition says it's Claudia Bernelli."

"I wouldn't know. But I can tell you this, if I'd been in Bill's shoes and read that *Tribune* article, I would've done a lot worse than just break off a relationship."

She looked incredulous. "*C'mon*, Ryan. You think I had a choice about doing that goddamn piece? You have *any* idea what it's like to work under Chip Sonsky?"

"That has nothing to do with blowing facts on the case, attributing quotes to people who didn't say them, and using Bill."

She slid her sunglasses back onto the top of her head and narrowed her eyes. "You know what's tough on this island, Ryan? Being a newcomer. It would've been different if I'd been one of you."

"One of who?"

"The Fritters. Key West has its Conks and Tango has its Fritters. That's what you and Bernelli, Bill and Aline are. And you don't take to newcomers. Right from the beginning, it was pretty obvious that none of you really liked me, that you were tolerating me just because you liked Bill, because he was one of your own. It's almost like . . . well, like this incestuous family or something. It's pretty disgusting, really, it's—"

"Molly, I've got to finish preflighting the plane."

"Don't let *me* hold you up."

"Look, I'm not the person you should be talking to. Bill is. If you have something to say to him, then go see him."

"I will," she snapped, and walked off, cutting through the hot wind like a scythe.

2

Despite the buffeting winds, Aline's takeoff was smooth, Kincaid thought. The map was folded into a neat square in her lap, and she followed the route she'd set from Tango to Marathon and then up the east coast toward Miami. She cruised at about 3,000 feet, below the cloud ceiling. He would've climbed above the ceiling, where the ride would've been smoother and more economical, but her choice suited her experience. She felt comfortable with it, and that was what counted.

Once they'd turned north, they had a tailwind that moved them along at a swift clip and put them in Miami half an hour earlier than he'd anticipated. At 11:15, a taxi let them off in front of the Immaculate Conception Church in Coral Gables.

It was set back in a copse of rustling palms, on an old quiet street where the buildings were predominantly Spanish style. Attached to the church on either side, like the extended wings of an insect, were an elementary school and a convent. They walked along a shaded path that threaded through palms with twisted trunks and bushy crowns, palms that soared, palms the winds had bent so they looked hunched over, as if afflicted with arthritic spines. They passed no one. The wind moaned through the church's eaves and played the long, slen-

der leaves of the palms. *God is breathing,* Kincaid thought.
That was how you were meant to feel here, as though the
very air you drew into your lungs was sacred.

The path emptied into a garden surrounded by a cobbled
courtyard bordered on three sides by low buildings. Somewhere a bell tolled, and the sound echoed eerily in the silence. "It feels like we're the last people on Earth," Aline
whispered. "Where *is* everyone?"

"Vespers?"

"Why're we whispering?" she whispered.

Kincaid laughed and in a normal tone said, "I don't know.
Let's track down the mother superior."

As the bell stopped tolling, women appeared in the courtyard—not a lot of them, perhaps a dozen in all, and except
for their veils and their sensible shoes, they didn't look like
nuns. They wore street clothes and chattered like schoolgirls.
Aline stopped one of them and asked where they could find
the mother superior. She pointed out a corpulent woman at
the end of the courtyard who was speaking to the gardener.

They paused a couple of feet away, and the mother superior
finished giving the gardener instructions, then looked over at
them. "Yes? May I help you with something?"

Her face was pleasant and plump, the face of a matronly
aunt, perhaps, who had never married but harbored no bitterness about it. Her street clothes were plain, simple, made
of cotton. Her shoes were the most eccentric thing about her;
they were blue-and-white Nikes.

". . . with the Tango Key Police Department," Aline was
saying, "and this is Ryan Kincaid, a private investigator."

The mother superior turned her soft, kind eyes on him,
eyes that were magnified by the thick glasses she wore, and
extended her hand. Her grip was firm; he guessed she wasn't
going to be an easy customer. "A police detective and a
private eye all in one day. My. Nice to meet you, Mr. Kincaid. Why don't we talk over there." She gestured toward a
picnic table at the far side of the garden. "It's private and
much cooler than my office. The air conditioner broke last
night. I suppose it's God's way of testing my resilience to
heat." She let out a small laugh, as if to say she didn't quite
believe God gave a damn. They started walking. "Now what
is it that's brought you all the way up here to Miami, Detective?"

"A series of murders that seem to be related to Jimmy Ray Luskin."

She didn't ask who Luskin was. She didn't deny that she knew the name. "I'm not quite sure what the connection is, since he was executed last August."

"The connection is Lenore," Kincaid told her.

Those gray eyes slid toward him. "Lenore."

"Jimmy Ray's sister."

She smiled slightly. "Yes, I know who Lenore was, Mr. Kincaid."

They reached the picnic table. The mother superior swept the dried leaves off with her hand and sat down. Aline and Kincaid settled across from her. "What we'd like to know," she said, "is whether Lenore had a child, and if so, where the child is."

"Why?"

"Because we think it may be relevant to this case."

"Why have you come to me?"

"So you could explain this." Kincaid brought a brown envelope from his flight bag, opened it, and removed the bank statements Mrs. Feld had surrendered.

The mother superior looked down at the statements, then up, then she gazed off to the right, across the courtyard, where the gardener was now trimming the hibiscus hedges. "About thirteen years ago I worked as a nurse at a hospital and home for unwed mothers here in Miami. Most of the women we treated were either quite young or quite poor. We operated strictly on donations and were not having a very easy time of it. Lenore heard about us through one of the stories in the press and donated close to a hundred thousand dollars to the home." She turned her attention back to them. "Perhaps it was a prudent tax write-off for her. Perhaps she was hoping to buy her way into God's graces. I don't know. But three or four months after she'd made the donation, she came to the home to live."

"So she *was* pregnant," Aline said.

"Yes. She wanted to have the child. She said she'd considered an abortion, but decided against it because the father was a man whom she loved deeply."

"Who was the father?" Kincaid asked.

"He was married, Mr. Kincaid. That's all I know. But even if I knew more, I wouldn't be able to divulge it. That's part of the pledge I made to Lenore.'' She looked down at her hands, smoothed one over the other in a gesture that was almost a caress. A clap of thunder brought her head up. She studied the sky a moment, then continued. ''During the months she was with us, Lenore and I spent a great deal of time talking. In a sense, I became her counselor, the mother she never really had, I guess, her psychiatrist, her friend. Although she wanted to keep the child, she already had Jimmy Ray to take care of and she wasn't willing to change her way of life. I convinced her to give up the child for adoption and to set up a trust fund of some sort that would ensure the child's adoption by a . . . well, a more traditional family, if you will.'' She touched the bank statements. ''That's what she did.''

''From the sale of her art collection?'' Kincaid asked.

''Yes.''

''And you became trustee of the money?''

''That's right. Maybe it's what she had in mind all along. I don't know. It was difficult to ever be sure of anything with Lenore. But, after all, with her money, she could have gone anywhere to have the child. She didn't need us.''

''And Travis Feld dispenses it to the adoptive parents.''

''Yes.''

''Who're the parents?'' Aline asked.

''I can't tell you that, Detective Scott.''

''Then tell me this. Do the adoptive parents know the child's mother was a prostitute? Were they told?''

''No.'' Thunder rumbled; it started to sprinkle. ''They didn't know anything about Lenore, and Lenore, at her own request, was told nothing about them. That was the condition that came with the trust fund. They could have declined to accept the trust, of course, but they didn't.''

''But the parents know now?'' Kincaid asked.

''Yes. The father hired someone. That's all I know.'' She pressed her hands against the edge of the table, pushing herself to her feet. ''But if you're thinking that one of the parents could be responsible for these murders, you're wrong. And that's all I can tell you. I'm sorry. I wish I could be of more help, but I honestly believe that none of this is related to the murders you've mentioned.''

''Before you leave, Sister, I'd like you to take a look at something.'' Aline reached into her purse and pulled out the same manila envelope Kincaid had taken with him to the safe house last night. She let the photographs slide out, and as her fingers stepped through them, raindrops splattered them. Kincaid saw the nun's eyes widen, saw her mouth open as though she were going to say something, then close. "Two of these victims were children. Their only mistakes were being in the wrong place at the wrong time. This woman was a social worker. You know what her crime was? She sat on Jimmy Ray's jury. And these . . ."

Her fingers kept trekking through the photos, then she tossed Renie's sketches on top of them. "And here's what the witness has to live with. A twelve-year-old girl named Renie Foreston saw the murders of the judge and his family. The sketches are her way of trying to break through the block. So I'm going to leave all this with you, Sister. Think about how if this lunatic gets to the rest of the jurors, their murders are going to be on *your* conscience. Think about *that*, and if you change your mind, my number's in the envelope."

Aline got up and walked off through the light rain, leaving Kincaid and the nun standing at the table. The mother superior stared after Aline for a long, pensive moment. The photos and sketches fluttered in the wind, drawing her eyes back to the table where Kincaid was sliding everything back into the envelope. She looked at him. "You don't understand."

"What I understand, Sister, is that Aline arrested Luskin. She's already been threatened. If something happens to her that could've been prevented by some cooperation from you, then I'll be back. That's a promise."

He strode back through the courtyard, into the wind and the rain.

3

Prentiss was in his office, shuffling through paperwork he didn't feel like doing, wishing he were anywhere but here. He picked up the phone and dialed Bernelli's office. He swiveled in his chair as it rang, and watched rain smearing against the window, the light gray, muted.

"Tango Key Police Department."

"Detective Bernelli, please."

"I'll see if she's in."

He was put on hold. Every now and then a beep sounded, indicating their conversation was being taped. Such privacy, he thought.

He and Bernie hadn't spent any time alone together since the night at the safe house. Every time he'd wanted to suggest they go someplace for a beer, his guilt over Molly kept interfering. But why should he feel guilt after what *she* had done to *him*?

"This is Detective Bernelli."

"Hi, Bernie."

He sensed she was going to hang up on him. But she didn't. In a somewhat cool voice, she said, "Hi yourself, Dr. Bill."

"Did I catch you at a bad moment?"

"No worse than usual."

"Any repercussions from the Forestons about last night?"

"Not yet."

"Good."

An awkward silence ensued. The beep sounded. Prentiss rubbed at his throbbing temple. "Bernie, I . . ."

"Bill, I . . ."

They had spoken at the same instant, and now they both laughed, and it broke the tightness. "You first," he said.

"No, you."

"You free tonight?"

"So far."

"How about dinner? A real dinner? Just the two of us."

"At my place. Danny's visiting his dad for a few days."

"What time?"

"Barring any disasters, I should be out of here by five or six. Let's say seven, how's that?"

"What should I bring?"

She laughed, a low husky sound. "Just your bod, Dr. Bill."

"See you then."

When he hung up, he was smiling. He was still smiling when he turned back around, and then his smile faded by degrees. Molly was standing in the doorway. He gazed at her with incredulity.

"You have a minute, Bill?"

"I don't have anything to say, Molly."

"I do." She came into the office and shut the door. "I want to explain. About the article." She looked forlorn and contrite as she eased herself into one of the chairs across from his desk. "I don't blame you for being pissed about it."

He started to laugh then, and couldn't stop. He laughed at the absurdity of it all, the pathos. He laughed because he couldn't believe she really believed they were going to have a conversation about this. But sure enough, she launched into a diatribe against Sonsky, making it sound as if he had held a gun to her head. She talked rapidly, stumbling over words, her hands working frantically in her lap, and then she smoked one of her occasional cigarettes with quick, urgent puffs, the smoke stinking up his office.

"It's bullshit," he said when she'd finished, his voice tightly controlled. "It's bullshit, and I'm sick of the bullshit, Molly. I'm sick of it. So before I throw you out, just get the hell out of here."

She gaped. "You didn't hear a word I said."

He lost it. His temper flew up out of him like a wild bird, a huge bird, flapping its long, hot wings, its beak pecking at her, at her mouth, her eyes, pecking until her face bled. "You knew about the goddamn article when you pulled that *very* convincing act about how heartbroken you were over the demise of our relationship. Now get out."

He didn't realize he'd gotten to his feet until he took her by the arms and yanked her up and pushed her toward the door. He had never in his life been violently physical with a woman until yesterday morning, and now he was doing it again. Not only was he doing it, but that terrible urge to hurt her returned and nearly overwhelmed him. He wanted to sink his fist into her face, God help him, he did. He wanted to see her bleeding and broken because he had loved her and she'd betrayed him, she'd twisted everything.

"You're hurting me," she whined, and jerked free of his grip. Then her voice lifted shrilly, a piercing sound: "Can't you understand what I'm going through? For once in your life, can't you see what kind of position I've been in?"

He trembled with rage. He nearly grabbed her by the shoulders again, but instead, stepped away from her quickly, as if the air around her were scorched. He waited a beat, two, three, waited a full thirty seconds before his fury had receded enough for him to speak in a calm, even voice. *A dead voice.*

You're more comfortable with the dead than the living, good buddy.

"Whether I understand or don't understand doesn't matter, Molly. It's over. With you and me. It's finished. That's as simple as I can put it. Now please, just go."

She opened her mouth to say something, but nothing came out, no words, no syllables, just a long sibilant hiss, the sound of a balloon losing gas. Her eyes bulged in their sockets. Her hands flew to her chest. She tried again to speak, but the rasp deepened. Molly sucked, trying to draw in oxygen, but nothing happened. She clutched herself at the waist, but Prentiss was already moving toward her, scooping her up in his arms. He hurried to the couch, set her down, grabbed his black bag from the floor at the side of his desk. She kept rasping, struggling for air. Her eyeballs threatened to pop from their sockets. He dug inside the bag for one of the Tornalate inhalers he kept inside.

He quickly tilted her head, slipped one end of the inhaler between her lips, and told her to breathe as deeply as she could. But she still couldn't draw in air, so he pulled the inhaler out and pressed his mouth to hers and started resuscitating her until her chest rose and fell. Then he worked the inhaler between her lips and resuscitated her again, an almost impossible task because the inhaler took up most of the space in her open mouth. In the middle of the breath, he pushed down on top of the inhaler, releasing a puff of mist.

He did this twice, and gradually the asthma attack subsided, the color returned to her face, and enormous waves of guilt washed through him. *I caused this. Me.*

She whispered something. He shook his head and touched a hand to her sweating forehead. "Don't talk. Just relax, Molly. I'm going to drive you home. You'll be okay."

He had one of the nurses follow him in Molly's jeep to her apartment. She sat slumped and boneless in his Mercedes, her eyes closed. Her chest rose and fell evenly now, but every so often he heard echoes of that terrible rasp. The rain drummed the windshield, the roof, and it was like a chant. *This is your fault your fault your fault.*

In her bedroom, he undressed her and pulled the covers over her and brushed his mouth to her forehead. He whispered that he was sorry, but he didn't know if the words were for her or for himself.

22: THE DEFENSE ATTORNEY

I

Five days a week, Vic Xaphes swam three miles in the Olympic-sized pool at the Tango Health Club, then spent half an hour in the Jacuzzi room. It was something he did with an almost religious fervor, regardless of how tight his schedule was, and had more to do with vanity than with health. Swimming kept him trim and fit; he considered it his hedge against aging.

Today he'd actually canceled a meeting with a client to get down here for his swim, and then the weather had turned against him. Before he'd gone a mile and a half, it had started to pour and the club had closed the pool because of lightning. So here he was, languishing in the empty Jacuzzi room, consoling himself with a Campari and soda. Steam drifted from the surface of the swirling water and rose toward the tiny lights in the ceiling that were supposed to parody stars. For some strange reason, this room was painted black—black walls and ceiling, black floors, even the tubs were black. Perhaps it was intended as a metaphor for the womb—darkness, the warm embryonic waters, the sound of the tub pumps like a heartbeat: the ultimate in relaxation.

The Campari and the heat made him drowsy, and he rested his head against the edge of the tub and closed his eyes. He thought about the sweet young thing he'd met at the Pink Moose last night and brought home. She was a junior at Sarah Lawrence, one of those erudite types with fancy airs. But when it got right down to it, when she was naked, turned on, and shuddering against him, she was no different from a waitress or a stew or a stockbroker. Over the years, he'd come to realize that women were not the startlingly diverse creatures he had once believed. Most women fit into one of maybe half a dozen categories, and once he'd figured out *which* category, he usually lost interest.

The nice thing about the woman last night, however, was her age. Xaphes had a particular fondness for women in their late teens or early twenties. He liked the softness of their skin, the firmness of their breasts, the flatness of their bellies, their resilience. They were direct, and he liked that, too. The honey last night, for instance, hadn't been the least bit shy. At the secluded spot on the Tango Inlet where they'd ended up, she'd shucked her clothes in full view of his two body-guards, who were nearby, and then later, at the house, paraded out into the kitchen in the buff for a bottle of wine while the men were playing cards at the kitchen table. At the Moose, she had wanted to know, of course, why he had Body Boys—that was what she called them—and when he told her, she kept questioning him about the murders. Later, at the house, she'd questioned him some more, and then wanted to go at it again, for the third time, as if she'd gotten off on the talk of murder and mayhem.

She would be on the island for another week, and maybe he would call her again. Snowbirds were usually good bets because they were looking for fun, not commitment. But the Body Boys were something of a problem. Although the woman last night hadn't been inhibited by their presence, she was the exception. And frankly, the constant companionship, the way the two men shadowed him—even to the goddamn john this morning at work—was beginning to bug him. When they'd arrived at the health club this afternoon, he'd told them to go lift weights or something while he did his laps and enjoyed some solitude in the hot tub. After all, the odds of anything happening to him here were damn remote.

A wedge of light fell into the room as the door opened. Xaphes didn't look back to see who had come in; it didn't matter. He resented any intrusion on his solitude. He'd been hoping to have the place to himself for the half hour. The room wasn't much larger than his bedroom, and most of it was raised decking where the three Jacuzzis were. If you got a couple of noisy idiots in one of the tubs, it ruined the mood because the tubs were so close together.

He opened his eyes and frowned. The little overhead stars had winked out, and the air was pitch black. Distantly, he heard a clap of thunder and realized the electricity had probably gone off. But if that were true, then why was the pump in the tub still working?

You're jumpy, boy.

Yeah, he *had* been jumpy lately. Ever since Lloyd Watkins's plane had gone down, he'd felt like he was being watched. Followed. *Spied on.* It was an insidious paranoia, the kind that could get under your skin if you let it. Even last night, after the honey had gone to sleep, he'd lain in the dark, listening to the night sounds, and he could've sworn he'd heard something outside his window. He'd turned on the floodlights at the side of the house and had sent one of the Body Boys out to investigate. He hadn't found anything, of course, but it was still a long time before Xaphes had fallen asleep.

It was this same paranoia that whispered, *Safer in the tub until you find your matches*, that kept him in the hot waters, blinking against the wall of blackness as he patted the decking for his canvas bag. He thought he heard something below, at the bottom of the decking steps, but he couldn't see anything. Hell, he couldn't make out his hand when he brought it up close enough to his face to feel the heat of his own palm: that's how dark it was.

No one was down there. He was imagining it. Sure. He was spooked. *Don't like the dark.* Stupid. It was likely that whoever had opened the door hadn't come in, they'd only been looking to see if the tubs were occupied. Probably a couple of rich teenagers from the Cove who'd cut out of school for the day and figured the Jacuzzi room would be a good place to screw.

Sure.

Then haul your ass outa the tub, numbnuts.

But he didn't. He pushed away from the side of the tub until he was treading water out in the middle, his head jerking right, left. Where were the stairs? What was that noise? A creaking step? Someone clearing his throat? What was that smell? And wasn't the water a lot hotter now? Christ almighty, it was. "Goddamn," he hissed, his arms and feet propelling him forward, the heat burning his skin now, the swirling water splashing up onto his cheeks, scorching them.

He scrambled out of the tub and bumped into the railing.

That smell was stronger here. *Gasoline? Is that it? Is that what I smell?* Impossible. There couldn't be gasoline in here. It was the steam he smelled. And breathing that he heard. "Hey, who's there?"

Silence.

His hands moved one over the other across the railing, with his feet trailing reluctantly behind. *Why's the deck so slippery? Is gas on the deck?* The breathing seemed louder now, but he was probably imagining it, just like he'd imagined that the water had gotten hotter, that he smelled gasoline. The water was always an even ninety degrees. *A balmy ninety.* A bubble of laughter started up his throat and then lodged there, huge and sticky, as he remembered that the temperature and light switches were on a panel near the door. *The door that opened a little while ago. The door the door the . . .*

Was it also his imagination that it was tougher to breathe in here now? That he was sweating like a pig? That his hands were sliding all over the railing like the damn thing had been greased? Was he imagining that, too?

And the breathing: it's much louder. I'm not imagining that. I'm not. The heat, the gas, the steam, the breathing, the . . .

"Easy does it," he whispered, and stumbled over his canvas bag. He laughed out loud as he crouched and dug his hands inside, looking for the matches he kept in here. Matches for when he went camping in the Everglades, matches for serendipitous poolside meetings with sweet young things who smoked, matches that meant *light*.

He fumbled with several matches, but couldn't get them lit because they were wet. He dug for more, struck two, and they flared. The light was so beautiful, so simple, he nearly wept. He held the little torch above his head, squinting as he peered through the dark. *Nothing. There's nothing, you fool.* He stood slowly, scooping up his canvas bag, pinching the matches between his thumb and forefinger, wanting to laugh, but unable to. The fear was still crouched inside him, a horrid, wrinkled gremlin, clawing at his eyes, his mouth, pounding at the inside of his chest, coiled in his gut.

He spotted the stairs eight or nine feet away, and he could see the decking, the water darkening the wood, the . . .

Gasoline. Sweet Christ. It's gasoline all over the deck. It is. Jesus . . . He quickly blew out the matches and tossed them into the hot tub. The dark entombed him again, a hot, heavy dark that turned his knees rubbery, and now that smell, thickening in his nostrils, and oh Christ, light, he wanted light, needed it, thirsted for it, but the gas . . .

From where? Where did the gas come from?

His bare feet were sliding in the stuff. It stung his soles as he stumbled and slipped toward the stairs. His heart thundered in his chest. Sweat sprang from the pores of his skin. Just when he thought he was going to reach the stairs, a flame leaped into the dark directly in front of him and a woman whispered, ''Bye, bye, Vic,'' and tossed the match to the deck.

In the blink of an eye, a tongue of fire was racing toward him and sprang onto his feet. He screamed. He threw himself into the tub, where the temperature had soared to nearly two hundred degrees, and never uttered a second scream because his mouth was open as he struck the water.

It rushed down his throat, scorching the roof of his mouth, turning his tongue rawer than liver, and searing his vocal cords. He lost consciousness in about ten seconds. But it was a long ten seconds.

Long enough for the skin over ninety-five percent of his body to suffer third-degree burns, damaging the epidermis, dermis, and the subcutaneous tissue. Long enough for his major organs to leap into shock as blood was diverted to the damaged areas. Long enough for the flames to start sputtering and hissing out because the gasoline had covered only three square feet to the right of the stairs and there was too much dampness in the room for them to feed. Long enough for Vic Xaphes to realize the worst mistake he ever made was taking Luskin on as a client.

The second worst mistake was losing the case.

23: UNRAVELING

I

When it came to aviation, Kincaid didn't take risks; she liked that. He was thorough in his preflight checks, he had the plane serviced every hundred hours, he worked out fuel requirements before any extended trips. But best of all, he respected the weather.

And because of that, they were stranded in Miami until six that evening, when the storm that had plagued South Florida most of the day had moved out to sea. Since the airport traffic was heavy and it was dark, Kincaid took them off, then turned the controls over to her once they were twenty five miles south. It was the first time Aline had flown cross-country at night. It disoriented her. The sky was black, because clouds obscured the moon and most of the stars. The space beneath them was black, because they were flying ten miles offshore. She had to rely on instruments—the altimeter, VOR navigation, the compass. But instruments had been known to fail, and how would she know she'd made a mistake until it was too late?

Lloyd Watkins hadn't known.

It was an uneasy thought, and she shoved it aside.

Shortly after eight the Cessna touched down and Kincaid got on the radio and closed their flight plan. The controller said, ''Uh, November Tango four niner niner, there's an urgent message for you here. Please swing by aviation.''

''Tower, can you read the message?'' Kincaid said.

''Roger. It says, 'Come straight to Tango Health Club. The fifth fat crow is gone.' It's signed, 'Bernelli.' ''

* * *

The kitchen clock ticked. Branches scratched at the bedroom window. Wolfe's claws clicked across the floor. The air conditioner whispered. More distantly, she heard the screech of brakes, the mournful bay of a dog, a cat fight. Ordinary sounds from which treachery was absent, Aline thought. And yet it seemed that each noise possessed its own peculiar peril, something that would burst from its camouflage any second and become what it truly was.

Aline sat up, reached for her robe, and slipped it on as she got out of bed quietly so she wouldn't awaken Kincaid. She climbed down the ladder from the loft and padded into the kitchen. Nightmare Chaser: that was what she needed. She reached for the light switch, then yanked her hand back as though the wall had shocked her.

No lights.

Not until she checked outside.

She moved silently through the house, parting the blinds with her hands, peering out from behind curtains and closed windows, eyes sweeping through the dark that embraced the house. In the living room, she gazed down into the driveway, where the Saab and her rental Buick were parked. *She might've wired the cars. . . . They're just sitting out there, waiting for her. . . . Or the trees, maybe she's hidden somewhere in the trees, watching the house. . . .*

No. Not yet. She wouldn't move yet. So far, she had never killed two people on the same day, and there was no reason to think she would break this particular routine now. *But the murders have been happening closer together. . . .*

But who was *she*? Louisa Almott? She was beginning to doubt it. Even if the killer *was* Almott, she wouldn't be outside now; she was under surveillance. So why was she still spooked?

Aline backed away from the window, and when her legs rubbed up against the armrest of the couch, she leaned into it, slid over it on the cushions, shifted, and pulled her legs up against her. She covered her knees with her robe and hugged them, resting her chin on her kneecap. She started to tremble. She clamped her mouth shut so her teeth wouldn't chatter. She squeezed her eyes shut. Dimly, she thought: *I'm having an anxiety attack, not a coronary. It will pass.*

But it didn't pass. It got worse. Sweat seeped from her

pores like blood. Her heart thudded. Adrenaline pumped
through her. Now her eyes burned and the inside of her mouth
had gone dry. Her tongue seemed thick, huge. She sensed
the woman now, hurling toward her through the dark, across
the few miles that separated them. Aline felt the hot wind of
her approach in the same way you sometimes did a nightmare
in the seconds before it slammed into you. Her head snapped
toward the door; she expected it to explode inward, spewing
glass and wood. A bitterness surged in her throat. She bit
into her lip to keep from crying out and brought her arms up
around her head and squeezed as she pressed her face against
her knees.

Blood pounded in her ears.

She smelled her fear. She smelled burned skin. She smelled
vengeance.

Something popped in her chest and a sob burst from her
mouth. It was muffled against her knees. Tears stung her
cheeks. She dropped her head back against the couch and
pressed her hands to her mouth to keep the second sob in. It
died in her throat. A long moment passed. She felt the next
sob forming, struggling, but she pushed it farther and farther
back, and after a while she let her hands drop away from her
mouth and breathed deeply once, twice, three times. She
stopped shaking. Okay. It would be okay now.

But she didn't stretch out her legs or drop her feet to the
floor, which was alive with shadows. She didn't loosen her
hold on her legs. She rubbed her nose against her robe and
waited, and little by little she regained some of the footing
she'd lost. She felt like she was trying to steal a base, knowing that any second the pitcher was going to glimpse her
peripherally and the ball would fly and the first baseman
would catch it before she made it back, and then the fear
would pounce on her again, tearing her to bits.

Pick through it.

Louisa Almott had been at school, and her alibi checked
out.

Burned skin.

Sheila Reiner was having dinner at the Hibiscus Inn, and
there were five people who testified to it.

Boiled alive.

The records of the Tango Health Club had told them very
little. Each member had a plastic electronic card that granted

ingress to the club at the front lobby and with which he or she could purchase everything needed. Although the time of arrival was automatically entered on the computer, the card wasn't used to leave the club. So the killer, knowing Xaphes swam at the club every day, could've been there when it opened and waited around or could've checked into the club sometime after he did, after four. There was just no way of telling.

The heaviest use at the club had been between 8:00 that morning and 3:30 in the afternoon. Between 4:00 and 7:00, it was usually pretty slow, then picked up again until 11:00, when it closed. Xaphes was found at 5:32 by one of his body-guards, within fifteen to thirty minutes of his death, Prentiss had estimated. More than fifty people had used the club by the time Xaphes had arrived, and of those, more than a dozen were corporate names, which meant any number of people could've been there without having signed in under their own names.

Gas on the deck.

Face it, she thought. Kincaid was wrong: belief that she was going to solve this case wasn't enough. Belief didn't cut it. They had reached a dead end, and the wall in front of her had her name on it.

She went into the den and opened the closet doors. Stuff fell out—it always did: papers that slipped from precarious perches, a stack of paperback books, old galleys that had arrived at the bookstore and which she hadn't tossed out, computer supplies. She ignored everything and patted around on the upper shelf, looking for a particular box. When she found it, she removed it from the shelf, stepped over the things on the floor, and carried the box over to her desk.

Working quickly, she put together the smoke-gray carbon polymer components. The weapon was a Heckler and Koch MPK5, a machine pistol in vogue these days among Colom-bian drug boys. It was about ten inches long, with no dis-cernible barrel, and what she liked most about it was that it was exactly what it appeared to be—sinister and deadly.

A couple of years ago she had lifted it during a drug raid, christened it "Gringo," and had never turned it in. She snapped a clip into the gun, and pulled back on the cocking lever. A round fit into the chamber. The sound was sharp, definite, not something you could argue with.

Even a lunatic would not argue with a weapon like this. *Would she?*

2

At five-thirty that morning, a van drew up to the gate of the safe house and drove through when the gate opened. On the side of the van was written PLUMBING MART. Bill Prentiss was at the wheel. He left the engine running as Gene Frederick slid open the side doors and hurried up to the house. The door opened before he'd even rung the bell, and Dr. Stratton and Renie Foreston hustled out, with Carol Foreston bringing up the rear.

Stratton and the girl sat in the back with the chief, while Carol Foreston slid into the passenger seat next to Prentiss. Since the night of the hypnosis, she'd been staying here at the safe house with her daughter, and the stress was beginning to show. The brief glimmer of light that spilled across her features before she shut the door revealed a China doll face that was developing tiny fissures at the eyes, around the mouth. It was like looking at a piece of Kleenex, thought Prentiss, which had been wadded up and then smoothed out. She sipped gratefully at one of the cups of coffee Prentiss handed out before they got started. During the ride, she lapsed into a silence so deep it was as if she'd toppled into a coma.

Instead of driving to the Pier House in Key West, as they had planned, Prentiss turned in at the Flamingo Hotel and continued around to the back, where the employees parked. Bernelli was waiting on the steps and hurried over as he pulled into the parking space. They split up. Bernelli, Frederick, and the girl hopped into one of the two golf carts, and Prentiss, Dr. Stratton, and Carol Foreston got into the other. They putted through two miles of green in the predawn stillness, the golf carts whirring, birds fussing in the trees that bordered the golf course. Halfway between the ninth hole and the tenth, Frederick swung his golf cart off into the trees at the left, and Prentiss followed.

The land sloped toward the Tango Inlet. The trees and brush thickened. The sky to the east was oozing gray. A mile into the woods, about a hundred yards from the banks of the inlet, Frederick stopped. Prentiss parked alongside him. Everyone got out and walked quickly toward an old fire ranger station that rose some sixty feet above the golf course, the trees, sixty feet into the Tango sky.

A catwalk surrounded the station, and positioned at each of the four points was a man from the Monroe Country SWAT team. Inside the station were four small rooms—a fully stocked kitchen, a living room, two bedrooms, and a bath—and two cops from vice. Quarters were going to be cramped for the next twenty-four to forty-eight hours, Prentiss thought, but so what. The article would be in tomorrow's paper, the Sunday issue of the *Tribune*, and no one was taking chances.

He and Frederick stuck around for a few minutes, checking last-minute things, and at some point he ended up alone in the kitchen with Carol Foreston. She radiated a grim tightness that seemed to cover the air around them like a net. It suffocated him, and, more to break the silence than anything else, he asked, "Is your husband going to be in town?"

"I don't know." She was starting breakfast, cracking eggs into a bowl, setting strips of bacon into a black iron frying pan. "I haven't spoken to him."

Odd, Prentiss thought, and pushed on. "What was he afraid of that night at the bungalow?"

She turned her head toward him then, her expression painfully vulnerable, her dark eyes misted. "I wouldn't know, Dr. Prentiss. You'll have to ask him."

"What were *you* afraid of?"

Her smile was thin, resigned. "Everything."

"I don't understand."

For a split second he thought she was going to spill her guts, that she was going to vomit every bitterness she harbored, every disappointment. He thought she was going to confess something. Her mouth opened a little, her eyes took on a strange, feverish sheen, he could feel her wanting to reach out, to open up. But then she averted her eyes. "Be glad you don't," she said, and walked out, leaving bacon sizzling in the pan.

Bands of dark gray light sutured the sky to the east, where clusters of thunderheads grew like stalks of cauliflower. The high pressure trough that had stalled over South Florida had pushed the temperature to ninety-one, and it wasn't even ten A.M. yet. By mid-afternoon, Aline thought as she stood at her office window, the air would be blistered and she'd be waiting around at the safe house for Molly to show, anxious to get this goddamn interview over with.

It had been Frederick's idea to have it at the safe house, as though it would somehow lend credence to the information he'd given Sonsky, even though the "witness" would no longer be there. So it'd be just Aline and Prentiss and maybe a cop or two in the guardhouse to make it look like the witness had been moved only recently.

She was a little unclear on what was supposed to happen once the article was published. Presumably, the killer would panic when she read that the police expected to make an arrest within the next two to three days and would do one of several things: attempt to locate the girl, move against the remaining jurors, move against Aline, or all three. But again, they were working only with *theory.*

It seemed just as likely to Aline that the woman would call their bluff and not do anything, or that she would flee the island. And by Monday or Tuesday, the Tango Key Police Department would have about as much credibility as the Three Stooges. Another possibility was that the woman knew where Renie Foreston had been moved. In that case, she probably wouldn't do anything, unless she was equipped with a small army. The most likely scenario was that nothing at all would happen. The woman would wait. The cops would wait. Maybe the waiting would stretch into a second or even a third day, but Aline doubted it. At some point, Frederick would call the whole thing off. Then Renie would return to her parent's home, resume her life, and continue therapy while the cops kept investigating. By then, of course, Aline and the other two jurors might be dead.

Some of last night's anxiety leaked into her, and she let her fingers rest lightly against the box in her drawer, the box with Gringo in it. It helped ease the chill fanning out across her back, and she thought: *This is sick.* She had killed one person in her five years with the department, and that was nearly three years ago, a matter of kill or be killed.

But three years ago she'd been face-to-face with the man; her enemy this time had no face, no identity, no name. She was nothing more than a concrescence of facts clustered like malignant cells around the corpses she'd left in her wake.

Aline moved away from her window, unable to recall what she'd been looking at. *Keep busy. Do paperwork. Put your head down on the desk and take a nap. Go downstairs for coffee. But don't just sit around thinking.*

4

Kincaid stood at the bookcase under the window in Aline's office at Whitman's, perusing the collection: old telephone and city directories; county records on births and deaths on Tango for the last twenty years; dictionaries in three languages. Aline, the pack rat. She could've set up a research library with the stuff she had in here. He didn't understand why she saved it, but for once he was grateful.

The county records were arranged in five-year bundles. He picked out the one that covered 1975 through 1979, then located the phone directories from 1975 to 1977. He sat at the table and went to work.

Something Aline had said last night about Renie Foreston had triggered this, and he'd lain awake, mulling it over, seeking the right connections. He hadn't found them, but by this morning, he'd known where to look.

He flipped open the 1975 phone directory to the F's. Frank and Carol Foreston were listed, but at a different address, in a less prestigious part of the island. He turned to the yellow pages, looking for Foreston Builders. Only a number was listed next to it, and it was the same as the home phone. So thirteen years ago, Frank had been operating his business out of his home.

Kincaid consulted the 1976 directory and found the same situation had been true a year later. But 1977 looked like a real busy year for the Forestons—a new home address and an office for Foreston Builders with an 800 number listed under it, as well as three Tango Key exchanges. The Forestons had apparently come into quite a bit of money that year.

Just to make sure he was on the right track, he went through the phone directories prior to 1975. It took him a while, but he finally determined that the Forestons had moved to the island during 1973, the first year they were listed in the phone directory.

From the bookcase, he removed a plump volume and set it on the table. He turned to the county birth records for 1976, checked the list twice, and even checked for 1975 and 1977. He found no birth records for Renie Foreston. It was possible Carol Foreston had decided to have her child in Key West or even Miami, since the Tango hospital had been much smaller then. But he felt that wasn't what had happened.

He dialed the Immaculate Conception Church in Miami and asked to speak to the mother superior. He was put on hold. He spun around in the chair and gazed down at the Tango boardwalk and beach. The hard-cores were already out in full force, bodies slick with suntan lotion, their bright towels like islands against the wheat-colored sand.

"This is Mother Superior, may I help you?"

"Hi, Sister, it's Ryan Kincaid."

"Oh. Mr. Kincaid."

Such enthusiasm. "I was hoping you could answer a question for me."

"I've given our conversation a great deal of thought, Mr. Kincaid. And I'm afraid that in good conscience, I can't help you with—"

"Sister, all I need is a simple yes or no."

She sighed. In the background, he heard the tolling of the church bell. "I can't promise anything, but what's your question?"

"Was Lenore's child adopted by Frank and Carol Foreston?"

He heard a click, and then a dial tone. It was all the answer he needed.

The Foreston home looked unaffected by the heat. Sprinklers whirled in the yard, shooting out sprays of water that fractured the light. Plants glistened with moistness, the lawn was a deep green carpet, even the air here seemed cooler, pristine.

Foreston's navy-blue Volvo was in the driveway. Either he'd taken his wife's car to work or he hadn't gone in yet. It didn't make much difference to Kincaid; if Foreston wasn't here, he would just go to his goddamn office and make a scene there.

He rang the doorbell. No answer. He rang it twice more, then walked around to the side of the house. A wooden fence enclosed the backyard. Kincaid unlatched the gate, took in the clusters of ferns and wildflowers, the thick hibiscus hedge with the hot-pink blooms, and the swimming pool and its cool blue waters.

Foreston was in the pool, spreading suntan lotion on the bare and very tan back of a young woman. He couldn't see her face, because her cheek was pressed against the raft. But judging from her laugh, she was a lot younger than Foreston, who looked to be having the time of his life. He was running his hands over the woman's hips, her buttocks, and down along the inside of her thighs, which were conveniently parted. Kincaid just stood there, watching them, a slow rage working through him. The bastard's daughter was going through the worst crisis of her young life, and here he was, diddling a ditzy bimbo, acting like some horny teenager at the drive-in.

The woman giggled. "C'mon, Frank, that tickles."

"C'mon what, baby?" he crooned, and let his hand slip under her. "Bet that doesn't tickle, does it?"

The woman moaned a little and managed to turn onto her back without tipping the raft. Foreston, right on cue, squirted more suntan lotion into his hands and rubbed it across the woman's belly. He nibbled at her knees and she giggled again. His tongue licked at the water on her upper thighs, skipping upward to her belly, teasing her, lingering at her naval. Sunlight poured over them and struck Kincaid in the face as he moved silently toward the pool, thinking of Renie.

Foreston and the woman were so oblivious they weren't

even aware of Kincaid until he'd been standing at the side of the pool for a full minute. It was long enough for him to clamp down on his fury, long enough for the young woman to screech when Kincaid moved again and his shadow fell over her.

"Hey! Who the hell are you?"

She bolted upward from the raft, it tipped, and she rolled, sputtering, into the water. Foreston had spun around, cheeks bright red with embarrassment and rage. He propelled himself toward the side of the pool, where the towels were puddled. Kincaid whipped them up, along with Foreston's swimming trunks and a skimpy bikini.

"Get off my property!" Foreston demanded, hands gripping the side of the pool, his head tipped back, one eye winked shut against the harsh light. "You're trespassing, Kincaid!"

"You're going to have to answer a few questions first."

"I want my towel," the young woman shouted. The water cut her off at the throat, but beneath it, Kincaid could see that her arms formed an X over her breasts. She was young, all right, eighteen or nineteen, and as Kincaid looked at her, she glanced away and swam toward the raft. When she reached it, she used it as a shield. "I said I want my towel. Frank, tell him I want my towel."

"The lady would like her towel, Kincaid."

"Then I guess you'd better tell me who Renie's father is, Foreston. Then the lady can have her towel *and* her bikini."

"What?"

Kincaid pointed at his mouth. "Watch my lips. *Who the fuck is Renie's real father?*"

"What's he talking about, Frank? What's going on?" the girl whined.

"Shut up!" Foreston barked.

"Fuck you," she shot back, and grabbed hold of the end of the raft and kicked her way to the deep end.

"I'm Renie's father. Now leave, Kincaid, before I call the cops."

Kincaid crouched, so he was almost eye-level with Foreston. "Renie's adopted. The school told Detective Scott that much. Now who're her real parents, Foreston? That's what you've been afraid of, right? That, and your wife finding out about your little lady friend."

Foreston cast an uneasy glance toward the end of the pool, where the young woman was all ears. He wiped the back of his hand across his mouth. "What difference does it make?"

"Oh, I figure it makes a difference of about seventy-five grand a year—money from a trust fund Lenore Luskin set up for her daughter and which you've sure used to your own advantage. I wonder what would happen if your wife knew about your honey over there and divorced you, Foreston. She would get custody of Renie, of course, since judges on Tango are old-fashioned and don't look too kindly on adultery. And I imagine that in the event of a divorce, all the money would go to the parent with custody. Right, Foreston? Now who was her biological father? Travis Feld? Who?"

He wiped at his mouth again; the seams of his jaws tightened. In another day and age, the look on the man's face could've struck down giants, Kincaid thought. "Get outa here before I call the cops."

Kincaid exploded with laugher. "The cops. Right. You're going to call the cops, and the first person *I'll* be calling is your wife. Count on it."

He blinked; water flew off his lashes. He'd been gripping the side of the pool so hard his knuckles had turned the color of milk. "Judge Michael. Her father was Judge Michael."

Good Christ.

"Okay?" Foreston spat. "You satisfied?"

"We're just getting warmed up. Let me see if I've got this right, Foreston. Renie and your wife were arguing that night at dinner about who her real parents were."

"I wasn't there. I was out of town."

Another piece of the riddle shifted into place. Foreston hadn't been out of town; he'd been with his young mistress, and Carol Foreston suspected as much. In fact, maybe Carol Foreston knew about her husband's affair. And maybe Renie did, too, but didn't know how to label it. *At night sometimes, when Daddy's out of town, I hear Mom crying. . . . I heard her say she found something on Daddy's shirt. . . .*

"Let's go back to the argument, Foreston. Your wife refused to tell her about Lenore because Lenore was a call girl. Hardly the sort of genetic legacy a kid can handle. So instead, she tells Renie about her daddy. The rich judge on the hill. That evening when your wife leaves the house, Renie decides she's going to visit Daddy. But someone else beat her to it.

A woman who hacked the family to death while your daughter watched. She saw her real father murdered, and you were just going to let the whole thing pass, you sack of shit.''

In the blink of an eye, Foreston was out of the pool. If Kincaid had been standing, he might've avoided the punch. But he was squatting, and he was close enough to the pool so that Foreston's fist slammed into the side of his jaw, knocking him over. Blood filled his mouth. Pain sang through his jaw and the tip of his tongue, where he'd bitten it. Before he could scramble to his feet, Foreston was on top of him, his knee sinking into Kincaid's gut, his hands squeezing around Kincaid's throat, pressing down against his windpipe. He started to gag, his vision went fuzzy at the edges. *The fucker's going to kill me.*

Kincaid bucked, jerked his right arm free, and jammed it into the underside of Foreston's jaw, in the soft, fleshy place just above his Adam's apple. He bellowed and fell back, and Kincaid rolled and leaped up, coughing, spitting blood. He locked an arm around Foreston's neck and hurled him into the pool.

Foreston smacked the water, sank, shot to the surface sputtering and coughing, shaking his head, treading water as he headed back to the edge to get at Kincaid. ''Don't, Foreston,'' he shouted, and pulled his .38 from the holster inside his windbreaker, flicked off the safety, and fell forward on one knee, both hands gripping the weapon. ''One move and you're history, asshole.''

The girl started shrieking. Without taking his eyes from Foreston, Kincaid told her to shut up. She did.

Foreston stammered, ''I'll sue you, Kincaid. I swear to Christ I'll sue and—''

''Reserve the bullshit for your little friend, Foreston. You're not calling anyone, not with seventy-five grand a year at stake.'' He engaged the safety, slipped the gun back into his shoulder holster, and spit out a mouthful of blood. He got up and walked away, feeling old and miserable. He had the key to Renie Foreston's memory, but he didn't know what the hell he was going to do with it.

He passed through the gate in the fence, slamming it behind him.

24: COUNTDOWN

I

As Aline left town at four it started to sprinkle, and by the time she cruised into the Tango hills it was raining. The rain wasn't bad, but the wind was. It whipped the stuff horizontally across the road, slicking the asphalt to a smoothness like silk, bending the treetops, tearing leaves from branches and plastering them against the windshield. The only good thing about the weather was that it thinned Saturday traffic along the Old Post Road.

And maybe Molly won't show and we can do this over the phone. Then she would have time to take care of more pressing issues, like talking to Carol Foreston about the little matter of her daughter's true parentage. Yes, she would very much enjoy telling China doll what she thought of her sin of omission.

Kincaid had called her shortly before she'd left and given her the rundown on what had happened. She tried to imagine Judge Michael and Lenore Luskin as lovers, but the only thing that came to mind was two bodies that could've been any man, any woman, humping and sweating in the old Luskin homestead. The judge had died with his secret, and Lenore with hers.

Aline slowed as she approached the turnoff for the safe house and slipped the box with Gringo in it under her raincoat on the passenger seat. Since it technically was against the law for her to even have the gun in the first place, it was wisest to keep it out of sight until she'd passed the guardhouse.

As she swung onto the dirt road, the wind whistled against

the Buick's windows. The pines and ficus trees curved in, creating a canopy of green overhead. The gray light darkened, and she switched on her headlights. It was like moving through a tunnel, light dancing off the trees pressing in on either side of her, the rain slicing through her field of vision at an angle, the road already turning muddy and difficult.

The guardhouse was empty, the door swinging back and forth in the wind. Except for Prentiss's Mercedes in the driveway and the lights shining in the windows, the place looked as if it had been abandoned for years. Leaves pinwheeled through the front yard. The door to the guardhouse creaked and moaned. Leaves and twigs had blown across the front steps of the porch.

She wondered why Prentiss was here so early when Molly wasn't due until four-thirty and would probably be late to boot. For that matter, why had he come at all? She had his statement, and considering who was doing the interviewing, she really hadn't expected him. But on the other hand, maybe he had a score to settle with Molly about misquotes in her last article. Maybe he wanted to be damn sure she got the record straight this time. Who could blame him?

Aline pulled up behind the Mercedes, plucked her raincoat and Gringo from the seat, and dashed toward the front door. It was unlocked, and when she stepped into the hall, she shook the raincoat and hooked it on the back of the door.

"Bill?" Her voice echoed. It was so quiet in the house she heard the moan of the wind and the way it rattled the sliding glass doors that opened onto the deck. "Bill? It's Al. You're early."

"Down here," he called. "In the basement."

Aline locked the front door behind her and went into the living room. The hospital computer equipment hadn't been removed yet, but she supposed that was part of Frederick's stab for authenticity.

The phone pealed and she answered it.

"Al, it's Ryan."

"I just walked in the door. Good timing. What's up?"

"A surprise. Remember the mysterious tutor, Joe Waldo? He'd left a message on the machine here at the house. He called the station but you'd just left. Anyway, I called him back. He was on Big Pine Key, setting up an educational program or something, and he's on his way to the house."

"Goddamn, that's great. I shouldn't be more than an hour."

"If he can't stick around, I'll get what I can out of him."

"And make sure he gives you his home number."

"Right. See you later."

She left Gringo's box by the phone and trotted down the spiral staircase to the basement. "Hey, Bill, that was Ryan. Remember that Joe Waldo fellow who . . ." She stopped, her eyes sweeping through the empty basement living room. A slow dread pulsed in her throat. "Bill?"

Her voice curled into the quiet, barely above a whisper. She let go of the railing. She'd been gripping it so tightly the tendons in her hand ached. Her gaze paused on the yawning black that was the open bedroom doorway. *He's using the john and can't hear me.* Sure. A simple explanation. The bathroom was off the bedroom. It was difficult to hear anything in there, especially if the ventilation fan was on.

But tiny spicules of sweat formed on her upper lip as she neared the bedroom doorway. She moved into the room, and by the time she realized the box Gringo was in was next to the phone upstairs, it was too late. The door suddenly slammed into her, smacked her in the temple, and knocked her out.

2

Joe Waldo was short and plump, a koala bear of a man. He wore navy-blue slacks and a pale blue guayabera shirt that barely covered his considerable paunch. His brown hair was longish and curly, and he kept running his fingers through it as if to make sure it hadn't disappeared since he'd arrived. He was uptight, although Kincaid couldn't tell if it was due to the subject matter or if it was just Waldo's nature.

He listened to Kincaid's synopsis of the murders and their connection to the Luskin case. When he frowned, it thrust two plump lines down between his brows. "I guess I'm not clear on exactly what sort of information it is you want from me."

"You must've known him pretty well if you were his tutor, right?" Kincaid asked.

Waldo's lips pursed. "I guess that would depend on what you mean by 'well.' Death row inmates aren't anything like the general population of inmates you find in my line of work, Mr. Kincaid. They don't run a line of bullshit, because they know they don't have anything to gain. They either like you or dislike you, and you usually know within minutes of meeting them which it is. But Luskin was a real odd duck, even on the row. I never knew whether he liked me or hated my guts. I know he enjoyed the curriculum I designed for him, and that he liked me as a teacher, but I don't know what he felt about me personally. So although I knew him well on one level, I didn't know him at all on another."

"Was there any woman in his past who would've perpetrated this sort of vendetta against the people responsible for putting him behind bars?"

"Not that I know of. But then, the only woman he ever mentioned to me was his sister. There *is* something that happened, though, which may be connected to all this. I don't know. You'd probably be a better judge of that than me."

About three years ago, the dean at his junior college instituted a program at Florida State Prison to provide college education for death row inmates. "We were like subcontractors, I guess you could call it. I was paid by the college but put my hours in at the Rock. Basically, my job entailed designing specific curriculums for about a dozen guys on the row. It had to be individual instruction rather than classroom, because guys there aren't permitted association with other inmates. About a year and a half into the program, Jimmy Ray became one of my students. Before he went to prison, he'd had a year of college and then dropped out because he was bored. That's when he was living here on Tango. So I tried to put together something that would meet the specs for a degree but also hold his interest. He wanted to write so that's what we focused on."

Waldo started his curriculum by assigning Luskin certain books to read and analyze—everything from the classics to contemporary horror. He learned the basics of plotting, characterization, grammar, and syntax. "About three months into the program, he mentioned he wanted to write a book about his prison experiences. I told him to keep a journal. He said he already was. I didn't hear anything more about the book thing for, oh, maybe four months, so I brought it up. " 'Naw,' he says, 'that's okay, Joe. I already got some outside help.' "

"What'd he mean by 'outside'?" Kincaid asked.

"Inmates are always making reference to 'life on the outside.' But in this case, I figured Luskin meant that someone on the educational staff was helping him out. Maybe the prison librarian. But when I asked him, he said no, the only contact with Luskin he ever had was bringing him the books I recommended. As far as he knew, no one else had much contact with him. So I got real curious." He paused and a small dimple appeared in a corner of his mouth. "And what I learned is that if you work in a prison, don't *ever* be *too* curious because you don't have to look very far to find something haywire in the system. It's okay to break the rules and do whatever the hell you want within the context of the system, as long you don't get caught at it—or point the finger at someone else."

Thunder rumbled, startling Waldo, silencing him for a second. Raindrops tapped the windows. When he resumed speaking, Kincaid noticed that his voice had changed somewhat, grown slower, more cautious. He started snooping, he said, and discovered that someone from the governor's office had arranged meetings between a journalist and a couple of death row inmates.

"My mistake was that I didn't have proof. There were no records of the visits. All I had was hearsay. But just the same, I went to the warden. The warden went to the governor. I was asked to leave the prison, and if I hadn't had tenure with the college, I would've been fired. As it was, I was demoted. I finally got a transfer within the state university system, but they couldn't start me until two days ago, so I took some leave time I had coming. Part of the reason I didn't get Detective Scott's message until last night was that the switchboard at the college hadn't been notified of the change."

"Who was the journalist?" Kincaid asked.

"A woman, that's all I know. I heard from some of the other inmates that something was going on between her and Jimmy Ray. He would brag about it—how much she loved him, what he did with her sexually when they met, how she was going to be his ticket out of the joint.''

"Sexually? Where the hell were they meeting?''

"In one of the offices, apparently. I know how it sounds. Believe me. But that's what I meant about the system. If you work within the parameters, anything can happen—and does. And the governor's office is very definitely part of that system. It's the apex of power. The governor has the right to grant stays of execution. He grants clemency. He says the word, and you're out. The only other unit with almost equal power is the parole board. So you can imagine the kind of clout this turkey from the governor's office had. If he wanted to get someone in without there being a record, fine. No problem. He could probably do anything short of smuggling weapons into the compound.''

"Why were you asked to leave?''

"Ah.'' Waldo sighed. "The biggie. It took me a while to trace it back to the source, but I think it went something like this. The governor confronts his lackey about the accusation. The lackey denies it. But now the lackey knows who I am, so he pays off a guard to plant some coke in my desk. Then it's discovered and I'm given a choice—resign or face criminal prosecution. So I resigned. The only reason I know who set me up is because about eight months later in Jacksonville, I was at a party one night and met a guy who'd worked as a guard at the Rock. He roomed with the bastard who did it. Funny, isn't it, all these marvelous coincidences life tosses your way.''

The rain was coming down harder now. The wind had risen and moaned against the glass, the doors, and sent Wolfe scampering into the living room. He stopped short when he realized someone besides Kincaid was present and his nose worked busily at the air, investigating.

"Jesus, a skunk,'' Waldo said with a laugh.

"He's been de-stinkoed.'' Kincaid clicked his tongue against his teeth, and Wolfe waddled over and lifted his front paws and Kincaid picked him up, stroking him. The skunk settled into his lap, raising his head so his throat could be scratched.

"Let's backtrack a second to the woman. What do you know about her?'' Kincaid asked.

"Virtually nothing. I was never able to find out her name

or what she looked like, except that she supposedly had an awesome body. But that doesn't mean a hell of a lot, either, because Totie Fields would look great to an incarcerated man. I figure she must've lived in or around Tallahassee, since the governor's office is there and that's where Bradley worked.''

Bradley: now why did that name stick in his mind? Where had he heard it? From Aline? Prentiss? Had it been in one of those files they'd put together weeks ago? "Who's Bradley?"

"The dude who worked for the governor's office. Bradley Higgins."

"When was all this going on? A year ago? Eighteen months ago? What?"

Tallahassee . . .

"Well, let's see. . . ."

Left-handed . . .

"Luskin went to the chair in early August."

Respiratory ailment . . . asthma . . .

"So it must've been six months previous to that."

Planes. She knows enough about planes to trim an aileron cable. A journalist. Kincaid closed his eyes. The color drained from his face. The inside of his head rang.

Impossible. He opened his eyes. The stormy dusk hugged the window. The wind cackled through the eaves. *The eye, the hat pin in the eye.* "Christ," he spat, and leaped to his feet, his face utterly white as he tore toward the phone.

3

His head felt as if firecrackers had gone off inside it. The inside of his mouth tasted metallic, of blood. Prentiss knew his eyes were open, but there was only a terrible blackness, thick as tar. Panic boiled up inside him. *My eyes Jesus she poked out my eyes oh God please*

No. My eyes don't hurt.

He hurt everywhere else, but not there. She hadn't touched his eyes. *Then where the fuck am I?*

The floor. He was on his side on the bathroom floor. In the dark. His hands were tied. His ankles were tied. *Because*

she'll be back for you, Bill. She told you she would. After
Aline had arrived and Molly had cocked the .38 in her hand,
demanding that he answer Aline's call, she had knocked him
out. That explained the warm ooze from his temple. The
throb in his head. But how had she locked him in? *And what's
she done with Aline?*

Slowly, carefully, grimacing at the flare of pain in his temple, he shifted around until he could hook his toes under the
vanity, then he pulled himself forward. He couldn't understand why Molly had tied his hands in front of him but was
grateful that she had. He patted his way to the wall, then up
to the switch. He flipped it. Nothing happened. She'd removed the bulb. *Or the electricity has gone out.* He could
still hear the distant rumble of thunder. It was the way it
would sound if he were buried alive six feet under.

He scooted left until he bumped into something. The door.
He patted the wood until he reached the knob, turned it, but
nothing happened. He knew the door opened inward. That
meant she must've tied something to the outside knob that
was holding the door shut. *Guess what, good buddy, you're
in a world of shit.*

The panic started leaking into him again. He could feel it
stuffed into a closet in his mind, could hear it pounding
against the walls of his skull, screeching, *Lemme out.* He
forced himself to take deep breaths. How long had he been
out? How much time had passed from when he'd opened the
front door of the safe house, shocked that Molly was so early
for her interview?

Think.

All right, it must've been close to four when she'd arrived.
And it was only a few minutes later, when he was in the
kitchen, that she came up behind him with the .38 in one
hand and the hat pin in the other. *Know what this is, Billy
boy?*

And in that split second, when he'd seen the light glinting
off the sharp point of the hat pin, he had understood what
terror was. He had understood what pain was. And death. He
had peered into the abyss. The hat pin was his terror button.
He had seen its effects firsthand. He had described the effects
in detail. His terror button, yes, sweet Christ, yes, and she
knew it. She knew it and she used it to control him. *Down*

into the basement now, Billy boy. Into the bedroom now, Billy boy. Sit on the toilet seat, Billy boy.

And he had. He had done everything she had told him to do.

But he was not going to die.

And he was not going to allow Aline to die because of him.

He tried the knob again. The switch. He rolled onto his knees, hooked the rope on his wrists around the knob, and rattled it.

Nothing.

And then he remembered Renie saying, *Did you know there's a secret passage in the basement bathroom, Dr. Bill? No kidding. Where is it?*

She'd giggled, a small, girlish giggle. *If I told you that, it wouldn't be a secret anymore.*

He'd forgotten about it and had neglected to ask her about it later.

Floor? No way. It was tile. *A secret passage to where?* As long as it led out of here, who gave a shit where it went, he thought, and frantically groped for the door to the vanity.

He dug his hands through the stuff inside—shampoo and hair dryers, curlers, a first-aid kit, things Stratton and Carole Foreston had left here. He knocked everything out, patting the walls inside, tapping his knuckles lightly against them. *Nothing. No hollow spots, no loose panels, not a goddamn thing.*

A little more panic bled into him. *Maybe Renie was joking.* He squeezed his eyes shut, wiped the backs of his hands across his sweaty forehead, started tapping the walls again, certain he must've missed a spot. But he hadn't. Hopelessness clawed up his throat and he leaned into the wall and something rattled. *The old air-conditioning grate.* A large grate. Large enough for a child, but was it big enough for a man?

He swung his legs around and worked at the edges of the grate with his fingers. It was already loose, the screws just balanced in their holes, and lifted out easily. He set it on the floor and stuck his head into the hole. Air no longer poured out of this particular grate; the vents were now all along the ceiling, and were smaller. No telling where it went, but Renie had said "passage" not "door," and "passage" implied that it led somewhere.

Say your prayers, good buddy, and he climbed through the hole.

25: GROUND ZERO

I

Aline came to in a chair, each of her arms wrapped tightly with masking tape to the armrests. Her ankles were bound with rope. Pain fluttered along her left temple. Her body ached—her hips, legs, thighs, shoulders—and when she realized where she was, she understood why. She was in the living room on the main floor; Molly had pulled her up the spiral staircase. Not a bad feat for a woman working alone, she thought dimly. And it had to be Molly, who had arrived early and done something to Prentiss and now intended to do something to her.

She was facing the sliding glass doors, which were open. Wind and rain blew into the house, chilling her face, her arms. It was nearly dark. Now she heard footfalls behind her and a *slap, slap* that burned the back of her neck. Molly appeared on her left side, smiling, slapping the flat edge of a blade against her open palm. *What we have here, ladies and gentlemen, is a repeat:* this was how the social worker had died.

"Well, the princess wakes up. Hello, princess."

Aline didn't say anything. A part of her mind was struggling through her body's complaints, seeking a weakness in her bonds. She found it, in the ankles; the rope was awfully loose. Molly had apparently been in a big goddamn hurry.

"I said, *Hellooooo*, Aline," and she leaned close enough so Aline could see the blue in her eyes and smell the faint scent of mint on her breath.

Don't piss her off. You're sitting here for a reason. Molly wants an audience. Give her one. "Where's Bill?"

"Asleep. Not dead, Aline, don't worry. Billy boy isn't dead. I have no personal beef with him, except for Bernelli, of course, but that's a different story, isn't it?" *Slap, slap,* sang the blade, and then she brought it up under her hair, flicking it off her shoulder. It was a strange, violent gesture, and Aline felt some of her control slipping. "A very different story."

"What about the other two jurors, Molly? You won't get to them."

"Not now, maybe. But eventually I will. Really. I always keep my word, Aline," and her smile grew.

"Joe Waldo knows who you are, Molly. Do you know who he is? He was Jimmy Ray's tutor. In prison. He knew about you. And right now he's telling everything he knows to the chief of police, who of course knows you're coming up here for an interview, Molly. I don't think you're going to have an easy time leaving the island."

Slap, slap went the knife as she moved slowly around in front of the chair and stopped. "I guess that does change the picture a little. But that's fine. I'm very adaptable, Aline. When one plan doesn't seem to be working out, I just come up with another one. It's a little trick my father taught me. He's a pianist, you know, and he loves to jam with other musicians. And when you jam, you improvise. It was probably the best thing he ever taught me, really."

The cold glint in her eyes was terrifying. It was not madness; it would almost have been better if it were. It was simply—*cold*. Void of emotion. *Dead.* "All this for Jimmy Ray? Why?"

The smile stretched as far as it could go without sliding right off the edge of her face. "Why not?"

Aline blinked, her terror digging deeper. "Your life was that empty?"

Slap, slap, slap. "It's not a matter of emptiness or fullness, Aline. It never is. Look at Norman Mailer's involvement with Gary Gilmore. It's a matter of satisfaction. He satisfied something in me. In a sense, he completed me. I owed him for that. I owed him vindication."

"I don't understand." And suddenly it seemed vital that she did. "How?"

"None of you will ever forget him, will you? And as long as there are people to remember him, remember him in a *big* way, he isn't really dead, now is he?"

A gust of wind swept into the room, blowing Molly's hair around her face, blinding her momentarily. Aline worked her legs. The ropes loosened a little more. *Slap, slap*, whispered the knife once Molly had brushed the strands of hair away from her eyes. "So tell me about our little witness, Aline."

"She's Jimmy Ray's niece."

Molly frowned. The knife paused in its relentless slapping. The cold in her eyes flicked off, on again. She laughed. "That's a fucking lie, Aline."

"It's a lot of things, but lie isn't among them. One of Lenore's clients was Judge Michael. He was the father of the child she gave up for adoption. An attorney here on Tango receives money from a nun in Miami who receives money from a bank in the Caicos, which draws on an account Lenore set up from the sale of her art collection. Does that sound like a lie, Molly?"

For a full minute, Molly said nothing. There was only the sharp *slap, slap* as she moved slowly around to the other side of the chair—and then behind it. *Slap, slap.* . . . Aline worked her feet some more; the rope gave a little. She moved them again; the ropes slipped farther.

"So where're they keeping her, Aline?"

She didn't answer until Molly had circled the chair and stopped in front of her again. "Why? You want to tell her about her Uncle Jimmy Ray? About how he shoved glass up her mommy's twat?"

Molly winced. "That was cruel and unnecessary, Aline," and from somewhere around the pocket of her slacks she withdrew a hat pin, and before Aline had barely registered what it was, Molly drove it between Aline's second and third knuckles. The excruciating pain slammed into her, and she shrieked and kicked, and Molly smiled and smiled.

Air. Rain. Dark.

Prentiss, dazed, was lying on the wet ground, rain beating against his head, wind roaring in his ears. He had slid down a chute feet first, his back scraping painfully over metal. His shoes had slammed into the thick plastic panel at the other end, knocking it loose, and he'd barreled out of the chute onto the ground.

The left side of his face was scraped raw and bleeding. The water and dirt stung. His hands were bleeding. His shirt was torn, and he thought, but wasn't sure, that his left shoulder was also bleeding. He wiggled like a worm through the mud and rain, wanting only to get as far away from the chute as he could. He didn't know which side of the house he was on, where the driveway was, where the cliff was. It was too dark to see anything.

The wind: it's stronger here.

Okay: he was toward the back of the house, near the deck. Had to be, because the wind had always been stronger when you faced the cliff.

He rolled into a hedge. *Gardenias.* He was on his stomach now, hands digging into the dirt, the mud, inching forward, trying to keep his face up. From inside the house, piercing the sound of the wind, he heard Aline shriek.

Prentiss rolled into the hedge, breathing hard, dirt smeared across his eyes, his mouth, in his ears, and gnawed at the ropes on his wrists. When his jaw started to ache, he rubbed the ropes back and forth on the end of a branch. Now and then his hands slipped, he lost the rhythm, he panted, he cursed, the muscles in his neck screamed and he let his face fall to the ground, into the mud. The wind moaned around him. He heard another shriek. He moved his hands faster. Slipped again. A sob of frustration broke loose from his throat. He chewed at the ropes again.

Then he felt them start to give, a little at a time at first, as though he were being rewarded, and then more and more as he gnawed harder. The chords began to fray. His frustration collapsed into fury; he yanked on his wrists, and the ropes loosened and he flung them away, relief roaring into him.

The woods were primeval, dark, filled with secrets, and Kincaid inadvertently stumbled over two of them: a dead cop who'd been dragged off into the trees, and Molly Chapman's jeep. He raced at a crouch through the black, into the wind, toward the guardhouse. He paused in the doorway long enough to determine that the phone was dead.

Just like the phone in the house. Molly had been thorough.

He stole through the gate, then sprang for the shadows to the left side of the house, intending to enter through the back. And that was when he saw something leaping up from the ground, rushing toward him.

It was Prentiss.

Kincaid sprinted the few yards that separated them, and both men skidded through the mud, flattening against the wall, the wind whistling past them, through them. "Where's Aline?"

"Inside."

Christ. Kincaid flicked the safety off the .357 and from an ankle strap produced a knife. He passed it to Prentiss. "We're on our own."

"Ryan, she's . . . she's . . ." Prentiss stammered.

"C'mon, man," he hissed. "They're two of us and only one of her."

He grabbed Prentiss's wet arm and yanked him to his feet. He started toward the deck. *"No,"* Prentiss said loudly, over the din of the wind. "There's a better way."

Kincaid followed him toward the deck, and behind a hedge. Prentiss dropped to his knees and then ducked into a hole. Kincaid unhooked the flashlight from his belt, switched it on, and followed.

4

"So what'll it be, Aline? The knife? A bullet? You can have your choice. I'll be fair with you that way. It's more than anyone gave Jimmy Ray, you know. No one gave him any choice at all.''

She leaned forward, her hands bearing down against Aline's arms, hair falling at the sides of her face. Pain had blurred Aline's perceptions because Molly's little hat pin had been busy busy busy. But she could smell Molly now, smell the dank, sweaty stink of her skin, an odor like rotting fish that she could drown in. And worse, she could smell herself. The wind mixed the odors until they were a confluence of smells, a dark rushing river of smells, horrible and terrifying.

She worked her feet again.

She worked her feet as Molly's voice droned on, taunting her, flicking the hat pin in front of her face, those blue eyes, those cold eyes boring into her, patting her all over inside, eyes that would haunt her for the rest of her life, eyes that would blaze in her dreams. And then, suddenly, her feet were free. The rope slipped below her ankles. She blinked, afraid to hope, no longer trusting her senses.

Free?

Hey, feet, are you free?

They groaned. They twitched. And when Molly rolled back on her heels, away from Aline, those feet lifted swiftly, suddenly, and the tips of Aline's running shoes slammed into Molly's stomach. The impact threw her back and tipped the chair Aline was tied to. Her head struck the floor, nearly knocking her into next week. She felt herself about to pass out and, through an effort of sheer will, tipped the chair again, onto its side, her feet working in a frenzy for purchase. And then she was up, arms still taped to the sides of the chair, her vision fuzzy, her body on fire with pain, nothing but pain, oh God, so much pain, everywhere, all over, igniting her skin, her bones. She hurled herself toward Molly.

Her right arm ripped free of the armrest. She flung the chair, her left arm still connected to it, and something tore in her shoulder. She heard it before she felt it, a protracted ripping, the sound of fabric being shorn, and then it lit up the right side of her body and wrenched a scream from someplace so deep inside her, she hadn't even known the place existed. The chair smashed into Molly's right side, knocking her back, back, back onto the deck and to the floor.

The knife flew from her hand and skittered like a bug.

The hat pin slipped between the boards.

The .38 tucked into the waistband of Molly's pants dug into her hip, taking the brunt of her fall. She cried out.

Aline dived into the wind, toward the knife. It slipped away from her and fell between the boards. She saw it slip. She saw it vanish. She saw and she nearly wept, and then, remembering Molly, she rolled, but it was too late, Molly was stumbling to her feet, the wind whipping her hair into her eyes and around her head like bleached seaweed. She drew the .38 from her waistband.

5

Prentiss reached the top of the stairs first. In the glow of the single lamp in the room, he saw Molly. He saw Aline. He knew the knife wouldn't do it. He turned, grabbed the .357 from Kincaid, lifted it with both hands, aimed, and fired.

The explosion threw him back into Kincaid, who grabbed hold of the railing to keep from falling. His hands shot out and connected with Prentiss's back, shoving him forward. He stumbled into the living room, the gun still clutched in his hand.

Molly had fallen. Aline had fallen. There was only the wind, whipping across the deck, and then Aline moved, she rolled, she rolled and leaped up and ran, and Prentiss stood over Molly, gazing down at the blood seeping through her blouse, a bib across her chest.

Her eyes fluttered open.

Blood bubbled from the corners of her mouth.

Bill, she mouthed, and her hand raised the .38 she was still clutching. Her hand moved, he saw it move, he would forever after tell himself he *saw her hand move*. His arms jerked up and the barrel pointed down and he squeezed the trigger once. Twice. A third time. He squeezed and the explosions rocked the air, shredded the wind, the dark, and he squeezed and squeezed, emptying the gun into her.

And then he dropped to his knees, the gun slipping from his hand. He stared at Molly, at what was left of her, and the wind lifted him, filled him, and he floated away.

EPILOGUE: APRIL

"You sure this thing will get off the ground with four of us in here?" Bernelli asked, leaning forward from the backseat. "Four of us and *all* our luggage?"

"Relax, Bernie." Aline was taxiing *Cat* toward runway 90. Kincaid was in the passenger seat, and Prentiss and Bernie were in the back. The plane *did* seem heavier, but she kept that to herself. "If I mess up, Ryan can always take over."

"Great, Al. That's a real comfort. Bill, I feel sick. You have anything for air sickness?"

"Hey, Ryan," said Prentiss. "Are there any puke bags up there?"

Kincaid wagged a white bag over his shoulder. "If you get sick in here, Bernie, we'll let you off at the next stop."

"Stop picking on me, Ryan."

"Quiet," Aline bellowed. "I need quiet so I can concentrate."

This elicited a groan from Bernelli, but after that she was quiet, and Aline continued to runway 90, where she did her runup check. Then she pulled up behind a slick twin-engine Beechcraft.

The weather was mild, sunny, and winds were out of the east at six knots. The weather, in fact, looked good all the way to Pensacola, where they would spend the night. From Pensacola, they would head west across the Southwest to California. There they would let off Bernelli and Prentiss, and a week later Aline and Kincaid would board a commercial flight to Auckland. No rain was forecast. But Kincaid's shoulder, which had become sensitive to nuances in barometric pressure, said differently. She was betting on rain before they hit Tampa—not a deluge, not anything that would mean delays or detours, just scattered showers.

The radio crackled, and the controller signaled the Beechcraft in front of them that it was cleared for takeoff. Aline gave Cat a little gas and inched forward to the line. She had completed her license a month ago, several days after the chief had tracked down Bradley Higgins, Molly's Tallahassee lover. He hadn't been exactly cooperative, but they'd been able to piece together some of what had happened during the six months before Luskin had been electrocuted.

Molly had been working on a series of free-lance pieces on capital punishment, and Higgins had arranged for her to meet on the sly with two death row inmates—Luskin and another man. Molly and Luskin met alone in one of the offices several times a month. When Higgins told her the meetings had to stop, she threatened to expose him, so the meetings continued until the day Luskin fried. It still left a lot of questions unanswered, but maybe that was just as well.

"Tango Niner Niner, you're cleared for takeoff," said the controller.

"Roger, tower." Aline swung into position. The sun struck the windshield, and she skewed up her eyes. "Hey, Ryan, could you—"

"Got them right here." He fixed her sunglasses onto the bridge of her nose. "I thought this was going on your checklist."

"Picky, picky."

From the backseat, Bernelli said, "C'mon, Allie. Get this heap into the air, will you?"

Aline pushed in the throttle, and the Cessna sped down the runway, the nose perfectly parallel to the yellow line. At seventy-five, she pulled back gently on the wheel, Bernelli gasped in the backseat, and *Cat* lifted smoothly into the blue Tango sky.

About the Author

Alison Drake lives in South Florida. She is the author of
TANGO KEY.

CHARLES WILLEFORD

TOP-NOTCH CRIME NOVELS ABOUT THE MIAMI SCENE...

FEATURING DETECTIVE HOKE MOSELEY

Available at your bookstore or use this coupon.

___ MIAMI BLUES	32016	$2.95
___ NEW HOPE FOR THE DEAD	33839	$3.50
___ SIDESWIPE	34947	$3.95

BB **BALLANTINE MAIL SALES**
Dept. TAF, 201 E. 50th St., New York, N.Y. 10022

Please send me the BALLANTINE or DEL REY BOOKS I have checked above. I am enclosing $............. (add 50¢ per copy to cover postage and handling). Send check or money order — no cash or C.O.D.'s please. Prices and numbers are subject to change without notice. Valid in U.S. only. All orders are subject to availability of books.

Name _____

Address _____

City _____ State _____ Zip Code _____

12   Allow at least 4 weeks for delivery   TA-203